THE
PARATIME
POLICE
CHRONICLES

VOLUME II

EDITED BY
JOHN F. CARR

Pequod Press

THE PARATIME POLICE CHRONICLES: Volume II
A Pequod Press Anthology

First Edition

Printed in the United States of America
First Printing 2020

V 10 9 8 7 6 5 4 3 2 1

ISBN: 978-0-937912-75-1

ACKNOWLEDGEMENTS

Special thanks to Victoria Alexander for all her help editing the early drafts and her expertise as editor.

Special thanks to my hard working copy editors, Dwight Decker, Mark Moeser and Victoria Alexander.

To the Paratime Study Group, Jim Landau, Jevon Kasich and Eric Fisher.

Finally, to H. Beam Piper who created the template.

TABLE OF CONTENTS

GUNPOWDER GOD

H. BEAM PIPER

I

1964 A.D.

Tortha Karf, Chief of Paratime Police, told himself to stop fretting. Only two hundred-odd days to go to Year-End Day, and then, precisely at midnight, he would rise from this chair and Verkan Vall would sit down in it, and after that he would be free to raise grapes and lemons and wage guerrilla warfare against the rabbits on the island of Sicily, which he owned on one uninhabited Fifth Level timeline. He wondered how long it would take Vall to become as tired of the chief's seat as he was now.

Vall was tired of it already, in anticipation. He'd never wanted to be chief; prestige and authority meant little to him, and freedom much. It was a job that somebody had to do, though, and it was

11

the job for which he'd been trained, so Vall would take it, and do it, he suspected, better than he himself had done. The job, policing a near-infinity of different worlds, each one of which was this same planet, Earth, would be safe in the hands of Verkan Vall.

Twelve thousand years ago, facing extinction on an exhausted planet, the First Level race had discovered the existence of a second, lateral, dimension of time, and a means of physical transposition to and from the world of alternate probability parallel to their own. So the conveyers had gone out by stealth, to bring back wealth in abundance to First Level Home Time Line, a little from here, a little from there, never enough to be missed.

It all had to be policed. Some Paratimers were unscrupulous in dealing with outtime peoples—he'd have retired five years ago, but for the discovery of a huge paratemporal slave trade, only recently smashed. More often, by somebody's bad luck or indiscretion, the Paratime Secret would be endangered, and that had to be preserved at any cost. Not merely the technique of Paratime Transposition, that went without comment, but the very existence of a race possessing it. If for no other reason, and there were many others, it would be utterly immoral to make any outtime people live with the knowledge that there were among them aliens indistinguishable from themselves, watching and exploiting. So there was the Paratime Police.

Second Level: it had been civilized almost as long as the First, but there had been long Dark-Age interludes. Except for Paratemporal Transposition, it almost equaled First. Third Level civilization was more recent, but still of respectable antiquity. Fourth Level had started late and advanced slowly; some Fourth Level genius was inventing agriculture when the coal-burning steam engine was obsolescent on Third. And Fifth Level—on a few time-lines, subhuman brutes, fireless and speechless, were using stones to crack nuts and each other's head; on most of it nothing even humanoid had evolved.

Fourth Level was the big one. The others had devolved from low-probability genetic accidents; Fourth had been the maximum probability. It was divided into many sectors and subsectors, on most of which civilization had first appeared on the Nile and Tigris-Euphrates valleys, and, later, on the Indus and the Yangtze. Europo-American Sector; they might have to pull out of that entirely, that would be Chief Verkan's decision. Too many thermo-nuclear weapons and too many competing national sovereignties, always a disaster-fraught combination. That had happened all over Third Level within Home Time Line experience. Alexandrian-Roman, off to a fine start with the pooling of Greek theory and Roman engineering, and then, a thousand years ago, two half-forgotten religions had been rummaged out of the dustbin and their respective proselytes had begun massacring each other. They were still at it, with pikes and matchlocks, having lost the ability to make anything better. Europo-American could come to that if its rival political and economic sectarians kept on. Sino-Hindic, that wasn't a civilization, it was a bad case of cultural paralysis. Indo-Turanian, about where Europo-American had been a thousand years ago.

And Aryan-Oriental; the Aryan migration of three thousand years ago, instead of moving west and south, as on most sectors, had rolled east into China.

And Aryan-Transpacific, there was one to watch. An offshoot of Aryan-Oriental; the conquerors of Japan had sailed north and east along the Kuriles and the Aleutians, and then spread south and east over North America, bringing with them horses and cattle and iron-working skills, exterminating the Amerinds, splitting into diverse peoples and cultures. There was a civilization along the Pacific coast, and nomads on the plains herding bison and cross-breeding them with Asian cattle, another civilization in the Mississippi Valley, and one around the Great Lakes. And a new one, only four centuries old on the Atlantic seaboard and back in the Appalachians.

The technological level was about that of Europe in the Middle Ages, a few subsectors slightly higher. But they were going forward. Things, Tortha thought, were about ripe to start happening on Aryan-Transpacific.

Well, let Chief Verkan watch that.

II

Rylla tried to close her mind to the voices around her, and stared at the map between the two candlesticks on the table. There was Tarr-Hostigos overlooking the gap, just a tiny fleck of gold on the parchment, but she could see it in her mind: the walls, the outer bailey, the citadel and keep, the watchtower pointing a blunt finger skyward. Below, the little Darro glinted, flowing north to join the Listra and, with it, the broad Athan to the north and east. The town of Hostigos, white walls and slate roofs and busy streets; the checkerboard of fields and forests.

A voice, louder and harsher than the others, brought her back to reality.

"He'll do nothing at all? Well, what in Dralm's name is a Great King for but to keep the peace?"

She looked along the table, from one to another of them. The speaker for the peasants, at the foot, uncomfortable in his feast-day clothes and ill at ease seated among his betters, the speakers for the artisans and the merchants and the townsfolk, the lesser family members, the sworn land-holders. Chartiphon, the captain-in-chief, his blond beard streaked with gray like the gray lead splotches on his gilded breastplate, his long sword on the table in front of him. Old Xentos, the cowl of his priestly robe thrown back from his snowy head, his blue eyes troubled. And her father, Prince Ptosphes of Hostigos, beside whom she sat at the table's head, his mouth tight between pointed mustache and pointed beard. How long it had been since she had seen a smile on her father's lips!

Xentos passed a hand negatively in front of his face. "The Great King, Kaiphranos, said that it was every prince's duty to guard his own realm; that it was for Prince Ptosphes to keep the raiders out of Hostigos."

"Well, great Dralm, didn't you tell him it wasn't just bandits?" the other voice bullyragged. "They're Nostori soldiers; it's war!" Gormoth of Nostor means to take all Hostigos, as his grandfather took Sevenhills Valley after the traitor we don't name sold him Tarr-Dombra."

That was a part of the map her eyes had shunned, the bowl valley to the east, where Dombra Gap split the mountains. It was from thence the Nostori raiders came.

"And what hope have we from Styphon's House?" her father asked. He knew the answer; he wanted all to hear it at first hand.

"Chartiphon spoke with them," Xentos said. "The priests of Styphon hold no speech with priests of other gods."

"The Archpriest wouldn't talk to me," Chartiphon said. "Only one of the upper priests. He took our offerings and said he would pray to Styphon for us. When I asked for fireseed, he would give us none."

"None at all?" somebody cried. "Then we are under the ban!"

Her father rapped with the pommel of his poignard.

"You've heard the worst, now," he said. "What's in your minds to do? You first, Phosg."

The peasant representative rose awkwardly, cleared his throat.

"Lord, my cottage is as dear to me as this fine castle is to you. I'll fight for mine as you would for yours," he said.

There was a quick mutter of approval along the table. The others spoke their turns, a few tried to make speeches. Chartiphon said only, "Fight. What else."

"Submission to evil is the worst of all sins," Xentos said. "I am a priest of Dralm, and Dralm is a god of peace, but I say, fight with Dralm's blessing."

"Rylla?" her father asked.

"Better die in armor than live in chains," she said. "When the time comes, I will be in armor with the rest of you."

Her father nodded. "I expected no less from any of you." He rose, and all with him. "I thank you all. At sunset, we will dine together; until then, servants will attend you. Now, if you please, leave me with my daughter. Xentos, you and Chartiphon stay."

There was a scrape of chairs, a shuffle of feet going out, a murmur of voices in the hall before the door closed. Chartiphon had begun to fill his stubby pipe.

"Sarrask of Sask won't aid us, of course," her father said.

"Sarrask of Sask's a fool," Chartiphon said shortly. "He should know that when Gormoth's conquered Hostigos, his turn will come next."

He knows it," Xentos said calmly. "He'll try to strike before Gormoth does, or catch Gormoth battered from having fought us. But even if he wanted to, he'd not aid us. Not even King Kaiphranos dares aid those whom the priests of Styphon would destroy."

"They want that land in Wolf Valley, for a temple farm," she said slowly. "I know that would be bad, but—"

"Too late," Xentos told her. "Styphon's House is determined upon our destruction, as a warning to others." He turned to her father. "And it was on my advice, Lord, that you refused them."

"I'd have refused against your advice. I swore long ago that Styphon's House should never come into Hostigos while I lived, and by Dralm neither shall they! They come into a princedom, they build a temple, they make a temple farm and make slaves of the peasants on it. They tax the prince, and force him to tax the people, till nobody has anything left. Look at that temple farm in Sevenhills Valley!"

"Yes, you'd hardly believe it," Chartiphon said. "They make the peasants on the farms around them cart their manure in, till they have none left for their own fields. Dralm only knows what they do with it." He puffed at his pipe. "I wonder why they want Wolf Valley."

"There's something there that makes the water of those springs taste and smell badly," she considered.

"Sulfur," Xentos said, "But why do they want sulfur?"

III

Corporal Calvin Morrison, Pennsylvania State Police, crouched in the brush at the edge of the old field and looked across the brook at the farmhouse two hundred yards away, scabrous with peeling yellow paint, and festooned with a sagging porch roof. A few white chickens pecked disinterestedly in the littered barnyard; there was no other sign of life, but he knew that there was a man inside. A man with a rifle, who would use it; a man who had murdered once, broken jail, would murder again.

He looked at his watch; the minute hand was squarely on the nine. Jack French and Steve Kovac would be starting down on the road above where they had left the car. He rose, unsnapping the retaining-strap of his holster.

"I'm starting. Watch that middle upstairs window."

"I'm watching," a voice behind assured him. A rifle-action clattered softly as a cartridge went into the chamber. "Luck."

He started forward across the weed-grown field. He was scared, as scared as he had been the first time, back in '52, in Korea, but there was nothing he could do about that. He just told his legs to keep moving, knowing that in a few moments he wouldn't have time to be scared. He was almost to the little brook, his hand close to the butt of his Colt, when it happened.

There was a blinding flash, followed by a moment's darkness. He thought he'd been shot; by pure reflex, the .38-special was in his hand. Then, all around him, a flickering iridescence of many colors glowed, in a perfect hemisphere thirty feet across and fifteen feet high, and in front of him was an oval desk or cabinet, with an instrument panel over it, and a swivel-chair from which a man was turning and rising. Young, well-built; wore loose green trousers and black ankle boots and a pale green shirt; a shoulder holster under his left arm, a weapon in his right hand.

He was sure it was a weapon, though it looked more like an electric soldering-iron, with two slender rods instead of a barrel, joined at the front in a blue ceramic knob. It was probably something that made his own Colt Official Police look like a kid's cap-pistol, and it was coming up fast to line on him.

He fired, held the trigger back to keep the hammer down on the fired chamber, and threw himself down, hearing something fall with a crash, landing on his left hand and his left hip and rolling, until the nacreous dome was gone around him and he bumped hard against something. For a moment, he lay still, then rose to his feet, letting out the trigger of the Colt.

What he'd bumped into was a tree. That wasn't right, there'd been no trees around, nothing but brush. And this tree, and the others, were huge, great columns rising to support a green roof through which only a few stray gleams of sunlight leaked. Hemlocks, must have been growing here while Columbus was still conning Isabella into hocking her jewelry. Come to think of it, there was a stand of trees like this in Alan Seeger Forest. Maybe that was where he was.

He wondered how he was going to explain this.

"While approaching the house," he began, aloud and in a formal tone, "I was intercepted by a flying saucer, the operator of which threatened me with a ray pistol. I defended myself with my revolver, firing one round—

No. That wouldn't do at all.

He swung out the cylinder of his Colt, ejecting the fired round and replacing it. Then he looked around, and started in the direction of where the farmhouse ought to be, coming to the little brook and jumping across.

IV

Verkan Vall watched the landscape flicker outside the almost invisible shimmer of the transposition field. The mountains stayed the same, but from one time-line to another there was a great deal of randomness about which tree grew where. Occasionally there were glimpses of open country and buildings and installations, the Fifth Level bases his own people had established. The red light overhead winked off and on, a buzzer sounded. The dome of the conveyer became a solid iridescence, and then a cold, inert metal mesh. The red light came on and stayed on. He was picking up the sigma-ray needler from the desk in front of him and holstering it, when the door and a lieutenant of the Paratime Police looked in.

"Hello, Chief's Assistant. Any trouble?"

In theory, the Ghaldron-Hesthor transposition-field was impenetrable from the outside, but in practice, especially when two paratemporal vehicles going in opposite paratemporal directions interpenetrated, it would go weak and outside objects, sometimes alive and hostile, would intrude. That was why Paratimers kept weapons at hand, and why conveyers were checked immediately on emergence; it was also why some Paratimers didn't make it home.

"Not this trip. My rocket ready?"

"Yes, sir. Be a little delay about an aircar for the rocketport." The lieutenant stepped aside, followed by a patrolman, who began taking the transposition record tape and the photo-film record out of the cabinet. "They'll call you when it's in."

Verkan and the lieutenant strolled out into the noise and color of the conveyer-head rotunda. He got out his cigarette case and offered it; the lieutenant flicked his lighter. They had only taken a few first puffs when another conveyer quietly materialized in a vacant circle a little to their left. A couple of Paracops strolled over as the door opened, drawing their needlers. One peeped inside, then holstered his weapon and snatched a radio phone from his belt; the other entered cautiously. Throwing away his cigarette, he strode toward the newly arrived conveyer, the lieutenant following.

The chair was overturned; a Paracop, his tunic off and his collar open, lay on the floor, a needler a few inches from his out-flung hand. His shirt, pale green, was darkened with blood. The lieutenant, without touching him, looked at Verkan.

"Still alive," the lieutenant said. "Bullet or sword-thrust?"

"Bullet; I can smell nitro powder." Then Verkan saw the hat lying on the floor, and stepped around the fallen man. Two men were entering with an antigrav stretcher; they and the patrolman got the wounded man onto it. "Look at this, Lieutenant."

The lieutenant glanced at the hat. It was gray felt, wide-brimmed, the crown peaked with four indentations. "Fourth Level," he said. "Europo-American."

Verkan picked it up, glancing inside. The sweatband was lettered in gold, JOHN B. STETSON COMPANY. PHILADELPHIA, PA., and, hand-inked, Cpl. Calvin Morrison. Penna. State Police, and a number.

"I know that crowd" the lieutenant said. "Good men, every bit as good as ours."

"One was a split second better than one of ours." He got out his cigarette case. "Lieutenant, this is going to be a real baddie. This pickup's going to be missed, and the people who'll miss him will be one of the ten best constabulary organizations in the world, on their time-line. They won't be put off with the sort of lame-brained explanations that usually get by on Europo-American. They'll want factual proof and physical evidence. And we'll have to find where he came out. A man who can beat a Paracop to the draw won't sink into obscurity on any time-line. He's going to kick up a fuss that'll have to be smoothed over."

"I hope he doesn't come out on a next-door time-line and turn up at a duplicate of his own police post, where a duplicate of himself is on duty. With duplicate fingerprints," the lieutenant said. "That would kick up a small fuss."

"Wouldn't it?" Verkan went to the cabinet and took out the synchro-nized transposition record and photo film. "Have the rocket held; I'll want it after a while. But I'm going over these myself. I'm going to make this operation my own personal baby."

V

Calvin Morrison dangled black-booted legs over the edge of the low cliff and wished, again, that he hadn't lost his hat. He knew exactly where he was; he was on the little cliff, not more than a big outcrop, above the road where they'd left the car, but there was no road under it now, or ever had been. And there was a hemlock four feet thick at the butt growing right where the farmhouse ought to be, and no trace of the stone foundations of it or the barn. But the really permanent features, like the Bald Eagles to the north and Nittany Mountain to the south, were exactly as they should be.

That flash and momentary darkness could have been subjective; put that in the unproven column. He was sure the strangely beautiful dome of shimmering light had been real, and so had the oval desk and the instrument panel and the man with the odd weapon. And there was certainly nothing subjective about all this virgin forest where farmlands ought to be.

He didn't for an instant question either his senses or his sanity; neither did he indulge in dirty language like "incredible" or "impossible." Extraordinary; now there was a good word. He was quite sure that something extraordinary had happened to him. It seemed to break into two parts: (One), the dome of pearly light and what had happened inside of it, and, (Two), emerging into this same-but-different place.

What was wrong with both was anachronism, and the anachronisms were mutually contradictory. None of (One) belonged in 1964 or, he suspected, for many centuries to come. None of (Two) belonged in 1964, either, or any time within two centuries in the past. His pipe had gone out; for a while he forgot to relight it, while he tossed those two facts back and forth. Then got out his lighter and thumbed it, and then buttoned it back in his pocket.

In spite—no, because—of his clergyman father's insistence that he study for and enter the Presbyterian ministry, he was an agnostic. Agnosticism, to him, was refusal either to accept or reject without factual proof. A good philosophy for a cop, by the way. Well, he wasn't going to reject the possibility of time machines; not after having been shanghaied out of his own time in one. Wherever he was now, it wasn't the Twentieth Century, and he was never going to get back to it. He made his mind up on that once and for all.

Climbing down from the low cliff, he went to the little brook, and following it to where it joined a larger stream. A bluejay made a fuss at his approach. Two deer ran in front of him. A small black bear regarded him with suspicion and hastened away. Now, if he could only find some Indians who wouldn't throw tomahawks first and ask questions afterward....

A road dipped to cross the stream. For an instant he accepted that calmly, then caught his breath. A real, wheel-rutted road! And brown horse-droppings in it, they were the most beautiful things he had seen since he came into this here-and-now. They meant he hadn't beaten Columbus here, after all. He'd have trouble giving a plausible account of himself, but at least he could do it in English. Maybe he was even in time to get into the Civil War. He waded through the ford and started west along the road, toward where Bellefonte ought to be.

The sun went down in front of him. By now, the big hemlocks were gone, lumbered off, and there was a respectable second growth, mostly hardwoods. Finally, in the dusk, he smelled freshly-turned earth. It was full dark when he saw a light ahead.

The house was only a dim shape; the light came from the narrow horizontal windows near the roof. Behind, he thought he could make out stables and, by his nose, pigpens. Two dogs ran into the road and began whauff-whauffing in front of him. "Hello, in there!" he called. Through the open windows he heard voices, a man's, a woman's, another man's. He called again. A bar scraped, and the door swung in. A woman, heavy-bodied, in a dark dress, stood aside for him to enter.

It was all one big room, lighted by one candle on a table, and one on the mantel and by the fire on the hearth. Double-deck bunks along one wall, table spread with a meal. There were three men and another woman besides the one who had admitted him, and from the comer of his eye he could see children peering around a door that seemed to open into a shed-annex. One of the men, big and blond-bearded, stood with his back to the fire, holding something that looked like a short gun in his hands. No, it wasn't, either. It was a crossbow, bent, with a quarrel in place.

The other two men were younger, the crossbowman's sons for a guess; they were bearded, too, though one's beard was only a fuzz. They all wore short-sleeved jerkins of leather and cross-gartered hose. One of the younger men had a halberd and the other an axe. The older woman spoke in a whisper to the younger; she went through the door, pushing the children ahead of her.

He lifted his hands pacifically as he entered. "I'm a friend," he said. "I'm going to Bellefonte; how far is it?"

The man with the crossbow said something. The man with the halberd said something. The woman replied. The youth with the axe said something, and they all laughed.

"My name is Calvin Morrison. Corporal, Pennsylvania State Police." Hell, they wouldn't know the State Police from the Swiss Marines. "Am I on the road to Bellefonte?"

More back-and-forth. They weren't talking Pennsylvania Dutch—he knew a little of it. Maybe Polish. No, he'd heard enough of that in the hard-coal country to recognize it, at least. He looked around while they argued, and noticed in the far corner left of the fireplace, three images on a shelf. He meant to get a closer look at them. Roman Catholics used images, so did Greek Catholics, and he knew the difference.

The man with the crossbow laid his weapon down, but kept it bent and loaded, and spoke slowly and distinctly. It was no language he had ever heard before. He replied just as distinctly in English. They looked at one another, passing hands in front of their faces in bafflement. Finally, by signs, they invited him to sit and eat, and the children, six of them, trooped in.

The meal was roast ham, potatoes and succotash. The eating tools were knives and a few horn spoons; the men used their sheath knives. He took out his jackknife, a big switchblade he'd taken off an arrest he'd made. It caused a sensation, and he had to demonstrate it several times. There was also elderberry wine, strong but not particularly good. Then they left the table for the women to clear, and the men filled pipes from a tobacco jar on the mantel, offering it to him. He filled his pipe, lighted it, as they did theirs, with a twig at the fire. Stepping back, he got a look at the images.

The central figure was an elderly man in a white robe with a blue eight-pointed star on the breast. He was flanked, on one side, by a seated female figure, exaggeratedly pregnant, crowned with grain and holding a cornstalk, and on the other by a masculine figure in a mail shirt, holding a spiked mace. The only really unusual thing about him was that he had the head of a wolf. Father-god, fertility goddess, war-god. No, this crowd wasn't Catholic, Greek, Roman or any other kind. He bowed to the central figure, touching his forehead, and repeated the gesture to the other two. There was a gratified murmur behind him; anybody could see he wasn't any heathen. Then he sat down on a chest against the wall.

They hadn't re-barred the door. The children had been chased back into the shed after the meal. Nobody was talking, everybody was listening. Now that he remembered, there had been a vacant place at the table. They'd sent one of the youngsters off with a message. As soon as he finished his pipe, he pocketed it, and unobtrusively unsnapped the strap of his holster. It might have been half an hour before he heard galloping hooves down the road. He affected not to hear; so did everybody else. The older man moved to where he had put down the crossbow; his elder son got the halberd and a rag as though to polish the blade. The horses clattered to a stop outside, accoutrements jingled. The dogs set up a frantic barking. He slipped the. 38 out and cocked it.

The youngest man went to the door. Before he could touch it, it flew open in his face, knocking him backward, and a man—bearded face under a high-combed helmet, steel breastplate, black and orange scarf— burst in, swinging a long sword. Everybody in the room shouted in alarm; this wasn't what they'd been expecting, at all. There was another helmeted head behind the first man, and the muzzle of a short musket. Outside, a shot boomed and one of the dogs howled.

Kalvan rose from the chest and he shot the man with the sword. Half-cocking with the double-action and thumbing the hammer back the rest of the way, he shot the man with the musket. The musket went off into the ceiling. A man behind him caught a crossbow quarrel through the forehead and pitched forward on top of the other two, dropping a long pistol unfired.

Shifting the Colt to his left hand, he caught up the sword the first man had dropped. It was lighter than it looked, and beautifully balanced. He tramped over the bodies in the doorway, to be confronted by another swordsman outside. For a few moments they cut and parried, and then he drove the point into his opponent's unarmored face and tugged his blade free. The man in front of him went down. The boy who had been knocked down had gotten hold of the dropped pistol and fired it, hitting a man holding a clump of horses in the road. The older son dashed out with his halberd, chopping a man down. The father got hold of the musket and ammunition, and was ramming a charge into it.

Driving the point of the sword into the ground, he holstered the .38-special; as one of the loose horses dashed past, he caught the reins and stopped it, vaulting into the saddle. Then, stopping, he retrieved the sword, thankful that even in a motorized age the State Police insisted on teaching their men to ride. The fight was over, at least here. Six attackers were down, presumably dead. The other two were galloping away. Five loose horses milled about, and the two young men were trying to catch them. Their father, priming the pan of the gun, came outside, looking around.

This had only been a sideshow fight, though. The main event was a half mile down the road; he could hear shots, yells and screams, and where a sudden orange glare mounted into the night. He was wondering just what he had cut himself in on when the fugitives began streaming up the road. He had no trouble identifying them as such; he'd seen enough of that in Korea. Another fire was blazing up beside the first one.

Some of them had weapons spears and axes, a few bows, and he saw one big musket. His bearded host shouted at them, and they paused.

"What's going on down there?" he demanded loudly.

Babble answered him. One or two tried to push past; he hit at them with the flat of his sword, cursing them luridly. The words meant nothing, but the tone did. That had worked for him in Korea, too. They all stopped, in a clump, a few cheered. Many were women and children, and not all the men were armed. Call it twenty effectives. The bodies in the road were quickly stripped of weapons; out of the corner of his eye he saw the two women of the house passing things out the door. Four of the riderless horses had been caught and mounted. More fugitives came up, saw what was going on, and joined.

"All right, you guys!" he bawled. "You guys want to live forever?" He swung his sword to include all of them, then stabbed down the road with it. "Let's go!"

A cheer went up, and as he started his horse the whole mob poured after him, shouting. They met more and more fugitives, who stopped, saw that a counterattack had been organized, if that was the word for it, and joined. The firelight was brighter, half a dozen houses must be burning now, but the shooting had stopped. Nothing to shoot at, he supposed.

Then, when they were halfway to the burning village, there was a blast of forty or fifty shots in less than ten seconds, and more yelling, most of it in alarm. More shots, and then mounted men began streaming up the road; this was a rout. Everybody with guns or bows let fly at them. A horse went down, and another had its saddle emptied. Considering how many shots it had taken for one casualty in Korea, that wasn't bad. He stood up in his stirrups, which were an inch or so too short for him as it was, and yelled, "*Chaaarge!*—like Teddy, in *Arsenic and Old Lace.*

A man coming in the opposite direction aimed a cut at his bare head. Kalvan parried and thrust, his point glanced from a breastplate, and before he could recover, the other man's horse had carried him on past and among the spears and pitchforks behind. Then he was trading thrusts for cuts with another rider, wondering if none of these imbeciles had ever heard that a sword had a point. By this time, the road for a hundred yards in front, and the open field on the left, was a swirl of horsemen, chopping and firing at each other.

He got his point in under his opponent's armpit, almost had the sword wrenched from his hand, and then saw another rider was coming at him, unarmored and wearing a wide hat and a cloak, aiming a pistol almost as long as the arm that held it. He urged his horse forward, swinging back for a cut at the weapon, and knew he'd never make it. *O.K., Cal; your luck's run out!* There was an upflash from the pan of the pistol, and something sledged him in the chest.

He hung onto consciousness long enough to kick his feet free of the stirrups. In that last moment, he was aware that the rider who had shot him had been a girl.

VI

Verkan Vall put the lighter down on the desk and took the cigarette from his mouth. Tortha Karf leaned back in the chair in which he, himself, would be sitting all too soon.

"We had one piece of luck, right at the start. The time-line is one we've already penetrated. One of our people, in a newspaper office in Philadelphia, that's the nearest large city, reported the disturbance. The press associations have it already, there's nothing we can do about that."

"Well, just what did happen on the pickup time-line?"

"This Corporal Morrison and three other state police officers were closing in on a house in which a wanted criminal was hiding. Morrison and another man were in front; the other two were coming in from behind. Morrison started forward, his companion covering for him with a rifle. This other man is the nearest thing to a witness there is, and was watching the front of the house and only marginally aware of Morrison. He heard the other two officers pounding on the back door and demanding admittance, and then the man they were after burst out the front door with a rifle in his hands. Morrison's companion shouted at him to halt; the criminal raised his rifle, and the State Police officer shot him, killing him instantly.

"Then, he says, he realized that Morrison was nowhere in sight. He called to him, without answer. The man they were after was dead, he wouldn't run off, so all three of them hunted for Morrison for almost half an hour. Then they took the body to the county seat and had to go through a lot of formalities, and it was evening before they were back at their substation. A local reporter happened to be there at the time. He got the story, including the disappearance of Morrison, phoned it to his paper, and the press association got it from there. Now the State Police refuse to discuss, and are even trying to deny the disappearance."

"They believe their man lost his nerve, bolted, and is ashamed to come back," Tortha Karf said. "Naturally, they wouldn't want anything like that getting out. Are you going to use that line?"

Verkan nodded. "The hat he lost in the conveyer. It will be planted about a mile from the scene, along a stream. Then one of our people will catch a local, preferably a boy of twelve or so, give him a hypno-injection and instruct him to find the hat and take it to the State Police. The reporter responsible for the original news break will be notified by an anonymous phone call. Later, there will be the usual spate of rumors of Morrison being seen in all sorts of unlikely places."

"How about his family?"

"We're in luck there, too. Unmarried, parents both dead, only a few relatives with whom he didn't maintain contact."

"That's good. How about the exit?"

We have it approximated; Aryan-Transpacific. We're not quite sure of the area, because the transposition field was weak for several thousand parayears and we can't determine the exact instant he broke out of the conveyer. We have one positive indication to look for at the scene."

The Chief nodded. "The empty revolver cartridge."

"Yes. He used a revolver, they don't eject automatically. As soon as he was out and no longer immediately threatened, he would open his revolver, remove the empty, and replace it. I'm as sure of that as though I saw him do it. We may not be able to find it, but if we do, it'll be positive proof."

VII

He woke, in bed, under soft covers, and for a moment lay with his eyes closed. There was a clicking sound near him, and from a distance an anvil rang, and there was shouting. Then he opened his eyes. He was in a fairly large room, paneled walls and a painted ceiling; two windows on one side, both open, and nothing but blue sky visible through them. A woman, stout and gray-haired, sat under one knitting. His boots stood beside a chest across the room, and on top were piled his clothes and his belt and revolver. A long unsheathed sword with a swept handguard and a copper pommel leaned against the wall by the boots. His body was stiff and sore, and his upper torso was swathed in bandages.

The woman looked up quickly as he stirred, then put down her knitting and rose, going to a table and pouring a cup of water for him. Pitcher and cup were of heavy silver, elaborately chased. He took the cup, drank and handed it back, thanking her. She replaced it on the table and went out.

He wasn't a prisoner, the presence of sword and revolver proved that. This was the crowd that had surprised the raiders at the village. That whole business had been a piece of luck for him. He ran a hand over his chin and estimated about three days' growth of stubble. His fingernails had grown enough since last trimmed to confirm that. He'd have a nasty hole in his chest and probably a broken rib.

The woman returned, accompanied by a man in a cowled blue robe with an eight-pointed white star on the breast. Reversed colors from the image on the peasants' farm; a priest, doubling as doctor. The man laid a hand on his brow, took his pulse, and spoke in a cheerfully optimistic tone; the bedside manner seemed to be a universal constant. With the woman's help, he changed the bandages and smeared the wound with ointment. The woman took out the old bandages and returned with a steaming bowl. It was turkey broth, with finely minced meat in it. While he was finishing it, two more visitors entered.

One was robed like the doctor, his cowl thrown back. He had white hair, and a good face, gentle and pleasant. His companion was a girl with blonde hair cut in what would be a page-boy bob in the Twentieth Century; she had blue eyes and red lips and an impudent tilty little nose dusted with golden freckles. She wore a jerkin of something like brown suede, stitched with gold thread, a yellow under-tunic with a high neck and long sleeves, knit hose and thigh-length boots. There was a gold chain around her neck, and a gold-hilted dagger on her belt. He began to laugh when he saw her; they'd met before.

"You shot me!" he accused, aiming an imaginary pistol and saying "Bang!" and pointed to his chest.

She said something to the older priest, he replied, and she said something to him, pantomiming shame and sorrow, covering her face with one hand and winking at him over it. When he laughed, she laughed with him. Perfectly natural mistake, she hadn't known which side he'd been on. The two priests held a lengthy colloquy, and the younger one brought him about four ounces of something in a tumbler. It tasted alcoholic and medicinally bitter. They told him, by signs, to go back to sleep, and went out, all but the gray-haired woman, who went back to her chair and her knitting. He dozed off.

Late in the afternoon he woke briefly. Outside, somebody was drilling troops. Tramping feet, a voice counting cadence, long-drawn preparatory commands, sharp commands of execution, clattering equipment. That was another universal constant. He smiled; he wasn't going to have much trouble finding a job, here-and-now, whenever now was.

It wasn't the past. Penn's Colony had never been like this. It was more like Sixteenth Century Europe, but no Sixteenth Century cavalryman who was as incompetent a swordsman as that gang he'd been fighting, would have lived to wear out his first pair of issue boots. And two years in college and a lot of independent reading had given him at least a nodding acquaintance with most of the gods of his own history, and none, back to Egypt and Sumer, had been like that trio on the peasant's shrine shelf.

So it was the future. A far future, maybe a thousand years later than 1964, AD; a world devastated by atomic wars, blasted back to the Stone

Age, and then bootstrap-lifted to something like the end of the Middle Ages. That wasn't important, though. Now was when he was, and now was when he was stuck.

Make the best of it, Cal. You're a soldier; you just got re-assigned, that's all.
He went back to sleep.

VIII

The next morning, after breakfast, he sign-talked the woman watching over him to bring him his tunic, and got out his pipe and tobacco and lighter from the pockets. She brought him a stool to set beside the bed to put things on. The badge on the tunic breast was twisted and lead-splotched; that was why he was still alive.

The old priest and the girl were in, an hour later. This time she was wearing a red and gray knit frock that could have gone into Bergdorf Goodman's window with a $200 price-tag any day, but the dagger she was wearing with it wasn't exactly Fifth Avenue. They greeted him, then pulled chairs up beside the bed and got to business.

First they taught him the words for "You," and "Me," and "He" and "She," and names. The girl was Rylla. The old priest was Xentos. The younger priest, who came to see his patient, was Mytron. Calvin Morrison puzzled them; evidently they didn't have surnames here-and-now. They settled for calling him Kalvan. They had several shingle-sized boards of white pine, and sticks of charcoal, to draw pictures. Rylla smoked a pipe, with a small stone bowl and a cane stem, which she carried on her belt along with her dagger. His lighter intrigued her and she showed him her own. It was a tinderbox, the flint held down by a spring against a semicircular striker which was pushed by hand and returned for another push by a spring. With a spring to drive the striker instead of returning it, it would have done for a gunlock. By noon, they were able to tell him that he was their friend and he was able to tell Rylla he didn't blame her for shooting him in the skirmish on the road.

They were back in the afternoon, accompanied by a gentleman with a gray mustache and imperial beard, wearing a garment like a fur-collared bathrobe, with a sword-belt over it. He had a large chain around his neck. His name was Ptosphes and after much pantomime and picture-writing it emerged that he was Rylla's father, that he was Prince of this place, and that this place was Hostigos. Rylla's mother was dead. The raiders with whom he had fought had come from a place called Nostor, to the north and east, ruled by a Prince Gormoth. Gormoth was not well thought of in Hostigos.

The next day, Kalvan was up in a chair, and they began giving him solid food, and wine to drink. The wine was excellent; so was the tobacco they gave him. He decided he was going to like it here-and-now. Rylla was in at least twice a day, sometimes alone, and sometimes with a big man with a graying beard, Chartiphon, who seemed to be Ptosphes' top soldier. He always wore a sword and often an ornate but battered steel back-and-breast. Sometimes he visited alone, and occasionally accompanied by a younger officer, a cavalryman named Harmakros. Harmakros had been in the skirmish at the raided village, but Rylla had been in command.

"The gods," he explained, "did not give our Prince Ptosphes a son. A Prince should have a son. A Prince should have a son to rule after him, so the Princess Rylla must be a son for him."

The gods, Kalvan thought, ought to be persuaded to furnish Ptosphes with a son-in-law, named Calvin Morrison, no, Kalvan. He made up his mind to give the gods a hand on that.

Chartiphon showed him a map, elaborately illuminated on parchment. Hostigos appeared to be all of Centre and Union Counties, a snip of Clinton south and west of where Lock Haven ought to be, and southeastern Lycoming, east of the West Branch, which was the Athan, and south of the Bald Eagles, the Mountains of Hostigos. Nostor was the West Branch Valley from above Lock Haven to the forks of the river, and it obtruded south into Hostigos through Ante's Gap, Dombra Gap, to take in Nippenose, Sevenhills Valley. To the west, all of Blair County, and parts of Huntington and Bedford, was the Princedom of Sask, ruled by Prince Sarrask. Sarrask was no friend; Gormoth an open enemy.

On a bigger map, he saw that all Pennsylvania and Maryland,

Delaware and the southern half of New Jersey, was the Great Kingdom of Hos-Harphax, ruled from Harphax City at the mouth of the Susquehanna by King Kaiphranos. Ptosphes, Gormoth, Sarrask and a dozen other princes were his nominal subjects. Judging from what he'd seen on the night of his advent here-and-now, Kaiphranos' authority would be maintained for about one day's infantry march around his capital and ignored elsewhere.

He had a suspicion that Hostigos was in a bad squeeze, between Nostor and Sask. Something was bugging these people. Too often, while laughing with him—she was teaching him to read and write, now, and that was fun—Rylla would remember something she wanted to forget, and then her laughter would be strained. Chartiphon was always preoccupied; occasionally he'd forget, for a moment, what he had been talking about. And he never saw Ptosphes smile.

Xentos showed him a map of the world. The world, it seemed, was not round, but flat like a pancake. Hudson's Bay was in the exact center, North America was shaped rather like India, Florida ran almost due east, and Cuba north and south. The West Indies were a few random spots to show that the mapmaker had heard about them from somebody. Asia was attached to North America, but it was still blank. An illimitable ocean stretched around the perimeter. Europe, Africa and South America simply weren't. Xentos wanted him to show the country from which he had come. He put his finger down on central Pennsylvania's approximate location. Xentos thought he misunderstood.

"No, Kalvan. This is your home now, and we want you to stay with us always, but where is the country you came from?"

"Here," he insisted. "But at another time, a thousand years from now. I had an enemy, an evil sorcerer. Another sorcerer, who was my friend, put a protection on me that I might not be slain by sorcery, so my enemy twisted time around me and hurled me far into the past, before my first known ancestor had been born, and now here I am and here I must stay."

Xentos' hand described a quick circle around the white star on his breast, and he muttered rapidly. Another universal constant.

"What a terrible fate!"

"Yes. I do not like to speak of it, but it was right that you should know. You may tell Prince Ptosphes and Princess Rylla and Chartiphon, but beg them not to speak of it to me. I must forget my old life, and make a new one in this time. You may tell the others merely that I come from a far country. From here." He indicated the approximate location of Korea. "I was there, once, fighting in a great war."

"Ah; I knew you had been a warrior." Xentos hesitated, then asked "Do you also know sorcery?"

"No. My father was a priest, as you are, and wished me to become a priest also, and our priests hated sorcery. But I knew that I would never be a good priest, so when this war came, I left my studies and went to fight. Afterwards, I was a warrior in my own country, to keep the peace."

Xentos nodded. "If one cannot be a good priest, one should not be a priest at all, and to be a good warrior is almost as good. Tell me, what gods did your people worship?"

"Oh, we had many gods. There was Conformity, and Authority, and Opinion. There was Status, whose symbols were many and who rode in the great chariot Cadillac, which was almost a god itself. And there was Atombomb, the dread Destroyer, who would some day end the world. For myself, I worshiped none of them. Tell me about your gods, Xentos."

Then he filled his pipe and lit it with the tinderbox he had learned to use in place of his now fuelless Zippo. He didn't need to talk any more; Xentos was telling him about his own gods, Dralm, and about Yirtta the AllMother and wolf-headed Galzar the god of battle, and Tranth, the lame craftsman god—funny how often craftsman gods were lame—and about all the others.

"And Styphon," Xentos added grudgingly. "Styphon is an evil god, and evil men serve him, and are given great wealth and power."

IX

After that, he noticed a subtle change in manner toward him. He caught Rylla regarding him in wondering pity. Chartiphon merely clasped his hand and said, "You'll like it here with us, Kalvan." Prince Ptosphes hemmed and hawed, and said: "Xentos tells me there are things you don't want to talk about, Kalvan. Nobody will mention them to you ever. We're all happy to have you with us. Stay, and make this your home."

The others treated him with profound respect. They'd been told that he was a prince from a distant land, driven from his throne by treason. They gave him clothes, more than he had ever owned before, and weapons. Rylla gave him a pair of her own pistols, one of which had wounded him in the skirmish. They were two feet long but lighter than his .38 Colt, the barrels almost paper thin at the muzzles. They had locks operating on the same principle as the tinderboxes, and Rylla's name was inlaid in gold on the butts. They gave him another, larger room, and a body servant.

As soon as he could walk unaided, he went outside to watch the troops being drilled. They had no uniforms but scarves or sashes of Ptosphes' colors, red and blue. The infantry wore leather or canvas jacks sewn with metal plates, and helmets not unlike the one he'd worn in Korea. Some had pikes, some halberds, and some hunting spears, and many had scythe blades with the tangs straightened out on eight-foot shafts. Foot movements were simple and uncomplicated; the squad was unknown, and they maneuvered by platoons of forty or fifty.

A few of the firearms were huge fifteen-pound muskets, aimed and fired from rests. Most were lighter, arquebuses, calivers and a miscellany of hunting guns. There would be two or three musketeers and a dozen calivermen or arquebusiers to each spear-and-scythe platoon. There were also archers and crossbowmen. The cavalry were good; they wore cuirasses and high-combed helmets, and were armed with swords and pistols and either lances or short musketoons. The artillery was laughable; wrought-iron six to twelve pounders, hand-welded tubes strengthened with shrunk-on bands, without trunnions. They were mounted on four wheel carts. He made up his mind to do something about that.

He also noticed that while the archers and crossbowmen practiced constantly, not a single practice shot was fired with any firearm.

He took his broadsword to the castle bladesmith and wanted it ground down into a rapier. The bladesmith thought he was crazy. He called in a cavalry lieutenant and demonstrated with a pair of wooden practice swords. Immediately, the lieutenant wanted a rapier, too. The blacksmith promised to make both of them real rapiers. By the next evening, his own was finished.

"You have enemies on both sides, Nostor and Sask, and that's not good," Kalvan said one evening as he and Ptosphes and Rylla and Chartiphon sat over a flagon of wine in the Prince's study. "You've made me one of you. Now tell me what I can do to help."

"Well, Kalvan," Ptosphes said, "you could better tell us that. You know many things we don't. The thrusting sword"—he glanced down admiringly at his own new rapier—"and what you told Chartiphon about mounting cannon. What else can you give us to help fight our enemies?"

"Well, I can't teach you to make weapons like that six-shooter of mine, or ammunition for it" He tried, as simply as possible, to explain about machine industry and mass production; they only stared in uncomprehending wonder. "I can show you a few things you don't know but can do with the tools you have. For instance, we cut spiral grooves inside the bores of our guns to make the bullets spin. Grooved guns shoot harder, farther and straighter than smoothbores. I can show your gunsmiths how to do that with guns you already have. And there's another thing." He mentioned never having seen any practice firing. "You have very little powder, fireseed, you call it. Is that it?"

"We haven't enough in Hostigos to fire all the cannon of this castle once," Chartiphon said. "And we can't get any. The priests of Styphon will give us none, and they send cart after cart to Nostor."

"You mean, you get fireseed from the priests of Styphon? Can't you get it from anybody else, or make your own?"

They all looked at him, amazed that he didn't know any better.

"Only Styphon's House can make fireseed, and that by Styphon's aid," Xentos said. "That was what I meant when I said that Styphon gives his servants great wealth, and power even over the Great Kings."

Kalvan gave Styphon's House the grudging respect any good cop gives a really smart crook. No wonder this country was a snakepit of warring princes and barons. Styphon's House wanted it that way; it kept them in the powder business. He set down his goblet and laughed.

"You think nobody can make fireseed but Styphon's House?" he demanded. "Why, in my time, even the children could do that." Well, children who got as far as high school chemistry; he'd almost gotten expelled, once. "I can make fireseed, right here on this table!"

Ptosphes threw back his head and laughed. Just a trifle hysterically, but it was the first time Kalvan had ever heard the Prince laugh. Chartiphon banged a fist on the table and shouted, "Ha, Gormoth!" Now see how soon your head goes up over your own gate." And no War Crimes foolishness about it, either. Rylla flung her arms around him. "Kalvan! You really and truly can?"

"But it is only by the power of Styphon..." Xentos began.

"Styphon's a big fake; his priests are a pack of impudent swindlers. You want to see me make fireseed? Get Mytron in here; he has everything I need in his dispensary. I want sulfur, he has that, and saltpeter, he has that." Mytron gives sulfur mixed with honey for colds; saltpeter was supposed to cool the blood. "And charcoal, and a couple of brass mortars and pestles, and a flour-screen, and balance scales."

"Go on, man; hurry!" Ptosphes said. "Bring him anything he wants."

Xentos went out. Kalvan asked for a pistol, and Ptosphes brought one from a closet behind him. He opened the pan, and dumped out the priming on a sheet of parchment, touching a lighted splinter to it. It scorched the parchment, which it shouldn't have done, and left too much black residue. Styphon wasn't a very honest powder maker; he cheapened his product with too much charcoal and not enough saltpeter. Xentos returned, accompanied by Mytron; the two priests carried jars, and a bucket of charcoal and the other things. Xentos seemed dazed; Mytron was scared and trying not to show it.

He put Mytron to work grinding charcoal in one mortar and Xentos to grinding saltpeter in the other. The sulfur was already pulverized. Screening each, he mixed them in a dry goblet, saltpeter .75, charcoal .15, sulfur .10; he had to think a little to remember that.

"But it's just dust," Chartiphon objected.

"Yes. The mixture has to be moistened, worked into a dough, pressed into cakes and dried, and then ground and sieved. We can't do all that now, but this will flash. Look."

Kalvan primed the pistol with a pinch of it, aimed at a half-burned log in the fireplace, and squeezed. The pistol roared and kicked. Ptosphes didn't believe in reduced charges, that was for sure. Outside, somebody shouted, feet pounded, and the door flew open. A guard with a halberd looked in.

"The Lord Kalvan is showing us something with a pistol," Ptosphes said. "There may be more shots; nobody is to worry."

"All right," Kalvan said, when the guard closed the door. "Now, we can see how it fires." He poured in about forty grains, wadded it with a bit of rag, and primed it, handing it to Rylla. "You fire. This is a great moment in the history of Hostigos, I hope."

She pushed down the striker, aimed into the fireplace and squeezed. The report wasn't quite as loud, but it did fire. Then they tried it with a bullet, which went into the log half an inch. He laid the pistol on the table. The room was full of smoke, and they were all coughing, but nobody cared. Chartiphon went to the door and shouted into the hall for more wine.

"But you said no prayers," Mytron faltered. "You just made fireseed. Just like cooking soup."

"That's right. And before long, everybody will make fireseed."

And when that day comes, the priests of Styphon will be out on the sidewalk beating a drum for pennies. Chartiphon wanted to know how soon they could be able to march on Nostor.

"It will take more fireseed than Kalvan can make on this table,"

Ptosphes told him. "We will need saltpeter, and charcoal, and sulfur. We will have to teach people how to get these things, and grind and mix them. We will need many things we don't have and tools to make them. And nobody knows all about this but Kalvan, and there is only one of him."

Well, glory be, Ptosphes had gotten something from the lecture on production, if nobody else had.

"Mytron knows a few things, I think. Where did you get the sulfur and the saltpeter?" Kalvan asked the doctor-priest.

Mytron had downed his first goblet of wine at one gulp. He had taken three to the second; now he was working his way down the third and coming out of shock nicely. It was about as Kalvan thought. The saltpeter was found in crude lumps under manure piles and refined; the sulfur was gotten by evaporating water from the sulfur springs in Sugar Valley, Wolf Valley here-and-now. For some reason, mention of this threw both Ptosphes and Chartiphon into a fury. Mytron knew now to extract both on a quart-jar scale. He was a trifle bewildered when told how much would be needed for military purposes.

"But this'll take time." Chartiphon objected. "And as soon as Gormoth hears about it, he'll attack, before we can get any made."

"Don't let him hear about it. Clamp down the security." Kalvan had to explain that. "Cavalry patrols, on all the roads and trails out of Hostigos; let anybody in, but don't let anybody out. And here's another thing. I'll have to give orders, and people won't like them. Will I be obeyed?"

"By anybody who wants to keep his head on his shoulders," Ptosphes said. "You speak with my voice."

"And mine, too, Lord Kalvan!" Chartiphon was on his feet, extending his sword for him to touch the hilt. "I am at your order; you command here."

X

They gave him a little room inside the main gateway of the citadel, across from the guardroom, a big flagstone-floored place with the indefinable but unmistakable flavor of a police court. The walls were white plaster; he could write and draw diagrams on them with charcoal. Paper was unknown here-and-now. He decided to do something about that, after the war. It was a wonder these people had gotten as far as they had without it. Rylla attached herself to him as adjutant. He gathered in Mytron and the chief priest of Tranth, all the master-artisans in Tarr-Hostigos and some from Hostigos Town, a couple of Chartiphon's officers and some soldiers to carry messages.

Charcoal was going to be easy, there was plenty of that. For sulfur evaporation he'd need big iron pans, and sheet iron, larger than a breastplate or a cooking pan—all unavailable. There were bog-iron mines over in Bald Eagle, Listra Valley, and iron works, but no rolling mill. They'd have to beat the sheet iron by hand in two-foot squares and weld them together like a patch quilt. Saltpeter could be accumulated from all over. Manure piles, at least one to a farm, were the best source, and stables, cellars, underground drains. He set up a saltpeter commission, headed by one of Chartiphon's officers, with authority to go anywhere and enter anything, to hang any subordinate who abused that authority out of hand and to deal just as summarily with anybody who tried to obstruct.

Mobile units, oxcarts loaded with cauldrons, tubs, tools and the like, to go from farm to farm. Peasant women to be collected and taught to leach nitrated soil and purify nitrates.

Grinding mills; there was plenty of water power, and the waterwheel was known here-and-now. Gristmills could be converted. Special grinding equipment, designing of. Sifting screens, cloth. Mixing machines, big casks with counter-rotating paddle wheels inside. Presses to squeeze dough into cakes. Mills to grind caked powder; he spent considerable thought on a set of regulations to prevent anything from striking a spark around them, with bloodthirsty enforcement threats.

During the morning, he ground up the cake he'd made the night before, running it through a couple of sieves to about FFFg fineness. A hundred-grain charge in one of the big eight-bore muskets drove the two-ounce ball an inch deeper into a hemlock log than an equal charge of Styphon's Best and fouled the bore much less.

By noon, he was almost sure that most all of his War Production Board understood most of what he'd told them. In the afternoon, there was a meeting in the outer bailey of as many of the people who would be working on the Fireseed Project as could be collected. There was an invocation of Dralm by Xentos. Ptosphes spoke, bearing down heavily on the fact that the Lord Kalvan had full authority and would be backed to the limit, by the headsman if necessary. Chartiphon made a speech, picturing the howling wilderness they were going to make of Nostor. He made a speech, himself, emphasizing that there was nothing of a supernatural nature about fireseed. The meeting then broke up into small groups, everybody having his own job explained to him. He was kept running back and forth from one to another to explain to the explainers.

In the evening, they had a feast. By that time, he and Rylla had gotten a rough table of organization charcoaled onto the wall in his headquarters.

Of the next four days, he spent eighteen hours each in that room, talking to five or six hundred people. The artisans, who had a guild organization, objected to peasants invading their crafts. The masters complained that the apprentices and young journeymen were becoming intractable, which meant they had started thinking for themselves. The peasants objected to having their dunghills forked down and the ground under them dug up, and to being put to unaccustomed work. The landlords objected to having the peasants taken from the fields, and predicted that the year's crop would be lost.

"Don't worry about that," Kalvan told them. "If we win, we'll eat Gormoth's crops. If we lose, we'll all be too dead to eat."

And the Iron Curtain went down, itinerant packtraders and wagoners began to collect in Hostigos Town, trapped for the duration. Sooner or later, Gormoth and Sarrask would start wondering why nobody was leaving

Hostigos and send spies in through the woods to find out. Organize some counterespionage; get a few spies of his own into both princedoms.

By the fifth day, the sulfur-evaporation plant was operating and salt-peter production had started, only a few pounds of each, but that would increase rapidly. He put Mytron in charge of the office and went out to supervise mill construction. It was at this time that he began wearing armor, at least six and often eight hour a day—helmet over a padded coif, with a band of fine-linked mail around his throat and under his chin, steel back-and-breast over a quilted arming-doublet with mail sleeves, mail under the arms, and a mail skirt to below his hips, and double leather hose with mail between. The whole panoply weighed close to forty pounds and his life was going to depend on accustoming himself to it.

XI

Verkan Vall watched Tortha Karf spin the empty revolver cartridge on the top of his desk. It was a very valuable empty cartridge; it had cost over ten thousand man-hours of crawling on hands and knees and pawing among dead hemlock needles to find it, not counting transposition time.

"A marvel you found it, Vall. Aryan-Transpacific?"

"Oh, yes. We were sure of that from the first. Styphon's House Subsector." Verkan gave the exact numerical designation of the exact time-line.

"Styphon's House. That's that gunpowder theocracy, isn't it?

That was it. At one time, Styphon had been a minor god of healing. Still was, on most of Aryan-Transpacific. But, three or four hundred years ago, on one time-line, a priest of Styphon, trying to concoct a new remedy for something, had mixed a batch of saltpeter, charcoal and sulfur—fortunately for him a small batch—and put it on fire. For fifty years, the mixture had been a temple miracle, and then its propellant properties were discovered, and Styphon had gone out of medical practice and into the munitions business. The powder had been improved by priestly researchers; weapons to use it were designed. Now no king or prince without gunpowder stood a chance against one with it. No matter who sat on any throne, Styphon's House was his master, because Styphon's House could throw him off it at will.

"I wonder if this Morrison knows how to make gunpowder," Tortha Karf said.

"I'll find that out. I'm going out there myself."

"You know, you don't have to. You have hundreds of men who could do that."

Verkan shook his head obstinately. "After Year-End Day, I'm going to be chained to that chair of yours. But until then, I'm going to work out-time as much as I can." He leaned over to the map-screen and twiddled the selector unit until he had the Great Kingdom of Hos-Harphax. "I'm going in about here," he said. "I'll be a pack trader, they go anywhere without question. I'll have a saddle horse and three pack horses, with loads of appropriate merchandise. That's in the adjoining Princedom of Sask. I'll travel slowly, to let word travel ahead of me. I may even hear something about this Morrison before I enter Hostigos."

"What'll you do about him when you find him?"

He shrugged. "That will depend on what he's doing, and particularly how he's accounting for himself. I don't want to, the man's a police officer like ourselves, but I'm afraid I'm going to have to kill him. He knows too much."

"What does he know, Vall?"

"First, he's seen the inside of a conveyer. He knows that it was something completely alien to his own culture and technology. Then, he knows that he was shifted in time, because he wasn't shifted to another place, and he will recognize that the conveyer was the means effecting that shift. From that, he'll deduce a race of time-travelers.

"Now, he knows enough of the history of his own time-line to know he wasn't shifted into the past. And he will also know he wasn't shifted into the future. That's all limestone country, where he was picked up and dropped, and on his own time-line it's been quarried extensively for the past fifty or more years. Traces of those operations would remain for tens of thousands of years, and he will find none of them. So what does that leave?"

"A lateral shift and people who travel laterally in time," the Chief said. "Why, that's the Paratime Secret itself."

XII

There would be a feast at Tarr-Hostigos that evening. All morning cattle and pigs, lowing and squealing, had been driven in and slaughtered. Woodcutters' axes thudded for the roasting pits, casks of wine came up from the cellars. He wished the fireseed mills were as busy as the castle kitchens and bakeries. The whole day's production shot to hell. He said as much to Rylla.

"But, Kalvan, they're all so happy." She was pretty excited about it herself. "And they've worked so hard."

He had to grant that, and maybe the morale gain would offset a day's work lost. And they had a full hundredweight of fireseed, fifty percent better than Styphon's Best, and half of it made in the last two days.

"It's been so long since anybody had anything to be really happy about. When we had feasts, everybody would get drunk as soon as they could, to keep from thinking about what was coming. And now, maybe it won't come at all."

And now, they were all drunk on a hundred pounds of black powder. Five thousand arquebus rounds at most. They'd have to do better than twenty-five pounds a day; have to get it up to a hundred. Mixing, caking and grinding was the bottleneck, that meant still more mill machinery, and there weren't enough able men to build it. It would mean stopping work on the rifling machinery and on the carriages and limbers for the light four-pounders the ironworks were turning out.

It would take a year to build the sort of an army he wanted, and Gormoth of Nostor would attack in two months at most.

He brought that up, that afternoon, at the General Staff meeting. Like rifling and trunnions on cannon and teaching swordsmen to use the point, that was new for here-and-now. You just hauled a lot of peasants together and armed them; that was Organization. You picked a marching route, that was Strategy. You lined up your men somehow and shot or hit anybody in front of you, that was Tactics. And Intelligence was something mounted scouts, if any, brought in at the last minute from a mile ahead. It cheered him to recall that that would probably be Gormoth's idea of the Art of War. Why, with ten thousand men, Gustavus Adolphus or the Duke of Parma, or Gonzalo de Córdoba could have gone through all five of these Great Kingdoms like a dose of croton oil.

Ptosphes and Rylla were present *ex officio* as Prince and Heiress-Apparent. The Lord Kalvan was Commander-in-Chief. Chartiphon was Field Marshal and Chief of Operations. Harmakros was G-2, an elderly infantry captain was drillmaster, paymaster, quartermaster, inspector-general and head of the draft board. A civilian merchant, who wasn't losing any money at it, had charge of supply and procurement. Xentos, who was Ptosphes' chancellor as well as chief ecclesiastic, attended political matters, and also fifth-column activities, another of Lord Kalvan's marvelous new ideas, mainly because he was in touch with the priests of Dralm in Nostor and Sask, all of whom hated Styphon's House beyond expression.

The first blaze of optimism had died down, Kalvan was glad to observe. Chartiphon was grumbling:

"We have three thousand at most; Gormoth has ten thousand, six thousand mercenaries and four thousand of his own people. Making our own fireseed gives us a chance, which we didn't have before, but that's all."

"Two thousand of his own people," somebody said. "He won't take the peasants out of the fields."

"Then he'll attack earlier," Ptosphes said. "While our peasants are getting the harvest in."

Kalvan looked at the map painted on one of the walls. Gormoth could invade up the Listra Valley, but that would only give him half of Hostigos—less than that. The whole line of the Mountains of Hostigos was held at every gap except one, guarded by Tarr-Dombra, lost by treachery three quarters of a century ago, and Sevenhills Valley behind it.

"We'll have to take Tarr-Dombra and clean Sevenhills Valley out," he said.

Everybody stared at him. It was Chartiphon who first found his voice.

"Man! You never saw Tarr-Dombra, or you wouldn't talk like that. It's smaller than Tarr-Hostigos, but it's even stronger."

"That's right," the retread captain who was G-1 and part of G-4 supported him.

"Do the Nostori think it can't be taken, too?" Kalvan asked. "Then it can be. Prince, have you plans of the castle?"

"Oh, yes. On a big scroll, in one of my coffers. It was my grandfather's, and we always hoped...."

"I'll want to see them. Later will do. Do you know of any changes made on it since then?"

None on the outside, at least. Kalvan asked about the garrison; five hundred, Harmakros thought. A hundred regular infantry of Gormoth's, and four hundred cavalry for patrolling around the perimeter of Sevenhills Valley. They were mercenaries, and they were the ones who had been raiding into Hostigos.

"Then stop killing raiders who can be taken alive." Prisoners can be made to talk. The Geneva Convention was something else unknown here-and-now. Kalvan turned to Xentos. "Is there a priest of Dralm in Sevenhills Valley? Can you get in touch with him, and will he help us? Explain that this is a war against Styphon's House."

"He knows that, and he will help, as he can, but he can't get into Tarr-Dombra. There is a priest of Galzar there for the mercenaries, and a priest of Styphon for the lord of the castle. Among the Nostori, Dralm is but a god for the peasants."

That rankled. Yes, the priests of Dralm would help.

"All right. But he can talk to people who can get inside, can't he? And he can send messages, and organize an espionage apparatus among the peasants. I want to know everything that can be found out, no matter how trivial. Particularly, I want to know the guard-routine at the castle, and how it's supplied. And I want it observed all the time; Harmakros, you find men to do that. I take it we can't storm the place, or you'd have done that long ago. Then we'll have to surprise it."

XIII

Verkan the pack trader went up the road, his horse plodding unhurriedly and the three pack horses on the lead-line trailing behind. He was hot and sticky under his steel back-and-breast, and sweat ran down his cheeks from under his helmet into his new beard, but nobody ever saw an unarmed pack trader, so he had to endure it. They were local made, from an adjoining, nearly identical time-line, and so were his clothes, his sword, the carbine in the saddle sheath, his horse gear, and the loads of merchandise, all except a metal coffer on top of one pack load.

Reaching the brow of the hill, he started down the other side, and as he did he saw a stir in front of a thatched and whitewashed farm cottage. Men mounting horses; glints of armor, and the red-and-blue Hostigi colors. Another cavalry post, the third since he'd passed since crossing the border from Sask. The other two had ignored him, but this crowd meant to stop him. Two had lances, and a third a musketoon, and the fourth, who seemed to be in command, had his holsters open and his right hand on his horse's neck.

Verkan reined in his horse; the pack horses came to a well-trained stop. "Good cheer, soldiers," he greeted.

"Good cheer, trader," the man with his hand close to his pistol-butt replied. "From Sask?"

"Sask last. From Ulthor, this trip; Grefftscharr by birth." Ulthor was the lake port to the northwest; Grefftscharr was the kingdom around the Great Lakes. "I'm for Agrys City."

One of the troopers laughed. The captain asked "Have you any fireseed?"

"About twenty charges." He touched the flask on his belt. "I tried to get some in Sask, but when the priests of Styphon heard that I was coming through Hostigos they'd give me none."

"I know; we're under the ban, here." It did not seem to distress him greatly. "But I'm afraid you'll not see Agrys soon. We're on the edge of war with Nostor, and the Lord Kalvan wants no tales carried, so he's ordered that no one may leave Hostigos."

Verkan cursed; that was expected of him.

"I'd feel ill-used, too, in your place, but you know how it is," the captain sympathized. "but when princes and lords command, common folk obey. It won't be so bad, though. You can get good prices in Hostigos Town or at Tarr-Hostigos, and then, if you know a skilled trade, you can find work at good wages. You're well-armed and horsed; the Lord Kalvan welcomes all such."

"The Lord Kalvan? I thought Ptosphes was Prince of Hostigos?"

"Why, so he is, Dralm guard him, but the Lord Kalvan, Dralm bless him, too, is the war leader. It's said he's a prince himself, from a far land. It's also said that he's a sorcerer, but that I doubt."

Ah, yes; the stranger prince from afar. And among these people, Corporal Calvin Morrison—he willed himself no longer to think of the man as anything but the Lord Kalvan—would be suspected of sorcery. He chatted pleasantly with the captain and the troopers, asking about inns, about prices being paid for things; all the questions a wandering trader would ask, then bade them good luck and rode on. He passed other farms along the road. At most of them, work was going on; men were forking down dunghills and digging under them, fires burned and cauldrons steamed over them. He added that to the cheerfulness with which the cavalrymen had accepted the ban of Styphon's House.

Styphon, it seemed, had acquired a competitor.

Hostigos Town spread around a low hill and a great spring as large as a small lake, facing the mountains, which on the Europo-American Sector, had been quarried into sheer cliffs. The Lord Kalvan wouldn't fail to notice that. Above the gap stood a strong castle; that would be Tarr-Hostigos, *tarr* meant castle, or stronghold. The streets were crowded with carts and wagons; the artisans' quarter was noisy with the work of smiths and joiners. He found the sign of the Red Halberd, the inn the sergeant had commended to him. He put up his horses and safe-stowed his packs, all but his personal luggage, his carbine and the metal coffer. A servant carried the former; he took the coffer over one shoulder and followed him to the room he had been given.

When he was alone, he set the coffer down. It was an almost feature-less block of bronze, without visible lock or hinges, with only two bright steel ovals on the top. Pressing his thumbs to these, he heard a slight click as the photoelectric lock inside responded to his thumbprint patterns. The lid opened. Inside were four globes of gleaming coppery mesh, a few instruments with dials and knobs and a little sigma-ray needler, a ladies' model, small enough to be covered by his hand, but as deadly as the big one he usually carried. It was silent, and it killed without a trace that any autopsy would reveal.

There was also an antigrav unit, attached to the bottom of the coffer; it was on, the tiny pilot light glowed red. When he switched it off, the floor boards under the coffer creaked. Lined with collapsed metal, it now weighed over half a ton. He pushed down the lid, which only his thumb-prints could open, and heard the lock click.

XIV

The common room downstairs was crowded and noisy. Verkan found a vacant place at one of the long tables and sat down. Across from him, a man with a bald head and a small straggling red beard grinned at him.

"New fish in the net?" he asked. "Welcome. Where from?"

"Ulthor, with three horse loads. My name's Verkan."

"Mine's Skranga." The bald man was from Agrys City. "They took them all, fifty of them. Paid me less than I asked, but more than I thought they would, so I guess I got a fair price. I had four Trygathi herders, they're all in the cavalry now. I'm working in the fireseed mill."

"The what?" Verkan was incredulous. "You mean these people make their own fireseed? But nobody but the priests of Styphon can do that."

Skranga laughed. "That's what I thought, when I came here, but anybody can do it. No more a trick than boiling soap. See, they get the saltpeter from under dunghills, and...."

Skranga detailed the process step by step. The man facing him joined the conversation; he even understood, dimly, the theory. The charcoal was what burned, the sulfur was the kindling, and the saltpeter made the air to blow up the fire and blow the bullet out of the gun. And there was no secrecy about it, at least inside Hostigos. Except for keeping the news out of Nostor until he had enough fireseed for a war, the Lord Kalvan simply didn't care.

"I bless Dralm for bringing me into this," the horse trader said. "When people can leave here, I'm going to go to some place and start making fireseed myself. Why, I'll be rich in a few years and so can you."

Skranga finished his meal, said he had to return to work, and left. A cavalry officer who had been sitting a few places down the table picked up his cup and flagon and took the vacant seat.

"You just came in?" he asked. "From Nostor?"

"No, from Sask." The answer seemed to disappoint the cavalryman; he went into the Ulthor-Grefftscharr story again. "How long will I be kept from going on?"

"Till we fight the Nostori and beat them. What do the Saski think we're doing here?"

"Waiting to have your throats cut. They don't know anything about your making fireseed."

The officer laughed. "Ha! Some of them'll get theirs cut, if Prince Sarrask doesn't mind his step. You say you have three horse loads of Grefftscharr wares; any weapons?"

"Some sword blades. Some daggers, a dozen gunlocks, three good shirts of rivet-link mail, a lot of bullet-molds. And brassware, and jewelry, of course."

"Well, take your loads up to Tarr-Hostigos. They have a little fair each evening in the outer bailey, you can sell anything you have. Go early. Use my name"—he gave it—"and speak to Captain Harmakros. He'll be glad of any news you have."

Verkan re-packed his horses, when they had eaten, and led them up the road to the castle above the gap. Along the wall of the outer bailey, inside the gate, were workshops, all busy. One thing he noticed was a gun carriage for a light field piece being put together, not a little cart, but two big wheels and a trail, to be hauled with a limber. The gun for it was the sort of wrought-iron four-pounder, normal for this sector, but it had trunnions, which was not. The Lord Kalvan, again.

Like all the local gentry, Captain Harmakros wore a small neat beard. His armor was rich but well battered, but the long rapier on his belt was new. He asked a few questions, then listened to a detailed account of what Verkan the trader had seen and heard in Sask; the mercenary companies Sarrask had hired, the names of the captains, their strength and equipment.

"You've kept your eyes and your wits about you," Harmakros commented. "I wish you'd come through Nostor instead. Were you ever a soldier?"

"All free-traders are soldiers, in their own service."

"Yes, well, when you've sold your loads, you'll be welcome in ours. Not as a common trooper, as a scout. You want to sell your pack horses, too? We'll give your own price for them."

"If I can sell my loads, yes."

"You'll have no trouble doing that. Stay about, have your meals with the officers here. We'll find something for you."

Verkan had some tools, for both wood and metal work. He peddled them among the artisans, for a good price in silver and a better one in information. Besides cannon with trunnions on regular field-carriages, Kalvan had introduced rifling in small arms. Nobody knew whence Kalvan had come, but they knew it had been a great distance.

The officers with whom he ate listened avidly to what he had to tell them about his observations in Sask. Nostor first, and then Sask, seemed to be the schedule. When they talked about the Lord Kalvan, the coldest expressions were of deep respect, and shaded up to hero-worship. But they knew nothing about him before the night he had appeared at a peasant's cottage and rallied a rabble fleeing from a raided village.

Verkan sold the mail and sword blades and gunlocks as a lot to one of the officers; the rest of the stuff he spread to offer to the inmates of the castle. He saw the Lord Kalvan strolling through the crowd, in full armor and wearing a rapier and a Colt .38 special on his belt. He had grown a small beard since the photograph the Paratime Police had secured on Europo-American had been taken. Clinging to his arm was a beautiful blonde girl in male riding dress; Prince Ptosphes' daughter Rylla, he was told. He had already heard the story of how she had shot him by mistake in a skirmish and brought him to Tarr-Hostigos to be cared for. The happy possessiveness with which she held his arm, and the tenderness with which he looked at her, made him smile. Then the smile froze on his lips and died in his eyes as he wondered what Kalvan had told her privately.

Returning to the Red Halberd, he spent some time and a little money in the tap room. Everybody, as far as he could learn, seemed satisfied that Kalvan had come, with or without divine guidance, to Hostigos in a perfectly normal manner. Finally, he went up to his room.

Pressing his thumbs to the sensitized ovals, he opened the coffer and lifted out one of the gleaming copper-mesh balls. It opened at pressure on a small stud; he drew out a wire with a mouthpiece attached, and spoke for a long time into it.

"So far," he concluded, "there seems to be no suspicion of anything paranormal about the man in anybody's mind. I have not yet made any contacts with anybody who would confide in me to the contrary. I have been offered an opportunity to take service under him a scout; I intend doing this. Some assistance can be given me in carrying out this work. I will find a location for a conveyer-head; this will have to be somewhere in the woods near Hostigos Town. I will send a ball through when I do. Verkan Vall, ending communication."

Then he set the timer for the transposition field generator and switched on the antigrav unit. Carrying the ball to the open window, he released it. It rose quickly into the night, high above, among the many visible stars, there was an instant flash. It could have been a meteor.

XV

Kalvan sat on a rock under a tree, wishing he could smoke, and knowing that he was beginning to be scared. He cursed mentally. It didn't mean anything, as soon as things got started he'd forget to be scared, but it always happened before, and he hated it. It was quiet on the mountain top, even though there were two hundred men sitting or squatting or lying around him, and another five hundred, under Chartiphon and Prince Ptosphes, five hundred yards behind. There were fifty more a hundred yards ahead and a skirmish line of thirty riflemen. Now there was a new word in the here-and-now military lexicon. A few of the rifles were big fifteen- to twenty-pound muskets, eight- to six-bore; mostly they were calivers, sixteen- and twenty-bore, the size and weight of a Civil War musket. They were commanded by the Grefftscharr trader, Verkan. There had been objection to giving an outland stranger so important a command; he had informed the objectors, stiffly, that he had been an outland stranger himself only recently.

Out in front of Verkan's line, in what the defenders of Tarr-Dombra thought was cleared ground, were fifteen sharpshooters. They all had big-bore muskets, rifled and fitted with peep-sights, zeroed in for just that range. The condition of that supposedly cleared approach was the most promising thing about the operation. The trees had been felled and the stumps rooted out, but the Nostori thought Tarr-Dombra couldn't be taken and that nobody would try to take it, so they'd gone slack. There were bushes all over it up to a man's waist, and many of them were high enough to hide behind standing up.

His men were hard enough to see even in the open. The helmets had all been carefully rusted, so had the body-armor and every gun-barrel or spearhead. Nobody wore anything but green or brown, most of them had bits of greenery fastened to helmets and clothes. The whole operation, with over twelve hundred men, had been rehearsed a dozen times, each time some being eliminated until they were down to eight hundred of the best.

There was a noise, about what a feeding wild-turkey would make, in front of him, and a voice said, "Lord Kalvan!" It was Verkan, the Grefftscharrer; he had a rifle in his hand, and wore a dirty gray-green hooded smock; his sword and belt were covered with green and brown rags.

"I never saw you till you spoke," Kalvan commented.

"The wagons are coming. They're around the top switchback, now."

He nodded. "We start, then." His mouth was dry. What was that thing in *For Whom the Bell Tolls* about spitting to show you weren't afraid? He couldn't do that, now. He nodded to the boy squatting beside him; he picked up his arquebus back toward where Ptosphes and Chartiphon were waiting.

And Rylla! He cursed vilely in English; there was no satisfaction in taking the name of Dralm in vain, blaspheming Styphon. She'd announced that she was coming along. He'd told her she was doing nothing of the sort. So had her father, and so had Chartiphon. She'd thrown a tantrum; thrown other things, too. In the end, she had come along. He was going to have his hands full with that girl, when he married her.

"All right," he said softly. "Let's go earn our pay."

The men on either side of him rose, two spears or scythe-blade things to every arquebus, though some of the spearmen had pistols in their belts. He and Verkan went ahead, stopping at the edge of the woods, where riflemen crouched in behind trees, and looked across the open four-hundred yards at Tarr-Dombra, the castle that couldn't be taken, its limestone walls rising beyond the chasm that had been quarried straight across the mountain top. The drawbridge was down and the portcullis was up, and a few soldiers in black and orange scarves—his old college colors; he oughtn't shoot them—loitered in the gateway. A few more kept perfunctory watch from the battlements.

Chartiphon and Ptosphes brought their men, one pike to every three calivers and arquebuses, up with a dreadful crashing and clattering that almost stood his hair on end under his helmet and padded coif, but nobody at the castle seemed to have heard it. Chartiphon wore a long brown sack, with neck and arm holes, over his cuirass, and what looked like a well-used dishrag wrapped around his helmet. Ptosphes was in brown, with browned armor; so was Rylla. They all looked to the left, where the road came up the side and onto the top of the mountain.

Four cavalrymen, black and orange scarves and lance-pennons, came into view. They were only fake Princeton men; he hoped they'd remember to tear off that stuff before some other Hostigi shot them by mistake. A long ox-wagon followed, piled high with hay and eight Hostigi under it, then two more cavalrymen in false Nostori colors, another wagon, and six more cavalry. Two more wagons followed.

The first four cavalrymen clattered onto the drawbridge and spoke to the guards at the gate, then rode through. Two of the wagons followed. The third rumbled onto the drawbridge and stopped directly under the portcullis. That was the one with the log framework on top and the log slung underneath. The driver must have cut the strap that held that up, jamming the wagon. The fourth wagon, the one loaded to the top of the bed with rocks, stopped on the outer end of the drawbridge, weighting it down. A pistol banged inside the gate, and another; there were shouts of "Hostigos!" and "Hostigos!" The hay seemed to explode off the two wagons in sight as men piled out of them.

He blew his Pennsylvania State Police whistle, and half a dozen big elephant-size muskets bellowed, from places he'd have sworn there had been nobody at all. Verkan's rifle platoon began firing, sharp whip-crack reports like none of the smoothbores. He hoped they were remembering to patch their bullets; that was something new to them. Then he blew his whistle twice and started running forward.

The men who had been showing themselves on the walls were all gone: a musket-shot or so showed that the snipers hadn't gotten all of them. He ran past a man with a piece of fishnet over his helmet, stuck full of oak twigs, who was ramming a musket. Gray powder smoke hung in the gateway, and everybody who had been outside had gotten in. Yells of "Hostigos!" and "Nostor!" and shots and blade-cutting from within. He broke step and looked back; his two hundred were pouring after him, keeping properly spaced out, the arquebusiers not firing. All the shooting was coming from where Chartiphon—and Rylla, he hoped—had formed a line two hundred yards from the walls and were plastering the battlement, firing as rapidly as they could reload. A cannon went off above when he was almost at the end of the drawbridge, and then, belatedly, the portcullis came down to stop seven feet from the ground on top of the log framework hidden under the hay on the third wagon.

All six of the oxen on the last wagon were dead; the drivers had been furnished short-handled axes for that purpose. The oxen on the portcullis-stopper had also been killed. The gate towers on both sides had already been taken. There were black-and-orange scarves lying where they had been ripped off, and more on corpses. But shots were beginning to come from the citadel, across the outer bailey, and a mob of Nostori were pouring out from its gate. This, he thought, was the time to expend some .38s.

XVI

Feet apart, left hand on hip, Kalvan aimed and emptied the Colt, killing six men with six shots, timed fire-rate. He'd done just as well on silhouette targets many a time; that was all this was. They were the front six; the men behind them stopped momentarily, and then the men behind him swept around him, arquebuses banging and pikemen and halberdiers running forward. He holstered the empty Colt; he had only eight rounds left, now, and drew his rapier and poignard. Another cannon on the outside wall thundered; he hoped Rylla and Chartiphon hadn't been in front of it. Then he was fighting his way through the citadel gate.

Behind, in the bailey, something else besides "Nostor!" and "Hostigos!" was being shouted. It was:

"Mercy, comrade! Mercy; I yield!"

He heard more of that as the morning passed. Before noon, the Nostori garrison had either been given mercy or hadn't needed it. There had only been those two cannon-shots, though between them they had killed and wounded fifty men. Nobody was crazy enough to attack Tarr-Dombra, so they'd left the cannon empty, and had only been given time to load and fire two. He doubted they'd catch Gormoth with his panzer down again.

The hardest fighting was inside the citadel. He ran into Rylla there, with Chartiphon trying to keep up with her. There was a bright scar on her browned helmet and blood on her sword; she was laughing happily. He expected that taking the keep would be even bloodier work, but as soon as they had the citadel it surrendered. By that time he had used up all his rounds for the Colt.

They hauled down Gormoth's black flag with the orange lily and ran up Ptosphes' halberd-head, blue on red. They found four huge bombards, throwing hundred-pound stone cannon balls, and hand-spiked them around, to bear on the little town of Dyssa, at the mouth of Pine Creek, Gorge River here-and-now, and fired one round from each to announce that Tarr-Dombra was under new management. They set the castle cooks to work cutting up and roasting the oxen from the two rear wagons. Then they turned their attention to the prisoners herded into the inner bailey.

First, there were the mercenaries. They would enter the service of Ptosphes, though they could not be used against Nostor until their captain's terms of contract with Gormoth had run out. They would be sent to the Sask border. Then, there were Gormoth's own troops. They couldn't be used at all, but they could be put to work, as long as they were given soldiers' pay and soldierly treatment. Then, there was the governor of the castle, a Count Pheblon, cousin to Prince Gormoth, and his officers. They would be released on oath to send their ransoms to Hostigos. The priest of Galzar elected to go to Hostigos with his parishioners.

As for the priest of Styphon, Chartiphon wanted him questioned under torture, and Ptosphes thought he should be beheaded on the spot.

"Send him to Nostor with Pheblon," Kalvan said. "With a letter for his highpriest—no, for the Supreme Priest, Styphon's Voice. Tell Styphon's Voice that we make our own fireseed, that we will teach everybody to make it, and we will not rest until Styphon's House is utterly destroyed."

Everybody, including those who had been making suggestions for novel and interesting ways of putting the priest to death, shouted in delight.

"And send Gormoth a copy of the letter, and a letter offering him peace and friendship. Tell him we'll teach his soldiers how to make fireseed, and they can make it in Nostor when they're sent home."

"Kalvan!" Ptosphes almost yelled. "What god has addled your wits? Gormoth's our enemy!"

"Anybody who can make fireseed will be our friend, because Styphon's House will be his enemy. If Gormoth doesn't realize that now, he will soon enough."

Verkan the Grefftscharrer trader commanded the party that galloped back to Hostigos with the good news—Tarr-Dombra taken, with over two hundred prisoners, a hundred and fifty horses, four tons of fireseed, twenty cannon. And Sevenhills Valley was part of Hostigos again. Harmakros had destroyed a company of mercenary cavalry, killing twenty and capturing the rest, and he had taken Styphon's temple farm, a richly productive nitriary, freeing the slaves and butchering the priests and guards. And the once-persecuted priest of Dralm had gathered all the peasants for a thanksgiving, telling them that the Hostigi came not as conquerors but as liberators.

Verkan seemed to recall having heard that before, on a number of paratemporal areas, including Calvin Morrison's own.

He also brought copies of the letters Prince Ptosphes had written, or, more likely, which Kalvan had written and Ptosphes had signed to the Supreme Priest of Styphon House and to Prince Gormoth. Dropping a couple of troopers in town to spread the good news, he rode up to the castle and reported to Xentos. It took a long time to tell the old priest-chancellor the whole story, counting interruptions while Xentos told Dralm about it. When he got away, he was immediately dragged into the officer's hall, where a wine barrel had been tapped. By the time he got back to the Red Halberd in Hostigos Town, it was after dark, and everybody was roaring drunk, and somebody had a little two-pounder in the street and was wasting fireseed that could have been better used to kill Gormoth's soldiers. The bell at the town hall, which had begun ringing while he was riding in through the castle gate, was still ringing.

Going up to his room, he opened the coffer and got out another of the copper balls, putting it under his cloak. He rode a mile out of town, tied his horse in the brush, and made his way to where a single huge tree rose above the scrub oak. Speaking into the ball, he activated and released it. Then he got out his cigarettes and sat down under the tree to wait for the half hour it would take the message-ball to reach Fifth Level Police Terminal Time-Line, and the half hour it would take a mobile antigrav conveyer to come in.

XVII

The servant brought him the things, one by one, and Lord Kalvan laid them on the white sheet spread on the table top. The whipcord breeches; he left the billfold in the hip pocket. He couldn't spend United States currency here, and his identity cards belonged to another man, who didn't exist here-and-now. The shirt, torn and blood-stained; the tunic with the battered badge that had saved his life. The black boots, one on either side; the boots they made here were softer and more comfortable. The Sam Browne belt, with the holster and the empty-looped cartridge-carrier and the handcuffs in their pouch. Anybody you needed handcuffs for, here-and-now, you just shot or knocked on the head. The Colt Official Police; he didn't want to part with that, even if there were no more cartridges for it, but the rest of this stuff would seem meaningless without it. He slipped it into the holster, and then tossed the blackjack on top of the pile.

The servant wrapped them and carried the bundle out. There goes Calvin Morrison, he thought, long live Lord Kalvan of Hostigos. Tomorrow, at the thanksgiving service before the feast, these things would be deposited as a votive offering in the temple of Dralm. That had been Xentos' idea, and he had agreed at once. Besides being a general and an ordnance engineer and an industrialist, he had to be a politician, and politicians can't slight their constituents' religion. He filled a goblet from a flagon on the smaller table and sat down, stretching his legs. Un-chilled white wine was a crime against nature; have to do something about refrigeration—after the war, of course.

That mightn't be too long, either. They'd already unsealed the frontiers and the transients who had been blockaded in would be leaving after the feast. They all knew that anybody could make fireseed, and most of them knew how. That fellow they'd gotten those Trygathi horses from; he'd had a few words with him, and Skranga was going to Nostor. So were half a dozen agents to work with Xentos' fifth column. Gormoth would begin making his own fireseed, and that would bring him under the ban of Styphon's House.

Gormoth wouldn't think of that. All he wanted was to conquer Hostigos, and without the help of Styphon's House, he couldn't. He couldn't anyhow, now that he had lost his best invasion route. Two days after Tarr-Dombra had fallen, he'd had two thousand men at the mouth of the Gorge River and lost at least three hundred by cannon fire trying to cross the Athan before his mercenary captain had balked, and the night after that Harmakros had come out of McElhattan Gap, Vryllos Gap, with two hundred cavalry and raided western Nostor, burning farms and villages and running off horses and cattle, devastating everything to the end of Listra Valley.

Maybe they'd thrown Gormoth off until winter. That would mean, till next spring. They didn't fight wars in the winter, here-and-now; against mercenary union rules. By then, Kalvan should have a real army, trained in new tactics he'd dredged from what he remembered of Sixteenth and Seventeenth Century History. Four or five batteries of little four-pounders, pieces and caissons each drawn by four horses, and as mobile as cavalry. And plenty of rifles, and men trained to use them. And get rid of all those boar spears and scythe-blade things, and substitute real eighteen-foot Swiss pikes; they'd hold off cavalry.

Styphon's House was the real enemy. Beat Gormoth once, properly, and he'd stay beaten, and Sarrask of Sask was only a Mussolini to Gormoth's Hitler. But Styphon's House was big; it spread over all five Great Kingdoms, from the mouth of the St. Lawrence to the Gulf of Mexico.

Big but vulnerable, and he knew the vulnerable point. Styphon wasn't a popular god, as, say, Dralm was; that was why Xentos' fifth column was building strength in Nostor. Styphon's House had ignored the people and even the minor nobility, and ruled by pressure on the Great Kings and their subject princes, and as soon as they could make their own powder, they'd turn on Styphon's House and their people with them. This wasn't a religious war, like the ones in the Sixteenth and Seventeenth Centuries in his own former history. It was just a job of racket-busting.

He set down the goblet and rose, throwing off the light robe and began to dress for dinner. For a moment, he wondered whether the Democrats or the Republicans would win the election this year—he was sure it was the same year, now, in a different dimension of time—and how the Cold War and Space Race were coming along.

XVIII

Verkan Vall, his story finished, relaxed in his chair. There was no direct light on this terrace, only a sky-reflection from the city lights below, so dim that the tips of their cigarettes glowed visibly. There were four of them: the Chief of Paratime Police; the Director of the Paratime Commission, the Chairman of the Paratemporal Trade Board and Chief's Assistant Verkan Vall, who would be chief in another hundred days.

"You took no action?" the Director asked.

"None at all. The man's no threat to the Paratime Secret. He knows he isn't in his own past, and from things he ought to find and hasn't, he knows he isn't in his own future. So he knows he's in the corresponding present in a second time dimension and he knows that somebody else is able to travel laterally in time. I grant that. But he's keeping it to himself. On Aryan-Transpacific, in the idiom of his original time-line, he has it made. He won't take any chances on unmaking it.

"Look what he has that the Europo-American Sector could never give him. He's a great nobleman; they've gone out of fashion on Europo-America, where the Common Man is the ideal. He's going to marry a beautiful princess, that's even out of fashion for children's fairy-tales. He's a sword-swinging soldier of fortune, and they've vanished from a nuclear-weapons world. He's in command of a good little army, and making a better one of it, and he has a cause worth fighting for. Any speculations about what space-time continuum he's in he'll keep inside his own skull.

"Look at the story he put out. He told Xentos that he had been thrown into the past from a time in the far future by sorcery. Sorcery, on that time-line, is a perfectly valid scientific explanation of anything. Xentos, with his permission, passed the story on, under oath of secrecy, to Ptosphes, Rylla and Chartiphon. The story they gave out is that he's an exiled prince from a country outside local geographical knowledge. Regular defense in depth, all wrapped around the real secret and everybody has an acceptable explanation."

"How'd you get it then?" the Board Chairman asked.

"From Xentos, at the feast. I got him into a theological discussion, and slipped some hypno truth-drug into his wine. He doesn't even remember, now that he told me."

"Well, nobody on that time-line'll get it that way," the Commission Director agreed. "But didn't you take a chance getting those things of Morrison's out of the temple?"

"No. We ran a conveyer in the night of the feast, when the temple was empty. The next morning, the priests all cried, 'A Miracle! Dralm has accepted the offering!' I was there and saw it. Morrison doesn't believe that, he thinks one of those pack traders who left Hostigos the next morning stole the stuff. I know Harmakros' cavalrymen were stopping people and searching wagons and packs. Publicly, of course, he has to believe in the miracle."

"Was it necessary," the Director asked.

"As to the necessity, yes. This stuff will be found on Morrison's original time-line, first the clothing with the numbered badge still on the tunic, and, later, in connection with some crime we'll arrange for the purpose, the revolver. They won't explain anything, they'll make more of a mystery, but it will be a mystery in normal terms of what's locally accepted as possible."

"Well, this is all very interesting," the Trade Board Chairman said, "but what have I to do with it, officially?"

"Trenth, you disappoint me," the Commission Director said. "This Styphon's House racket is perfect for penetration of that subsector, and in a couple of centuries it'll be a good area to have penetrated. We'll just move in on Styphon's House and take it over, the way we did the Yat-Zar temples on the Hulgun Subsector, and build that up to general economic and political control."

"You'll have to stay off Morrison's time-line, though," Tortha Karf said.

"You certainly will!" Verkan was vehement about it. "We'll turn that time-line over to the University, here, for study, and quarantine it absolutely to everybody else. And about five adjoining time-lines, for control study. You know what we have here?" He was becoming excited about it. "We have the start of an entirely new subsector, and we have the divarication point absolutely identified, the first time we've been able to do that except from history. Now, here; I've already established myself with those people as Verkan the Grefftscharr trader. I'll get back, now and then, about as frequently as possible for traveling by horse, and set up a trading depot. A building big enough to put a conveyer-head into...."

Tortha Karf began laughing. "I knew it," he said. "You'd find some way!"

"All right. We all have hobbies; yours is fruit growing and rabbit-hunting on Fifth Level Sicily. Well, my hobby is going to be the Kalvan Subsector, Fourth Level Aryan-Transpacific. I'm only a hundred and twenty years old, now. In a couple of centuries, when I'm ready to retire...."

D☉WN STYPH☉N!

H. Beam Piper

I

1964 A.D.

In the quiet of the Innermost Circle, in Styphon's House Upon Earth, the great image looked down, and Sesklos, Supreme Priest and Styphon's Voice, returned the carven stare almost as stonily. Sesklos did not believe in Styphon, or in any other god; if he had, he would not be sitting here. The policies of Styphon's House were too complicated to entrust to believers. The image, he knew, was of a man—the old high priest who, by discovering the application of a half-forgotten secret, had taken the cult of a minor healer-god out of its mean back-street temples and made it the power that ruled the rulers of all the Five Great Kingdoms. If it had been in Sesklos to worship anything, he would have worshipped that man's memory.

And now, the first Supreme Priest looked down upon the last one. He lowered his eyes, flattened the parchment on the table in front of him, and read again:

PTOSPHES, *Prince of Hostigos, to* SESKLOS, *calling himself Styphon's Voice, these:*

False priest of a false god, impudent swindler, liar and cheat!

Know that we in Hostigos, by simple mechanic arts, now make for ourselves that fireseed which you pretend to be the miracle of your fraudulent god, and that we propose teaching these arts to all, that hereafter Kings and Princes minded to make war may do so for their own defense and advancement, and not to the enrichment of Styphon's House of Iniquities.

In proof thereof, we send you fireseed of our own make, enough for twenty musket charges, and set forth how it is made, thus:

To three parts of refined saltpeter add three fifths of one part of charcoal and two fifths of one part of sulfur, all ground to the fineness of bolted wheat flour. Mix these thoroughly, moisten the mixture, and work it to a heavy dough, then press the dough into cakes and dry them, and when they are fully dry, grind and sieve them.

And know that we hold you and all in Styphon's House of Iniquities to be our mortal enemies, and the enemies general of all men, to be dealt with as wolves are, and that we will not rest content until Styphon's House of Iniquities is utterly cast down and ruined.

PTOSPHES

That had been the secret of the power of Styphon's House. No ruler, Great King or petty lord, could withstand his enemies if they had fireseed and he had none. Given here, armies marched to victory; withheld there, terms of peace were accepted. In every council of state, Styphon's House had spoken the deciding word. Wealth had poured in, to be lent out at usury and return more wealth.

And now, the contemptible prince of a realm a man could ride across without tiring his horse was bringing it down, and Styphon's House had provoked him to it. There were sulfur springs in Hostigos, and of Styphon's Trinity, sulfur was the hardest to get. When the land around the springs had been demanded of him, Ptosphes had refused, and since none could be permitted to defy Styphon's House, his enemy, Prince Gormoth of Nostor, had been raised against him, with subsidies to hire mercenaries and gifts of fireseed. When Gormoth had conquered Hostigos, he was pledged to give the sulfur springs to Styphon's House. Things like that were done all the time.

But now, Ptosphes was writing thus to Styphon's Voice Himself. For a moment, the impiety of it shocked Sesklos. Then he pushed aside Ptosphes' letter and looked again at the one from Vyblos, the highpriest of the temple of Nostor Town. Three moons ago, a stranger calling himself Kalvan and claiming to be an exiled prince from a far country—the boast of every needy adventurer—had appeared in Hostigos. A moon later, Ptosphes had made this Kalvan commander of his soldiers, and had set guards on all the ways out of Hostigos, allowing any to enter but none to leave. He had been informed of that at the time, but had thought nothing of it.

Then, six days ago, the Hostigi had captured Tarr-Dombra, the castle guarding Gormoth's easiest way into Hostigos. The castellan, a Count Pheblon, had been released on ransom-oath, with a letter to Gormoth in which Ptosphes had offered peace and friendship, and the teaching of fireseed making. A priest of Styphon, a black-robed believer, who had been at the castle, had also been released to bear Ptosphes' letter of defiance to him.

It had, of course, been the stranger, Kalvan, who had taught Ptosphes the fireseed secret. He wondered briefly if he could be a renegade from Styphon's House. No; only yellow-robed priests of the Inner Circle knew the full secret as Ptosphes had written it, and had one of these absconded, the news would have reached him as swiftly as galloping relays of horses could bring it. Some Inner Circle priest could have written it down, a thing utterly forbidden, and the writing fallen into unconsecrated hands, but he questioned that. The proportions were different, more saltpeter and less charcoal. He would have Ptosphes' sample tried; it might be better than their own.

A man, then, who had rediscovered the secret? That could be, though it had taken many years and the many experiments to perfect the process, especially the caking and grinding. He shrugged. That was not important; the important thing was that the secret was broken. Soon anyone could make fireseed, and then Styphon's House would be only a name, and a name of mockery.

Perhaps, though, he could postpone the end for as long as it mattered. He was near his ninetieth year; soon he would die, and for each man, when he dies, the world ends.

Letters of urgency to the Archpriests of the five Great Temples, telling them all. A story to be circulated among the secular rulers that fireseed, stolen by bandits, was being smuggled and sold. Prompt investigation of all stories of anyone collecting sulfur or saltpeter or building or altering grinding mills. Immediate death by assassination of anyone suspected of knowing the secret.

And, of course, destruction of Hostigos, none in it to be spared. Gormoth had been waiting until his crops were harvested; he must be made to strike now. And an Archpriest of Styphon's House Upon Earth to Nostor, this was quite beyond poor Vyblos' capacities, with more silver, and fireseed and arms for Gormoth.

He glanced again at Vyblos' letter. A copy of Ptosphes' letter to him had been sent to Gormoth; why, then Gormoth knew the fireseed secret himself! It had been daring, and fiendishly clever, of Ptosphes to give this deadly gift to his enemy.

And, with the Archpriest, fifty mounted Guardsmen of the Temple, their captain to be an Inner Circle priest without robe, and more silver to corrupt Gormoth's nobles and his mercenary captains.

And a special letter to the high priest of the temple at Sask Town. It had been planned to use Prince Sarrask of Sask as a counterpoise to Gormoth, when the Gormoth had grown too mighty by the conquest of Hostigos. The time for that was now. Gormoth was needed to destroy

Hostigos; then he, too, must be destroyed, before he began making fire-seed in Nostor.

He struck the gong thrice, and as he did he thought again of the mysterious Kalvan. That was nothing to shrug off; it was important to learn whence he had come before he appeared—he was intrigued by Vyblos' choice of the word—in Hostigos, and with whom he had been in contact. He could have come from some country in which fireseed was commonly made. He knew of none such, but it could be that the world was larger than he thought.

Or could there be other worlds? The idea had occurred to him, now and then, as an idle speculation.

II

It was one of those small late-afternoon gatherings, with nobody seeming to have a care in the world, lounging indolently, smoking, sipping tall drinks, nibbling canapés, talking and laughing. Verkan Vall, who would be Chief of Paratime Police after Year-End Day, flicked his lighter for his wife, Hadron Dalla, then applied it to his own cigarette. Across the low table, Tortha Karf, the retiring chief, was mixing another drink, with the concentrated care of an alchemist compounding the Elixir of Life. The Dhergabar University people—the elderly professor of Paratemporal Theory, the lady who was professor of Outtime History (IV), and the young man who was Director of Outtime Study Operations—were all smiling like three pussycats at a puddle of spilled milk.

"You'll have it all to yourselves," Verkan told them. "The Paratime Commission has declared that time-line a study-area, and it's absolutely quarantined to everybody but University personnel and accredited students. And five adjoining near-identical, time-lines for comparison study. And I will make it my personal business to see that the quarantine is rigidly enforced."

Tortha Karf looked up. "After I retire, I'll have a seat on the Paratime Commission, myself," he said. "I'll make it my business to see that the quarantine isn't revoked or diluted."

"I wish we could account for those four hours, after he was caught in the transposition field, before and until he made his way to that peasant's cottage," the Paratemporal Theorist fretted. "We have no idea what he was doing."

"Wandering in the woods, trying to orient himself," Dalla said. "I'd say sitting and thinking, for a couple of hours, trying to figure out what happened to him. A paratemporal shift like that is a pretty shattering experience for an outtimer. I don't think he was changing history all by himself, if that's what you're worrying about."

"You can't say that," the Paratemporal Theorist reproved. "He might have killed a rattlesnake which would otherwise have fatally bitten a child who would otherwise have grown up to be an important personage. That sounds farfetched and trivial, but Paratemporal Alternate Probability is built on such trifles. Who knows what started the Aryan migration east-ward instead of westward on that sector? Some chief's hangover, some tribal wizard's nightmare."

"Well, that's why you're getting those five control-study time-lines," the Operations Director said. "And that reminds me; our people stay out of Hostigos on all of them for a while. We don't want them massacred along with the resident population by Gormoth's gang, or forced to use First Level weapons in self-defense."

"What bothers me," the lady professor of history said over the rim of her glass, "is Vall's beard."

"It bothers me, too," Dalla said, "but I'm getting used to it."

"He grew it when he went out to that time-line, and he hasn't shaved it off since. And Dalla's a blonde, now; blondes are less conspicuous on Aryan-Transpacific. They're both going to be on and off that time-line all the time, now."

"Well, your exclusive rights don't exclude the Paratime Police," Verkan said. "I told you I was going to give that time-line my personal attention."

"Well, you'll not introduce a lot of probability contamination, will you?" the paratemporal theorist asked anxiously. "We want to observe the effect of this man's appearance on that time-line—"

"No, of course not. But I'm already well established with these people. I am Verkan, a free-trader from Grefftscharr, that's the kingdom around the Great Lakes. I am now supposed to be traveling on horseback to Zygros, about where Quebec is on Europo-American; I have promised to recruit brass-founders to teach the Hostigi how to cast brass cannon. He needs light field-pieces badly."

"Don't they have cannon of their own?" the historian asked. "I thought you said—"

"Wrought iron, welded up and strengthened with shrunk-on rings. They have iron works, there's a lot of bog iron mined in that section, but no brass foundries. There are some at Zygros, they get their copper and tin by water from the west." Verkan turned to the operations director. "I won't be able to get back, plausibly, for another thirty days. Can you have your first study team ready by then? They'll be the Zygrosi brass founders."

The young man nodded. "They have everything now but local foundry techniques and correct Zygrosi accents. They'll need practice, you can't get manual dexterity by hypno-mech. Yes, thirty days will be plenty."

"Good. We have two Paratime Police agents in Hostigos now, a supposed blind minstrel and a supposed half-witted boy. As soon as I show up with your crowd, they can take off their coats and go to work, and they won't even have to hunt for coathooks. And, I'll set up a trading depot to mask your conveyer-head. After that, you'll be in business."

"But you're helping him win," the Paratemporal Theorist objected. "That's probably contamination."

"No, it isn't. If I didn't bring in fake Zygrosi founders, he'd send somebody else to get real ones. I will give him information, too, just what any other wandering pack trader would. I may even go into battle with him, as I did at Tarr-Dombra, with a local flintlock. But I want *him* to win. I admire the man too much to hand him an unearned victory."

"He sounds like quite a man," the lady historian said. "I'd like to meet him, myself."

"Better not, Eldra," Dalla warned. "This princess of his is handy with a pistol."

"Yes. The man's a genius. Only a police corporal on his own time-line, which shows how outtimers let genius go to waste. We investigated his previous history. Only son of a clergyman; father named him for a religious leader, and wanted him to be a clergyman, too. As a boy, he resisted, passively; scamped all his studies at college except history, and particularly military history, in which he was much interested. Then they had this war in Korea, you know what that was, and it offered him an escape from the career he was being forced into. Father died while he was at war, mother a year later. After the war he entered the Pennsylvania State Police. Excellent record, as far as his opportunities went; held down by routine because nobody recognized him for what he was. Then he blundered into the field of that conveyer, just when it went weak, and—"

III

Three months ago—no, just "at another time," he was sure of that—he had been Corporal Calvin Morrison, Pennsylvania State Police. Now he was Lord Kalvan, in command of the army of Prince Ptosphes of Hostigos, and soon he would marry Ptosphes' daughter and become heir-matrimonial to the princely throne. That couldn't have happened in his own world.

Hostigos, of course, was no vast realm. It was only as big as Centre and Union Counties, Pennsylvania, with snips of Clinton and Lycoming. That was precisely what it was, too, except that here-and-now there was no Commonwealth of Pennsylvania, it was part of the Great Kingdom of Hos-Harphax—*Hos* meant great—ruled by a King Kaiphranos. No, just reigned over lightly; outside his own capital at the mouth of the Susquehanna, Kaiphranos' authority was nonexistent, the present situation for example.

When he was less evident. Going to arrest a perfectly routine hillbilly murderer, he had entered what could only have been a time-machine; emerging from it, he had landed on what could only have been another time-dimension. He had theorized a little about that, and his theories had demolished themselves half-constructed. Then he had given it up and dismissed the whole subject. He had other things to think about.

Rylla, for one; it was hard not to think about her all the time. And commanding an army, once he got it made into one. And manufacturing gunpowder in competition with Styphon's House. And fighting a war, against uncomfortably steep odds. And, at the moment, a meeting of the General Staff, all of whom were new at it. So, for that matter, was he, but he had a few vague ideas of military staff organization which put him several up on any of the others. And he was hot and sweat-sticky, because he was wearing close to thirty pounds of armor, to accustom himself to the weight.

They all stood around the big table, looking at the relief map of Hostigos and surroundings which covered the entire top. Just to show you, none of this crowd had ever realized that maps were weapons of war. Maps, here-and-now, were illuminated parchment scrolls, highly artistic and wildly inaccurate. This one had taken over a month, he and Rylla doing most of the work, from what he remembered of the U.S. Geographical Survey maps he'd used on the State Police, from hundreds of talks with peasants, soldiers, woodsmen and landlords, and from a good deal of personal horseback reconnaissance.

"The bakeries in Nostor work night and day." That was old Xentos, the blue-robed priest of Dralm, who was also Prince Ptosphes' chancellor and because of contacts with his co-religionists in Nostor, head of espionage and fifth-column operations. "And milk cannot be bought at any price, it is all being made into cheese, and most of the meat is being ground for smoked sausages."

Field rations, stuff a soldier could carry in his haversack and eat uncooked. That could be stored, but Xentos also had reports of wagons and oxen being commandeered and peasants impressed as drivers. That wouldn't be done too long in advance.

"Then they'll strike soon," somebody said. "Taking Tarr-Dombra hasn't stopped Gormoth at all."

"It delayed him," Prince Ptosphes said. "He'd be pouring troops in through Sevenhills Valley if we hadn't."

There was a smile on his thin lips, between the pointed gray mustache and the small chin-beard. Ptosphes had been learning to smile again, since the powder mill had gone into production. He hadn't before.

Chartiphon, bulky and grizzle-bearded, stood glowering at the map. He had been chief captain of Hostigos for as long as Ptosphes had been Prince; now he was second in command—Field Marshal and Chief of Operations—and gratifyingly unresentful at Lord Kalvan being placed over him. His idea of war was to hit every head you saw, and whoever hit the most heads first won. All this staff-stuff, maps and fifth columns and logistics and intelligence and security, he did not understand, and he was happy to let somebody do it who did. Lord Kalvan had been hurled into the past from a thousand years in the future by sorcery, and he probably half-suspected that Lord Kalvan was a sorcerer, himself.

"Yes, but where?" Kalvan wanted to know.

Ptosphes drew his sword. It was a rapier; the bladesmiths of Tarr-Hostigos had been swamped with orders for rapiers, since this crowd had learned that a sword has a point and that a thrust beats a swinging cut. He used his point now to trace the course of the West Branch—the Athan, here-and-now—from the otherwhen site of Muncy down to where Milton ought to be. The point rested on the river midway between them.

"Marax Ford," he said.

"Oh no, Prince!" Chartiphon growled. "Go all the way around the mountain and all the way up East Hostigos? He won't do that. Here's where he'll try to come in."

He drew his own sword—long, heavy and double-edged, none of these newfangled pokers for him—and pointed to the juncture of Bald Eagle Creek and the river, at the site of Lock Haven.

"Listra Mouth," he said. "He can move his whole army west along the river, cross here—if we let him—and go up the Listra Valley to the Saski border. And that's where all our ironworks are."

Now that was something. Not so long ago, Chartiphon had taken weapons for granted. Now he was realizing they had to be produced.

That started an argument. Somebody thought Gormoth would

try to force one of the gaps. Not Dombra—Antes Gap—that was too strong. Maybe Vryllos—McElhattan—or the gap back of where South Williamsport ought to be.

"He'll attack where he can best use his cavalry," young Harmakros, who was a cavalryman himself, declared. "That's what he has the most of."

That was true. Gormoth's cavalry superiority was something to worry, not to say be frightened about.

"He'll attack where we don't expect him to."

That was Rylla, in male riding dress, a big dagger on her belt and a pheasant feather in her cap, leaning forward on the map table across from him.

Rylla was the nicest of many nice things here-and-now. She was beautiful—blonde hair almost shoulder-length, laughing blue eyes, impudent tilty little nose dusted with golden freckles—vivacious and fun-loving. She was utterly fearless; Kalvan had first seen her riding into a cavalry skirmish at the head of her father's troopers. But best of all, after the wonderful very-best that she loved him and was going to marry him, the girl had a brain and wasn't afraid to use it.

"That's right," Kalvan agreed. "Where don't we expect him?"

"You know what that means?" Ptosphes asked. He had a pretty good brain, himself. "It means we'll have to be strong enough to resist everywhere." His rapier point swung almost from one end of the map to the other.

"With five thousand, and that counts boys with bows and arrows and peasant grandfathers with pitchforks," Chartiphon demanded. "Don't joke about such things, Prince."

It came to a little over that, but not much. Twenty-five hundred regular infantry, meaning organized into something like companies and given a modicum of drill, a thousand arquebusiers and calivermen, with fifteen hundred pikemen to keep the cavalry off them. Two thousand militia, peasant levies, anybody who could do an hour's foot-drill without dropping dead, armed with anything at all. And slightly less than a thousand cavalry, with steel cuirasses, helmets and thigh-guards. And against that, Prince Gormoth had four thousand of his own subjects, including neither the senile nor the adolescent and none of them armed with bows or agricultural implements, and six thousand mercenaries, of whom four thousand were cavalry.

"Then we'll just have to be able to move what men we have around faster," Rylla said.

Well, good girl. She'd grasped what neither her father nor Harmakros had, that mobility can make up for a numerical inferiority.

"Yes, Harmakros, how many horses can you find to mount our infantry? They don't have to be good horses, just good enough to get the men where they can fight on foot."

Harmakros was scandalized. Mounted troops were *cavalry*; anybody ought to know it took years to train a cavalryman. So was Chartiphon; infantry were foot soldiers and had no business on horseback.

"It'll mean one out of four holding horses in a battle, but they'll get to the battle before it's over, and they can wear heavier armor. Now, how many infantry can we mount?"

Harmakros looked at Kalvan, decided that he was serious, and was silent for a while. It always took Harmakros a little time to recover from the shock of a new idea. Then he grinned and nodded. "I'll find out," he said, grabbing the remount officer by the arm and pulling him off to the side. Rylla joined them with a slate and a piece of soapstone. Rylla was the math wizard; she'd learned how to do up to long division in Arabic numeration. While they argued, Kalvan began talking to Ptosphes and Chartiphon about artillery.

That was the one really hopeful situation. Here-and-now cannon didn't have trunnions. The guns were bedded into timbers like huge gunstocks, or timber frames for the heavier pieces. What passed for field artillery was mounted on four-wheeled carts, usually ox-powered. He blamed Styphon's House for that. They did the weaponeering, and they didn't want bloody and destructive wars, which were bad for business, or decisive wars which established peace, which were worse. They wanted a lot of little wars, all the time, to burn a lot of fireseed.

In the past two months, along with everything else and by methods which would have made Simon Legree look like the Model Employer, he had ordered six new four-pounders built, with trunnions, on field carriages with limbers. Drawn by four horses apiece, they would keep up with cavalry on any sort of decent ground. He also had trunnions welded onto some old pieces, mostly eight-pounders and mounted them on makeshift field carriages. They would *not* keep up with cavalry, but they were five hundred percent better than anything Gormoth had ever heard of.

They were still talking when Harmakros and Rylla came over.

"Two thousand," Rylla said. "They all have four legs. We think they were all alive yesterday evening."

"We'll need some for pack trains and replacements. Sixteen hundred mounted infantry. Eight hundred arquebusiers, with arquebuses, not rabbit guns, and eight hundred pikemen, with pikes, not hunting spears or those scythe-blade things." Kalvan turned to Chartiphon, "Can you manage that?"

Chartiphon could. Men who wouldn't fall off their horses, too.

"And all the riflemen." Fifty of them, all the muskets and calivers and arquebuses he'd been able to get rifled to date. That was fifty more than the combined rifle strength of all five Great Kingdoms. "And five hundred cavalry, swords and pistols, no lances or musketoons."

Everybody heard that, and everybody howled. There weren't that many, not uncommitted. Swords flashed over the map, pointing to places where there were only half enough now. One of these days, somebody was going to use a sword in one of those arguments for something besides map-pointing. Finally, they scraped up five hundred cavalry for the new Mobile Force.

"You'll command," he told Harmakros. "You'll have all six four-pounders and the best four eights. You'll be based in Sevenhills Valley; be ready at any notice to move either east or west from there."

"As soon as I get it all organized, which will be tomorrow afternoon at latest, I'll be ready to go to Sevenhills. I can promise I'll be there by noon the next day."

That meant he'd be there before then; that was another thing about Harmakros.

"Oh, and before I forget." He addressed them all. "Battle cries." They had to be shouted constantly to keep from being killed by your friends. "Besides 'Ptosphes!' and 'Hostigos!' we will also shout, '*Down Styphon!*'"

That met with general approval. They all knew who the real enemy was.

IV

Gormoth, Prince of Nostor, set down the goblet and wiped his bearded lips on the back of his hand. The candles in front of him and down the long tables to the side flickered. Tableware clattered, voices were loud.

"Lost everything!" The speaker was a baron driven from Sevenhills Valley when Tarr-Dombra had fallen. "My house, a score of farms, a village—"

"You think we've lost nothing? They crossed at Vryllos and burned everything on my land; it was Styphon's miracle I got out at all."

"For shame!" Vyblos, the high priest cried rebukingly. "What of the Sevenhills temple-farm, a holy place pillaged and desecrated? What of the blood of fifteen consecrated priests and novices and a score of lay guards, all cruelly murdered? 'Dealt with as wolves are,'" he quoted.

"Well, we have an army, haven't we?" somebody at the side table on the left hectored. "Why don't we use it?"

Weapons clattered outside, and somebody else sneered: "That's Ptosphes, now; under the tables, everybody."

A man in black leather entered, advancing and saluting; the captain of the dungeons.

"Lord Prince," he said, "the special prisoner will tell all."

"Ha!" Gormoth knew what that meant. Then he laughed at the anxious faces along the tables; not a few of his nobles dreaded the thought that somebody was telling all about something. He drew his poignard and cut a line across the candle in front of him; a thumbnail's length from the top.

"You bring good news. I'll hear him in that time."

He nodded in dismissal. As the captain backed away, he rapped loudly on the table with the dagger-pommel.

"Be silent, all of you. I've little time, so give heed." He turned to Klestreus, the elected captain-general of the mercenaries. "You have four thousand horse, two thousand foot, and ten cannon. Add to them a thousand of my infantry, choose which you will, and such cannon of mine as you need. You'll cross the river at Marax Ford. Be on the road before the dew's off the grass tomorrow; before dawn of the next day, take and hold the ford, put the best of your cavalry across and let the others follow as speedily as they can.

"Netzigon," he addressed his own chief-captain, "you'll gather every man you can, down to the very peasant rabble, and such cannon as Klestreus leaves you. With half of them, confront all the gaps into Nostor, from Nirfe up. You'll take the other opposite Listra-Mouth and Vryllos Gap. As Klestreus moves west through Hostigos, he will attack each gap from behind. When he does, your men will cross the river and attack from the north. Dombra we'll have to starve out, the rest must be stormed. When Klestreus is back of Vryllos Gap, the force you have at Listra-Mouth will cross and move up Listra Valley. After that, we'll have Tarr-Hostigos to take. Galzar only knows how long we'll be at that, but by the end of the moon-half, all else in Hostigos should be ours."

There was a gratified murmur along the tabled; this made good hearing to all. Only the high priest, Vyblos, was ill-pleased.

"But why so soon, Prince?" he asked.

"Soon?" Gormoth roared. "By the Mace of Galzar, you've been bawling for it like a weaned calf! Well, now you have your invasion; thank your god for it."

"A few more days would not be too much, Lord Prince,' Vyblos said. "Today I had word from Styphon's House Upon Earth, from the pen of His Divinity Himself. An Archpriest, His Holiness Krastokles, is coming here to Nostor, with rich gifts of fireseed and money, and the blessing of Styphon's Voice. It was poor reverence not to await His Holiness' coming."

Gormoth turned to the two captains. "You heard me," he said. "I rule here, not the priest. Be about it; send orders at once. You move tomorrow."

Then he rose, pushing back the chair before the servant could withdraw it. The line was still visible at the top of the candle.

Guards with torches attended him down the winding stairs into the dungeons. The air stank. His breath congealed; the heat of summer never penetrated here. From the torture chambers shrieks told of some wretch being questioned; idly he wondered who. Stopping at an iron-bound oaken door, he unlocked it with a key from his belt and entered alone, closing it behind him.

The room within was large, warmed by a fire on a hearth in the corner and lighted by a great lantern from above. Under it, a man bent over a littered table. He had a bald head and a straggling beard, and wore a most unprisoner-like dagger on his belt. A key for the door lay on the table and a pair of heavy horseman's pistols. He straightened, turning.

"Greetings, Prince. It's done. I tried it; it's as good as they make in Hostigos, and better than the priests' trash."

"And no prayers to Styphon, Skranga?"

Skranga was chewing tobacco. He spat brownly on the floor.

"In the face of Styphon! Try it yourself, Prince; the pistols are empty."

There was a dish half full of fireseed on the table. Gormoth measured in a charge, loaded and wadded a ball on top of it, primed the pan, readied the striker, then fired into a billet of wood by the fire and went to probe the hole with a straw. The bullet had gone in almost a little finger's length; Styphon's powder wouldn't do that. He carried the pistol back and laid it on the table.

"Well, Skranga," he laughed. "You'll have to hide here for a while, but from this hour you're first nobleman of Nostor after me. Style yourself Duke. There'll be rich lands for you in Hostigos, when Hostigos is mine."

"And the Styphon temple-farm of Nostor?" Skranga grinned. "If I'm to make your fireseed, there's all there that I'll need."

"Yes, that too, by Galzar! After I've downed Ptosphes, I'll deal with Vyblos, and he'll envy Ptosphes before I let him die."

Snatching up a pewter cup without looking to see if it were clean, he went to the wine keg and drew for himself, tasted the wine, then spat it out.

"Is this the swill they've given you?" he demanded. "By Galzar, whoever's at fault won't see tomorrow's sun set!" He flung open the door and bellowed into the hall: "Wine! Wine for Prince Gormoth and Duke Skranga! And silver cups! And see it's fit for nobles to drink!"

V

Mobile Force HQ had been the mansion of a Nostori noble driven from Sevenhills Valley on D-for-Dombra Day; Kalvan's name had been shouted ahead as he rode through the troop-crowded village, and Harmakros and his officers met him at the door.

"Great Dralm, Kalvan!" Harmakros laughed. "Are you growing wings on horses, now? Our messengers only got off an hour and a half ago."

"I know; I met them at Vryllos Gap." They crossed the outer hall and through the doorway to the big room beyond. "We got the news at Tarr-Hostigos just after dark. What have you heard since?"

At least fifty candles burned in the central chandelier. Evidently the cavalry had gotten here before the peasants, and hadn't looted too destructively themselves. Harmakros led him to an inlaid table on which a map, scorched with hot needles on white deerskin, was spread.

"We have reports from all the watchtowers along the mountains. They're too far to see anything but dust, but the column's three miles long; first cavalry, then infantry, then wagons and guns, then more infantry and cavalry. They halted at Nirfe at dusk and built hundreds of campfires. Whether they left them burning and moved on after dark, and how far ahead the cavalry are, we don't know. We expect them at Marax Ford by dawn."

"We got a little more than that," Kalvan replied. "The priest of Dralm at Nostor got a messenger off a little after noon, it was dusk before he could get across the river. Your column's commanded by Klestreus, four thousand mercenary cavalry and two thousand mercenary infantry, a thousand of Gormoth's infantry, fifteen guns, he didn't say what kind, and a wagon train that must be creaking with loot. At the same time, Netzigon's moving west, probably toward Listra-Mouth and we don't know what with. The messenger had to dodge troops all the way up to Vryllos. Chartiphon's going to Listra-Mouth with what he can scrape up; Ptosphes is occupying Vryllos Gap."

"That's it; a double attack," Harmakros said. "We can't help Chartiphon, can we?"

"We can help him by beating Klestreus." Kalvan had got out his pipe; as soon as he had filled it, one of the officers provided a light. "Thank you. What have you done so far?"

"I started my wagons and the eight-pounders down the main road. They'll stop just short of Fitra, here"—Harmakros pointed on the map—"and wait for us. As soon as I'm all collected, I'm taking the cavalry and mounted infantry and the four pounders down the back road. After we're on the main road, the wagons and the eights will follow on. I have two-hundred militia, the usual odds-and-sods, marching with the wagons."

"That was smart."

Puffing on his pipe, Kalvan looked at the map. The back road, adequate for horsemen and the four-pounders but not for wagons, followed the mountains and then bent south away from them to join the main valley road at the village of Fitra. Harmakros had started his slow stuff off first, and could overtake without being impeded by it, and he was waiting till he had all his striking force in hand, not dribbling it in to be chopped up by detail.

"Where had you thought of fighting?"

"Why, on the Athan, of course." Harmakros was surprised that he should ask. "Klestreus will have some cavalry over before we get there, that can't be helped, but we'll wipe them out or chase them back, and then defend the line of the river."

"Huh-uh," Kalvan touched the Fitra road-junction with his pipe stem. "We fight here."

"But that's miles inside Hostigos!" one of the officers cried. Maybe he owned an estate down there. "We can't let them get that far."

"Lord Kalvan," Harmakros began stiffly. He was going to be insubordinate, he never bothered with titles otherwise. "We cannot give up a foot of Hostigi ground. The honor of Hostigos forbids it."

Here we are, back in the Middle Ages! He seemed to hear the voice of the history professor, inside his head, calling a roll of battles lost on points of honor. Mostly by the French; they'd been the worst, though they weren't the only, offenders. He decided to fly into a rage.

"To Styphon with that!" he yelled, banging his fists on the table. "Honor won't win this war, and real estate won't win this war. The only thing that'll win this war is killing Nostori.

"Now, here," he continued quietly, the rage having served its purpose, "is where we can kill the most of them, and get the fewest of our own men killed doing it. Klestreus will cross the Athan here, at Marax Ford." That would be a little below where he remembered Watsontown to have been. "He'll rush his best cavalry ahead to secure the ford, and the rest of his cavalry will cross next. They'll want to get in on the best looting ahead of the infantry; they'll push ahead without waiting. By the time the infantry are over, they'll be stringing west in bunches.

"Now, that army Klestreus has could walk all over us, if they were all together. But they won't be. And they'll be tired, and we'll have reached Fitra by daylight, have our position prepared, our men and horses will be rested, we'll even be ready to give everybody a hot meal. And Klestreus will be strung out for ten miles by the time his advance elements come up to us. Now, what troops have we east of here?"

A hundred cavalry along the river; a hundred and fifty regular infantry and about twice as many militia; about five hundred militia and regulars, at posts in the gaps.

"All right; get riders off at once. Somebody who won't be argued with. Have all that force along the river move back; to Fitra, if possible, and if not they can reinforce the posts at the gaps. The gaps'll have to look out for themselves, we can't help them. The cavalry will keep just in front of Klestreus, skirmishing but doing nothing to delay him."

Harmakros looked at the map, thought for a little and nodded.

"East Hostigos," he said, "will be the graveyard of the Nostori."

That was all right; that took care of the honor of Hostigos.

"Well, mercenaries from Hos-Agrys and Hos-Ktemnos, anyhow." That reminded Kalvan of something. "Who hired those mercenaries;

Gormoth or Styphon's House?"

"Why, Gormoth. The money came from Styphon's House, but the mercenary captains contracted with Gormoth; they serve him."

"The reason I asked, the Rev. Whatshisname, in Nostor, included a bit of gossip in his message. It seems that this morning Gormoth had one of his under-stewards put to death. Had a funnel forced into his mouth and half a keg of wine poured into him. The wine was of inferior quality, and had been given to a prisoner for whom Gormoth had commanded good treatment."

One of the officers made a face. "Sounds like Gormoth." Another laughed and said he could think of a few tavern keepers in Hostigos Town who deserved that.

"Who was the prisoner?" Harmakros asked. "Count Pheblon?"

"Oh no, Pheblon's out of favor, but he isn't a prisoner. You know his fellow. An Agrysi horse-trader named Skranga."

"Yes, he got caught in Hostigos during the Iron Curtain." Like Fifth Column, Iron Curtain was now part of the Hostigi vocabulary. Then Harmakros blinked. "He was working in the fireseed mill, while he was here. You think he might be making fireseed for Gormoth?"

"He is if he's doing what I told him to do." There was an outcry at that. Kalvan laughed. "And if Gormoth begins making his own fireseed, Styphon's House'll hear about it, and you know what'll happen then. That's why I asked about those mercenaries. I was wondering whether Gormoth would use them against Styphon's House, or Styphon's House against Gormoth." He shrugged. "Not that it matters. If everybody does his job tomorrow, nobody'll use those mercenaries. Except, maybe, us. That's another thing. We don't bother with Nostori prisoners, but take all the mercenaries who'll surrender. We may need them later."

VI

Dawn was only a pallor in the east, and the whitewashed walls were dim blurs under dark thatches, but the village of Fitra was awake, light pouring from open doors and a fire blazing on the small common. There was a crowd, villagers and cavalrymen who had ridden ahead. Behind him, hoofs thudded and armor and equipment clattered; away back, Kalvan could hear the four-pounders thumping over the pole bridge at the mill. The shouting started, of course: "Lord Kalvan! Dralm bless Lord Kalvan!" He was used to it, now; it didn't give him the thrill it had at first. He had to make a speech, while orders were shouted and re-shouted to the rear, and men and horses got off to the sides off the road to make way for the guns.

Then he and Harmakros and four or five other officers turned left and cantered down the main road, reining in where it began to dip. The eastern pallor had become a bar of yellow light. The Mountains of Hostigos were blackly plain on the left, and the jumble of ridges to the right were taking shape. Nearby trees began to detach themselves from the obscurity. In a few hours, they'd all be down. He pointed to the right.

"Send two hundred cavalry around that ridge, over there, to where those three farms are clumped together," he told Harmakros. "They're to wait till we're engaged and the second mob of Nostori cavalry come up; then they'll come out and hit them from the flank and rear."

An officer galloped away to attend to it. The yellow light was spreading upward in the east, only the largest and brightest stars were still visible. In front, the ground fell away to a little hollow, with a brook running through it to the left, to join a larger stream at the foot of the mountain, which rose steeply, then sloped up to the summit. On the right was broken ground, mostly wooded. A few trees around them, in the hollow and on the slope beyond; open farmland in front. This couldn't have been better if he'd had Dralm create it to order.

The yellow light was past the zenith, and the eastern horizon was a dazzle. Harmakros squinted at it and said something about fighting with the sun in their eyes.

"No such thing; it'll be overhead before they get here. Now, you go take a nap. I'll wake you in time to give me some sack-time. As soon as the wagons get here, we'll give everybody a hot meal."

An ox-cart appeared on the brow of the hill across the hollow, piled high, a woman and a boy trudging beside the team and another woman and more children riding. Before they were down to where the road crossed the stream, a wagon was coming up.

"Have them turned aside," Kalvan ordered. "Don't let them get into the village." This was only the start; there'd be a perfect stream of them before long. They couldn't be allowed on the main road past Fitra, not until the wagons and the eight-pounders got through. "And use wagons for barricades, and the oxen to help drag trees."

The village peasants were coming out now, leading four- and six-ox teams, chains dragging. Axes began thudding. One thing, if anybody was alive here then, this village wouldn't have to worry about winter firewood. More refugees were coming in; loud protests at being diverted, and at the seizure of wagons and teams. The axemen were across the hollow, now, and men shouted at straining oxen as trees were dragged in to build an abatis.

Kalvan strained his eyes against the sunrise; he couldn't see any smoke. Too far away. He was sure, though, that the mercenary cavalry was across the Athan, and they ought to be burning things. Pyromania was as fixed in the mercenary character as kleptomania. Of course, he could be misjudging here-and-now mercenaries; all he knew was what he'd learned reading Sir Charles Oman's *History of the Art of War*, when he should have been studying homiletics and scriptural exegesis and youth-organization methods at college, but there were universal constants. One was that mercenary soldiers' hearts were full of larceny. Another was that they liked being alive to spend their loot. He was pretty confident of what Klestreus' cavalry were doing down toward the river.

The abatis began to take shape, trees dragged into line, the tops to the front, with spaces for three of the six four-pounders on either side

of the road and a barricade of peasant wagons at either end. Kalvan rode
forward a couple of times to get an enemy's-eye view of it; he didn't want
it to look too formidable. He made sure that none of the guns would be
visible. Finally, he noticed smears of smoke against the horizon, maybe
five or six miles down the valley. Klestreus' mercenaries weren't going to
disappoint him, after all.

A company of regular infantry, a hundred and fifty, three pikes to
two calivers, came up in good order. They'd marched all the way from the
Athan, reported firing behind them, and were disgusted at marching away
from it. He told them they'd get all the firing they wanted by noon, and
to fall out and rest. A couple of hundred militia dribbled in, some with
crossbows. There were more smokes in the east, but he still couldn't hear
anything. At seven-thirty, the supply wagons and the eight-pounders, and
the two hundred militia wagon-guards came in from the west. That was
good; the refugees, now a steady stream, could be sent on up the road.

Kalvan found Harmakros asleep in one of the village cottages, wakened him, and gave him the situation to date.

"Good; I'll get the men fed. When do you want me to wake you?"

"As soon as you see smoke two miles down the valley, as soon as our
cavalry from the east begin coming in and in any case in two hours."

Then he pulled off his boots and helmet, unbuckled his belt, and lay
down in the rest of his armor on the cornshuck tick Harmakros had va-
cated, hoping that it had no small inhabitants or, if so, that none of them
would move in under his arming-doublet. It was comparatively cool in
here, behind the stone walls and under the thick thatch; the wet heat of
his body became a clammy chill. He shifted positions a few times, finally
deciding that fewer things dug into him if he lay flat on his back.

So far, everything had gone nicely; all he was worried about was who
would let him down, and how badly. If some valiant fool got a rush of
honor to the head and charged at the wrong moment—

If he could bring this off just half as well as he'd planned it, which
would be about par for the course for any battle, he could go to Valhalla
when he died and drink at the same table with Richard Coeur-de-Lion
and the Black Prince and Henry of Navarre. A complete success would

entitle him to take a salute from Stonewall Jackson. He fell asleep receiving the commendation of George S. Patton.

VII

An infantry captain wakened him at a little before ten.

"They're burning Systros now," Kalvan said. That was a town, of about two thousand, two and a half miles away. "A couple of the cavalry who've been keeping just in front of them came in. The first batch are about fifteen hundred; there's another lot, maybe a thousand, two miles behind them. We don't know where the infantry and the wagons are, but we've been hearing those big bombards at Narza Gap."

That would be Klestreus' infantry on this side, probably supported by Netzigon's ragtag-and-bobtail from the other side. He pulled on his boots and buckled on his sword, and, after eating a bowl of beef stew with plenty of onion in it, he put on his helmet and drank a mug of wine. Somebody brought his horse, and he rode up to the line. On the way, he noticed that the village priest of Dralm and the Mobile Force Uncle Wolf had set up a field hospital in the common and that pole-and-blanket stretchers were being prepared. No anesthetics, here-and-now, though the priests of Galzar used sandbags. He hoped he wouldn't be wounded himself. The last time had been bad enough.

A big column of smoke dirtied the sky above Systros. Silly buggers; first crowd into it had fired it, here-and-now mercenaries were the same as any other, and now the ones behind would have to bypass it. They'd be handling Klestreus' army in retail lots.

The abatis was finished, over a hundred felled trees ox-dragged into line, butts to the rear and tops to the front. Between them, men sat smoking or eating, or lay on the ground resting. The horse lines were back of the side road, with the more poorly-armed militiamen holding horses. At each end of the abatis were two of the four eight-pounders, then an opening big enough for cavalry to sortie out through, and then barricades of farm carts.

He could hear a distant, and then not so distant, popping of small arms. Away off, one of the bombards at Narza Gap boomed, and, after a while, the other. Good; they were still holding out. Cavalry came drifting up the road, some reloading pistols. The shots grew louder and more cavalry, in more of a hurry, arrived. Finally, a dozen or so topped the rise across the hollow and galloped down; the last fired a pistol over his shoulder. By the time he was splashing across the brook, Nostori cavalry appeared, ten or fifteen of them.

Immediately, a big eight-bore rifled musket bellowed from behind the abatis. His horse dance-stepped daintily; another, and another, roared. Across the hollow, a horse went down kicking, and another just went down. Another, with an empty saddle, trotted down to the stream and stopped to drink. The Nostori turned and galloped back out of sight. Nobody else had fired; riflemen were a law to themselves, but the arquebusiers were waiting for orders. He was wondering where the rest of the rifles were when a row of white smoke puffs blossomed along the edge of the bench above the stream on the left, and shots banged like a string of firecrackers. There were yells from out of sight across the hollow, and musketoons thumped in reply.

Wasting Styphon's good fireseed; four hundred yards, they couldn't hit Grant's Tomb at that range with smoothbores. Along the abatis, everybody was on his feet, crowding into position; there were a few yells of "Hostigos!" and "Down Styphon!" More confused noise from the dead ground beyond the brow of the hill, a steady whip-cracking of rifles, fired as fast as they could be reloaded and aimed, from the bench. He wished he had five hundred rifles up there.

Hell, while he was wishing, why not wish for twenty medium tanks and half a dozen Sabre-Jets?

Then the mercenary cavalry came up in a solid front on the brow of the hill, black and orange lance-pennons and helmet-plumes and scarves, polished breastplates. Lancers all in front, musketoon-men behind. A shiver ran along the line as the lances came down; the advance paused to dress front.

As though that had been the signal, which it had been, six four-pounders and four eight-pounders went off as one, not a noise, but a palpable blow on the ears. His horse started to buck; by the time he had him under control again, the smoke was billowing out over the hollow, and several perfect rings were floating up against the blue, and everyone was yelling, "*Down Styphon!*"

Roundshot; he could see the furrows it had torn into the block of black and orange cavalry; men were yelling, horses rearing, or down and screaming horribly as only wounded horses can. The charge had stopped, briefly, before it had started. On either side of him, gun captains were shouting, "Grapeshot! Grapeshot!" and cannoneers were jumping to their pieces before they had stopped recoiling with double-headed swabs, one end wet to quench lingering powder-bag sparks and the other dry.

The charge slid forward in broken chunks, down the dip into the hollow. When they were twenty yards short of the brook, four hundred arquebuses blazed; the whole front went down, horses behind tripping over fallen horses in front. The arquebusiers stepped back, drawing the stoppers of their powder-flasks with their teeth. *Memo: self-measuring spring power flasks; start making them as soon as possible.* When they were half reloaded, the other four hundred arquebuses crashed. The way those cavalry were jammed down there, every bullet must have hit something. The smoke was clogging the hollow like spilled cotton now; through it he could see another wave of cavalry coming up on the brow of the hill. A four-pounder spewed grape into them, and then another. *Down Styphon!* Before they could begin the descent, another four-pounder went off.

Gustavus Adolphus' four-pounder crews could load and fire faster than musketeers, a dry lecture-room voice was telling him. Lord Kalvan's weren't doing quite that well, but almost. The first one had fired on the heels of the third arquebus volley. Then one of the eight-pounders fired, and that was a small miracle.

A surprising number of Klestreus' cavalry had survived the fall of their horses. Well, horses were bigger targets, and they didn't wear breastplates. Having nowhere else to go, they were charging up on foot, their lances as pikes. Some of them were shot in front of the abatis, quite a few were piked trying to get through it. As Kalvan galloped to help deal with one party of these, he could see militiamen with scythe-blade things, he had never decided on the correct name for those weapons, and billhooks and axes, running forward from the horse lines. At that moment, he heard a trumpet sound on the right, and another on the left, and there were great shouts of *"Down Styphon!"* at both ends. Harmakros and the cavalry.

Then he was in front of a dozen Nostori cavalrymen, pulling up his horse and aiming a pistol at them.

"Yield, comrades! We spare mercenaries!"

An undecided second and a half, then one raised his reversed musketoon.

"We yield; oath to Galzar."

That they would keep. Galzar didn't like oath-breaking soldiers; he always let them get killed at the next opportunity. *Memo: cult of Galzar; encourage.*

Some peasants ran up, brandishing axes. Kalvan waved them back.

"Keep your weapons," he told the mercenaries. "I'll find somebody to guard you."

He found a couple of Mobile Force arquebusiers; and then he had to save a couple more mercenaries from having their throats cut. Damn these civilians! Have to detail prisoner-guards. Disarm the mercenaries, and the peasants would butcher them; leave them armed in the rear, and maybe the temptation would be too great even for the fear of Galzar.

Along the abatis, the firing had stopped, but the hollow below was a perfect hell's bedlam—*Down Styphon!*—and, occasionally, *Gormoth!* Over his shoulder, he could see villagers, even women and children, replacing militiamen on the horse lines. Captains were shouting, "Pikes forward!" and pikemen were dodging out among the felled trees. Dimly, through the smoke, he saw red and blue colors on the horsemen at the brow of the opposite hill. The road had been left open; he trotted forward and down toward the brook.

What he saw in the hollow made his stomach heave. After being de-mobbed on the West Coast, he had made a side trip into Mexico on the way home, and had seen a bullfight in Juarez. One horse gored to death by a bull hadn't bothered him much, but this would have sickened the most hardened *aficionado*. The infantrymen going forward, were stopping to brain wounded horses or cut their throats or shoot them with pistols from saddle-holsters. They oughtn't to stop to do that, but he couldn't blame them. The Hostigi soldier was a farmer and couldn't let horses suffer.

Stretcher-bearers were coming forward too, and so were villagers to loot. Corpse-robbing was the only way the civil population, here-and-now, had of getting some of their own back after a battle. Most of them had clubs or hatchets, to make sure that what they were robbing really were corpses. A lot of good weapons lying around, too. They ought to be collected before they rusted into uselessness, but no time to do that now. Stopping to do that, once, had been one of Stonewall Jackson's few mistakes.

Away ahead there was another uproar of battle, and more *Down Styphon!* That would be the two hundred cavalry from the far right hitting the second batch of mercenaries, who would be disorganized by now, by fugitives from the fight at the hollow. Gormoth wasn't going to have to pay a lot of mercenaries, if this kept up. The infantry were beginning to form up on the opposite hill, blocks of pikemen and smaller blocks of arquebusiers between, and some were running back to fetch the horses. And Nostori cavalry were coming in in groups, holding their helmets up on their sword-points and crying, "We yield; oath to Galzar." One of the officers of the flanking party, with four men, was bringing in close to a hundred of them. He was regretful that so many had escaped. The riflemen on the bench were drifting east, firing as they went. All the infantry from the Athan and many of the militia had mounted themselves on captured horses.

There was a clatter behind him, and he got his horse off the road to let the four-pounders pass in column. Their captain waved to him and told him, laughing, that the eights would be along in a day or so.

"Where do we get some more shooting?" Kalvan asked.

"Down the road a piece. Just follow along; we'll show you."

He looked at his watch. It was still ten minutes to noon, Hostigos Standard Sundial Time.

VIII

By 1700, they were well down the road, and there had been a lot of shooting on the way. Now they were two miles west of the Athan, where Klestreus' wagons and cannon were strung out for half a mile each way along the road, and Kalvan was sitting, with his helmet off, on an up-ended wine keg, at a table made by laying a shed door across a couple of boxes, with Harmakros' pyrographed deerskin map spread in front of him and a mug where he could reach it. There were some burned-out farm buildings beside the road, and the big oaks which shaded him had been yellowed on one side by the heat. Several hundred prisoners were squatting in the field beyond, eating food from their own wagons. Harmakros, and the chief captain of mounted infantry, he'd be about two-star rank, and the major-equivalent Galzar chaplain, and the brigadier in direct command of the cavalry, sat or squatted around him. The messenger from Sevenhills Valley, who had just caught up with him, was trying to walk the stiffness out of his legs, carrying a mug from which he drank as he paced and talked.

That's all we know," the messenger said. "All morning, there was cannon fire up the river, and then small-arms fire, a lot of it, and when the wind was right, we could hear shouting. A little after noon, some cavalry, who'd been patrolling the strip between the river and the mountain, came in; they said Netzigon was crossing in force in front of Vryllos Gap, and they couldn't get through to Ptosphes and Princess Rylla."

Kalvan cursed; some of it was comprehensible in local cursing terms. "Is she at Vryllos Gap, too?"

Harmakros laughed. "You ought to know her by now, Kalvan. Try and keep her out of a battle."

He'd probably be doing that the rest of his life. Or hers, which mightn't be so long if she wasn't careful. The messenger stopped, taking a deep drink, then continued:

Finally, a rider came in from this side of the mountain. He said that the Nostori were over the river and pushing Prince Ptosphes back into the gap. He wanted to know if the captain of Tarr-Dombra could send him help."

"Well?" Kalvan asked.

"We only had two hundred regulars and two hundred and fifty militia, and it's ten miles up to Vryllos along the river, and the Styphon's own way around the mountains on the south side. So the captain left a few cripples and kitchen-women to hold the castle, and took everything else he had across the river. They were just starting when he sent me off. I could hear cannon fire when I was crossing Sevenhills Valley."

"That was about the best thing he could do."

There'd be a couple of hundred men at Dyssa—about Jersey Shore—just a holding force. If they could run them out, burn the town, and start enough of a scare, it might take some of the weight off Ptosphes at Vryllos and Chartiphon at Listra-Mouth.

"I hope nobody expects any help from us," Harmakros said. "Our horses are ridden into the ground; half our men are mounted on captured horses, and they're in worse shape now than the ones of our own we have left."

"Some of my men are riding two to a horse," Phrames, the mounted infantry CO, said. "You figure what kind of a march they can make."

"It would be midnight before any of us could get to Vryllos Gap," Harmakros said. "That would be less than a thousand."

"Five hundred, I'd call it," the cavalry brigadier said. "We've been losing by attrition all the way east."

"But I'd heard that your losses had been very light," the rider said.

"You heard? From whom?"

"Why, the men guarding prisoners. Great Dralm, Lord Kalvan, I never saw so many—"

"That's our losses: prisoner-guard details, every one as much out of it as though he'd been shot through the head."

But Klestreus' army had simply ceased to exist. It was not improbable that as many as five hundred had safely crossed the Athan at Marax Ford.

There would be several hundred more, singly and in small bands, dodging through the woods to the south. And some six hundred had broken through at Narza Gap. The rest had all either been killed or captured.

First, there had been the helter-skelter chase east from Fitra. For instance, twenty-five riflemen, firing from behind trees and rocks, had stopped and turned back two hundred cavalry making for the next gap down. Mostly, anybody who was overtaken held up an empty hand or a reversed sword and evoked Galzar. Kalvan only had to fight once, himself; he and two Mobile Force cavalrymen caught up with ten fleeing mercenaries and charged them, shouting to them to yield. Maybe the ten were tired of running, maybe they thought it was insulting for three men to try and capture them, or many they were just contrary. Instead, they had turned and charged. He had half-dodged and half-parried a lance and spitted the lancer through the throat, and had been parrying with two swordsmen, when a dozen mounted infantrymen had come up.

Then, they had fought a small battle a half mile west of Systros. Fifteen hundred infantry and five hundred cavalry, all mercenaries, had just gotten to the main road after passing around both sides of the burning town and were forming up when the wrecks of cavalry from Fitra had come pelting into them. Their own cavalry and the fugitives were trying to force a way to escape, and the infantry were trying to pike them off, when the Hostigi, mounted infantrymen dismounted to fight on foot. Then the four-pounders arrived and began throwing case-shot, leather tubes full of pistol balls. Gormoth's mercenaries had never been exposed to case-shot before. Several hundred were killed and the rest promptly hoisted their helmets, tore off Gormoth's colors and cried for quarter.

That had been where the mercenary general, Klestreus, had surrendered. Phrames had attended to that; he and Harmakros had kept on with the cavalry, now down to three hundred, pistoling and cutting down fugitives. A lot of these toward Narza Gap.

Hestophes, the Hostigi CO there—about United States captain equivalent, he'd be a full colonel this time tomorrow—had been a real cool cat. He'd had two hundred and fifty men, mostly regulars with calivers, two old twenty-pound bombards and several smaller pieces. Klestreus' infantry had attacked Nirfe Gap, the one below him, and, with the aid of Netzigon's men from the other side, had swamped it. A few survivors had escaped along the mountaintop and brought the news to Narza. An hour later, Hestophes' position was under attack from both sides, too.

He had beaten off three assaults, a probable total of a thousand men. Then his lookout on the mountain reported seeing the Fitra-Systros fugitives streaming east. Hestophes promptly spiked his guns and pulled his men up out of the gap. The infantry who had been besieging him were swept along with the fleeing cavalry; from the mountainside, Hestophes spattered them with caliver bullets to discourage loitering and let them escape to spread panic on the other side. By now, they would be spreading it in Nostor Town.

Fitra had been a turkey shoot, Systros had been a roundup and the rest of it had been a fox hunt. Then they ran into the guns and wagon train, inching along under ox-power. There had been, with the train, a thousand of Gormoth's own infantry and five hundred mercenary cavalry. This had been Systros over again, except it had been a massacre. The fugitive cavalry had tried to force their way through, the infantry had resisted, and then the four-pounders—only five, one was off the road below Systros with a broken axle—had arrived and begun firing case-shot, and then one of the eight-pounders arrived. Some of the mercenaries tried to put up a serious fight; when they later found the pay chests in one of the wagons they understood why. The Nostori infantry simply emptied their calivers and threw them away and ran. Along with *Down Styphon!* the pursuers were now shouting *Dralm and No Quarter!* Kalvan wondered what Xentos would have thought of that. Dralm wasn't supposed to be that kind of god.

"You know," Kalvan said, getting out his pipe and tobacco, "we didn't have a very big army to start with. Just what do we have now?"

"Five hundred here, and four hundred at the river," Phrames said. "The rest are guarding prisoners all the way back to Fitra."

"Well, I think we can help Ptosphes and Chartiphon best from here," he said. "That gang Hestophes let through at Narza Gap will be panting out their story all the way to Nostor Town." He looked at his watch. If he ever broke that thing, he'd be sunk! "By this time, Gormoth will be getting ready to fight the Battle of Nostor." He turned to Phrames. "How many men do you absolutely need, here?" he asked. "Two hundred?"

Phrames looked up and down the road, and at the prisoners, and then, out of the corner of his eye, at the boxes under the shed door that formed the table top. They hadn't gotten around to weighing all that silver yet, but there was too much of it to be careless with.

"I ought to have twice that many, Lord Kalvan."

"The prisoners are mercenaries, and they have agreed to take Prince Ptosphes' colors" the priest of Galzar said. "Of course, they cannot bear arms against Gormoth or against any in his service until released from their oaths to him by the end of the war. In the sight of the Wargod, helping you to guard these wagons would be bearing arms against Gormoth, for it would free your own soldiers to do so. But I will speak to them, and I will answer that they will not break their surrender. You will need no guards for them."

"Two hundred, then," Phrames said. "I can use the walking wounded for some things."

"All right. Take two hundred, the ones with the worst beat-up horses, and mind the store. Harmakros, you take three hundred and two of the four-pounders and cross at the next ford down. I'll take four hundred across at Marax and work east and north. You can divide into two columns of a hundred men and one gun apiece, but no smaller. There will be companies and parts of companies over there trying to re-form. Break them up. And burn the whole country out, set fire to everything that'll make a smoke, or a blaze after dark. Any refugees going north, give them a good scare but don't stop them. We want Gormoth to think we have three or four thousand men across the river. That'll take some pressure off Vryllos Gap and Listra-Mouth."

Kalvan rose, and Phrames took his seat. Horses were brought; he and Harmakros and the others mounted. The messenger from Sevenhills Valley refilled his mug and sat down, stretching his legs in front of him. Kalvan rode along the line of wagons, full of food the people of Nostor wouldn't eat this winter, and curse Gormoth for the lack, and kegs of fireseed the slaves in Styphon's temple farms would have to toil to replace. He came to the guns, and saw one at which he stopped. A long brass eighteen-pounder, on a two-wheeled cart, with a four-wheeled cart for ammunition and to support the tail of the heavy timber stock. There was another behind it and an officer in gilded armor sitting on the cart, morosely smoking a pipe.

"Your guns, Captain?" Kalvan asked.

"They were. Prince Ptosphes' guns, now."

"They're still yours, and good pay for their use. Gormoth of Nostor isn't our only enemy."

The mercenary artilleryman grinned. "Then I'll take Ptosphes' colors, and my guns with me. You're Lord Kalvan? Is it really true that you make your own fireseed?"

"What do you think we were shooting at you today, sawdust?" He looked at the guns again. "We don't see brass guns around here."

They'd been made, as he suspected, in Zygros. He looked at them again, critically; there wasn't a thing wrong with Zygrosi brass-casting. The captain was proud of them, and glad he wasn't going to lose them; he boasted about good shots they had made.

"Well, you'll find one of my officers, Count Phrames, back by that burned house and those big trees. Tell him I sent you. He's to get those guns to Hostigos Town. Where are your men?"

"Some of them got killed before we cried quits. The rest are back there with the others. They'll all take the red and blue along with me."

"I'll talk to you later. Good luck, Captain, and glad to have you with us."

There were many dead infantry all along the road, mostly killed from behind, while running. Infantry who stood firm had a chance, usually a very good one, against cavalry. Infantry who ran had none at all. It grew progressively worse until he came to the river, where the four-pounder crews were swabbing and polishing their pieces, and dark birds rose cawing and croaking and squawking when disturbed at their feast. Must be every crow and raven and buzzard in Hos-Harphax; he even saw a few eagles.

And the river, horse-knee deep at the ford, was tricky. Crossing, their mounts stumbled continuously on armor-weighted corpses. This one had been a real baddie for Nostor.

IX

"So your boy did it, all by himself," the lady history professor was saying.

Verkan Vall nodded, grinning. They were in a seminar room at the University, lounging in seats facing a big map of Fourth Level Aryan-Transpacific Hostigos, Nostor, northeastern Sask and northern Beshta.

"Didn't I tell you he's a genius?"

"Just how much genius did it take to lick a bunch of klunks like that?" the operations director challenged. "From the reports I got on it, they licked themselves."

"Well, a great deal, accurately to predict the mistakes they'd make and then plan to take advantage of them," the elderly professor of Paratemporal Probability theory pronounced. He saw it as a brilliant theoretical accomplishment, vindicated by experiment. "I agree with Chief's Assistant Verkan; the man is a genius. Wait till we get this worked up a little more completely!"

"He knew the military history of his own time-line," the historian said. "And he knew how to apply it." She wasn't going to let her own subject be ignored. "Actually, I think Gormoth planned a good campaign—against Ptosphes and Chartiphon. Without Kalvan, they'd never have won."

"Well, Ptosphes and Chartiphon fought a battle of their own and won, didn't they?"

"More or less. Netzigon was supposed to wait across the river till Klestreus got up to Vryllos Gap, but Chartiphon started cannonading him—ordnance engineering by Kalvan—and Netzigon couldn't take it."

"Well, why didn't he pull back out of range? He knew Chartiphon couldn't get his cannon over the river."

"Oh, that wouldn't have been honorable. Besides, he didn't want the mercenaries to win the war, he wanted the honor of winning it."

"How often I've heard *that* one!" the historian laughed. "But don't the Hostigi go in for all this honor jazz, too? On that cultural level—"

"Sure, till Kalvan talked them out of it. As soon as he started making better-than-Styphon's powder, he gained a moral ascendancy over them. And then, the new swordplay, the new tactics, the artillery improvements; now it's 'Trust Lord Kalvan; Lord Kalvan is always right!'"

"He'll have to keep working at that. He won't dare make any mistakes. But what happened to Netzigon?"

"He made three attempts to cross a hundred yards of river in the face of artillery superiority. That was when he lost most of his cavalry. Then he threw his infantry across at Vryllos, pushed Ptosphes back into the gap, and started a flank attack on Chartiphon up the south bank of the river. Ptosphes didn't stay pushed; he counter-attacked and flanked Netzigon. Then the girl, Rylla, took a hundred-odd cavalry across, burned Netzigon's camp, slaughtered a lot of camp-followers and started a panic in Netzigon's rear."

"That was too bad about Rylla," the lady historian said.

Verkan shrugged. "That can happen in battles, any size. That's why Dalla's always worried when she hears I've been in one. Well, then everything went to pieces and the pieces began breaking up. We had a couple of conveyers in on antigrav last night. They had to stay above twenty thousand feet; we didn't want any heavenly portents on top of everything else, but they got some good infrared telephoto pictures. Fires all over the western end of Nostor, and for a two-mile radius around Dyssa, and in the southeast, that was Kalvan and Harmakros. And a lot of entrenching and fortifying around Nostor Town; Gormoth thinks he's going to have to fight the next battle there."

"That's ridiculous," the operations director declared. "It'll be a couple of weeks before Kalvan has his army reorganized, after those two battles. And powder; how much do you suppose he has left?"

"Five or six tons. That came in just before a little after noon, from our people in Hostigos Town. After he crossed the river, Harmakros captured a wagon train. An Archpriest of Styphon's House, on his way to Nostor

Town, with four tons of fireseed for Gormoth—and seven thousand ounces of gold."

The operations director whistled, "Man! That's making war support war, now!"

"And another ton or so in Klestreus' supply train, Klestreus' pay-chests," he added. "Hostigos came out of this deal pretty well."

"Wait till we get this all worked up," the old Paratemporal Probability theorist was cackling. "Absolute proof of the decisive effect of one superior individual on the course of history. Kalthar Marth and his Historical Inevitability, and his vast, impersonal, social forces, indeed!"

X

Gormoth of Nostor stood with an arm over his companion's shoulder—nobly clad, freshly bathed and barbered, with a gold chain about his neck, Duke Skranga looked nothing like the vagrant horse trader who had come to Nostor half a moon ago. Together they stared at the crowd in the Presence Chamber. Netzigon, who had come stumbling in after midnight with all his guns and half his army lost and the rest a frightened rabble; his cousin, Count Pheblon, his ransom still unpaid; the nobles of the Elite Guard who had attended him yesterday, waiting with him for news of victory until news of defeat had come; three officers of Klestreus' mercenaries who gotten through Narza Gap, and several more who had managed to cross at Marax Ford alive. And Vyblos, the highpriest, and with him Krastokles, the Archpriest of Styphon's House Upon Earth, and his black-armored guard captain, who had arrived with half a dozen men on broken-down horses at dawn.

Gormoth hated the sight of all of them, and the two priests most of all, and wasted no words on them.

"This is Duke Skranga. Next to me, he is first nobleman of Nostor. He takes precedence over all here."

The faces in front of him went slack with amazement, then stiffened angrily. A mutter of protest was hushed almost as it began.

"Do any object? Then he'd better be one who's served me half as well as Skranga, and I see none such here." Gormoth turned to Vyblos. "What do you want here, and who's this with you?"

"His Sanctity the Archpriest Krastokles, sent by His Divinity Styphon's Voice," Vyblos began angrily. "And how has he fared, coming here? Set upon by Hostigi heathens, hounded through the hills like a deer, his people murdered, his wagons pillaged—"

"His wagons, by the Mace of Galzar! My gold and fireseed, sent to me by Styphon's Voice in his care, and look how he cared for it! He and Styphon between them!"

"Blasphemy!" A dozen voices said it at once. Vyblos', Krastokles', and the guard captain's. And, among others, Netzigon's.

Now, by Galzar, didn't he have a fine right to open his mouth here? Anger sickened him; in a moment he thought he would vomit pure bile. He strode to Netzigon, snatching the golden chief-captain's chain from over his shoulders and striking him in the face with it, reviling him with obscenity upon malediction.

"Out of my sight! I told you to wait at Listra-Mouth for Klestreus, not throw your army away with his. By Galzar, I ought to flay you alive! Go now, while you can!"

"Speak not of your fireseed and your gold," Krastokles told him. "They were the god's gold and fireseed, to be given to you for use in the god's service at my discretion."

"And lost at your indiscretion; you witless fool in a yellow bedgown. Didn't you know a battle when you saw one in front of you? Vyblos, take this fellow you brought, and get you back to your temple with him, and come here again at my bidding or at your peril. Now go!"

He looked at the golden chain in his hand, then tossed it over the head of his cousin Pheblon.

"I still don't thank you for losing me Tarr-Dombra, but that's a handful of dried peas to what that son of a horseleech's daughter lost me. Now, Galzar help you, you'll have to make an army out of what he's left you."

"My ransom still needs paying," Pheblon reminded him. "Till that's done, I'm still oath-bound."

"So you are. Twenty thousand ounces of silver, do you know where I can find it? I don't."

"I do, Prince," Duke Skranga said. "There should be five times that much in the treasure vault of the temple of Styphon, here."

XI

Kalvan's horse stumbled, jerking him awake, and he got back onto the road. Behind him clattered fifty-odd men, most more or less wounded, but none seriously. There had been a score on horse litters, or barely able to cling to their mounts, but they had been left at the base hospital in Sevenhills Valley. He couldn't remember how long it had been since he had had his clothes off, or even all his armor. Except for pauses of a quarter-hour now and then, he hadn't been out of the saddle since daybreak, when he had crossed the Athan with the smoke of southern Nostor behind him.

That had been as bad as Phil Sheridan in the Shenandoah, but every time some peasant's thatch blazed up, he knew it was burning holes in Prince Gormoth's morale. He'd felt better about it after seeing the mile-wide swath of devastation along the main road in East Hostigos; at Systros there wasn't a house unburned. It stopped dramatically short at Fitra, and that made him feel best of all.

And the story Harmakros' stragglers had told him—fifteen eight-horse wagons, four tons of fireseed, seven thousand ounces of gold, that was at least one hundred and fifty thousand dollars, three hundred new calivers and six hundred pistols; a wagon load of plate armor. Too bad the Archpriest got away, his execution would have been a big public attraction in Hostigos Town.

He had passed prisoners marching west, mercenaries, under arms and in good spirits, at least one pike or lance in each detachment sporting red and blue colors. Some of them shouted "Down Styphon!" as he rode past. The back road from Fitra to Sevenhills Valley had not been so bad, but now, in what he had formerly known as Nittany Valley, the traffic became heavy again. Militia from Listra-Mouth and Vryllos, marching like regulars, which was what they were, now. Lines of farm wagons, piled with sacks and barrels and furniture that must have come from manor houses. Droves of cattle, and droves of prisoners not in good spirits and not armed, under heavy guard: Nostori headed for labor camps and intensive Styphon-is-a-fake indoctrination. And guns, on four-wheel carts, that he couldn't remember from any Hostigi ordnance inventory.

Hostigos Town was in an all-time record traffic-jam. He ran into the mercenary artillery captain, wearing his sword and dagger, with a strip of blue cloth that seemed to have been torn from a bedspread and a red strip from the bottom of a petticoat. He was magnificently drunk.

"Lord Kalvan!" he shouted. "I saw your guns; they're wonderful! What god taught you that? Can you mount mine that way?"

"I think so. I'll have a talk with you about it tomorrow, if I'm awake then."

Harmakros was on his horse in the middle of the square, his rapier drawn, trying to untangle the chaos of wagons and carts and riders. He shouted to him, above the din:

"What the Styphon; when did we start using three-star generals for traffic cops around here?"

MP's, of course; how the devil had he forgotten about that? *Memo: Organize soonest.*

"Just till I get a detail here, I sent all my own crowd up with the wagons." Harmakros started to say something else, stopped, and asked, "Did anybody tell you about Rylla?"

Kalvan went cold under his scalding armor. "Great Dralm, no. What about her?" It seemed an eternity before Harmakros answered:

"She was hurt; late yesterday, across the river. Her horse threw her, or something; I only know what one of Chartiphon's aides told me. She's at the castle—"

"Thanks; I'll see you later."

Kalvan plowed his horse into the crowd. People got out of his way and yelled to those beyond. Outside town, the road was choked with things too big and slow to get out of the way, and mostly he rode in the ditch.

The wagons Harmakros had captured were going up to Tarr-Hostigos, huge covered things like Conestogas with drivers riding the horses. He thought he'd never get past them, there was always another one ahead. Finally he rode through the outer gate of Tarr-Hostigos.

Throwing his reins to somebody, he stumbled up the steps to the keep and through the door. From the Staff Room, he heard laughing voices, Ptosphes' among them. For an instant he was horrified, then a little reassured. If Ptosphes could laugh, maybe it wasn't so bad.

He was mobbed as soon as he entered, everybody was shouting his name and thumping him on the back, he was glad for his armor. A goblet of wine was thrust into his hand. Ptosphes, Xentos, Chartiphon, most of the General Staff— And a dozen officers decked with red and blue, whom he had never seen before.

"Kalvan, this is General Klestreus," Ptosphes was saying to introduce a big man with gray hair and a florid face."

"An honor, General; you fought most brilliantly and valiantly." He'd fought like a damned imbecile, and his army had been chopped to hamburger, but let's be polite. Kalvan raised his goblet to the mercenary and drank. It was winter wine, set out in tubs to freeze and the ice thrown off until it was almost as strong as brandy. Maybe sixty proof, the closest they had to spirits here-and-now. It made him feel better and he drank more.

"Rylla? What happened to her?" he asked her father.

"Why, she broke a leg," Ptosphes began.

That scared him. People had died of broken legs in his former world, when the level of medical art was at least up to here-and-now. They used to amputate—

"She's all right, Kalvan," Xentos was saying. "None of us would be here if she were in any danger. Brother Mytron is with her. If she's awake, she'll want to see you."

"Then I'll go to her." Kalvan finished his wine and put the goblet down; drew off his helmet and coif and put them beside it, stuffed his gloves through his belt. "You'll all excuse me—"

Rylla, whom he had expected to find gasping her last, sat propped against a pile of pillows in bed, smoking a pipe with a cane stem and a silver-inlaid redstone bowl. She wore a loose gown, and her right leg was buckled into a huge contraption of saddle-leather. Mytron, the chubby and cherubic priest-physician was with her, as were several of the women who functioned as midwives, herb-boilers, hexers and general nurses. Rylla saw him first; her face lighted like sunrise.

"Hi, Kalvan! Are you all right? When did you get in? How was the battle?"

"Rylla, darling!" The women sprayed away from in front of him like grasshoppers. She flung her arms around his neck as he bent over her; he thought, Mytron stepped in to relieve her of the pipe. "What happened to you?"

"You stopped in the Staff Room," she told him, between kisses. "I smell it on you."

"Well, what did happen?"

"Oh, my horse fell on me. We were burning a Nostori village, and he stepped on a hot ember." Yes, just like William the Conqueror, Nantes, 1087, the history professor in the back of his mind reminded him. "He almost threw me, and then fell over something, and down we both went. I had an extra pair of pistols down my boot-tops; I fell on one of them. The horse broke a leg, too, and they shot him."

"How is she, Mytron?"

"Nothing to worry about, Lord Kalvan! It's a beautiful fracture. A priest of Galzar set it—"

"And gave me Styphon's own lump on the head, too. And now, it'll be a couple of moons till we can have a wedding."

"Why, we could have it now—"

"I will not be married in my bedroom. I will be married in the temple, and I won't be on crutches."

"It's your wedding, Princess." Kalvan hoped the war with Sask everybody expected would be out of the way before she was back in the saddle. "Somebody," he said over his shoulder, "go and have a hot bath brought to my room, and tell me when it's ready. I must stink to the very throne of Dralm."

"I was wondering when you'd mention that, darling."

XII

Sesklos, Supreme Priest and Styphon's Voice, rested his elbows on the table and palmed his smarting eyes. Around him pens scratched and parchments rustled and tablets clattered. He longed for the cool quiet of the Innermost Circle, but there was so much to do.

The letter from the Archpriest of the Great Temple of Hos-Agrys lay before him. News of the defeat of Prince Gormoth's armies was spreading, and with it rumors that Prince Ptosphes of Hostigos was making fireseed for himself. Agents-inquisitory reported that the ingredients and even the proportions were being bandied about in taverns. To kill everyone who knew the secret was out of the question; even a pestilence couldn't do that. And how to check the spread of the secret without further divulging it?

He opened his eyes. Admit it; better that than try to deny and later be proven liars. Let everyone, even the lay Guardsmen, know the full secret, but, for believers, insist that special prayers and rites, which only the yellow-robe priests could perform, were necessary.

But why? Soon it would be known to all that fireseed made by unconsecrated hands would fire just as well.

Well, there were malignant demons of the netherworld. Everybody knew that. He smiled, imagining them thronging about, scrawny bodies, bat wings, bristling beards, clawed and fanged. In fireseed, there were many of them, and only the prayers of anointed priests of Styphon could slay them. If this were done, as soon as the fireseed was exploded, they would be set free into the world of men, to work manifold evils and frights. And, of course, the curse of Styphon was upon all who made fireseed unconsecrated.

But Ptosphes had made fireseed and had not been smitten, and he had pillaged a temple-farm and massacred priests, and after that he had defeated the armies of Prince Gormoth, who marched with Styphon's blessing. How about that, now?

But wait! Gormoth himself was no better than Ptosphes. He had made fireseed himself, both Krastokles and Vyblos were sure of it, and he had blasphemed Styphon and despitefully used a holy archpriest, and forced a hundred thousand ounces of silver from the Nostor temple, at as close to pistol-point as didn't matter. To be sure, most of that had been after the battle, but who outside Nostor would know that? Gormoth had suffered defeat for his sins.

Sesklos was smiling happily now. Of course, Hostigos must be utterly destroyed and ruined, and all in it put to the sword; the world must see, once and for all, what befell a land that turned its back on Styphon. Sarrask of Sask would have to do that; Gormoth couldn't, even if he could be trusted to. Sarrask and Balthar, Prince of Beshta; Sarrask had been seeking a Beshtan alliance, and now was offering his daughter, Amnita, in marriage to Prince Balthar's younger brother, Balthames. An idea began to seep up into his mind.

Balthames wanted to be a Prince, too. It needed only a poisoned cup or a hired dagger to make him Prince of Beshta, and Balthar knew it. He wanted Balthames and his ambitions removed; should have killed him long ago. Now, suppose Balthames married this wench of Sarrask's; suppose Sarrask gave up a little corner of Sask, and Balthar a little corner of Beshta, both adjoining Hostigos. Call it the Princedom of Sashta. To it could be added all western Hostigos south of the mountains; why, that would be a nice little Princedom for any young couple. He smiled benevolently. And the father of the bride and the brother of the groom could recompense themselves respectively, with the Listra Valley, rich in iron, and East Hostigos.

That should be done immediately, before winter set in; then, in the spring, Sarrask, Balthar and Balthames could hurl their combined armies out of conquered Hostigos into Nostor. He'd send out another Archpriest of Styphon's House Upon Earth...let's see who that should be...to Sask, to make arrangements—with lavish gifts of money and fireseed for Sarrask and Balthar. And this time, make sure the treasures of Styphon's House did not fall into the hands of the infidel.

H✛S-H✛STIG✛S

H. BEAM PIPER

I

1964 A.D.

Verkan Vall watched his wife pack tobacco into a little cane-stemmed pipe. Dalla preferred cigarettes, but on Aryan-Transpacific they didn't exist and everybody smoked pipes. No paper; in that alternate probability, the Aryans migrating east instead of west, had conquered China two thousand years before paper had been invented there, and their descendants, reaching North America via the Kuriles and the Aleutians, had never even thought of it.

Behind them, something thumped heavily; voices echoed in the barnlike prefab shed. Everything was temporary here; until they established a permanent conveyer-head at Hostigos Town, hundreds of thousands of parayears away, nobody knew where anything would go at Fifth Level Hostigos Equivalent. Talgan Dreth, the Dhergabar University Director of Outtime Study Operations, sitting on the edge of a packing-case with a clipboard on his knee, looked up. He saw what Dalla was doing, and watched too, while she got out her tinderbox, struck sparks, blew the tinder aflame, lit a pine splinter and was puffing smoke, all in fifteen seconds.

"Been doing that all your life, haven't you," he grinned.

"Why, of course," Dalla deadpanned. "Only savages rub sticks together and only sorcerers can make fire without flint and steel."

They had to be careful of things like that. They had hypnotic conditioning—language familiarity, culture details, situation responses which would be made automatically, and, behind everything else, a censor-mechanism which would suppress anything they weren't supposed to know. A conditioning like that would deceive even the lie-detectors of a Second Level civilization. But on this operation, they must be especially careful. There was a man at Aryan-Transpacific Hostigos Town who was an alien to that time-line.

To test his own conditioning, he tried to think of the name by which that man knew Zygros City, whence they would claim to have come. It danced tantalizingly just out of mental reach until he deliberately lifted the blockage. Quebec, of course. And the great Kingdom of Hos-Harphax included Pennsylvania, and the Princedom of Hostigos was Centre and Union Counties, and Hostigos Town was Bellefonte, which meant Beautiful Fountain, as Hostigos meant Great Spring, and the Listra Valley, across the mountains, was Bald Eagle Valley, and the Athan was the West Branch of the Susquehanna, and the Harph was the main Susquehanna including the North Branch. He left the blockage lifted for a while.

It had started, a hundred and fifty days ago, with a quite commonplace paratemporal traffic accident; two conveyers had interpenetrated in the middle of Fourth Level Europo-American, Hispano-Columbian Subsector, and their exclusion fields had weakened briefly. One, a Paratime Police vehicle, had made a pickup, an adult human male,

a Corporal Calvin Morrison, Pennsylvania State Police, who had shot
and badly wounded the operator and managed to break free before the
conveyer-field built back to full strength again. This had been a job
for the Paratime Police; two jobs, in fact. They had the vanishment of
Corporal Morrison to explain on his own time-line, and they had his
unaccountable appearance somewhen else to handle. The first had been
pure routine. It had taken forty-odd days to pinpoint the time-line on
which he had emerged.

That had been Aryan-Transpacific, Styphon's House Subsector;
eastern North America divided into five so-called Great Kingdoms, all
called Hos- something or other, *Hos-* meant Great, and each split into
an anarchy of petty princedoms, the whole thing tightly if unofficially
controlled by a racketeering theocracy called Styphon's House, through a
monopoly on the secret of making gunpowder, called fireseed.

When finally traced, Calvin Morrison had become the Lord Kalvan,
betrothed to a Princess Rylla, daughter of Prince Ptosphes of Hostigos,
in command of Ptosphes' army in a war with an enemy neighbor, Prince
Gormoth of Nostor, and manufacturing fireseed in competition with
Styphon's House, against which he had declared relentless enmity.

Verkan had taken personal charge of the operation. On Year-End
Day, Tortha Karf was retiring as Chief of Paratime Police; thereafter he
would be Chief, himself, and he was not looking forward happily to being pinned down at a desk on Home Time Line. He wanted to get as
much outtime work as possible first. Posing as a wandering pack-trader,
he had found that the Lord Kalvan, né Calvin Morrison, was no threat at
all to the Paratime Secret and was accounting for himself better than the
Paratime Police could have. Ptosphes, Rylla, and a couple of others had
been told that he had been hurled by sorcery out of the remote future;
for public consumption, they had put it out that he was an exiled prince
from a distant country. Local belief in sorcery was as unquestioned as
geographical ignorance was profound. Returning to Home Time Line,
he had so reported.

Then the Paratemporal Theory department of Dhergabar University
had gotten into the act. A new Probability subsector was starting, its

origin-point plainly identified; it ought to be studied intensively. At once, he had offered, for which read imposed, the cooperation of the Paratime Police; this would allow him to work outtime until Chief Tortha's retirement, and offer occasional pretexts for truancy from the Chief's desk afterward.

For one thing, he was already established in Hostigos Town as Verkan, the Grefftscharr trader; at the moment, he was supposedly returning from Zygros City, where he had gone to recruit brass-founders to teach the Hostigi to cast light field-pieces. The brass-founders and patternmakers, five men and three girls, were Talgan Dreth's first study team; with them were two Paratime Police officers, supposedly mercenary soldiers hired as guards. They would make the drop tonight in the mountains on the Hostigos-Nyklos border, thirty miles to the north.

"Well, you're not going to get into any more battles, are you?" Dalla was saying. She'd been worrying about that.

"There won't be any more battles," Talgan Dreth said. "Kalvan won the war for Ptosphes while Vall was away."

"He won *a* war. How long it'll stay won I don't know, and neither does he. His wars have just begun. He won't have peace till he's destroyed Styphon's House. And Styphon's House is big."

"Big but vulnerable," the Outtime Study Director said. "I think he destroyed it already, by showing that anybody can make gunpowder. It was doomed from the start. It was founded on a secret, and no secret can be kept forever."

"Not even the Paratime Secret?" Dalla asked innocently.

"Oh, Dalla. You know that's different!" the University man cried. "You can't compare that with a trick, like mixing sulfur and saltpeter and charcoal."

II

The morning sun baked the open horsemarket; heat and dust and dazzle, and flies at which the horses switched constantly. The Lord Kalvan was hot and sticky under forty pounds of armor—quilted arming-doublet with mail skirt and sleeves, quilted coif with mail throat-guard, plate cuirass, and plate tassets down his thighs into his jackboots, high-combed helmet, rapier and dagger. He was accustomed to the weight, he'd carried more, and less well distributed, in Korea. He questioned if anybody, even old Chartiphon, who'd worn it constantly for at least fifty years, became accustomed to the heat and lack of body ventilation. *Like a rich armor worn in heat of day. That scalds with safety;* if Shakespeare hadn't worn it himself, he'd talked to plenty of men who had, like that little Welsh pepperpot Williams, who'd been the original of Fluellen.

"Not a bad one in the lot," Harmakros, riding in the saddle beside him, was saying. He was young for his rank, lieutenant-general commanding the new Mobile Force. His armor, ornately gilded, was nicked and lead-splashed from hard fighting. "And the big ones'll do for gun-teams."

And fifty saddle horses; that meant, at second or third hand, fifty more pikemen and arquebusiers who'd be able to move faster, wear heavier armor, and get into line when and where they were needed. "And another lot coming in from Nyklos tonight."

There was considerable moonlight traffic between Hostigos and Nyklos over the north road, bootleg fireseed going up for Prince Armanes, and horses coming back. Armanes wasn't ready, yet, for an open break with Styphon's House, but he was secretly their enemy and a friend to Hostigos.

He turned in his saddle, starting to comment, when something sledged him on the breastplate with a loud clang, almost unhorsing him. He thought he heard the shot. He did hear the second shot, while struggling to keep his seat and clawing a pistol from his saddlebow.

Harmakros was yelling; so was everybody else. There was a kicking, neighing, confusion among the horses. An arquebus went off behind him. Across the alley beyond the corral, two puffs of smoke drifting from a pair of upstairs windows in of one of a row of lodginghouse-brothel-wine-shops beyond. His chest aching, he lifted the pistol and fired. Harmakros was firing, too, and a second arquebus banged. Hoping he hadn't gotten another broken rib, he holstered the pistol and drew its mate.

"Come on!" he yelled, spurring forward. "Take them alive; we want to question them."

Torture. He hated that, had hated even the relatively mild third-degree methods of his other world, but when you needed the truth out of somebody, you got it, no matter how. Men were throwing poles out of the corral gate; he sailed past them, put his horse over the fence across the alley, landing in the littered back yard. Harmakros was behind him, with a Mobile Force arquebusier and a couple of horse-wranglers with clubs on foot.

He decided to stay in the saddle; till he saw what that bullet had done, he didn't know how much good he'd be on foot. Harmakros flung himself from his saddle, knocked a half-clad slattern out of the way, drew his sword and ran through the back door, the others after him. Men were yelling, women screaming; commotion everywhere except behind the two open windows from which the shots had come. A girl was bleating that Lord Kalvan had been murdered. Looking right at him, too.

He managed to squeeze his horse between houses to the street beyond, where a mob was forming. Most of them were pushing into the house through the front door; from within came screams, yells and noises of breakage. Hostigos Town would be the better for one dive less if they kept at that.

Up the street, another mob was coagulating; people pushing together, arms and clubs rising and falling, savage yells of "Kill! Kill!" Cursing, he holstered the pistol and drew his rapier, knocking a man down as he spurred forward shouting his own name. The horse was brave and willing, but untrained for riot work; he wished he had a State Police horse under him, and a yard of locust riot-stick instead of this sword. Then the combination provost-marshal and police chief of Hostigos Town arrived with a dozen of his men laying about them with caliver-butts. Together, they rescued two men, bloodied, half-conscious and almost ripped naked. The mob fell back from around them.

He had time, now, to check on himself. There was a glancing dent on the right side of his breastplate, and a splash of lead; the armor was unbroken. *That scalds with safety*; Shakespeare could say that again. Good thing it'd been an arquebus and not one of those great armor-smashing brutes of 8-bore muskets. Then he saw Harmakros approaching with two soldiers, herding a potbellied, stubble-chinned man in a dirty shirt, a blowsy woman with "madam" written all over her and two girls in sleazy finery.

"That's them! That's them!" the man began, as they came up, and the woman was saying, "Dralm smite me dead, I don't know nothin' about it!"

III

As a child, he had heard his righteous Ulster Scots father speak scornfully of smoke-filled-room politics and boudoir diplomacy. The Rev. Alexander Morrison should have seen this; it was both, and for good measure two real idolatrous priests of two different heathen gods were sitting on it. They were in Rylla's bedroom, because she was a member of her father's Privy Council and she was immobilized there with a broken leg, encased in padded steel splints covered with saddle leather. They were all smoking. And because the October nights were chilly as the days were hot, the windows were all closed.

Rylla's usually laughing eyes were clouded with anxiety. "They could have killed you, Kalvan." She'd said that before. She was quite right, too. He shrugged.

"Glanced off, only gave me a bruise. The other shot killed a horse; I'm really provoked about that."

"Well, what's being done with them?" she demanded.

"They were questioned," her father said distastefully. He didn't like using torture, either. "They confessed. Guardsmen of the Temple, that's to say, kept cutthroats of Styphon's House, sent from Sask Town, with

Prince Sarrask's knowledge, by Archpriest Zothnes. They said there's a price of five hundred ounces gold on Kalvan's head and as much on mine. Tomorrow," he added, "they will be beheaded in the town square."

"Then it's war with Sask." She looked down at the saddler's master-piece on her leg. "I hope I'm out of this by then."

She wouldn't be. Keeping this crazy blonde sweetheart of his out of battles would have him gray-headed in another year. Only a good helmet had brought her through the taking of Tarr-Dombra alive, and she'd broken her leg when thrown by her horse during the harrying of western Nostor. Some time, her luck would run out, and his with it; his mind shied like a frightened horse from the thought of no more lovely, happy Rylla. Well, she wouldn't get in this one. Mytron, the priest of Dralm who was the castle physician, had been fixed. He'd keep that ten pounds of old sword-blades, cotton padding and top-grain skirting leather stayed on her leg till the battle had been fought. He could set his mind at rest about that.

"War with Sask means war with Beshta," grizzle-bearded Chartiphon, whose new titles were Field Marshal, Chief of Operations and CO Army of the Besh, grunted. "Together they outnumber us five to two."

"Then don't fight them together," Harmakros said. "We can smash either of them alone. Let's do that, Sask first."

"Must we always fight?" Xentos implored. "Can we never have peace?"

Xentos was a priest of Dralm, and Dralm was a god of peace, and in his secular capacity as Ptosphes' Chancellor, he regarded war as an evi-dence of bad statesmanship. Maybe so, but statesmanship was operating on credit, and sooner or later your credit ran out and you had to pay off in hard money or get sold out. Ptosphes saw it that way, too.

"Not with neighbors like Sarrask of Sask and Balthar of Beshta we can't," he told Xentos. "We'll have to fight Gormoth again in the spring, you know that. If we don't knock Sask and Beshta out before then, it'll be the end of us."

The other heathen priest nodded agreement. They called him Uncle Wolf, as they did all priests of Galzar the Wargod; his wolfskin cape and wolfhead were laid aside; now, as he lounged in one of the chairs with a mug of wine at his elbow, playing with one of the kittens who made Rylla's room their headquarters.

"You have three enemies to fight," *You*, not *we*; priests of Galzar never took sides in any war. "You can destroy each in turn; together, they will destroy you."

And after they had beaten all three, what? Hostigos was too small to stand alone, but Hostigos, dominating Sask and Beshta, with Nyklos allied and Nostor beaten again, could. Then, of course, they'd have the Great King, Kaiphranos of Hos-Harphax, to deal with, and back of him, back of everything, Styphon's House.

So it would have to be an empire. He'd reached that conclusion long ago.

Klestreus cleared his throat. He was portly and florid, with a neatly trimmed gray mustache and beard. He wore a sleeveless blue jerkin and a red undertunic and hose, Ptosphes' colors, but four weeks ago, as elected captain-general of mercenary companies, he had worn the black and orange of Prince Gormoth of Nostor. Then he had led an army across the Athan at Marax Ford and into East Hostigos, as far as the village of Fitra, where the invasion had stopped suddenly and bloodily. Klestreus and almost four thousand mercenaries who had surrendered with him had promptly taken Ptosphes' colors.

This change of allegiance on a still-smoking battlefield had been entirely in accordance with here-and-now mercenary ethics; the priests of Galzar, who were arbiters of such matters, were positive on that. Of course, neither Klestreus nor any of his men could bear arms against Gormoth until peace between him and Ptosphes relieved them of their contractual obligations, but the Code of Galzar said nothing about bearing tales, so Klestreus was now Chief of Hostigos Intelligence.

"If we fight Balthar first," he pronounced, "Sarrask being allied to Balthar, will deem it an attack on him and act at once. He wants war with Hostigos anyhow. But if we attack Sask, Balthar will vacillate, and take counsel of his fears, and consult his soothsayers, whom we are bribing, and do nothing. I know them both." He drained his goblet, refilled it, and continued:

"Balthar of Beshta is the most cowardly, and the most miserly, and the most treacherous, prince in the world. I served him, once, five years ago, and Galzar keep me from another like service! He goes about in an old black gown that wouldn't make a good dustcloth, all hung over with wizards' amulets. His palace looks like a pawnshop, and you can't go three lance lengths anywhere in it without having to shove some impudent charlatan of a soothsayer out of your way. He sees murderers in every shadow, and a plot wherever three gentlemen stop to give each other good day."

He drank some more, as though washing the taste from his mouth.

"And Sarrask of Sask's a vanity-swollen fool who thinks with his fists and his belly. By Galzar, I've known Great Kings who hadn't half his arrogance. He's in debt beyond belief to Styphon's House, and the money all gone for palaces and pageants and feasts and silvered armor for his guards and jewels for his light-o'-loves, and the only way he can get quittance is by conquering Hostigos for them."

"And his daughter's marrying Balthar's brother," Rylla observed. "They're both getting what they deserve."

This was the overt part of the alliance. Young Duke Balthames, who hated and envied his brother as Balthar feared and hated him, would marry Princess Amnita of Sask, and for them a new princedom, tentatively called Sashta, would be created from adjoining snips of Sask and Beshta. Sesklos, the Supreme Priest, who called himself Styphon's Voice, had sent an Archpriest to Sask Town to arrange it. It was easy to predict what would follow—a joint war, financed by Styphon's House, for the conquest and partition of Hostigos, and, next spring, a concerted attack on Nostor. Since he had begun making his own fireseed, Styphon's House didn't like Gormoth of Nostor any more.

It all came back to Styphon's House.

"If we smash Sask now and take over some of these mercenaries Sarrask's been hiring on Styphon's expense account, we might frighten Balthar into good behavior without having to fight him."

Ptosphes puffed slowly on his pipe. "If we could get our hands on Duke Balthames, we could depose Balthar and make him Prince of Beshta. We could control him, I think."

Xentos was delighted. He'd become reconciled to war with Sask, but this promised a bloodless—well, almost—conquest of Beshta. "Balthames would be willing. We could make a secret compact with him, and loan him, say, two thousand mercenary troops and all the Beshtan army and all the better nobles would join him."

"No, Xentos. We do not want to help Balthames take his brother's throne. "We want to depose Balthar ourselves and let Balthames do homage to Ptosphes for it. And if we beat Sarrask badly enough, we might depose him and make him do homage to get his back."

"Well, whatever we do in the end, we fight Sask now," Ptosphes said decisively. "Beat Sarrask before that old throttlepurse of a Balthar can help him."

That was something they'd have to make sure of; that was why they had two armies, the Army of the Listra to invade Sask and the Army of the Besh to keep Balthar's troops from coming to Sarrask's aid. Chartiphon would take care of the latter; as soon as war broke out, his Army of the Besh would drive through southern Sask to the Beshtan border.

"How about Esdreth Gap?" Chartiphon asked. He'd been worrying about that, too.

Tyrone Gap, as he'd known it formerly. The Hostigos-Sask border followed the eastern fork of the Besh, the Juniata; across the gap, two castles faced each other, Tarr-Esdreth-of-Hostigos and Tarr-Esdreth-of-Sask. Until one or the other was reduced, the gap was closed to both sides.

"Alkides can take care of that." He was the new commander of Tarr-Esdreth-of-Hostigos, a mercenary artilleryman who had surrendered at Marax, with three long brass eighteen-pounders which had since been fitted with trunnions and mounted on real field-carriages. He had them at the castle, and two fifty- and two-hundred pound bombards, old style. "Send him a couple of hundred infantry and some cavalry, to hold the east approach to the gap; the Army of the Listra will do the same for the other side."

"Well, how soon can we start the war?" Chartiphon wanted to know. "How much sending back and forth will there have to be first?"

Uncle Wolf set the kitten on the floor; she trotted over to Rylla's bed and jumped up to join her mother and a couple of brothers and sisters there.

"Well, strictly speaking, you're at peace with Prince Sarrask, now," he said. "You must send letters of defiance, setting forth your causes of enmity."

"Now, what would they be, I wonder?" Harmakros wondered. "Send him Kalvan's breastplate?"

"That's a valid cause, and you have plenty more. I will carry the letter myself." Among other things, priests of Galzar acted as heralds. "Put it in the form of a set of demands, to be complied with on pain of immediate war; that would be quickest."

"Insulting demands," Klestreus specified.

"Well, give me a slate and a soapstone, somebody," Rylla said. "Let's see how we can insult him."

"A letter to Balthar, too," Xentos considered. "Not of defiance, but of friendly warning against the treachery of Sarrask and Balthames. They plot together to involve Beshta in war, and then depose him and divide his Princedom between them. He'll believe that."

"Klestreus, that will be your job. "Leave for Beshta Town with it in the morning. You know him, and what he'll believe and what he won't," he said. "This may save a lot of fireseed."

It would save a lot of things. Klestreus was no soldier, he'd proved that at Fitra. He was a military businessman, with promotional and public relation skills, instead of operational and management abilities. A diplomatic assignment would be perfect for him, and it would keep him from commanding troops in combat without offending him.

"And a letter to Armanes of Nyklos," he added. "Advise him, if he hasn't done so already, to have trustworthy representatives in Sask Town as soon as possible, to report on what happens there. How soon can we get the letter to Sarrask off?"

"Well, we can get it ready tonight," Ptosphes said. "We will have to convoke the Full Council of Hostigos tomorrow. The nobles and people should have a voice in a decision for war."

As though war hadn't been decided upon already, here in Princess
Rylla's smoke-filled boudoir. Real democracy, this was; just like
Pennsylvania.

IV

Verkan Vall, currently known as Verkan the Grefftscharr trader, waited
until the others—Prince Ptosphes, old Xentos, the Priest of Dralm, and
the man of whom he must never under any circumstances think as Calvin
Morrison—were seated. Then he took a chair with them at the table in
Ptosphes' study.

"Have a good trip, Verkan?" the Lord Kalvan asked.

He nodded, and ran briefly over the details of his fictitious journey
to Zygros City, what he must claim he had done there, and his return,
checking them with the actual facts. Then he visualized the panel, and his
hand reaching out and pressing the black button. Other Paratimers used
other mental imagery, but the result was the same. The pseudo-memories
fed to him under narco-hypnosis took over, the real fact-memories were
suppressed, and a complete blockage imposed on anything he knew
about Fourth Level Europo-American, Hispano-Columbian Subsector.

"Not bad. I had a little trouble at Glarth Town, in Hos-Agrys.
I'd sold those two kegs of fireseed, and right away they were after me,
the Prince of Glarth's police and agents of Styphon's House. It seems
Styphon's House put out a story about one of their wagon-trains being
robbed by bandits, and everybody's looking for unaccountable fireseed.
They arrested and tortured the merchant I'd sold it to. I killed one and
wounded another, and got away from them."

"When was that?" Xentos asked.

"Three days after I left here."

"Only eight days after we took Tarr-Dombra and sent that letter to
Sesklos," Ptosphes said. "That story'll be all over the Five Kingdoms by
now."

"Oh, they've dropped that; they have a new story, now. They admit that some Prince in Hos-Harphax is making his own fireseed, but it's bad fireseed."

Kalvan laughed. "It only shoots half again as hard as theirs, with half as much fouling."

"Ah, but your fireseed has devils in it. There are devils in all fireseed, of course, that's what makes it explode, but the priests of Styphon perform secret rites which cause the devils to die as soon as they have done their work. When yours explodes, the devils escape alive. I'll bet East Hostigos is full of devils, now."

He began to laugh, then noticed that the others weren't amused. Kalvan cursed; Ptosphes mentioned a name.

"That story has appeared here," Xentos said seriously. "None of our people believe it, I hope. It comes from Sask Town."

"It came up in Full Council meeting, this morning," Kalvan said. "One of the nobles accused me of being a renegade priest of Styphon, myself. All priests of Styphon are circumcised; I'm not, and Mytron, the castle physician, could testify to it. That knocked that on the head, so he brought out this devil story."

"A kinsman by marriage of mine," Ptosphes added, "jealous of Kalvan's greatness among us. I think somebody from Sask has been at him. He was ridiculed by everybody on the Council, and, er, spoken to, afterward."

"They move swiftly," Xentos said, "and they act as one. Their temples are everywhere, and each temple has its post station, and relays of fast horses. Their Supreme Priest can speak today at Balph, in Hos-Ktemnos, and before the end of a moon-quarter his words will be heard in all the Five Kingdoms. Their lies can travel so swiftly that the truth will never overtake them."

"Yes, and see what'll happen," Kalvan said. "From now on, everything—plague, famine, drought, hailstorms, hurricanes, floods, forest-fires—will be blamed on the devils in our fireseed. Well, you got away from Glarth; what then?"

"I thought it best to travel by night, after that. It took me eight days to reach Zygros City. My wife, Dalla, met me there, as we'd arranged when I left Ulthor to come south. We recruited five brass-founders—two are cannon-founders, one's a bell-founder, one's an image-maker and knows the wax-runoff method and one's a foundry foreman. And three girls, wood-carvers and patternmakers, and two mercenary sergeants I hired as guards.

"I helped spread the fireseed secret there. I gave it and the secret of rifling gunbarrels to a gunsmith, in exchange for making up twelve long rifled fowling-pieces and rifling some pistols. They'd heard the devil story, but they didn't believe it. They will ship rifled gunbarrels to Hostigos as fast as they can make them. Then, I gave the secret to some merchants from Grefftscharr. They'll take it home, and by this time next year they'll be trading fireseed down the Great Middle River as far as the Warm Seas."

That pleased Kalvan. Then he asked: "How soon can this gang of yours be ready to pour cannon?"

"Two moons; a special miracle for every day less."

He started to explain about the furnaces and molding-sand; Kalvan understood.

"Then we'll have to fight this war with what we have. We'll be fighting inside a moon-quarter. Our Uncle Wolf left for Sask Town after the noon meal today with demands on Sarrask; if he hasn't delivered them already, he will in the morning. Then they'll have to chain Sarrask up to keep him from biting people."

Ptosphes laughed. "His alliance with Balthar to be repudiated, and the marriage of his daughter to Balthar's brother to be canceled. All the free-companies he's hired since last Midwinter Day to be dismissed. Tarr-Esdreth-of-Sask to be dismantled. And Archpriest Zothnes and the high-priest of the Sask Town temple of Styphon to be sent here in chains to be tried for plotting Kalvan's murder and mine, and Styphon's House to be banished utterly from Sask."

"You'll command the Mounted Rifles again, won't you, Verkan?" Kalvan asked. "It's carried on the Army List as a regiment, so you'll be a colonel. We got more calivers rifled; it's a hundred and twenty rifles, now."

Dalla wouldn't approve. Well, that was too bad, but people who didn't help their friends fight weren't well thought of around here. Dalla would have to learn to put up with it, the way she had with his beard.

"Where are they now?"

"At the south end of Listra Valley; Harmakros is in command there, now, and Chartiphon has an army on the other side of the mountains. That's why you didn't see either of them at dinner. We're only waiting here till we hear from Uncle Wolf.

"I'll go join them tomorrow."

Ptosphes finished his wine. "I'm glad you brought your wife with you, Verkan," he said. Charming girl, and she and Rylla made friends at once. She'll be company for Rylla while we're gone."

"Rylla's sore at us," Kalvan said. "She wants to go to war with us. That's why we want to get this war over with in a hurry; we can't keep that cast on her leg forever. Maybe Dalla will keep her amused."

He didn't doubt that. Rylla and Dalla would get along together; what he was thinking of was what they'd get *into* together. They were just two cute little sticks of the same brand of dynamite; what one wouldn't think of, the other would.

V

The common-room of the village inn was hot and stuffy in spite of the open door; it smelled of wet woolens drying, of oil and sheep-tallow smeared on armor against the rain, of wood smoke and tobacco and wine, ancient odors of cooking and unwashed humanity. The village outside was jammed with the Army of the Listra and its impedimenta; the inn with officers steaming and stinking and smoking, drinking mugs of mulled wine or strong sassafras tea, crowding to the fire or around the long table where the map was unrolled, spooning stew from bowls or gnawing meat impaled on dagger-points. Harmakros was saying, again and again, "Dralm-damn you, hold that dagger back; don't drip grease on this!" And the priest of Galzar, who had carried the ultimatum to Sask Town and gotten this far on his return sat half-clad on a stool with his back to the fire, his hood and cape spread to dry and a couple of village children wiping and oiling his mail shirt. He had a mug in one hand, and with the other was stroking the head of a dog that squatted beside him, and he was laughing jovially.

"So I read your demands, and you should have heard them! When I came to the part about the mercenaries, the captain-general of free companies howled like a branded calf. I took it on myself to tell him you'd hire all of them with no loss of pay; did I do right, Prince?"

"You did just right, Uncle Wolf," Ptosphes assured him. "When we come to battle, along with 'Down Styphon!' we'll shout, 'Quarter to mercenaries.' How about our demands touching Styphon's House?"

"Ha! The Archpriest Zothnes was there, sitting next to Sarrask, with the Chancellor of Sask shoved down one place to make room for him, which shows you who rules in Sask now. He didn't bawl like a calf; he screamed like a panther. Wanted Sarrask to have me seized and my head off right in the throne-room. Sarrask told him his own soldiers would shoot him dead if he ordered it, which they would have. The mercenary captain-general wanted Zothnes' head off, and half drew his sword for it. There's one with a small stomach to fight for Styphon's House. And this Zothnes was screaming that there was no god at all but Styphon; now what do you think of that?"

Gasps of horror, and exclamations of shocked piety. One officer was charitable enough to say that the fellow must be mad.

"No. He's just a—" A monotheist; there was no word in the language for it. "One who respects no god but his own." That was a difficult enough concept to express. "We had that in my own country." He caught himself just before saying, "In my own time;" only Ptosphes and Rylla and Xentos and Chartiphon had security-clearance for that version of his story. "They are people who believe that there is only one god and that the god they worship is the only true one, and all others are false. Then they believe that the only true god must be worshipped in only one way and that those who worship otherwise are vile monsters who should be killed." The Inquisition, the wicked and bloody Albigensian Crusade; Saint Bartholomew's Eve; Haarlem; Magdeburg. "We want none of that here."

"Lord Prince," the priest of Galzar said, "you know how we who serve

Father Wolfhead stand. The Wargod is the Judge of Princes, his court-room the battlefield. We take no sides. We minister to the wounded with-out looking at their colors, our temples are havens for the war-maimed. We preach only Galzar's Way: Be brave, be loyal, be comradely; obey your officers; respect yourselves and your weapons and all other good soldiers; be true to your company and to him who pays you.

"But, Lord Prince, this is no common war, of Hostigos against Sask and Ptosphes against Sarrask. This is a war for all the true gods against false Styphon and Styphon's foul brood. Maybe there really is some devil called Styphon, I don't know, but if there is, may the true gods, Great Dralm, and Galzar Wolfhead, Yirtta Allmother and cunning Tranth and the rest, trample him under their holy feet as we must trample those who serve him."

A shout rose of "Down Styphon!" So an old man in a dirty shirt, a mug of wine in his hand and a brown and white mongrel thumping his tail on the floor beside him, had spelled it out. A religious war, the vilest form an essentially vile business can take. Priests of Dralm and Galzar preaching fire and sword against Styphon's House. Priests of Styphon rous-ing the mob against the infidel devil-makers. *Styphon Wills It!* Atrocities. Massacres. *Holy Dralm and No Quarter!*

Well, what can't be dodged must be dealt with.

"And then?"

"Well, Sarrask was in a fine rage, of course; by Styphon, he'd meet Prince Ptosphes' demands where they should be met; in battle. The war would start as soon as I took my back out of sight over the border. That was just before noon. I almost killed a horse, and myself, getting here. I haven't done much hard riding, lately," he parenthesized. "As soon as I got here, Harmakros sent out riders."

They had reached Tarr-Hostigos at cocktail time, an alien rite insti-tuted by Lord Kalvan, and found him and Ptosphes and Rylla and Dalla and Xentos in Rylla's room. Hasty arming and saddling, hasty goodbyes, and then a hard mud-splashing ride through the rain, ending at night here in this village. The war was already on; from Esdreth Gap they could hear the dull thumping of cannon.

Outside, the Army of the Listra was still moving up; an infantry company marched by with a song:

Roll another barrel out, the party's just begun.
We beat Prince Gormoth's soldiers; you oughta seen them run!
And then we crossed the Athan, and didn't we have fun,
While we were marching through Nostor!

Clattering hoofs; cries of "Way! Way! Courier!" The song ended in shouted imprecations from mud-splattered infantry; the galloping horse stopped outside. The march, and the song, resumed:

Hurrah! Hurrah! We burned the buggers out!
Hurrah! Hurrah! We put them all to rout!
We stole their pigs and cattle and, we dumped their sauerkraut,
While we were marching through Nostor!

A muddy cavalryman stumbled into the room, looked about blinking, then made for the group at the table, saluting as he came.

"From Colonel Verkan, Mounted Rifles. He and his men have taken Fyk, then beat off a counter-attack, and now the whole Saski army's coming up. I found some Mobiles and a four-pounder on the way back; they're going to help him."

"By Dralm, the whole Army of the Listra's going to help him! Where the Styphon is this Fyk place?"

Harmakros pointed it out on the map—beyond Esdreth Gap, on the main road to Sask Town, which was U.S. Route 220; Fyk would be between Tipton and Bellwood. There was a larger town, Gour, a little beyond; call that the location of the East Altoona railroad yards. He pulled on his quilted coif and fastened the throat-guard; while he was settling his helmet on his head, somebody had gone to the door and was bawling into the dripping night for horses.

VI

The rain had stopped by the time they reached Fyk, an hour later. It was a small place, full of soldiers and lighted by bonfires. A four-pounder pointed up the road to the south, with the shape of an improvised barricade stretching into the dark on either side. Off ahead, a shot banged now and then, and he could distinguish the reports of Hostigos-made powder from the slower-burning stuff put out by Styphon's House. Maybe, as Uncle Wolf had said, this was a war between the true gods and false Styphon; it was also a war between two makes of gunpowder.

He found Verkan and a Mobile Force major in the kitchen-living room-bedroom of one of the larger cottages. There was no sign of the civil population, all refugeed out. They had a map, scorched with hot needles on white deerskin, spread on the table. *Paper, invention of*, he'd made that mental memo a thousand times already. The Grefftscharrer wore a hooded brown smock and carried a short chopping-sword on his belt and a powder-horn and a bullet-pouch slung from his shoulder. The major's armor was browned and smeared with tallow.

"There were about fifty cavalry here when we arrived," Verkan was saying. "We killed some and ran the rest out. In half an hour, they were back with a couple of hundred more. We beat them off, that was when I sent riders back. Then Major Leukestros came with some men and a gun, and more men came in later, Mobile cavalry and mounted arquebusiers on the flanks and out in front, that's the shooting you're hearing. There are at least a thousand mercenary cavalry as close as Gour, and probably all of Sarrask's army coming up behind them."

"I'm afraid we're going to make a wet night of it. We'll have to form our battle-line now; we can't take chances on what they'll do"

He shoved the map to one side, got a lump of charcoal from the hearth, and began scribbling an order of battle on the white-scrubbed table top. Guns to the right rear, in column with the four-pounders in front, horses to be fed and rested in harness, ready to move out quickly. Cavalry on the flanks, mounted infantry horses in the rear, infantry in a line on both sides of the road a thousand yards south of the village, Mobile Force infantry in the middle, straddling the road. A battle-order that could quickly be converted into march-order if they had to move on at daylight.

The army came stumbling in by bits and scraps for the next hour or so, got themselves sorted out and found their places on the slope south of the village. The air had grown noticeably warmer; he didn't like that. It threatened fog, and he wanted good visibility. Cavalry skirmishers began drifting back, reporting continued pressure of large troop-masses in front.

An hour after he had his line formed, the men lying in the wet grass on blankets or whatever bedding they could snatch from the village cottages coming through, the Saski began coming up. There was a brief explosion of small-arms fire as they ran into his skirmishers, then they pulled back and began forming their own battle-line.

Hell of a situation, he thought disgustedly, lying on a cornshuck tick that he and Ptosphes and Harmakros had stolen from some Saski peasant's bed. Two blind armies, not a thousand yards apart, and when daylight came—

A cannon went off, with a loud, dull *whump!* on the left; a couple of heartbeats later there was a whack like an axe striking a block. He rose on his hands and knees and peered into the darkness counting seconds. Two minutes later, he glimpsed an orange glow on the left and heard the report two seconds later. Call it eight hundred yards, plus or minus a hundred. The shot seemed to strike somewhere back of his own line. He hissed at a quartet of officers on a blanket next to him.

"They're overshooting us a little. Pass the word along for everybody to move forward three hundred paces. And not a sound; dagger anybody who speaks above a whisper. Harmakros, you get all the horses, cavalry and mounted infantry, back behind the village. Make a lot of noise going back."

The officers moved off, two to each side. He and Ptosphes picked up the cornshuck mattress and carried it forward, counting three hundred paces before they dropped it and lay down on it. Men were moving up on both sides, with a gratifying minimum of noise.

The Saski guns kept on firing. At first, there were yells of simulated fright; that would be Harmakros. Finally a gun fired almost in front of him; the cannonball passed above, with a swish and whack like a headsman's sword coming down. The next one was far on his left. Eight guns, firing at two minute intervals; fifteen minutes to reload between shots, which wasn't too bad in the dark and with what the Saski had. He relaxed, lying prone with his chin on his crossed elbows. After a while, Harmakros found his way back and joined him and Ptosphes. The cannonade went on in slow procession; once there was a bright flash instead of a dim glow, and a loud hard crack. Oh, goody-goody, one of their guns burst! After that, there were only seven rounds to the salvo. Once there was a rending crash behind, as though a roundshot had hit a tree. Every shot was a safe over.

Finally, the firing stopped. The distant intermittent dueling between the two Castles Esdreth had ceased, too. He let go of wakefulness and dropped into sleep.

VII

Ptosphes, stirring beside him, wakened him. His body ached and his mouth tasted foully, as every body and mouth on both battle-lines must. It was still dark, but the sky overhead was something less than black, and he could make out his companions as dim shapes. Fog.

By Dralm, that was all they needed! Fog, and the whole Saski army not five hundred yards away, and all their advantages of mobility and artillery superiority lost. Nowhere to move, no room to maneuver, visibility down to half pistol-shot, even the advantage of their hundred-odd rifled calivers nullified.

This looked like the start of a bad day for Hostigos.

They munched the bread and cheese and cold pork they had brought with them, and drank sour wine from a canteen, and talked in whispers, and other officers came creeping in, till there were a dozen around the headquarters mattress.

"Couldn't we draw back a little?" That was Mnestros, the mercenary "captain"—approximately major-general—in command of the militia. "This is a horrible position. We're halfway down their throats."

"They'd hear us and start with their guns again," Ptosphes said, "and this time they'd know where to shoot."

"Bring up our own guns and start shooting first," somebody offered.

"Same objection; they'd hear us before we had them in position. And for Dralm's sake keep your voices down. No, Mnestros is right, we're halfway down their throats now. Let's jump the rest of the way and kick their guts out from the inside."

The mercenary was a book-soldier. He was briefly dubious, then admitted:

"We're in line to attack, and we know where they are and they think we're back at the village. Cavalry on the flanks?"

He deprecated that. According to the here-and-now book, cavalry was posted in companies between blocks of infantry all along the line. French Wars of Religion stuff, Ivry, for instance.

"Yes, a thousand mercenaries on each end, and a solid line of infantry between, two ranks of pikes in front; arquebuses and calivers to fire over their shoulders. Verkan, have your men pass up and down the line with the word. Everybody keep quiet and stay put, every pan reprimed and every flint tight, all move off together. I'll take the extreme right; Prince, you'd better command the center; Mnestros, you take the left. Harmakros, you go back about five hundred yards with, say, five hundred Mobile infantry on foot and a thousand cavalry, Mobile Force and Hostigi regulars. If they flank us or break through, take care of it."

By now, the men around him were individually recognizable, but everything beyond twenty yards was fog-swallowed. Their saddle horses were brought up. He reprimed the pistols in the holsters, got a second pair from a saddlebag, renewed the priming and slipped one down the top of each jackboot. The line was stirring, with a noise that stood his hair on end under his helmet-coif, until he realized that the Saski would be making too much noise, themselves, to hear it. He slipped back the padded cuff under his mail sleeve and looked at his watch. Five forty-five;

be sunrise in another half hour. They all shook hands with him, and with Ptosphes and Harmakros and one another. He mounted and started off slowly toward the right.

Soldiers were rising, eating whatever they'd thought to bring with them, rolling cloaks and blankets and slinging them. There were quilts and ticks and things on the ground; mustn't be a piece of bedding left in Fyk. A few were praying, to Dralm or Galzar. Most of them took the attitude that the gods did what they wanted to, without impertinent human suggestions.

He stopped at the extreme end of the line, on the right of five hundred regular infantry. Like the rest, they were lined in four ranks, two of pikes and two of calivers. Behind, the mercenary cavalry were coming up, in a block fifty men to a rank and twenty ranks deep, the first ranks heavy-armed, plate rerebraces and vambraces on their arms instead of mail, heavy pauldrons on their shoulders, visored helmets, mounted on huge chargers, real old-style brewery-wagon horses. They came to a halt just behind him. He passed the word of readiness left, then sat stroking his horse's neck and talking softly to him.

After a while the word came back with a moving stir on his left. He lifted a long pistol from his right holster, said, "Forward now," and shook his reins. The line slid forward beside him, front rank pikes waist-high, rear rank pike-points a yard behind and breast-high, calivers behind them at high port, the cavalry following him with a slow fluviatile *clop-clatter-clop*. Things emerged from the fog in front—seedling pines, clumps of tall weeds, a rotting cartwheel, the whitened skull of a cow—but the gray nothingness marched just twenty yards ahead of them.

He recalled that Gustavus Adolphus had gotten himself killed, riding forward into a fog like this at Lützen.

An arquebus banged somewhere to the left; that was a charge of Styphon's Best. Half a dozen shots rattled on its heels, most of them Kalvan's Unconsecrated, and he heard yells of *"Down Styphon!"* and *"Sarrask of Sask!"* and *"Ptosphes!"* The pikemen stiffened; some of them missed a step and had to hop to make it up; calivers tilted forward over their shoulders. Among the cavalry, swords slithered out. By now, the firing was like an endless slate roof sliding off a house, and then, farther left, there was a ringing crash like sheet-steel falling into a scrap-car.

The Fyk corpse-factory was in full production.

But in front, there was only silence and the slowly receding curtain of fog, with pine-dotted pastureland broken by small gullies in which last night's rainwater ran yellowly. Ran straight ahead of them; that wasn't right. The Saski position was up the slope from where they had passed the night under the midrange trajectory of the guns; the noise of battle was not only left of but behind them. He flung up the hand that held the gold-mounted pistol.

"Halt!" he called out. "Pass the word along the line; stand fast!"

He knew what had happened. Both battle-lines, formed in the dark, had extended too far to the right, each beyond the opposite left. So he was out past the Saski left flank, and, naturally, they would have outflanked Mnestros.

"You two." He picked a pair of cavalry lieutenants. "Ride left till you come to the fighting. Find a good pivot-point, and one of you stay with it; the other come back along the line passing the word to swing left. We'll start the swing from this end. And send somebody to find Harmakros and tell him what's happened, if he hasn't found it out already. He probably has. No orders, just use his own judgment."

Everybody would have to use his own judgment. He wondered how Mnestros was making out. He hadn't the liveliest confidence in Mnestros' judgment. Then he sat, waiting for centuries, until one of the lieutenants came thudding back, and then gave the order and started the leftward swing.

The level pikes and slanting caliver-barrels kept line on his left; the cavalry clop-clattered behind him. The downward slope in front swung, until they were mounting a steep grade, and then the ground was level under their feet and he could feel a freshening breeze on his right cheek. He was shouting a warning when the fog tore apart in front and on both sides; out of it a mob of infantry, badged with Sarrask's green and gold, came running. He pulled his horse back and fired his pistol into them, holstered, drew its mate.

The infantry major blew a whistle, then screamed piercingly above the din: "Action front! Fire by ranks, odd numbers only!"

The front rank pikemen squatted as though simultaneously stricken with diarrhea. The second rank dropped to one knee, their pikes advanced. Over their shoulders, half the third rank blasted with calivers, then dodged, and the odd numbers in the rear rank fired over their shoulders. As soon as the second volley crashed, the pikemen were up and running forward at the disintegrating front of the Saski infantry, all shouting, "*Down Styphon!*"

He saw that much, then raked his horse with his spurs and then drove him forward, shouting, "Charge!" The heavy-armed mercenaries thundered after him, swinging long swords and firing pistols the size of small carbines, smashing into the Saski flank before the infantrymen could face left and form a new front. His pistoled a pikeman who was thrusting at his horse, then drew his sword.

Then the fog closed down again, and dim shapes on foot, nobody could be sure who they were, were dodging among the horses. A Saski cavalryman bulked in front of him, firing a pistol almost in his face; the bullet missed, but hot powder grains stung his cheek. Get a coalminer's tattoo out of that. Then his wrist hurt as he drove his point into the fellow's throat-guard, spreading the links. *Plate gorgets; issue to mounted troops as soon as can be produced.* He wrenched his point free, and the Saski slid gently out of his saddle.

"Keep moving!" he screamed. "Keep moving; don't let them slow you down!"

In a mess like this, halted cavalry were all but helpless; their best weapon was the momentum of a galloping horse, and once lost, that took at least thirty yards to regain. Cavalry horses ought to be crossed with jackrabbits; that was something he couldn't do anything at all about. One mass of cavalry, the ones who had been behind the heavy-armed troopers, had gotten hopelessly jammed in front of a bristle of pikes. He backed his horse hastily out of that, then found himself at the end of a line of Mobile Force infantry with short arquebuses and cavalry lances for pikes. Catching their captain's attention, he directed them to the aid of the stalled cavalry. Then he realized that he had ridden at right angles across the road, and that he was completely separated from his mercenaries. That meant that he, and also the battle, faced east instead of south.

A horseman came crashing out of the fog, shouting "Down Styphon!" and thrusting at him. He had barely time to beat the sword aside with his own and cry, "Ptosphes!" and, a moment later, "Ptosphes, by Dralm! How did you get here?"

"Kalvan! I'm glad you parried that one."

He told the Prince, briefly and as well as he could.

"We're east of the road, you know that? And the whole Dralm-damned battle's turned at right angles."

"I know it, too. Our whole left wing's gone. Mnestros is dead, I heard that from men who saw his body. The regular infantry on the extreme left are all but wiped out; what's left of them and the militia to their right must have re-formed on Harmakros behind our center. We've been push-ing the Saski east along their original line; I saw their guns on my left. I don't know where those left flank mercenary cavalry are, now; took to their heels out of this, I suppose."

"Well, their left isn't in any better shape than ours; I smashed it up." The battle seemed to have moved away from them; things were quiet in the immediate vicinity. "Where would you think our line, if that's the word for it, is?"

"It isn't; it's just a Styphon's own delight of a mess, all around. Watch over my shoulder, will you, Kalvan?" Ptosphes' lifted a pistol from his saddlebow and took a powder-flask from his belt. "Have you seen Sarrask, anywhere?"

He hadn't; he'd been looking for the Prince of Sask. They sat and talked while they reloaded pistols; all of his were empty, now, and so were Ptosphes'. Then, suddenly, a cannon went off in the fog; about an eight-pounder, loaded with Hostigos Special. On its heels came another, and another.

"That," Ptosphes said, "will be Harmakros. He's brought the guns up. Sounds toward the village."

"I hope he knows what he's shooting at." He had his fourth pistol loaded and down his left boot. "Where do you think we could do the most good?"

"Well, let's find some of our own cavalry and go hunting for Sarrask," Ptosphes suggested. "I want to kill or capture him myself; it might give me some kind of a claim on the throne of Sask. If this cursed fog would only clear."

Off to the right, a boiler-shop appeared to have started up; not much shooting, just steel-clashing. Everybody with empty guns and no time to reload. The battle-cries were an indistinguishable *waw-waw-waw-ing*. The fog was blowing in wet rags, but as fast as it blew away, more closed down from above. The sky overhead was glowing a little; this might be the end of it. Ptosphes finished repriming the second of his spare pair, slipped it into his left boot, and drew his sword. They started off toward what he thought would be the east, and then ran into fifty or so heavy-armed mercenary cavalry, the ones who had been with him at the start. They hadn't an idea where they were.

He hadn't any better idea; he was going toward the noise of battle, which is generally the proper direction in which to go, but he thought he was still going east until he saw, stretching on either side of him, a line of mud-trampled quilts and bedsheets and mattresses that had been appropriated from the village the night before and left on the ground when they'd moved forward at daybreak.

That meant that he was going north, instead, and it meant that the battle had made, not a right-angle, but a 180-degree turn. Everybody was facing in the direction from whence he had come; the rout of either army would be toward the enemy's country. Galzar, he thought irreverently, must have overslept this morning.

One thing, the fog was definitely clearing, gilded above by sunlight, and the gray tatters blowing around them were fewer and more threadbare, visibility better than a hundred yards. They found the line of battle extending, apparently, due east of Fyk, and came up behind a hodgepodge of militia, Regular Army infantry, and Mobiles, mixed inextricably, with Mobile Force cavalry trotting back and forth behind looking for soft spots where breakthroughs could happen.

He yelled to a Mobile Force officer who was fighting on foot: "Who's in front of you?"

"How the Styphon do I know? Same mess of odds-and-sods as we are. This Dralm-damned battle has no head or tail at all."

Before he could say anything else, there was a crash on the left like all the boiler-shops in creation at once. He and Ptosphes looked at one another.

"Something new has been added," he commented. "What was that, anyhow? *Lucky Strikes*, he thought. He wished he had a cigarette, any kind, even a Japanese cigarette. "Let's go see."

They started left with their picked-up mercenary horse, not too rapidly, and with pistols drawn. There was a lot of shouting—"*Down Styphon!*" of course, and "*Ptosphes!*" and "*Sarrask of Sask!*" There were also shouts of "*Balthames!*" That would be the retinue Balthar's brother had brought with him to Sask Town, about two hundred and fifty, he'd heard. Then, there were cries of "*Treason! Treason!*"

Now there was a hell of a thing to yell on any battlefield, let alone in a fog. He was wondering who was supposed to be betraying whom when he found the way blocked by the backs of Hostigi infantry at right angles to the battle line; not retreating but merely being pushed out of the way of something. The fog parted, and beyond their lines he could see a rush of cavalry, some wearing black and pale yellow surcoats over their armor. They'd be Balthames' Beshtans; they were firing and chopping indiscriminately at anything in front of them. Mixed with them, fighting both them and the Hostigi, were Saski. All he and Ptosphes and the mercenary men-at-arms could do was sit their horses and fire pistols at them over the heads of their own infantry.

Finally, the breakthrough, if that's what it had been, was over. The Hostigi foot closed in, shooting and piking, and there were cries of "We yield!" and "Comrade, spare mercenaries!"

"Should we give them a chase?" Ptosphes asked, nodding in the direction taken by the breakthrough or whatever it had been.

"I shouldn't think so; they're charging in the right direction. What the Styphon do you think happened?"

"Dralm knows," Ptosphes laughed. "I wonder if it really was treason."

"Well, let's get through, here." He raised his voice. "Come on, forward! Somebody's punched a hole, let's get through it. Let the cavalry through!"

VIII

Suddenly, the fog was gone. The sun shone from a cloudless sky; the mountainside, nearer than he thought, was gaudy with autumn colors; the drifting puffs and hanging bands of white were powder smoke. The village of Fyk, on his left, was ringed with army wagons like a Boer laager, guns pointing out between them. That was the strongpoint on which Harmakros had rallied the wreckage of Mnestros' left wing.

In front of him, the Hostigi were moving forward, infantrymen running beside the cavalry. In front of them, the Saski line was raveling away, men and squads and whole companies turning and taking to their heels, trying to join two or three thousand of their comrades who had made a porcupine. A Swiss hedgehog, as he knew if from Otherwhen history, a hollow circle bristling pikes in all directions. Hostigi cavalry were already galloping around it, firing into it, and Verkan's riflemen had dismounted and were sniping at it. Then three four-pounders came out from the village at a gallop, unlimbered at three hundred yards and began firing case-shot. When a pair of eight-pounders followed more sedately, helmets began going up on pike-points and caliver-muzzles.

Behind him, the fighting had ceased. Hostigi soldiers had scattered through the brush and the trampled cornstalks, tending to their own wounded, securing enemy prisoners, robbing corpses, collecting abandoned weapons. All the routine after-battle chores, and the battle wasn't over yet. Then he saw a considerable mass of cavalry approaching down the road from the south. That would be the gang that had smashed through, coming back for another round. He started to yell at the men around him to drop what they were doing and start earning their pay, and then he saw red and blue lance-pennons and saddle-cloths.

Some were mercenaries, some were Hostigi regulars; with them were a number of green-and-gold Saski, their helmets hung on their saddlebows. They shouted to him, asking where the Prince was.

"I saw him a little while ago, fighting on foot. How far did you go?"

"Almost to Gour. Better than a thousand of them got away; they won't stop short of Sask Town. The ones we have are the ones with the slow horses. Sarrask may have gotten away; we know Balthames did."

"Galzar and Dralm and all the True Gods curse that Beshtan whelp!" one of the prisoners cried. "Devils eat his soul forever! That lackwit son of a horseleech's daughter cost us the battle, and Galzar only knows how many dead and maimed."

"What happened? I heard cries of treason."

"Yes, that dumped the whole bagful of devils on us," the Saski said. "You want to know what happened? Well, in the darkness we formed with our right far beyond your left; yours beyond ours, I suppose. On our right, we carried all before us; our cavalry smashed yours and drove them from the field. Then this pimp from Beshta—we can fight our enemies, but Galzar save us from our allies—took his own company and near a thousand of our mercenaries off on a rabbit-hunt them, almost to Esdreth Gap. Well, you know what befell while he was gone; the whole Galzar-abandoned battle turned like a wheel, and there we were, facing in the way we'd come, when back comes Balthames, smashing into the rear of our center, thinking, Dralm forgive him for I won't, that he was saving the day.

"And to make it worse, the silly fool doesn't shout "*Sarrask of Sask*" when he hits us, no he and his company all shouted "*Balthames*," and the mercenaries with them to curry favor. Well, Great Dralm, you know how much anybody can trust a Beshtan; we thought the bugger'd turned his coat, and somebody cried treason. I'll not deny crying it myself, after I was near spitted on a Beshtan lance. Well, we were carried away in the rout, and I fell in with mercenaries from Hos-Ktemnos. We got almost to Gour, and tried to make a stand, and were ridden over and taken."

"Did Prince Sarrask get away? Galzar knows I want to spill his blood badly enough, but I want to do it honestly."

The Saski didn't know; he'd seen none of Sarrask's silver-armored guardsmen in the flight.

"Well, don't blame Balthames too much." There were at least a score of Saski and Saski-hired mercenary prisoners around him; too good an opportunity to neglect. "It was," he declared, "the work of the True Gods! Who do you think raised that fog? Lytris the Weather Goddess! Who confounded your captains in arraying your line, and made your gunners overshoot, harming not one of us; who but Galzar? And who but Great Dralm himself addled Balthames' wits, leading him on a fool's chase and bringing him back to strike you from behind? At long last," he cried, "the True Gods have raised their mighty hands against false Styphon!"

There were muttered amens, some from the Saski prisoners. Styphon's stock had dropped quite a few points. He decided to let it go at that and put them where they could talk to the other prisoners.

They rode to Fyk, where the Mobile Force infantry were leading out their horses and the four-pounders were being limbered up. Harmakros was getting sorted out to spearhead the pursuit to Sask Town. Ptosphes was shocked at the losses.

Well, they had been sort of shocking. Forty-two hundred survivors of fifty-eight hundred infantry; only eighteen hundred of three thousand cavalry left; only two hundred of the thousand on the left flank. The body-count didn't meet that, though, and he remembered what the Saski officer had said. Most of them had just bugged out; by now, they'd be fleeing unpursued down the Listra Valley, spreading news of a crushing defeat. He cursed; there wasn't anything else he could do about it.

Riders came in from Esdreth Gap. During the night, a force of infantry, Army of the Besh and Army of the Listra, had gotten to the mountain-top back of the Saski castle, and had stormed it just before daylight. Alkides had moved his three treasured eighteen-pounders down, and was holding the west end of the gap with them. As the fog had been blowing away, some Saski cavalry had tried to force their way through; they had been driven off by gunfire. He was perturbed about the presence of enemy troops that far north, having heard the noise of the battle. Riders were sent to reassure him, and to order the three eighteens brought up to Fyk.

Kalvan didn't know what they might have to break into before the day was over; long eighteen-pounders were excellent burglar tools.

Harmakros got off with the Mobile Force and all the four-pounders at ten, starting along the main road, more or less Route 220, for Sask Town, almost exactly Hollidaysburg. The captured mercenaries agreed to take Prince Ptosphes' colors; the Saski prisoners were disarmed and put to work digging trenches for mass graves and salvaging equipment. Mytron and his staff pre-empted the better cottages and several barns as hospitals. Taking five hundred of the remaining cavalry, he set out, himself, at eleven, leaving Ptosphes and the main army to await the guns from Esdreth Gap.

Gour was a market-town of some five thousand. He found bodies, already stripped of armor, in the square, and a mob of townsfolk and disarmed prisoners trying to put out several fires, guarded by a few lightly-wounded mounted arquebusiers. He dropped two squads to help them and rode on.

He thought he knew this section; he'd been stationed in Blair County for a while five Otherwhen years ago. He hadn't realized how much the Pennsylvania Railroad Company had altered the face of Logan Valley. About what ought to have been Allegheny Furnace, he was stopped by a picket-post of Mobile Force cavalry and warned to swing west and come in on Sask Town from behind; Tarr-Sask was being held, either by or for Prince Sarrask, and cannonading the town, which Harmakros had taken. While he talked with them, he could hear the occasional distant boom of a heavy bombard.

Tarr-Sask stood on the south end of Brush Mountain, above from where he remembered the Blairmont Country Club. From its tower flew Sarrask's golden rayed sun on a green field. The entrance of his cavalry from behind must have been observed; four bombards let go with strain-everything charges of Styphon's Best, hurling fifty and hundred pound stone balls into the town. This, he thought, wouldn't be improving relations between Sarrask and his subjects. Harmakros, who had nothing but four-pounders, which was to say nothing, was not replying. Wait, he thought, till Alkides gets here.

Battering-pieces, thirty-two-pounders; get cast as soon as Verkan's Zygrosi get the foundry going. And cast-iron shells, do something about.

There had been no fighting inside the town; Harmakros' blitzkrieg had hit it before any resistance could be organized. There had been some looting, that was to be expected, but no fires. Arson for arson's sake, without a valid strategic reason, as there had been in Nostor, was discountenanced in the Hostigos army. The civil population had either fled into the country or were down in the cellars.

Harmakros had taken the temple of Styphon first of all. It stood almost on the exact site of the Hollidaysburg courthouse, a circular building under a golden dome, with rectangular wings on either side. If, as he suspected, that dome were really gold, it would go a long way toward paying off the cost of the war. A Mobile Force infantryman was up a ladder with a tarpot and brush, painting DOWN STYPHON over the door. Entering, the first thing he saw was a twenty-foot image, its face newly spalled and pitted and lead-splashed. The Puritans had also been addicted to that sort of small-arms practice, he recalled. There was a lot of gold ornamentation inside, too, and guards had been posted.

Kalvan found Harmakros in the Innermost Circle, his spurred heels on the highpriest's desk. He sprang to his feet.

"Kalvan! Did you bring any guns?"

"No, only cavalry; the main army's three hours behind. What's been happening here?

"Well, as you see. Balthames got here a little ahead of us, and shut himself and his company up in Tarr-Sask. We sent the local Uncle Wolf up to parley with him. He says he's holding the castle in Sarrask's name, and won't surrender without Sarrask's orders as long as he has fireseed."

"Then he doesn't know where Sarrask is, either."

Sarrask could be dead; his body stripped on the field by common soldiers. It would be worth stripping, and then tumbled anonymously into one of those mass graves. They might never be sure; at least once a year for the next thirty years, some fake Sarrask would crop up in one of the Five Kingdoms, conning suckers into financing a war to recover his throne. That had happened, occasionally, in Otherwhen history.

"Did you get the priests along with the temple?"

"Oh, yes. Archpriest Zothnes, the temple highpriest, and a score of the lesser sort. They were still arguing about what to take with them when we arrived. They're all in irons in the town jail; do you want to see them?"

"Not particularly. We'll have to have their heads off tomorrow when we find time for it. How about the fireseed mill?"

Harmakros laughed. "Verkan has that surrounded with the Mounted Rifles. As soon as we get a dozen men dressed up in priestly robes, about a hundred more will chase them in, plenty of yelling and shooting. If that gets the gate open, we may take the place before some fanatic blows it up. You know, some of these underpriests really believe in Styphon."

"Well, what did you get here?"

Harmakros waved a hand about him. "All this gold and fancywork. Then there's specie and bullion in the treasure vault, I'd say around fifty thousand ounces of gold in value."

That was a lot of money. Around a million 1964 U.S. dollars. He could believe it, though; besides making fireseed, Styphon's House was in the loan-shark business, at something like ten percent per lunar month, compound interest. *Anti-usury laws; do something about.* Except for a few small-time pawnbrokers, Styphon's House was the only moneylender in Sask.

"Then, there's an armory and magazine; we didn't have time to take inventory, yet, but I'd guess ten tons of fireseed and three or four hundred stand of arquebuses and calivers, and a lot of armor. And one wing is packed with general merchandise, stuff they took in as offerings. I have that all under guard, too."

The guns of Tarr-Sask kept on firing slowly, smashing a house in the town now and then. The main army arrived about 1700; Alkides got his eighteen-pounders into position and began shooting back. They didn't throw the huge globes of granite the bombards did, but they fired every five minutes instead of every half hour, and with something approaching accuracy. A little later, Verkan rode in to report the fireseed mill taken intact. He didn't think much of the equipment, the mills were all slave-powered, but there had been twenty tons of fireseed and over a hundred of saltpeter and sulfur. He had had some trouble preventing a massacre of the priests when the slaves had been unshackled.

At 1815, in the gathering dusk, riders arrived from Esdreth, reporting that Sarrask had been captured, in the Listra Valley, while trying to reach the Nostor border and place himself under the questionable protection of Prince Gormoth.

"He was captured,' the sergeant in command finished, "by the Princess Rylla and Colonel Verkan's wife, Dalla."

Kalvan and Ptosphes and Harmakros and Verkan all shouted at once and, a moment later one of Alkides' eighteen-pounders was almost an anticlimax. Verkan was saying: "*That's* the girl who wanted *me* to stay out of battles!"

"But she can't even get out of bed," Ptosphes sputtered.

"I wouldn't know about that, Prince," the sergeant said. "Maybe that's what her Highness calls a saddle, but she was in a saddle when I saw her."

"Did she have that cast—that leather thing—on her leg?" he asked.

"No, sir. Just regular riding boots, with pistols in them."

He and Ptosphes cursed antiphonally. Well, at least they'd kept her out of that blindfold slaughterhouse at Fyk.

"Sound Cease Fire, and then Parley," he said. "Send Uncle Wolf up the hill again; tell Balthames we have his pa-in-law."

They got a truce arranged; Balthames sent out a group of neutrals to observe and report, and bonfires were lit along the road to the castle. It was full dark when Rylla arrived with a mixed force of mounted Tarr-Hostigos garrison-troops, fugitive mercenaries rallied along the road south and overage peasants on overage horses. With them were nearly a hundred of Sarrask's elite guard, in silvered plate that looked more like table-service than armor, and Sarrask himself in gold armor.

"Where's that lying quack of a Mytron?" Rylla began, as soon as she was within hearing distance. "I'll doctor him, when I catch him; a double orchiectomy! You know what? Yes, of course you do; you put him up to it! Well, Dalla had a look at my leg this morning, she's forgotten more about doctoring than Mytron ever knew, and she said that thing ought to have been off two moon-quarters ago."

"Well, what's the story?" Kalvan asked. "How did you pick all this up?" He nodded at Sarrask, glowering at them from his saddle, with his silver-plated guardsmen behind him.

"Oh, this band of heroes you took to a battle I had to stay out of," Rylla said bitterly. "About noon, they came pelting up to Tarr-Hostigos—the ones with the best horses and the sharpest spurs—screaming that all was lost, the army destroyed, you were killed, father was killed, Harmakros was killed, Mnestros was killed, Verkan was killed, why, they even had Chartiphon, down on the Beshtan border, killed!"

"Well, Mnestros *was* killed, I'm sorry to say" her father mentioned.

"Well, I didn't believe a tenth of it, but I thought something bad might have happened, so I gathered up everybody I could mount at Tarr-Hostigos, appointed Dalla my lieutenant, she was the best man around, and started south, gathering up what we could along the way. Then, we ran into this crowd, we thought they were the cavalry screen for a Saski invasion, and we gave them an argument. That was when Dalla captured Sarrask."

"I did not," Verkan's wife denied. "I only shot his horse. Some farmers captured him, and you owe them a lot of money, or somebody does. We rode into this gang on the road, and this big man in gilded armor came at me, swinging a sword as long as I am. I fired at him, and just as I did his horse reared and caught it in the chest and fell over backward, and some peasants with knives and hatchets and things jumped on him, and he was screaming, 'I am Prince Sarrask of Sask; my ransom is a hundred thousand ounces of silver!' Well, right away, they changed their minds about killing him."

"I'll have to make that good to them," Ptosphes said. "Who are they, I wonder?"

"Styphon will pay."

"Styphon ought to; he got Sarrask into this in the first place. What then?" Ptosphes asked.

"Well, when they saw we had Sarrask, the rest of them all pulled off their helmets and began crying, 'Oath to Galzar!'" Rylla said. "They admitted that they'd taken an awful beating, and were trying to get into

Nostor. Wouldn't that have been nice?"

"Our gold-plated friend here didn't want to come along with us," Dalla said. "Rylla told him we could take his head with us easier than all of him. You know, Prince, your daughter doesn't fool around. At least, Sarrask didn't think so."

She hadn't been, and Sarrask had known it. He had been sitting glaring at them in defiant silence; now he burst out:

"Prince Ptosphes!" I am a Prince, as you are. You have no right to let these—these girls—make sport of me!"

"They're as good soldiers as you are," Ptosphes snapped. "They captured you, didn't they?"

"It was the True Gods who made sport of you, Prince Sarrask!" Kalvan went into the same harangue he had given the captured officers at Fyk, in his late father's best denunciatory pulpit style. "I pray all the True Gods," he finished, "that now that they have humbled you, they may forgive you."

Sarrask was no longer defiant; he was a badly scared Prince, as badly scared as any sinner at whom the Rev. Alexander Morrison had thundered hellfire and damnation. Now and then he looked uneasily upward, as though wondering what the gods were going to hit him with next.

IX

It was almost midnight before he and Ptosphes could sit down privately in the small room behind Sarrask's gaudy presence-chamber. There had been the surrendered mercenaries to swear into Ptosphes' service, and the Saski subject troops to disarm and confine to barracks. Riders had been coming and going with messages. Chartiphon, on the Beshtan border, was patching up a field truce with Balthar's officers on the spot, and had sent cavalry to seize the lead mines in Sinking Valley; as soon as he could get things stabilized, he was turning over to his second of command and coming to Sask Town.

Ptosphes had let his pipe go out. Biting back a yawn, he drank some wine and leaned forward to light it at a candle.

"Well, what are we going to do now, Kalvan?" he asked. "We have a panther by the tail, haven't we?"

"Well, we clean Styphon's House out of Sask, first of all. We'll have the heads off every one of those priests, from Zothnes down."

"Oh, of course," Ptosphes agreed. "But how about Sarrask? If we behead him, the other Princes would criticize us for it."

"Oh, no; we want Sarrask as your vassal. Balthames, too; he'll marry that wench of Sarrask's if I have to stand back of him with a shotgun, and then, when we make him Prince of Sashta, we'll occupy all the territory Balthar ceded to him in that treaty. In return for this support, he'll do homage to you for his new throne, and give us the entire output of those lead mines. Lead, I am afraid, is going to be our chief foreign exchange monetary metal for a long time to come.

"To make it a little tighter," he continued, "we'll cede him some territory ourselves. All the Valley of Hostigos to the edge of the Barrens—"

"Are you crazy, Kalvan? Give up Hostigi land? Not as long as I'm Prince of Hostigos!"

"Oh, I'm sorry. I must have forgotten to tell you. You aren't Prince of Hostigos, any more. I am." Ptosphes half rose and half drew his dagger; his thin face was ashen with shocked incredulity. "You," he continued, before Rylla's father could speak, "are his Majesty, Ptosphes the First, Great King of Hos-Hostigos. As Prince by betrothal of Old Hostigos, let me be the first to do homage to your Majesty."

Ptosphes sat down again, stared at his goblet, and then drained it. This was a Hos- of a different color.

"If your people in that section don't want to live under Balthames' rule, for which I wouldn't blame them, we'll buy them out, Styphon's House will pick up the tab, and we'll resettle them elsewhere, and we'll fill that country with a lot of these mercenaries we've had to take over and don't want to carry on the payroll. Make landlords and barons of the officers, give each private forty acres and a mule, and make sure they all have something to shoot with. It'll keep them out of worse mischief and keep

Balthames' hands full, and if we need them we can call them up again.

"I don't know how long it'll take to get Beshta; not too long. We'll let Balthar find out how much money we get out of this temple here. There's a big Temple of Styphon in Beshta Town, and Balthar's fond of money. We had a king in the history of my own time, Henry VIII, who made a good thing out of expelling a hierarchy and seizing temples. Then, after he's broken with Styphon's House, he'll find he'll have to have our protection."

"Armanes, too," Ptosphes considered. "He owes Styphon's House money." He toyed with his golden chain. "Do you think Kaiphranos will take this?"

"Who cares? Kaiphranos doesn't have five thousand troops of his own; if he wants to fight us, he'll either have to hire a mercenary army, and there is a limit to how many mercenaries anybody, even financed by Styphon's House, can hire, or he can levy troops from his subject Princes. Half of them will refuse to help coerce a fellow Prince for fear their turn'll come next, and the other half will be too jealous of their own dignities to take orders from anybody.

Ptosphes had started to lift the chain from around his neck. He replaced it.

"No, Kalvan," he said firmly. "I must remain Prince of Hostigos. Old Hostigos, I mean. You must be Great King."

"Now, look here, Ptosphes; Dralm-damnit, you *have* to be Great King!" For a moment, he was ten years old again, arguing who'd be cops and who'd be robbers. "You're a Prince; you have some standing. Nobody knows me from a hole in the ground."

Ptosphes slapped the table till the goblets jiggled.

"That's just it. They don't know you, and they know me all too well. I'm just Prince of Hostigos, no better than they are. Every one of these other Princes would say he had as much right to be Great King as I have. But they don't know who you are. They just know what you've done. That and the story we put out in the beginning, that you are an exile from across the Western Ocean, around the Cold Lands, from whence our race first came. Why, that is the Home of the Gods! We oughtn't to claim that you're a god, yourself; the real gods wouldn't like that, but anybody can plainly see that you were taught and sent by the gods. Why, it would be nothing but blasphemy to deny it!"

He was right; none of these haughty Princes would kneel to one of their own ilk. But Kalvan, Galzar-taught and Dralm-sent; that, too, was a Hos- of, another color. Rylla's father had risen, and was about to kneel to him.

"Oh, sit down; sit down!" he said impatiently. "Leave that nonsense for people like Sarrask and Balthames. We'll have to talk to a few people tonight; best do that in the presence-chamber."

Harmakros was still up, and more or less awake. He took it quite calmly; by this time he was beyond surprise at anything. They had to wake Rylla; she'd had just a little too much for her first day out of bed. She merely nodded drowsily, then her eyes widened. "Hey, won't this make me Great Queen, or something?" Then she went back to sleep.

Chartiphon, who was informed as soon as he rode in from the Beshtan border, first asked, "Why not Prince Ptosphes?" When the reasons were explained, he agreed. He did not for a moment question the necessity for establishing a Great Kingdom. "What else are we, now? We'll have Beshta, next."

A score of others, Hostigi nobles and top army brass, were collected and let in on it. They were all half out on their feet—they'd only marched all yesterday, tried to sleep in a wet cow pasture with cannon firing over them, fought a "great murthering battle" in the morning fog, marched fifteen more miles, and taken Sask Town and Tarr-Sask—but they wanted to throw a party and celebrate. They were persuaded to take one drink to their new sovereign and then go to bed.

The rank-and-file were in no better shape; half a den of Cub Scouts could have beaten the lot of them and taken Tarr-Sask.

X

His orderly, who didn't seem to have gotten much sleep, wakened him at nine-thirty; should have done it earlier. He bathed, put on clothes he had never seen before—*have things brought from Tarr-Hostigos, soonest*—and breakfasted with Ptosphes, who had also been outfitted from some Saski nobleman's wardrobe. There were more messages: from Klestreus, in Beshta Town, who had bullied Prince Balthar into agreeing to an armistice and pulling his troops back from the Saski border, and from Xentos, at Tarr-Hostigos. Xentos was perturbed about reports of troop-mobilization in Nostor; Gormoth, he knew, had recently recruited five hundred new mercenary cavalry. This alarmed Ptosphes; Gormoth was going to invade Hostigos while they were busy in Sask. He wanted to march the army down Listra Valley at once.

"No, for Dralm's sake don't!" Kalvan expostulated. "You said it, last night; we have a panther by the tail, here. In a day or so, when we've established control, we can move a lot of these new mercenaries to Listra-Mouth, but we mustn't let this gang here think we're frightened."

"But if Gormoth's invading Hostigos—"

"Send Phrames with half the Mobile Force and four of the four-pounders; that'll hold anything Gormoth's moving against us for a couple days. And do it without any fuss, too."

Kalvan gave the necessary orders, and then tried to ignore the subject. He was glad, though, that Rylla had gotten out of her splint-harness and come to Sask Town; she'd be safer here. So they had Sarrask and Balthames brought in.

Both seemed to be expecting to be handed over to the headsman, and were trying, almost successfully, to be nonchalant about it. Ptosphes informed them, without preamble, of their new status as subjects of the Great King of Hos-Hostigos.

"Who's the Great King?" Sarrask demanded, with a truculence his position scarcely justified. "You?"

"Oh, no. I am Prince of Old Hostigos. His Majesty, Kalvan the First, is Great King."

They were both relieved. Ptosphes had been right; the sovereignty of the mysterious and possibly supernatural Kalvan was acceptable; that of a self-elevated equal was not. When the conditions under which they would reign as Princes of Sask and Sashta were explained, Balthames was delighted; he'd come out of this as well as though Sask had won at Fyk. Sarrask was less so, until he was told that he was free of all his debts to Styphon's House and could share in the loot of the Sask Town temple and be given the fireseed mill.

"Well, Dralm save your Majesty!" he cried, and then loosed a torrent of invective against Styphon's House and everybody in it. "You'll let me put these thieving priests to death, won't you?"

"The Great King will deal with them; they are subject to his Majesty's justice," Ptosphes informed him.

Then they had in the foreign envoys—representatives of the Prince of Ulthor, on Lake Erie, and Armanes of Nyklos, and Balthar of Beshta, and others. There hadn't been any diplomatic corps at Tarr-Hostigos since Hostigos had come under the ban of Styphon's House. The Ulthori minister wanted to know exactly what the new Great Kingdom included.

"Well, present, the Princedom of Old Hostigos, the Princedom of Sask, and the new Princedom of Sashta. Any other Princedoms which may elect to join us will be welcomed under our rule and protection; those which do not will be respected in their sovereignty. Or," he added, "what they may conceive to be their sovereignty subject to any allegiance they may hold to Great Kaiphranos of Hos-Harphax."

He shrugged that off as too trivial for consideration. Several of them laughed. The Beshtan minister was bristling.

"This Princedom of Sashta; is that contemplated as including territory now ruled by my master, Prince Balthar?"

"It includes the territory which Balthar agreed to cede to our subject, Prince Balthames, in a treaty with our subject Sarrask of Sask, which we realize and confirm, and which we are prepared to enforce. I hope I won't have to mention what happened at Fyk yesterday morning."

He turned to the others. "Now, if your respective Princes don't wish to accept our sovereignty, we hope they will accept our friendship," he said. "We also hope that mutually satisfactory agreements for trade can be arranged. For example, in the very near future we will be able to export fireseed in quantity, of a much better quality and at a lower price than that sold by Styphon's House."

"We know that," the Nyklosi envoy said. "I can't commit my Prince to accepting the sovereignty of Hos-Hostigos, though I will advise it, but in any case we'll be glad to get all the fireseed you can ship us."

"Well, look here" the Beshtan began. "What's this about devils? The priests of Styphon make the devils in fireseed die when it burns, and yours lets them loose."

The Ulthori nodded. "We've heard about that, too. We don't want Ulthor filled with evil spirits."

"We've been using Hostigos fireseed, and we haven't had any trouble with devils," Prince Armanes envoy said.

"There are no devils in fireseed, that's just another Styphon's House lie," he declared. "It's nothing but charcoal, sulfur and saltpeter, mixed without any prayers or magic whatever. Nobody's complained about devils around Fitra, and we burned enough fireseed there."

The Beshtan was unconvinced; the Ulthori dubious. The Nyklosi was ridiculing both of them. That devil-story was going to have to be answered, and how could you answer a lie about something that didn't exist? Particularly an admittedly invisible something?

They got rid of the diplomatic corps, and had in priests of Dralm and Galzar and priests and priestesses of all the other gods and goddesses. The one good thing about monotheism, he thought, was that it reduced the priesthood problem. The best thing about polytheism was that all the competing hierarchies had a mutual basis of belief and a respect for one another's deities. The highpriest of Dralm seemed to be the acknowledged dean of the local sacred college, or whatever it was; assisted by all his colleagues, he would make the invocation and proclaim the Great King in the name of the gods. Then they had in some of Sarrask's court functionaries; they bickered almost endlessly about precedence and protocol. And they made sure that all the mercenary captains swore fealty for themselves and their companies in the presence of a priest of Galzar.

After noon-meal, they assembled everybody in Prince Sarrask's throne room.

In Korea, he had soldiered with a man who'd seen Napoleon's throne room at Fontainebleau.

"I never really understood Napoleon till I saw that," his comrade had said, "If Al Capone had seen it, he'd have gone straight back to Chicago and ordered one for himself twice as big, because he couldn't possibly have gotten one twice as flashy or in twice as bad taste."

That described Sarrask's throne room exactly.

The highpriest of Dralm proclaimed him as Great King, chosen by all the True Gods; divine right of kings was another novelty here-and-now. He then seated Rylla on the throne beside him, and invested her father with the Princedom of Old Hostigos, emphasizing that he was First Prince of the Great Kingdom. Then he accepted the homage of Sarrask and Balthames, and invested them with their Princedoms. The rest of the afternoon was consumed in oaths of fealty from the Saski nobility.

When he left the throne, he was handed messages from Klestreus in Beshta Town and Xentos at Tarr-Hostigos. Klestreus reported that Balthar had surrounded the temple of Styphon with soldiers, to protect it from mobs incited by priests of Dralm and Galzar. Xentos had gotten confused rumors of internal fighting in Nostor, and reported peace on the border.

That evening, they had a feast.

The next morning, after assembling all the local nobility and true-gods hierarchy, and all the itinerant merchants and pack-traders who could be found, in the throne room, the priests of Styphon, from Zothnes down, were hustled in. They were a sorry lot, dungeon-soiled, captivity-scuffed and loaded with chains; prodded with pike-butts, they were formed into a line facing the throne, and booed enthusiastically by the court.

"Look at them!" Balthames jeered. "See how Styphon cares for his priests!"

"Throw their heads in Styphon's face!" Sarrask shouted.

Other suggestions were forthcoming, some of which would have horrified the Mau-Mau. A few, black-robe priests and white-robe underpriests, were defiant; he remembered what Harmakros had said about some on the lower echelons actually believing in Styphon. The majority didn't, and were in no mood for martyrdom. Zothnes, who should have been setting an example, was in a pitiable funk.

Finally, he commanded silence. "These people," he said, "are criminals against all men and all the true gods. They must be put to death in a special manner, reserved for them and those like them. Let them be blown from the muzzles of cannon!"

Well, the British had done that during the Sepoy Mutiny, in the reign of her enlightened Majesty, Victoria. You can't get any more respectable than that. There was a general shout of approval—original, efficient, uncomplicated and appropriate. One of the upperpriests fainted. He addressed the mercenary Chief of Artillery:

"Alkides, say we use the three eighteens and three twelves; how long would it take your men to finish off this lot?"

"Well, six at a time." Alkides considered. "If we started right after noon-meal, we could be through with them in time for dinner." He thought for a moment. "Look, Lord Kal-sorry, your Majesty, suppose we load them into these big bombards, here. We could stuff the skinny ones all the way in, and the fat ones up to the hips." He pointed at Zothnes. "I think we could get all of him into a fifty-pounder, almost."

"Well, I'd wanted to do it in the main square in Sask Town, so as many people as possible could see it."

"It'd make an awful mess in the square," Rylla said.

Another priest fainted.

"People could come out from town to watch," Sarrask pointed out. "More than could see it in the square."

He nodded inconspicuously at Ptosphes, on his left.

"Your Majesty, since this is the form of execution reserved for priests of Styphon," the Prince of Old Hostigos said, "I've been wondering what should be done with any of these who abjure their false god, recant their errors and profess faith in the True Gods?"

"Why, in that case, we'd have no right to execute them at all. If they make public abjuration of Styphon, renounce their priesthood, profess faith in the True Gods, and recant their false teachings, we would have to set them free. To those who enter our service, we will give honorable employment, appropriate to their condition. Now, if Zothnes, say, were to recant and enter our service, I'd think something around five hundred ounces of gold a year—"

A white-robed underpriest shouted that he would never deny his god; a yellow-robed upperpriest said, "Shut your fool's mouth!" and hit him across the face with the slack of his fetter-chain. Zothnes was giggling in half-hysterical relief.

"Bless your Majesty; of course we will, all of us!" he babbled. "Why, I spit in the face of Styphon! You think any true god would suffer his priests to be treated as we've been?"

XI

Xentos reached Sask Town that evening. The news from Nostor was a little definite; his sources there reported that Gormoth had started mobilizing for an attack on Hostigos on receiving the first false news of a Hostigi disaster at Fyk; as soon as he had learned the facts, he used his troops to besiege the temple of Styphon. Now there was savage fighting in Nostor Town and all over the countryside, between Gormoth's mercenaries and supporters of Styphon's House, and the Nostori regular army was split by mutiny and counter-mutiny.

The local highpriest of Dralm deferred at once to Xentos, who was evidently primate of the Great Kingdom. *Establish Church of Hos-Hostigos; think over seriously.* Xentos, advised by the other priests and priestesses, began working out a programme for the auto-da-fé. It was a big success. Procession of the penitents from Tarr-Sask to the Sask Town temple of Dralm, in sackcloth, guarded by enough pikemen to keep the mob from pelting them with anything more lethal than rotten cabbage and dead cats; token flagellation; public repudiation of Styphon—heavy emphasis on recanting the heresy that there were devils of any sort in fireseed—and, finally, after profession of faith in Dralm, Galzar, Yirtta, etc., absolution, and a triumphant procession, the repentant sinners robed in white and crowned with garlands and free wine for everybody. This was more fun for the public than blowing them out of cannons would have been.

They had another feast that evening.

By the next day, Klestreus reported that Balthar had seized the temple of Styphon and killed all the priests; the mob were parading their heads on pike-points. He refused, however, to renounce his sovereignty; evidently he never considered Great King Kaiphranos, which wasn't surprising. Late in the afternoon, a cavalry company from Nyklos Town arrived, escorting one of Prince Armanes' chief nobles, with a petition that Nyklos be admitted to the Great Kingdom, and a packhorse loaded with severed heads. Prince Armanes wasn't interested in making converts. Neither was Kestophes of Ulthor; he blew his priests of Styphon priests off the muzzles of the guns at his lakeside castle. Along with his homage, he gave Hos-Hostigos a port on the Great Lakes. By that time, work of demolition had commenced on the Sask Town temple of Styphon. The dome was gold, and it came to twelve thousand ounces, of which Sarrask received, after his ransom had been paid, three thousand.

When he returned in state to Tarr-Hostigos, Klestreus was there, seeking instructions. Prince Balthar was now ripe to submit to King Kalvan. It appeared that, after seizing the temple and massacring the priests, he had discovered that there was no fireseed-mill in Beshta. All the fireseed he had gotten from Styphon's House had been made in Sask, and as he was as far under the ban as anybody else, there was no place he could get more except Hos-Hostigos. He was, however, worried about the possible devil-content of Kalvan's Unconsecrated. The ex-Archpriest Zothnes, now in the Ministry of State at six thousand ounces of gold a year, was sent to Beshta forthwith to reassure him.

It took more reassurance to induce him to Tarr-Hostigos to do homage; Balthar was, outside his own castle, violently agoraphobic. He came, however, in a mail-curtained wagon, heavily guarded by Hos-Hostigi cavalry.

The news from Nostor was still confused. A civil war was going on, that was all that was clear about it. Netzigon, the former chief-captain who had been disgraced after the debacle of Listra Mouth, and Krastokles, the Archpriest who had escaped the earlier massacre at the temple, were in open revolt. There had been an unsuccessful attack on Tarr-Nostor, and fighting continued in the streets of the town. Count Pheblon, Gormoth's cousin and Netzigon's successor, controlled about half of what was left of the Nostori army; the other half had adhered to the former commander. The nobility, each with a formidable following, were split about evenly. Then there were minor factions: anti-Gormoth-and-anti-Styphon, pro-Styphon-and-pro-Gormoth, anti-Gormoth-and-pro-Pheblon. In addition, several large mercenary companies had come in and were looting indiscriminately while trying to auction their services.

Not liking all this anarchy next door, he wanted to intervene. Chartiphon and Harmakros were in favor of that. Xentos, of course, wanted to wait and see, and, surprisingly, he was supported by Ptosphes, Sarrask and Klestreus. He decided to wait, at least until he could get some unanimity.

Prince Tythanes of Kyblos—roughly Somerset, Westmoreland, and Cambria Counties—arrived with a large retinue to do homage. He brought with him a lot of priests of Styphon, yoked neck-and-neck like a Guinea Coast slave kaffle. Baron Zothnes talked to them; there was an auto-da-fé and public recantation. Some went to work in the fireseed mill; some became novices in the temple of Dralm. They were all kept under close surveillance.

Balthar was still at Tarr-Hostigos when the other Princes began arriving, including Kestophes of Ulthor. Tarr-Hostigos began to look like a convention hotel. *Royal Palace: get built soonest.* Something that could accommodate a crowd of subject Princes and their attendants, but not one of these castles. Something simple and homelike, on the order of Versailles. When the Princes had all arrived at Tarr-Hostigos, they had the wedding. And a two-day feast, and an extra day for hangovers. Sometime during the festivities, Balthames and Sarrask's daughter were married, too.

It was the first time he'd ever been married. He liked it. It couldn't possibly have happened with anybody better than Rylla.

Then they had the Coronation. Xentos crowned him and Rylla. Then he crowned Ptosphes, and then the others, in order of their submission. Then the Proclamation of the Great Kingdom was read. Quite a few hands had labored on it, emptying goblets between phrases. He had cribbed freely from The Declaration of Independence, and, touching Styphon's House, from Martin Luther. Everybody cheered it enthusiastically.

The Princes were less enthusiastic about the Great Charter. It wasn't anything at all like the one that Tammany Hall in chain mail had extorted from King John at Runnymede; Louis XIV would have liked it much better. For one thing, they didn't like having to renounce their right to hire mercenaries and levy war on one another, though they did like the tightening of authority over their subject barons, most of whom were quite unruly. Nor did the latter like the abolition of serfdom and, in Beshta and Kyblos, slavery. But it gave everybody security, without having to hire costly mercenaries or drag peasants out of the fields, and everybody saw what was going on at the moment in Nostor. So they all signed and sealed it.

Secret police, to make sure they lived up to the agreement; think of somebody for chief.

They feasted for a couple more days, had a tournament and a wolf-hunt, and then began taking their leave and drifting home, each of them carrying the flag of Hos-Hostigos—dark green, with a red keystone on it. Gradually, Tarr-Hostigos became comparatively empty and quiet.

XII

The weather stayed fine until what the first week in November, then turned cold, with squalls of rain, and finally the rain turned to snow. Outside, it was blowing against the window panes—*clear glass; do something about*—and the candles had been lighted, and he was still at work. Petitions, to be granted or denied or referred. Reports—Verkan's Zygrosi were going faster than any of them had expected with the brass foundry; they'd be pouring the first heat in ten or fifteen days. The rifle shop was up to fifteen a day, which was a real miracle. Fireseed production up, too; soon they could start exporting it in large quantities. News that the supreme Priest, Sesklos, Styphon's Voice, was calling a council of all his Archpriests at Balph, that would be Winchester, Virginia. Council of Trent, he nodded; the Counter-Reformation would be getting into high gear, now. And pardons, and death warrants. Be careful not to sign too many of the former and too few of the latter; that was how kings lost their thrones.

A servant announced a rider from Vryllos Gap, who informed him that a party from Nostor had just crossed the border. A priest of Dralm, a priest of Galzar, some cavalry, and Duke Skranga, First Noble of Nostor.

He laughed, remembering the last time he'd seen the now Duke Skranga, then a horse-trader from the Trygath who had been detained in Hostigos between the time they started making fireseed and the taking of Tarr-Dombra. A small man with a bald head and a straggling red beard and narrow eyes; the sort of a character Corporal Morrison, Pennsylvania State Police, would have kept a close eye on. He remembered the interview, in this room, just before the frontier had been re-opened.

"You worked in the fireseed-mill; you've learned how to make fireseed. If you take my advice, you'll get into Nostor, while you can. Speak to Prince Gormoth privately, don't let the priests of Styphon know about it. Offer to make fireseed for him. You'll be making your fortune, too."

"But, Lord Kalvan! Gormoth is your enemy!"

"If Styphon's House finds out he's making fireseed, they'll be his. I like my enemies to have all the other enemies they can. You worship Dralm? Then seek out the highpriest of Dralm in Nostor, tell him I sent you, and ask his advice. Don't let Gormoth find out about that. Dralm, or somebody, will reward you."

Dralm, or somebody, had, apparently. The former horse trader was richly clad, his robe lined with costly fur, a gold chain about his neck and a gold-hilted dagger on a belt of gold links. His beard was neatly trimmed.

"Well, you've come up in the world," Kalvan commented.

"So, if your Majesty will pardon me, has your Majesty." Then he produced a signet-ring—the ring given as pledge token by Count Pheblon of Nostor and returned on payment of his ransom. "So has the owner of this. He is now Prince Pheblon of Nostor, and he sends me to declare his desire to accept your Majesty's sovereignty and profess himself your Majesty's faithful subject."

"What, if it's a fair question, became of Prince Gormoth?"

"Prince Gormoth, Dralm receive his soul, is no longer among us. He was most foully murdered."

"Ah. And who seems to have done it?"

Skranga shrugged. "The then Count Pheblon and the Nostor highpriest of Dralm, whom your Majesty knows, and the Nostor Uncle Wolf, and I, were in Count Pheblon's apartment at Tarr-Nostor, when we heard a volley of shots from the direction of Prince Gormoth's private apartments. Snatching weapons, we rushed thither, to find the rooms full of mercenary guards who had entered just ahead of us. Our beloved Prince lay weltering in his gore, bleeding from a dozen wounds. He was quite dead. Uncle Wolf and the reverend highpriest will both testify—you Majesty won't doubt the word of such holy men—that he was dead when we found him, and the guards say the same. Count Pheblon then proclaimed himself Prince of Nostor by inheritance, as the late Prince Gormoth's next kinsman, and assumed the throne. We tortured a couple of servants lightly—we don't do so much of that in Nostor, since our late blessed Prince— Well, they all agreed that a band of men in black cloaks and masks forced their way into the Prince's bedchamber, shot him dead and then fled. In spite of the most diligent search, no trace of them can be found."

"Most mysterious," Kalvan said. "Fanatic worshippers of false Styphon, without question. You say Prince Pheblon will do homage to us for his Princedom of Nostor and become our subject?"

"On certain conditions, of course, Your Majesty. For example, he wishes to be confirmed in his possession of the temple of Styphon, and to have Your Majesty confirm me in the possession of the fireseed mill and sulfur-springs and nitriaries, all confiscated by his late Highness Prince Gormoth."

"Well, that's granted. And the act of his late Prince in elevating you to the title of Duke and First Nobleman of Nostor as well."

"Your Majesty is most gracious!"

"Your Grace earned it. Now, how about these mercenary companies?"

"Pure brigands, your Majesty! Prince Pheblon begs your Majesty to send troops to deal with them."

"Of course. What's happened to Krastokles, by the way?"

"Oh, we have him in prison, your Majesty. Netzigon, too. If your Majesty wishes, we'll bring both of them to Tarr-Hostigos."

"Don't bother about Netzigon; take his head off yourselves if you think he needs it. But we want that Archpriest. I hope our faithful Baron Zothnes can spare us the mess of blowing him off a cannon by talking some sense into him."

"I'm sure he can, your Majesty."

Kalvan wondered just who had arranged the killing of Gormoth; Pheblon, or Skranga, or both together, and which one would have the other killed next. He didn't care about Gormoth, Nostor hadn't been in his jurisdiction, then. It would be from now on, though.

General Order, to all Troops: Effective immediately, it shall be a court-martial offense for any member of the Armed Forces of the Great Kingdom of Hos-Hostigos publicly to sing, recite, play, whistle or otherwise utter the words and/or music of the song known as Marching Through Nostor.

XIII

Verkan Vall looked at his watch and wished Dalla would hurry, but Dalla was making herself beautiful for the party. A waste of time, he thought; Dalla had been born beautiful. But try and tell any woman that. Across the low table, Tortha Karf also looked at his watch, and smiled happily. He'd been doing that all through dinner and ever since, each time with more happiness in the smile, as more minutes till midnight leaked away.

Verkan hoped Dalla's preparations would allow them to reach Paratime Police Headquarters at least one hour before midnight. There'd be a crowd in the big assembly room, and tables loaded with bottles and jugs and huge platters of food, and they'd have to shake hands and have a drink with everybody. Then, a little before midnight, they'd all crowd into the Chief's office, and Tortha Karf would take a chair at the desk, and, exactly at midnight, he would rise, and they would shake hands, and the new Chief, Verkan Vall, would sit down, and the crowd would start that Fourth Level barbarian chant they used on such occasions.

And from then, he'd be stuck there—Dralm-damn-it!

He must have said that aloud. The soon-to-retire Chief grinned unsympathetically.

"Still swearing in Aryan-Transpacific. When do you think you'll be able to get back there?"

"Dralm knows, and he doesn't operate on Home Time Line. I'm going to have a lot to do. One, I'm going to start a flap, and keep it flapping, about this pickup business. Ten new cases in the last eight days!"

Tortha Karf laughed. "Pardon my mirth, but that's what I said to old Zarvan Tharg when I took over from him, and he laughed at me as I'm laughing at you, because that was what he'd said when he took over. Fortunately for the working cops, we're a longevous race. It's a long time between new Chiefs."

"Well, we know the causes, conveyer interpenetration. We'll have to eliminate it. We did it on the University Kalvan Project. We checked all the conveyer-heads equivalent with Hostigos Town, and ours doesn't co-incide with any of them."

"I'll bet you had a time. I'll bet they love you in Conveyer Registration, too. How many were there?"

"A shade under three thousand, all over Paratime, inside four square miles. You should have seen the map! Maybe fifty that didn't coincide with any other. I don't," he confessed, "know what can be done about that generally."

"Nobody does." Tortha Karf poured from his liqueur-glass into his coffee cup and filled it from the urn. Then he lit a cigarette and looked again at his watch. "Kalvan Project has their conveyer-head in?"

"Oh, yes. That was finished fifteen days ago, started just after the Battle of Fyk. We have a police outpost in Greffa, the capital of Grefftscharr, where Dalla and I are supposed to be; the University has study-teams in the capital cities of all the Great Kingdoms, now. They'll have to be care-ful; by spring there'll be a war that'll make the Conquest of Sask look like a schoolyard fight."

They were both silent for a moment. Tortha Karf was thinking about his farm on Fifth Level Sicily, where he'd be tomorrow. He, himself, was thinking about his friend, the Great King Kalvan, and the problems and dangers ahead of him. Then something else occurred to him, a disquieting thought suggested by something Dalla had said. He spoke of it:

"Chief, this pickup problem is a small facet of something big and seri-ous; something fundamental. Just how secret is the Paratime Secret?"

Tortha Karf looked up sharply, his cup half way to his lips.

"What's wrong with the Paratime Secret, Vall?"

"How did we come to discover Paratime Transposition?"

Tortha Karf had to think briefly. "Why, Ghaldron was working to develop a space-warp drive, to get us out to the stars, and Hesthor was working on linear time-travel, to get us into the past, before our forefa-thers had worn the planet out. Things were pretty grim on this time-line, twelve thousand years ago. And Rhogom, a little earlier, had worked up a two-dimensional time theory in an attempt to explain the phenomenon of precognition. Somehow, Ghaldron read a few of Rhogom's papers, and then got in touch with Hesthor—science was pretty tightly compartmented, in those days—and the two of them discovered paratemporal transposition. Why?"

"As far as I know, nobody off Home Time Line has developed any sort of time-machine, linear or lateral. There are Second Level civilizations, and one Third Level, that have over-light-speed drives for spaceships. But the idea of multidimensional time and worlds of alternate probability is all over Second and Third Levels. You can even find it on Fourth Level—a mystical concept on Sino-Hindic, and a science-fiction idea on Europo-American."

"And suppose some Sino-Hindic mystic, or some Europo-American science-fiction writer, gets picked up and dropped, say, on Second Level Interworld Empire Sector?"

"That would do it, maybe. It mightn't even be needed. Gunpowder is a simple little discovery; it's been made thousands of times, all over Paratime. Paratime Transposition is a huge, complicated, discovery; it was made once in twelve thousand years, on one of a near infinity of timelines. But that's no guarantee. There is no such thing as a single-shot discovery. Anything that has been discovered once can be discovered again."

Tortha Karf started to say something. Then he sat down his cup and rose, smiling.

"Well, now, Dalla! That gown! And how did you accomplish that hairdo?"

He rose and turned. Dalla was pirouetting slowly in the light from the room behind her. It hadn't been a waste of time, after all.

"But I kept you waiting ages! You're both dears, to be so patient. Do we go, now?"

"Yes, the party will be beginning already."

And Chief Verkan Vall would be beginning, in a little under two hours, to assume responsibility for guarding the Paratime Secret. No secret, he seemed to hear Talgan Dreth saying, can be kept forever.

What was the expression they used in Hostigos?

A panther by the tail.

KALVAN KINGMAKER

JOHN F. CARR

I

1966 A.D.

Paratime Police Chief Verkan Vall watched while the trees and scrub brush of Fourth Level flickered through the wavering silver sheen of the Ghaldron-Hesthor transposition-field, as the transtemporal conveyer carried him toward Fifth Level time-line on the Litzn Equivalent where former Chief Tortha Karf had his villa. The civilized Second and Third Levels were behind him now. Once in a while Verkan caught flickering glimpses of Fourth Level-buildings, airports, occasionally a raging battle. Fourth Level was the highest probability level of all the inhabited Paratime Levels. There the First Colony had come to complete disaster, in the past fifty thousand years, losing all knowledge of its origins. It was the most barbaric level, as well as the largest. Its cultures ranged from idol worshippers on Proto-Aryan to nuclear reactors and hydrogen bombs on Europo-American, Hispano-Columbian Subsector.

The conveyer was now entering the low-level probability Fifth Level, where nature, not man, was triumphant. The only humans—other than some sub-human apes—were Service and Industrial Sectors Proles and their First Level overseers who labored there to keep heavy and light industry off of First Level, Home Time Line. On Fifth Level only the mountains remained constant. Occasionally, a large beast could be made out, while several times large pools of water appeared and disappeared. There was always a bit of variability between time-lines, sometimes nothing more than trees growing in different spots, other times bodies of water flowing in otherwise deserts.

The Service Sector Proles were not indigenous to the Fifth Level, but were brought from time-lines of near savagery. The Paratime Transtemporal Code limited the colonization of Service Sector time-lines to natives below second-order barbarism. The Serv-Sec Proles were the ones who did most of the administration and record keeping for Home Time Line. The Proles who were dumped in the Fifth Level, Industrial Sectors, where the machines and robots of First Level were manufactured, were at the bottom rung of the Service Sector. Here also were the survivors of Paratime screw-ups, when policy or criminal mistakes had made it necessary to transplant entire tribes and sometimes nations to protect them from famine or hostile neighbors, or to protect the Paratime secret. No matter—it seemed—how diligently the undermanned and overworked Paratime Police worked, there were always new bodies to fill another industrial time-line on Fifth Level.

Few, on First Level, realized just how many of these uncountable time-lines had never seen man's imprint. Even after twelve thousand years of parasitism upon other Second, Third, and Fourth level time-lines, First Level Para-topographers—including the Paratime Police Survey Division—had described less than one tenth of one percent of all the 'known' time-lines. In actuality it was an impossible job; few Paratime theorists still believed they would ever completely map this near infinity of diverging time-lines.

In theory the transposition field was impenetrable; however, when two craft going in the opposite directions collided, other objects and life forms could and did pass through. It was why unscheduled trips like his were limited to the highest echelon of the Paratime Police. It was also Paratime policy to have a weapon drawn just in case the hitchhiker was dangerous, or a threat to the Paratime secret. Most human pickups were killed immediately and disposed of back at the conveyer-head. Only a few escaped, and even fewer flourished in their new 'homes.'

Fourth Level Aryan-Transpacific, where his friend Kalvan and his lovely wife, Rylla, ruled an unruly kingdom, was the exception. There Great King Kalvan, formerly Corporal Calvin Morrison of the Pennsylvania State Police, had accidentally boarded a conveyer in Europo-American, Hispano-Columbian as a Paratemporal hitchhiker, and was dumped off on Aryan-Transpacific, Styphon's House Subsector. Thrust into a ruder and deadlier culture, Kalvan not only survived, he prospered. In less than a year he'd married a princess, founded an empire, broken Styphon's House monopoly of gunpowder and more than held his own against the worst that band of priestly tyrants—who worshipped a gunpowder god named Styphon—could manifest, including the unholy Holy Host, the largest army ever assembled on that backward time-line.

Kalvan's intervention into local politics had created a new time-line. In many ways Kalvan's Time Line was unique. It was the first time in First Level history when Paratime observers had been present at the start of a new time-live and possible subsector, identified from the exact point of divarication. The Paratimers had been close before, the President John F. Kennedy assassination, only a few years earlier, had been the critical event in the formation of the Europo-American, Kennedy Subsector. The Kennedy assassination, while newsworthy, had not been considered a divarication event until months later. The Kalvan split had been discovered almost as it happened, since Verkan Vall himself had tracked down the Paratime conveyer that former Pennsylvania State Trooper Calvin Morrison had stumbled into and exited out onto Aryan-Transpacific.

Because of growing instability between the two competing nuclear-powered sovereignties, the Kennedy Subsector—where President Kennedy had survived his assassination attempt—was far too dangerous to risk intensive study and monitoring. Kalvan's Time Line, on the other hand, was backward enough there was little danger to outtimers. The Dhergabar University had sent out five Kalvan study teams to survey Kalvan Prime, as they called it, and a number of Kalvan 'control' time-lines.

True, there were some—mostly bleeding hearts and professors who'd never traveled outtime—who still believed it was Home Time Line's duty to colonize these barren time-lines, even here on Fifth Level. Or worse, that it was their duty to spread the 'benefits' of First Level civilization and Psycho-Hygiene.

Worlds without number, thought Verkan; only a politician or do-gooder would think they could be tamed in even ten thousand lifetimes.

Finally the conveyer came to rest outside a white marble villa. Solid mesh appeared overhead, out of the iridescence, and Verkan holstered his sigma-ray needler. He stepped out of the conveyer and saw two lovely prole girls, draped in white togas, tending flowers in the garden. *So much for ex-Chief Tortha Karf's solitude,* he thought!

Verkan watched with amusement as a small, brown, long-eared rodent scurried through the flowers causing the girls to squeal in assumed outrage. It appeared that Tortha was losing in his attempt to rid his hideaway, known in Fourth Level, Europo-American as Sicily, of its indigenous rabbit population. He caught the girls' coy glances in his direction, and was glad his wife, Dalla, wasn't along. A catfight would not be the proper introduction for the bad news he had to share with his former boss and the ex-Paratime Police Chief.

The commotion brought Tortha Karf to the doorway. "Verkan, from your message ball, I didn't expect you for several hours."

"We managed to home-in on the missing Paracop's beacon and were able to extricate him from the Fourth Level mess he'd fallen into. His mission was locating and then extracting French Impressionist paintings from a *Gauleiter's* mansion on a particularly nasty Fourth Level, Europo-American time-line. Unfortunately, someone had already removed the paintings and he was picked up by the *Gestapo,* a rather brutal quasi-police force."

"Must have been in the Hitler Belt or the Axis Subsector."

Verkan nodded.

"I remember that Subsector well," Tortha continued. "Its impact reverberated across the entire Fourth Level. Adolf Hitler's public works and culling of the regional populations on that subsector makes your Pennsylvania State Trooper's transtemporal interference look like a tempest in a teapot—to use a Europo-American Sector cliché! Remember when the Opposition Party claimed that Hitler was really a renegade Paracop?"

Verkan refused to be baited.

Tortha noticing his discomfort, added, "Come on in. I've been by myself too long. It seems I've forgotten all my manners."

Verkan gave a pointed look at the girls who were watching them closely.

Tortha gave an avuncular shrug of his shoulders in feigned ignorance, leading Verkan through the foyer and into the grand main room. The rich gold-veined white marble walls were covered with Cretan murals, while the floor was covered with Fourth Level, Etruscan-Zoroastrian rugs. There were several embroidered purple divans, decked with gold fringe, which appeared to be Alexandrian-Roman in origin.

"So this your 'little cottage?'" Verkan asked. "I don't remember it being so palatial on my previous visit."

Tortha smiled smugly. "I've made a few additions and changes. Compared to Paratime Headquarters, this place is tiny. And much quieter. So what brings you to paradise?"

To Verkan his ex-Chief looked a little twitchy. *Too much of a good thing?* Maybe paradise was better dreamed about than lived. He was sure Kalvan, in the midst of a war with three great kingdoms, might very well agree.

"It's the Wizard Traders."

"Wizard Traders. You mean slave traders, Verkan. We busted that outfit up just before I retired as Chief."

"You weren't so sure a year ago. True, we arrested the obvious ones;

those who were passing themselves off as wizards on backward Third and Fourth Level worlds, using their privileges to steal forbidden artifacts and buy and sell people to unscrupulous Home Time Liners. Plus, a couple of First Level dupes, who were manning their secret conveyer-heads. Now, we've uncovered evidence that they may be connected to the Opposition Party. Remember how you always told me 'follow the money trail.' I've been following your advice and we've found some evidence that much of it went into the Opposition Party coffers."

"But that doesn't make sense, Verkan. The Oppositionists run on a policy of non-interference and Prole equality. You're trying to tell me that blood money has been paying for Prole equality votes?"

"I think you've been on this big island for too long. Yes, I do. Don't you remember: the means justify the end. The lesser evil for the greater good!"

"Maybe I have been outtime too long. Could this be the break we've been looking for, Verkan? Get word of this out to our friends in the media and we can break their backs once and for all."

"Break is not the right word. The Opposition Party has been gaining adherents and I'm afraid they may well find a way to point the blame right back at the Department."

"How? We've never been linked to the Oppositionists—just the opposite."

"True, but it did happen on our watch. Didn't it?"

"Don't look at me like that, old son. It's not my watch anymore. I've got some lemons to harvest."

"What should I do about it?"

"What you have to do, according to your commission. You're the top Paracop. Find out who they are, who's supporting them; then root them out. Who's your goat?"

"Hadron Tharn."

"That fatuous prig. He's not smart enough to be behind stale bread much less the Wizard Traders."

"He's not behind them, but we've linked one of the Wizard Traders to his organization."

"It's too bad they used hypno-conditioning to commit suicide."

"We never got all the trigger words. Every one of the important Wizard Traders committed suicide, when one of the implanted suggestions froze the Vagus nerve—instant heart attack." Verkan shook his head. "No two of them shared the same trigger words either; it left the experts at Bureau of Psych-Hygiene in a state of paralysis. The rest of the Wizard Traders were just proles doing a job. I'm still getting bad press over the casualties."

"Not your fault, Verkan," Tortha said, shaking his head. "It does lend credence to the big conspiracy theory, though. That kind of deep conditioning doesn't come cheap. Anything more?"

"Yes, we've traced a new batch of Wizard Traders to Aryan-Transpacific."

Tortha's mouth dropped open. "Already!"

"Yes, they've gotten into bed with Styphon's House on every time-line they've entered. Trading the upperpriests weapons technology in exchange for young bodies and precious metals."

"Have they penetrated the Kalvan Time-Line?"

"No. Although we do have a suspected spy on one of the University study teams."

"Why don't you bring him in for questioning?"

"It's a she. And we don't have any evidence other than a relationship with Hadron Tharn. Besides, Tharn is too stupid to set up and run any decent spy ring. We suspect she's a red herring, as it's called on Fourth Level, Europo-American. Just as Tharn himself is just a cat's-paw to lead us astray."

"Good hunting. Every time I start to think back fondly of my time as Chief, you come along and remind me of why I retired."

"Tortha!" one of the girls called. "It's time for our swimming lessons. Will you be joining us?"

"Yes, of course. Must not neglect my guests. Please, excuse me Verkan, but I've got my duties here to contend with. Oh, do you have any presence on the study team."

"Verkan nodded. "One of our best agents."

II

The army Styphon's House had thrown at Hos-Hostigos had also let loose the great miracle of fireseed—the magic powder that made muskets and bombards such terrible weapons of destruction. Now anyone, even nonbelievers, could duplicate Styphon's Great Miracle or buy fireseed direct from King Kalvan. Now even those allies who still believed in Styphon's divinity were shaken in their faith by Kalvan's otherworldly ability to shake victory from almost certain defeat.

Grand Master Soton himself, ruler of a domain equal to that of any Great King's in the Sastragath border lands, was not pleased that the fanatics within Styphon's House had taken command of the Temple—aided and abetted by Supreme Priest Sesklos' growing senility. Yet, were it not for the Temple taking him in as an orphan thirty-some winters ago, he would now be a simple farmer or blacksmith in some isolated backwater village. For that and allowing him to raise himself so high—as Grand Master of the Order of Zarthani Knights and Archpriest of Styphon's House—the Temple had his undying loyalty.

Furthermore, there was no denying that Archpriest Roxthar and his followers had put new mettle into Styphon's Way On Earth. They had certainly given him an unlimited draft on the Temple's earthly resources; all of which, gold and arms especially, he was going to need if he was going to turn the broken Harphaxi Royal Army into any semblance of a military power.

Soton halted his party before the next steep grade and peered down onto Port Harphax, which appeared surprisingly busy for this late in the year. Galleys, hulks, and wide-bottomed carracks were scooting across the harbor below like water beetles. As he kneed the donkey into reluctant motion, Soton cursed the memory of Erasthames the Great, the legendary king who had conquered the Iroquois Alliance. Four hundred years ago it might have made sense to put Tarr-Harphax up at the top of these cliffs when the native Ruthani were an everyday threat; now it was a beastly nuisance.

It made feeding Harphax City and the castle a nightmare. Since the lower Harph flooded almost every spring, cutting off river transport, the city had to take in enough stores to last a long winter and spring as well. Food that arrived by sea had to be carted or packed up the Upper Road, at great expense in time and animals, or pulled up in great iron buckets by the rope tramway.

During a bad year such as this one, when fields had been trampled and burnt, most of Harphax City's food had to be imported by seagoing merchants. Thus the great number of boats crowding Harphax Port's limited docking facilities. Now there was less than a moon half before winter storms made sea passage impossible. Most of the captains were less than pleased at chancing the seas this late in the year and only generous gifts of Styphon's gold kept them at sea at all.

If all this weren't bad enough, the burnt fields and farms had brought tens of thousands of refugees into the already bursting-at-the-seams capital. Plus all the war casualties who were too crippled or maimed to work, yet had to be housed and fed. Already the strain of short rations and over-crowding were visible on the lean faces of the city's beggars. Only great need could force them to take their chances on the steep Upper Road and the occasional visitor's generosity.

At the top of the cliffs the city walls showed the abuse of more than a hundred years of neglect and civil complacency. Here and there teams of workmen were shoring up walls and replacing fallen stones, but—as far as Soton could see—it was clearly a case of too little, too late. He guessed that Kalvan's eight-pounder field guns would bring down most of these walls. As for the old castle itself, Tarr-Harphax, with proper siege guns Kalvan would have a dozen breaches in a moon quarter.

Soton shuddered to think of the slaughter Kalvan's veterans would make upon the shattered remnants of the Harphaxi Army. It was a good thing that acting Great King Lysandros, since his brother King Kaiphranos' death two moons ago, had taken his advice and appointed the mercenary Phidestros Captain-General of the Royal Army, rather than one of his cronies or aging mercenaries. Phidestros was young for such an appointment, but he had fought against Kalvan three times and lived to tell about it.

If anyone could turn this whipped rabble into a fighting force again, it was Phidestros. He had more ambition than an Archpriest of the Inner Circle of Styphon's House and as much gall as Kalvan himself. Even so, Phidestros would need Appalon's luck and Lyklos' cunning to forge this base metal into good fighting steel.

For all that, Phidestros was still a mercenary and owed his allegiance to the highest paymaster—gold before god. Therefore, he would have to make sure that the pupil did not come to best his master in the art of war.

The cobblestone and dirt streets of Harphax City were lined with makeshift tents and temporary housing. The stench alone was enough to bring tears even to the eyes of a seasoned soldier. Twice Soton had been forced to use his mace to beat off attempts by thieves to steal the trappings off his horse right under the noses of his guards. It took a full sandglass to navigate through the narrow city streets to Tarr-Harphax where Captain-General Phidestros had his headquarters.

Soton was pleased to note the severe appearance of Phidestros' audience room; the only adornments were a pair of crossed muskets, a well-used sword and a large deerskin map of Hos-Harphax, which included the new Great Kingdom of Hos-Hostigos outlined in red ink within its borders.

"Please take a seat, Grand Master."

"Thank you, Captain-General. My men will bring it in." This time he'd had his own seat brought with him from Balph and when he sat down on his elevated chair, he was eye-to-eye with Phidestros. The long-boned Captain-General looked thinner than he had last spring and the lines of his face were etched bolder and deeper. Soton sighed; at least, it showed that Phidestros had no illusions about the near impossible task set before him.

After Phidestros' aide had filled their wine goblets, Soton asked, "How does your command look these days?"

Phidestros frowned. "Not so good. The Harphaxi were not much of a fighting force before Kalvan ground them up. Now they're little better than a rabble."

"That bad?"

"Many of the units are at half strength—probably more due to desertions and the flux than Kalvan's lead. Some, like the Royal Lancers, were almost annihilated. That might have been a blessing, though. I would like to disband the entire unit if Lysandros would let me—or the nobles let him! The Lancers are more worried about gaining honor than winning battles, I fear."

"You might think that Kalvan's artillery would have taught them a thing or two."

"Those iron hats! No such luck. They see Kalvan's style of fighting as unjust and dishonorable. With the Succession Crisis, Prince Lysandros doesn't dare dismiss them. But, with Kalvan's help, I've reduced their number by almost half. I'm also turning them into more of a Household Guard than a line unit. I've also recruited about two thousand more mercenaries and brought the Royal Pistoleers back up to full strength. The Foot Guard is still seriously undermanned."

"How many troops could you muster if Kalvan were at the city walls tomorrow morning?"

"A little over four thousand Royal troops and another five thousand mercenaries. I am supposed to have about twelve thousand city militia, but they are next to worthless—even though I've made them spend at least one day a quarter-moon in training. Most of them would take off, as they did at Chothros Heights, at the first sound of cannon fire. At least I've managed to get them uniforms and guns that fire without exploding. You wouldn't believe the ordnance I had to replace—musket locks that were rusted shut, stocks half-rotted away and barrels fouled beyond belief."

'I believe it," Soton said. "Kaiphranos the Timid was more a tight-purse than a coward. I was aghast when his son asked to meet Kalvan on the field man to man; well, he paid for his impertinence. What you're telling me is that I'd better not depend upon the Harphaxi Royal Army for any duty more pressing than staying inside the City walls."

Phidestros looked crestfallen. "If Kalvan invades Hos-Harphax next spring, only the gods will be able to stop him from taking the entire

Kingdom, Tarr-Harphax included. The only bright news is that I don't believe Kalvan has any idea just *how* desperate our situation really is."

"I take it you have told no one else this."

"Only First Prince Lysandros and yourself, Grand Master. Kalvan has his intelligencers everywhere, even here in Harphax City. We almost caught a big one a moon ago. I've made a big show of parading the militia up and down the city streets in their new uniforms and arms. They look all right, but those whoresons couldn't be counted upon to stand before a good sneeze!"

"You've done well," Soton replied. "Now it is up to the gods and I believe they have done well by us. I have come up with a plan that will keep Kalvan busy all next year. And, with Galzar's Grace, it may even cost him his throne. "

"By the Wargod's Beard, tell me! What miracle is this?"

"I plan to let the nomads fight the war against Kalvan for us. The Mexicotal in their war against Xiphlon have driven the fierce southern pony warriors into the Sea of Grass, driving the nomads from their traditional hunting grounds into the Middle Kingdoms and over the Great River in their desire to find a safe haven. Only a few thousand have crossed the Great River thus far, but already the entire Lower Sastragath is aboil as new tribes move in and others use the disorder to settle old scores or build great clans. Three times this year the Order has had to fight battles against barbarians trying to move into Hos-Ktemnos and Hos-Bletha.

"Now things are beginning to settle down as the tribes search for shelter and forage for the coming winter. The Order has seen these migrations from the Plains many times before and events should come to a head next year. The nomads are caught between an anvil, the Middle Kingdoms, and the Ruthani hammer from the south. The only place they have to go is across the Great River and into the Sastragath. Next year will see ten times as many tribes fording the river, which will push all the tribes and clans of the Lower Sastragath either east into our forts, or north into the Upper Sastragath.

"Instead of fortifying the border and holding our forts, my plan is to move half our Lances into the Lower Sastragath and drive the nomads up the Pathagaros Valley into the Lydistros Valley and from there into Kalvan's backyard. With a nomad invasion threatening the Trygath and Kalvan's westernmost princedoms, he will be forced to go on the offensive and call back his troops on the Hostigos/ Harphaxi border."

"It is a brilliant plan, Grand Master. But surely things are not so bad that our only choice is to allow the barbarians to enter the Five Kingdoms through our own backdoor?"

"In words for your ears only, our situation *is* that desperate. If Kalvan invades Hos-Harphax, he will conquer it before the first moon of summer. With Hos-Harphax defeated, Great King Demistophon of Hos-Agrys will quickly sue for terms; especially after the beating he took with his army from Prince Ptosphes last summer. Great King Cleitharses of Hos- Ktemnos is still in shock over the losses his Sacred Squares took at the Battle of Phyrax; he won't go to battle again unless ordered to by the Innermost Circle. Hos-Bletha is too far away to be of any consequence and Great King Sopharar of Hos-Zygros is flirting with the League of Dralm. So, without the Great Kingdom of Hos- Harphax as an anchor, the war against Kalvan is doomed."

Phidestros massaged his temples as if he had the grandfather of all headaches. "Things wouldn't be so bad, Grand Master if I could hire more mercenaries. They are nowhere to be found. I know it is winter and that a lot of them died at Fyk, Tenabra, Chothros Heights, and Phyrax...but still?"

"In Balph I learned that Kalvan has been offering mercenaries bonuses and *year*-round pay for signing up in his Royal Army of Hos-Hostigos. That is where many of them have gone."

Phidestros groaned. "Why didn't I think of that?"

"The very idea of year-round pay for mercenaries hasn't been done in living memory," Soton replied. "So don't blame yourself. Besides, most of the available mercenaries have been hired by barons and princes for protection from the nomads," Soton replied. "In all of Hos-Ktemnos there are no sell-swords to be hired at any price; I understand that things are likewise in Hos-Agrys. Even if Kalvan defeats the nomads, he will do more than just give us breathing space."

"How so, Grand Master?"

"He will give us the greatest gift of all—time. Time for you to train the Harphaxi rabble. Empty the prisons and the gaols. Take the strongest and the toughest and forge them into an army."

"By what magic will I turn riffraff into real soldiers?"

"By the magic of Styphon's gold and your own will. I will go to Prince Lysandros and tell him that you will build an army twenty-thousand men strong. Styphon's House will supply the gold and victuals.'

"It could be done—the Royal Foot Guard can be my petty-captains. I can train them night and day until they drop. It doesn't take great marksmanship to make an arquebusier. It will take a lot of work—"

"Excellent, Captain-General, you are already thinking along the right lines. Kalvan will think twice about invading Hos-Harphax—*if* he defeats the nomads—and hears tell of a great army being assembled here."

Phidestros smiled for the first time. "I say a toast to Grand Master Soton and the *new* Royal Army of Hos-Harphax!"

Soton downed his goblet in a single gulp. When it was filled again, he made his own toast. "TO VICTORY! TO THE USURPER KALVAN'S DEATH! TO STYPHON'S HOUSE!"

III

Ranjar Sargos leaped out of the tree, flapped his wings, and caught an updraft which propelled him high into the sky. It was dawn and the sun was rising above the distant horizon, bathing the world in red flames. Looking down he saw a great herd of beasts flooding the Pathagaros Valley.

As he glided closer to the earth, he was able to discern the true nature of the teeming animals—only they weren't animals but thousands upon thousands of men—the two-legged beast. They were painted in war colors and carrying bows, spears, axes, and all the weapons of war.

He glided above their heads and they looked up at him. Suddenly they began to beat their weapons against their shields. It was as if he was the sign they had been waiting for and it came to him that it was his destiny to lead this sea of warriors.

At the other end of the valley there was a rumble like thunder; he flew closer to see another great clan of men wearing the metal skins of the dirtmen.

He shrieked a warning to his followers and raised his talons. The roar of war cries smashed against his ears like clubs—

"Ranjar, wake up! Wake up!"

Ranjar Sargos, Warlord of the Tymannes, removed his hands from his ears and slowly raised up on the cot he had been sleeping on. *Where am I?* The open door let in enough moonlight that he could see that he was inside the tribal longhouse where he had been sleeping during the clan gathering.

"What is it?" Ranjar asked.

"Ikkos has returned."

"Where are the others?" By the others, of course, he meant his eldest son, Bargoth, who against his private words had ridden off with the scouting party.

"I do not know, Chief. Only Ikkos has returned and he was on foot with many wounds."

Sargos brushed the sleep out of his eyes. Take me to him."

"Follow me."

Sargos, who still had enough wits about him to tuck his pistol into his belt, followed the sentry into the night. The tribe's longhouses and sweathuts filled most of the small upper valley and he could just make out another score of men gathered near the palisade's gateway. *If none of the sentries have stayed at their posts, there will be blood spilled this night!*

The Tymannes had come to this gathering, not as in the past to settle tribal boundaries or exchange furs before the coming cold, but to talk about the great movement of people that was taking place in the lowland valleys and along the Great River. Never in living memory had so many tribes and clans been uprooted from their traditional lands; already his tribe had been forced to defend their valley from invaders.

Interrogation of the prisoners had told them little, only that many tribes and bands were being forced to flee their homes by other tribes and the Black Knights. Sargos had never fought against the Black Knights, but he had heard stories of their war prowess from those who had and in old tales passed down by the clan fathers. Yet, in times past the Black Knights had not burned villages and slain whole tribes without provocation. So a gathering of all the Tymannes had been called at a time when men should be setting traps, hunting, and fishing.

I wonder if this has anything to do with my vision? Before he could mull this over, they had arrived at the circle of men surrounding Ikkos. A few held torches and he could see that Ikkos was bruised and shirt-less. Several tribesmen were trying to question Ikkos all at the same time; Sargos stilled their voices with a clap of his hands.

"Where is Bargoth?"

Ikkos shook his head as if dazed. "I left him with all the others when we were ambushed. He may be behind me, I don't know. The last I saw him, he was shooting his bow and telling me to escape."

Sargos mentally steeled himself for the worst. Bargoth had never been one to turn away from a fight, no matter what the odds. He was big for eighteen winters and could run, chase and fight as well as any man in the tribe; yet, Sargos had often wondered if he had the cunning necessary to make a good chief or lead his people. Tomorrow, at first light, he would send out a party to find out what had happened and if anyone else in the scouting party had survived.

"Did you recognize the tribe that set the ambush?"

"No, Chief Sargos. But one of them wore the blue tattoos of the Great River tribes."

Ikkos began to shake with fatigue and cold. Someone passed him a blanket and he wrapped it around his shoulders.

"We will get little more out of him tonight," Sargos pronounced. "Let him rest so that he can talk to the Council tomorrow. The rest of you, get back to your posts before our foes walk in through the gate!"

The men trotted off as if stung by bees. When everyone had left, Sargos squatted down in the grass and clenched his hands over his chest until tears streamed out of his eyes.

The next morning all the chiefs of the Tymannes sat in the clan's

Council Hut. Only Old Daron—who every winter survived his half-moon winter trail—had his son with him, a middle-aged man with too much belly and watery eyes. *Why, if the gods had to take a son, couldn't they have taken one such as this?* Sargos shook his head to help clear his thoughts, then he rose to make the opening prayers so the gods might bless the Folk in this year of trial.

When the rituals were complete, Sargos had Ikkos called into the hut.

"We traveled five days until we reached the banks of the Great River. Many times we had to hide from strange tribes and war parties. Many of the villages and camps we passed were burned out or deserted. At the camp of the Lyssos we discovered only the dead; the entire tribe had been massacred—even the women and children."

There was a collective shriek at this news. The Lyssos had long been allies of the Tymannes; all had lost friends in their unclean passing. To kill unarmed women and children was usually a sign of madness or great drunkenness.

"At the banks of the Great River we saw many grass people cross the ford on rafts so large they could hold the entire clan! We saw little fighting there, but the river was clogged with the bodies of the dead. Whether from some earlier battle, or one upstream, we never did learn.

"Downstream we came upon a great battle. The Black Knights were attacking a large village, ten times the size of our own camp. They burned the palisades and used great fire tubes to knock them down. When the walls collapsed they stormed the village, killing everyone who did not flee and burning everything left behind. We ran too, for fear they might attack us as well!

"Later we talked to some of the villagers who escaped and they told us the Knights were burning and destroying every village and camp in the Sastragath. They claimed the end of the world had come. They left us to flee north where they hope to join up with others of their people. After that we began our journey home when, three days later, we were ambushed by the grass people."

Hearing about the ambush brought the pain back again, but Sargos pushed it aside. Little new was told during the questioning so Sargos pondered over the death of his son and the vision he had been gifted with last night. *Was his son the god-price for leadership over all the clans, or was it all some jest of Lyklos, the Trickster?*

Before he could make sense of all this, his other son Larkander entered the hut. The boy's eyes were red and Sargos felt his stomach drop like a stone.

"Father, the last of the riders has returned. They brought Bargoth's body back with them. They say he died with honor, surrounded by dead foes. Why, Father, why?"

Before this son embarrassed them both, he ordered, "Sit down. The time has come for *you* to prepare for your place in the tribe."

Larkander stifled his emotions and sat down with all the dignity his fourteen winters could muster. Not for the first time, Sargos was proud of his young boy—no, man now. His voice had already broken and he was halfway through his last growth. The time had come for him to learn a man's duty and responsibility.

Sargos rose to speak. "Where there is one army of Black Knights, there are more. Either they or the grass people will soon come to drive us from our lands. We have two choices: we can stay and fight—and die, since our foes are in number like the summer grass. Or we can join the other tribes and clans and move up the Pathagaros Valley. How do you vote?"

There was little discussion. The clan leaders agreed to move north as their Warlord had suggested. The women and children would go into the hills with the warriors of Old Daron's tribe to protect them.

As they left the Clan Hut, Larkander moved close to his father and asked, "Father, may I come along with the rest of the warriors?"

Ranjar Sargos looked down at this youngest son— now his only son. *Was this to be the price of his visions? Both sons dead?* He shook his head.

"But Father, I can ride a horse and shoot a bow as good as any man in this camp."

Sargos knew this was no boast. "Larkander, you are my only son now. I need you safe."

"Will it be safe in the hills with the women and children? If it is my time, I can die anywhere. I am only a few moons from my manhood rites. It is time I learned how to lead our people; where better than at my father's side?"

Sargos clenched his fists until his palms bled. "If it is your wish, you can go. Tell your mother now."

Larkander let out a loud whoop and took off at a run. At another time it might have lightened Sargos' spirits, but at the moment all he could see in his mind were the hundreds of bodies drifting down the Great River. The gods were capricious: Sometimes they gave a man great gifts, but often they took even more in return.

IV

Chief Verkan sat at his horseshoe-shaped desk, watching the viewer replay the takeover of the Memphis conveyer-head on a minor Fourth Level, Nilo-Mesopotamian time-line in the Alexandrian-Roman sector. The Nile delta had been suffering from a famine due to a series of aqueducts built over a period of centuries that had finally reduced the flow of the major river to a trickle. Damning the Nile River was not unusual; it had been done on First Level and most Second Level sectors, even some of the more advanced Europo-American sectors had completed, or were finishing major dams. The result, of course—regardless of level—was always the same; too little silt and too little water, leaving the Nile valley an agricultural wasteland. Famine was not the surprise, the real question was: Why had the populace decided to attack the Consolidated Outtime Foodstuffs' conveyer-head?

The battle was fierce and the prole defenders were disadvantaged by having to employ local weapons. Despite using a motley collection of clubs, cutlery and agricultural implements, the populace extracted numerous casualties among the Paratime staff. A few of the attackers were armed with swords and spears, probably members of the local constabulary. The soldiers didn't arrive until the buildings had been looted and burned. Outtime Foodstuffs First Level employees had gotten out before the doors were blown apart by battering rams. Most of the outtimers had died, but five of them had gotten to the conveyer in time. Verkan made a note that he wanted copies of all the interrogations and would like to talk to at least one of the survivors. As he recalled, Outtime Foodstuffs had been peripherally involved in the Wizard Traders case. *Maybe there was a connection?*

Verkan looked up when he heard his secretary's voice announce, "Inspector, Skordran Kirv, to see you, Chief."

"Tell him to come in," he replied, wondering why one of his top men had arrived unannounced.

He motioned for Kirv to take a seat, as he shut off the viewer. "Kirv, I've got a question for you."

"Yes, Chief."

"Why would half the population of Memphis, Fourth Level Alexandrian-Roman, attack our local conveyer-head?"

Kirv replied, "Consolidated Outtime Foodstuffs runs the facility and there's a famine in all of Egypt."

"And what were they exporting?" Verkan asked.

"Hummingbird tongues, ibex steaks, crocodile livers, sir —there's a good market here for all of that right here in Dhergabar. Probably someone got careless and let some of the indigenes watch them bring foodstuffs into the building. People are starving in the streets—isn't that one of the sectors where they damned up the Nile, or some such nonsense?"

"Yes," Verkan said, enjoying the way Kirv had reached almost the identical conclusion he had after watching the clip. "It's almost always carelessness or stupidity that brings disaster to our outtime operations. Someday, someone is going to slip up and one of these more advanced Second Level, or even Fourth Level, time-lines and they are going to figure out that they're nurturing a colony of vampires at their breast and the big bill will finally come due."

The Paratime Secret: the one inviolate Home Time Line secret that had to be protected at any cost. Not only to preserve First Level society in all the luxury it had become accustomed to, but also because it wasn't right to let the poor outtime devils know that they were secretly being taken to the cleaners—as his friend Kalvan might have put it—by a secret race of parasites. But sometimes the parasites got careless and mistakes got made, and then it was up to the Paracops to clean up the resulting mess. This looked like it was going to be another one of those times. Sure, a few careers might be uprooted at Consolidated Outtime, but the real losers would be the families of the outtimers who'd died defending a place they neither built nor profited from.

Verkan shook his head. He'd have to think of a more appropriate punishment for those First Level incompetents; maybe a posting to that new Second Level Ashthor Rammis subsector, where the locals shaved all body hair, practiced ritual self-flagellation, were strict vegetarians and believed the highest state of being was to forego all pleasure. That might just be the place for these miscreants to cool their heels for a century or so.

"Good analysis," Verkan said. "I've got something pleasant in mind for those in charge, for a change."

"I don't like that look, Chief."

"How does a penal sentence to the Ashthor Rammis Subsector strike you?"

"Just rewards, comes to mind." Kirv shook his head. "But let me change the subject, for a moment. I have news you need to hear: Dalgroth Sorn is getting ready to announce his retirement at Year-End!"

Verkan bolted upright in his chair. "Dalgroth!" The Paratime Commissioner for Security was one of his and the Paratime Police's staunchest allies. Dalgroth Sorn was said to be older than time, but Verkan—preoccupied with events on Kalvan's Time Line—had not considered his retirement, certainly not so soon after former Paratime Chief Tortha Karf's. It appeared that all the men he'd looked upon as mentors and friends would be gone from active service by the end of the year. That left Verkan not only feeling alone, but also isolated and with more weight upon his shoulders than any man should have to bear.

Kirv added, "It wasn't unexpected. He is a half century older than Tortha and they are good friends."

"I know," Verkan said. "I should have anticipated this and had a candidate ready to step forward and take his place."

Skordran Kirv winced. "The Opposition Party has put forward

Councilman Aldron Ralth as their candidate."

"Already!" Ralth was the Opposition leader who had replaced Salgath Trod—who was assassinated during the Wizard Trader blow-up. "He's a good figurehead and rebuilt Opposition after the Wizard debacle, but he's probably the worst person—other than Hadron Tharn—to head the Paratime Security Commission."

"Ralth's sycophants in the Executive Council are saying that it's time the Commissioner stood on his own two feet, rather than being a rubber stamp for the Paratime Police force. He's getting a lot of media attention. Everyone knows that Dalgroth is a big Paratime Police booster."

"True, but he was no rubber stamp. Dalgroth had a very clear agenda, which was to protect the Paratime Secret and keep the Force strong and independent of the Executive Council. I've gotten more than one bawling out from Dalgroth, when he didn't agree with my policies or actions."

"You'll never convince the media or Executive Council of that."

Verkan shook his head wearily. For not the first time, nor last time, he wondered how Tortha Karf had run the Force for over two hundred years. "Who do we know that has the right background to serve as Paratime Commissioner?"

Skordran Kirv looked nervous. "We do have one exemplary candidate, Chief."

"And who might that be?"

"Tortha Karf. He's got the best background, great contacts and would back us to the hilt."

Verkan shook his head no. "Tortha's not about to give up his retirement; besides his nomination—after what Ralth has been saying—would stink all the way to Mars. Is there any way we can talk Dalgroth into staying in office for a few more years?"

Kirv shrugged his shoulders. "Maybe you could have a talk with him, Chief. I don't know anyone else, other than our ex-Chief, he'd listen to."

"Fine," Verkan said, in resignation. He knew when he was beat. "Set up an appointment for later this afternoon. I'll have to worry about Nilo-Mesopotamia tomorrow." *I'd better be able to convince Skordran not to retire; otherwise, this job of policing umpteen millions upon millions of time-lines is going to turn into a dead certain impossibility! If Aldron Ralth becomes Paratime Commissioner, it'll be time for me to retire—right to Kalvan's Time Line.*

V

Colonel Kronos nodded to his sovereign to signify that everyone was seated. Great King Kalvan banged his pistol on the table for silence. "Princes, lords and generals, we have very little time and a lot of items to cover. Please keep your questions to a minimum. General Baldour, would you bring us up-to-date on the nomad invasion?"

General Baldour was a former mercenary Grand Captain in the Army of Hos-Ktemnos and thus more familiar with the western territories and Middle Kingdoms than any of the Hostigi generals. He walked over to the deerskin map of the Middle Kingdoms and pointed to a spot just north of the Middle Kingdom city of Kythar (Louisville, Kentucky) with his sword point.

"Yesterday, I talked to a merchant just returned from Kyblos City; the word there is the northernmost horde is just outside Kythar Town. In years past, the nomads would have stopped there to sack Kythar Town, but not this year with Grand Master Soton's army less than five days behind.

"Soon they will have reached the Trygath. However, we must remember that this information was a moon-quarter old when it reached Kyblos City and it took another moon half to reach us here in Hostigos Town. We can expect the nomads to follow the trade routes along the Lydistros River so that by now they should be less than a moon-quarter from the Trygath border."

There was a collective sigh from around the plank table.

Queen Rylla asked, "Do you think the nomads might possibly move into Hos-Ktemnos or will they travel through the Trygath until they reach Kyblos and then invade Hos-Hostigos?"

"I believe the nomads would be going right into Hos-Ktemnos, as these migrations have done in the past, were they not being chased by the Zarthani Knights. The plunder is much richer in the Great Kingdom of Hos-Ktemnos than western Hos-Hostigos. Yet, if they travel east they are going to run straight into Tarr-Lydra, where they'd be caught between Soton's army and the Knights' garrison in Tarr-Lydra—which would be suicidal.

"Prince Tythanes of Kyblos and Prince Kestophes of Ulthor are right to believe the nomads are going northeast and will soon be invading their realms; thus, they have a legitimate claim to their overlord's protection. There is no way to avoid supporting them without our Great King acquiring the name of a king who advances himself at his princes' expense."

"That was my own analysis," Kalvan said.

Chancellor Chartiphon rose to speak. "Then it looks like we are going to have to delay the invasion of Hos-Harphax until the nomad problem has been settled."

Which is exactly what the Styphoni want, thought Kalvan, cursing Soton and his progenitors in four languages. Did he dare split the army into two smaller forces as he had done with such disastrous results last spring?

"Harmakros, what do you think of splitting the army in two, sending one half after the nomads; the other to invade Hos-Harphax?"

"I don't believe it would be wise, Your Majesty. We have reports that the nomad hordes number anywhere from one hundred thousand to just under a million—and that depends upon whether you're talking about the advance horde or the main horde and all its divisions. Nor do we know the proportion of fighting men to women, children and old men. We do not have enough information to judge what we may be up against. If we don't take at least thirty thousand troops we may be overwhelmed by sheer weight of numbers. In a situation this fluid I don't believe we can risk fighting a two-front war."

"On the other hand," Prince Ptosphes added, "we can be certain that the Army of Hos-Harphax is going to stay inside its borders and not be on campaign unless we attack first. If we do that now we may find ourselves fighting the Harphaxi in the east, the Ktemnoi in the south, and the nomads everywhere else. As our Great King has told us repeatedly, the only thing worse than fighting a two-front war is fighting one on three or four fronts, which is exactly what we will have if we undertake the invasion of Hos-Harphax."

Kalvan sighed and decided that in future he was going to have to be more careful about throwing out military maxims in front of his General Staff. Although he had to admit that his own advice struck him as frightfully sound. Here he was not only caught on the horns of a dilemma, but on the prongs and antlers as well!

At times like this he sometimes wondered if his friends and family might have been better off had he never been dropped off here-and-now by that cross-time flying saucer. It was when he landed that things began to get complicated. Hostigos was at the center of Pennsylvania, but nothing like the one he had known as a Pennsylvania State Policeman.

Here-and-now was an alternate world where the Indo-Aryan invasions had not stopped in India, but continued east across China, then by ships along the Aleutians until they reached the Pacific Coast as far down as Baja California. Later waves of related peoples had settled the in the Great Plains and the Mississippi River valley. They had brought with them horses, cattle and iron. A new civilization, five or six centuries old, had settled in the Appalachians and along the Atlantic Coast.

The new civilization, which called itself the Five Kingdoms, was the most advanced; they alone had discovered the secret of gunpowder. A theocracy called Styphon's House had grown up around the gunpowder miracle, dispensing the sacred fireseed to allies and subject states. Over the centuries they had used their monopoly of gunpowder to maintain their political status quo and enrich the priesthood. They almost matched the ancient Aztec priesthood of his own world for sheer bloody-mindedness.

It was a late-medieval to early Renaissance culture, with gunpowder and good hand weapons, including a modified flintlock. When Corporal Calvin Morrison, forcibly retired from the Pennsylvania State Police, had landed in the small Princedom of Hostigos, he had found himself in the midst of a war between Hostigos and Styphon's House—which wanted to annex the Princedom for its sulfur springs. After helping rout an enemy raid, he was accidentally shot by Prince Ptosphes' daughter, Rylla. He'd spent his convalescence in Tarr-Hostigos as a guest of the Prince.

Then he had fallen in love with the lovely Rylla and decided to stay and help them in their fight against Styphon's House. First, he had shown them how to make their own gunpowder, not only freeing them from Styphon's House but involving them in a war to the death with the gunpowder theocracy. After that Kalvan had been like a man hanging onto a runaway horse. There had been battles against Styphon's allies—the Battle of Listra-Mouth against Prince Gormoth of Nostor and the Battle of Fyk against Sask—both of which Kalvan had won.

Kalvan's knowledge of military history and stupid generalship by Kalvan's opponents had helped. So had new field artillery, with trunnions and proper field carriages, able to outshoot anything else in this world. A superior grade of gunpowder had helped too. Soon Hostigos was a major power, whether it wanted to be or not. There was nothing else, really, but to proclaim it the Great Kingdom of Hos-Hostigos. And Kalvan had become Great King and Rylla his Great Queen.

Following his enthronement, there had been a year of war, with attacks coming from Hos-Ktemnos to the south, Hos-Harphax to the east, and Hos-Agrys to the north. Kalvan had won three Great Murthering Battles and only lost one—the ill-fated Battle of Tenabra, where Prince Ptosphes had been given a good licking by Grand Master Soton. But three out of four weren't bad odds anywhere, even here-and-now, so Kalvan still held his throne—for now.

Kalvan rose to his feet. "I agree with Harmakros and First Prince Ptosphes. We must abandon our plans for the invasion of Hos-Harphax and draw up new ones for the defense of Kyblos."

All the assembled Princes and generals nodded their accord. Prince Sarrask of Sask stood up and said, "Let's raise our voices for Great King Kalvan, who has brought us several seasons of good fighting and now promises us more!"

There was a collective cheer and a chorus of 'Down Styphon!'"

Sarrask added, "Aye, and when we've finished giving the barbarians a good arse-kickin', let's come back and finish the job we started last year in Hos-Harphax!"

There were more cheers and Sarrask sat back down.

"Thank you, for the vote of confidence. Now, let's get down and work out the details of how we're going to get to the Trygath and which soldiers we're going to take. First, General Hestophes is going to need reinforcements for his Army of Observation at Tarr-Lorca in Beshta. We don't want to give the Harphaxi any cute ideas while we're away. What's Hestophes' army look like right now, Captain-General Harmakros?"

"Hestophes has four regiments of Royal Horse and one of infantry, plus about another two thousand Beshtan cavalry."

"That's only five thousand men," Kalvan said. "Let's send him the Second Musketeers, and the King's Heavy Horse and the Heavy Cavalry—they won't be of much use where we're going." Since so many of his cavalrymen, even the former mercenaries, were titled or the younger sons of the nobility, Kalvan had been forced to create three regiments of old-style fully armored cavalry. He had thought them almost useless until they had proved their mettle against the Zarthani Knights at the Battle of Phyrax.

Their real value now lay in the east where they could help shore up his defenses against the Harphaxi. In the Trygath they would be a liability in the hilly and broken terrain, and when matched against the much lighter nomad cavalry. Even the Roman heavy catiphracti had had serious problems with the Parthians.

"That will give Hestophes about seven thousand seasoned troops. Prince Phrames, do you think you can spare any men?"

"Some, Your Majesty. I can send a thousand musketeers and pikemen. But no cavalry, since I need all I have in order to train my recruits. I don't have to tell Your Majesty the shape I found the Beshtan Army in."

Prince Sarrask made a loud hoot. "Half-dead, half-starved and half-armed! Old Balthar the Black was a choke- purse, he was."

No one bothered to mention that Kalvan had taken the cream of the captured mercenaries—forty acres and a mule for each recruit—into the Royal Army, leaving only those free companions too infirm or too old to fight for Prince Phrames and the other princes. Still, all in all, Phrames had done wonders with the remnants of the old Army of Beshta and had managed to retake a border castle that had renounced fealty during the war with Beshta in the dead of winter.

"We'll leave Queen Rylla"—Kalvan ignored Rylla's grimace as she realized she wasn't going to be invited to the party—"four infantry regiments, including the Hostigos Rifles." That got a smile out of Rylla. "And a regiment of horse. The rest will form the nucleus of the Army of the Trygath."

"That will give us better than eleven thousand men for a start, not including the Royal Artillery," Harmakros said. "Are we going to take any of the field guns?"

"A light battery at most, four-and six-pounders," Kalvan answered. "The guns will only slow us down. We are going to be crossing countryside that's a nightmare—everything from ravines to swamps. Mobility is going to be all in this war against the nomads. If I can—and I'm going to try—I'll mount every infantryman in the Army of the Trygath. We'll be taking the entire Mobile Force, which will give us another five thousand men. "

"You're not leaving me with much of anything," Rylla complained.

"That's right. Because you're not going to need anything more than glorified garrison troops while I'm gone. I want you to stay right here at Tarr-Hostigos the entire time I'm gone. Unless Prince Lysandros is crazier than a rat in a shithouse drainpipe, he's going to be holding firm in Tarr-Harphax. Grand Master Soton is busy stirring up the Sastragath, while Great King Cleitharses of Hos-Ktemnos is back to counting scrolls in the Royal Library. You, my love, are staying here to keep everyone else honest. If it makes you feel better, I'll leave the Army of Hostigos and the Army of Sask here under the command of Prince Sarrask."

Sarrask rose to his feet sputtering, dropping half a cup of dark wine down his robes. "But Your Majesty, I'm not one to set watch over the Royal Nursery—Excuse me, Great Queen Rylla, no offense meant. But I'm a man of plain-spoken words."

Rylla was up and fumbling for her dagger as if she meant to beard Sarrask or cut off his tongue.

"Order, please!" Kalvan shouted. "Prince Sarrask, you are a valiant warrior and one of my best commanders. I would prefer to have you at my side fighting the nomads, but I need someone here I can trust to guard my home and household. I can think of no one better able to protect my throne in my absence." Actually Kalvan could think of half a dozen in a moment, but all of those he needed by his side and those he didn't, like Prince Ptosphes, would take it as a personal slight if he left them home.

Sarrask swelled up like a peacock on display and made a courtly bow. Rylla, who sat at Kalvan's right, turned so that no one else could see the horrible grimace she made at her husband.

"I will ask Prince Pheblon of Nostor to support the Army of the Trygath with three thousand of his troops, Prince Balthames of Sashta with another two thousand, three thousand from Nyklos, and I'm sure we can depend upon Ulthor and Kyblos for an additional eight to ten thousand men—since they will be defending their own lands and can call upon their lordly levies."

Harmakros grinned. "That should give us more than thirty thousand men for the Army of the Trygath. Enough teeth to grind the nomads' bones to dust." Everyone smiled at that thought and there was another chorus of "Down Styphon!" followed by an equally loud one of "Death to All Barbarians!"

Once the noise fell to a low roar, Kalvan said, "Harmakros and Chartiphon, I want you two to get together with General Baldour and decide which passage we take, the northern Nyklos Road or the Akyros Trail through Sask. Then I want you to go over possible foraging areas, ambush sites, bad stretches of road and where to set depots in case we have to make a hasty retreat. Also consider that we might want to link up with some of the more civilized kings and princes once we reach the Trygath. Duke Skranga and General Klestreus, I want you both to make a list of every Trygathi king, prince, baron and everything we know about them, from their fighting ability to whether they are pro- Styphoni or anti-Styphoni. I'd like it by tomorrow at the latest."

Duke Skranga nodded and smiled as if he'd just been thrown a tasty morsel. His other intelligence officer, General Klestreus, looked like a fish that had just been hooked.

"Now, one last thing before I let you all get back to work. The Pony Express route we've set up between Hostigos Town and the Army of Observation at Tarr-Lorca has given us a quarter-moon jump in our border communications. I'd like to run a similar route into Ulthor, and possibly Kyblos, so we can obtain adequate intelligence rather than having to depend upon itinerant peddlers and vagabonds. Colonel Kronos, I'd like for you to attend to that. Don't hesitate to pull as many of the experienced riders as you need off the Great King's Highway.

"That's it for now, gentlemen. This meeting is dismissed." Actually, Kalvan would have preferred a working semaphore system to the Pony Express, but he'd decided that building the Great King's Highway was more important.

He didn't have enough trained manpower to do both. By Father Dralm's Beard, he didn't have a tenth the trained manpower to do any of the things he wanted done, but give the new University of Hostigos a few years.... Then he would not only have good interior communications and roads, but he could start working on some more reliable vehicles, like a Butterworth stagecoach. Anything would be an improvement over the Conestoga-style wagons the Zarthani used for everything from overland transportation to mobile homes.

Note: After road is finished start stagecoach line. With leaf-springs, too!

VI

Thunder roared and shook the rooftree of Ranjar Sargos' temporary longhouse. For a few moments it drowned out the squeal of horses and the babble of more tongues than he had heard in all his days. Not since the time of his grandfather twice removed had such a great wave of humanity flooded over the Great River and spilled its way into the Sastragath. Like flotsam tossed by the Great River, Sargos and his tribe had been picked up and pushed into the Lydistros Valley.

Yet, like a flood which replenishes the land it destroys, there was good which came with this river of humanity. Since few of the chiefs knew these lands, they had been forced to rely upon the knowledge of those who did. Ranjar Sargos, having spent four years of his youth as a mercenary in the Trygath, knew more about this land than all but a few of the headmen in this great warband. This, along with Sargos' renown as a warrior, had placed him at the forefront of this human wave. Now only the constant pressure of the Black Knights gave the wave its form and kept it from dispersing into hundreds of separate warbands. Without cohesion, each tribe and clan would be destroyed piecemeal by the Trygathi iron men and their allies. The time had come for a great warlord to guide the horde and Ranjar Sargos knew that this was his destiny—for had not his own vision foretold of such triumphs?

Sargos took several deep breaths, held them, and waited for Thanor's banging on his sky anvil to cease. When the air was still, he spoke again to the assembled Plains headmen and Sastragathi chiefs. "The gods have allowed the Black Knights to take the field. They have allowed the demigod Kalvan of Hostigos to bring his army into the Trygath—"

"Demigod or demon, this Kalvan is no friend to the Trygathi, less so to the Black Knights," Chief Alfgar interrupted. "Let all three of them fight one another, I say. *This* is what the gods intend. Then let us pick the bones of the survivors!"

"Or Nestros and Kalvan swear brotherhood and pick *our* bones," Sargos replied, his voice growing in volume. He had never been even-tempered and knew it. He also knew that since the Tymannes had left their ancestral hunting grounds he had grown even sharper of tongue.

"By Galzar's Mace, this is as the gods will—" Chief Alfgar began.

A wordless muttering stopped him, as Headman Jardar Hyphos once more tried to form words with a jaw yet unhealed from the blow of a Knight's mace. His son leaned over and put his ear next to Hyphos' mouth for a time, then nodded.

"Father says he doubts the gods have willed it that we come so far only to fall to our pride as well as our enemies."

"You yapping puppy! Your father is a man. You are—"

"Silence," Sargos bellowed. He did not know what this would do, except perhaps make all the chiefs angry at him rather than at one another.

That could be a gain, if he was able to do something with their attention.

"To be proud is the mark of a warrior, as all here are," he began. "To let everything yield to that pride is the mark of a fool. More than four hands' worth of tribes in this great warband have set aside their pride and sworn to follow me. The gods have not punished them. Why should you fare otherwise?"

"Witlings and women," Alfgar muttered just loud enough that Sargos alone could hear. Sargos decided for the moment to ignore him.

"How many of these tribes are fighting as they please?" Chief Rostino asked. Of all those present, he appeared to have the most Ruthani blood as well as the most dignity.

Sargos chose an equally dignified answer. "I am not a Great King, with a host of armed slaves to punish disobedient warriors as if they were children. I am chief over the Tymannes, and those who swear to follow me as Warlord do so by choice."

"Then it is my choice," Chief Alfgar said, "not to swear any oaths to Ranjar Sargos or any other sachem or chieftain. We of the Sea of Grass have considered each chief his own master since the Great Mountains rose from the earth. Maybe the dirt scrapers and log builders of the Sastragath are more accustomed to following at the heels of their masters like curs!" Alfgar slammed his fist against his bone vest, making a sound like that of a gunshot.

The hands of about half the chieftains in the longhouse streaked for their knives, the only weapons allowed inside during the parley.

Sargos signaled for attention. "This is not the time to hurl baseless insults nor fight among each other. There is great booty to be won and much glory to be gained in fighting our real enemies."

Most of the chiefs sat back down and nodded their agreement to this sage advice.

But Hyphos' son stood his ground. "You have not fought Kalvan, Alfgar. We have fought others like him and know that to win we must stand as one, like wolves not dogs."

"Nor have you," Alfgar replied, his face twisted into an angry leer. "What has Sargos given you, that you take his word about Kalvan?"

Hyphos' son would have drawn his knife if his father's arm had not been sounder than his jaw—a bronzed arm gripped the young man's wrist and twisted. He gasped and dropped his knife.

"See! How the Sastragathi lick their master's hand. When Sargos nods his head, the old rein in the young. This is not the way of the plains!"

Rage flowed into Sargos, lifting him like a giant's hands—or perhaps the hands of the gods. Certainly he had never felt their presence more strongly, even in the steamhouse of his manhood rites.

"Let us submit this matter to the judgment of the gods." Sargos drew from the hides of his chieftain's chair the sacred axe of the chiefs of the Tymannes. "With this ax and no other weapon I will fight Chief Alfgar, this day, in this place. He may use any weapon his honor allows."

"No!" Chief Ulldar exclaimed. Next to Sargos, Ulldar Zodan was the wisest man in the room in the new ways of warfare. Two of his sons had served Chief Harmakros in Kalvan's wars and told him much. They had also brought him a tooled and engraved horse pistol that was the envy of every chief in the longhouse. "The gods have taken away Alfgar's wits. What if they have taken away his honor as well?"

Several of Alfgar's fellow chiefs had to restrain him from trying to kill Ulldar with his bare hands. When the uproar had subsided, Alfgar had found his voice again. "I will fight with the hand spear against your axe, you godless son-of-a-bitch who weaned you on stinkcat piss!"

"Let it be done, then," Sargos commanded. His rage was already fading, and in its place were doubts that he was really in the hands of the gods after all. If he fell—and Alfgar promised to be a formidable *foe*—his son would do well to see the Tymannes' great longhouse again.

Why not be hopeful? he thought. If you win, it will prove the gods' favor, and your own prowess as well. Then all the chiefs and clan headmen assembled here will proclaim you Warlord, and those lesser chiefs who were not here will quickly follow. Cast the bones and let the fates see to where they fall. By Galzar's Mace and Thanor's Hammer!

Sargos led the chiefs and headmen out to the square in the middle of the chiefs' longhouses. The rain was still falling and what had already fallen made the square a sea of foul-smelling mud. Sargos judged this would be to his advantage: Alfgar could seldom have fought on foot, on a slope, in mud up to his ankles.

So it went for a half-score of passes. Sargos quickly realized he had but one advantage. Alfgar was so confident of his greater youth and strength that he was careless of what fighting in mud would do to them. If the time ever came when Alfgar could not dance away in time—

As if to warn Sargos against hopefulness, on the next exchange Alfgar drew first blood. It was barely more than a thorn prick and on Sargos' left arm, but it held an arrogant message:

"I can do this at will. The next time, who knows where my spear will land?"

Both men's friends were shouting threats and promises. If Alfgar won, there would be a permanent breach between the plains and Sastragath chiefs. At first blood, all fell silent and remained so.

Sargos said nothing at all. He had better uses for his breath.

In time the rain stopped. Both men now bled in a hand of places, though nowhere seriously. Sargos began to wonder if he would have breath for any use at all before long. Beyond any doubt Alfgar was spending his strength freely. But he'd had rather more to begin with. The mud, it seemed, might not be the gods' way of saving Ranjar Sargos.

Alfgar made a thrust that would have disemboweled him had he not jumped in time and slipped in the mud. Sargos had to use all his arts in war while he still had the strength and speed to use them.

Silently he prayed to the gods: Guard my Folk and my son. Send them wisdom and courage, if there is justice in you. But if you sent Kalvan to be as a wolf to the flocks, then you are not gods and my spirit will tell my son to worship something else!

"Pray for an honorable home for your spirit, old man," Alfgar said with a sneer. "It will soon need one."

Then he sprang forward so fast that if Sargos had not been prepared, both in mind and body, for the final grapple, he would have been doomed. As it was he had already begun to turn, presenting his left thigh when Alfgar closed.

Offered a target, Alfgar thrust hard with his spear, forgetting that his target was mostly bone. As the spear point grated on that bone, Sargos' long arms whirled. His left gripped the spear, jerking it from Alfgar's hand.

His right arm brought the ax down hard on Alfgar's knife hand, as it leaped toward Sargos' groin. For an instant the gods might have turned both men into stone. Then the knife splashed into the mud.

The spear whirled in Sargos' hand, then seemed to sprout a red bloom in Alfgar's belly. The knowledge of what had happened was just dawning in his eyes when Sargos' axe came down on his head.

"The gods have spoken!" Sargos cried. He hoped if more needed to be said, the gods would say it themselves. Neither Sargos' wits nor his wind seemed to be fit for the task, and as for his legs, he prayed they would not tumble him into the mud beside his foe.

Sargos Ranjar, son of Cedrak Ranjar, you are too old for this and so you will learn the next time you confuse the voice of the gods with the memories of your own youth.

Egthar and Pydox, chiefs of his own clan, ran forward to aid him. "Stop treating me as if this was my first wound! It's more like my tenth, and one of the least." In truth it would need some care, and he would be riding more than walking in the coming battles. But only the flesh hurt.

Meanwhile the crowd around him had grown and was beginning to chant, "Sargos! Sargos! Warlord Sargos!" He wasn't sure if his own men had begun the chant or if it was a spontaneous outburst; regardless, he knew how to grasp the moment and squeeze it with both hands. He stepped back and raised his arms.

Together, Headman Jardar Hyphos and his son stepped forward and lifted Alfgar's motionless body.

Behind them came Chief Rostino. He knelt before Sargos and pressed his forehead against Sargos' hands.

"The gods have truly spoken. What do they wish that we swear to you?"

Had it been a Sastragathi chieftain making this pronouncement rather than a plainsman, there might have been jeers and catcalls—as it was there was naught but silence.

"They ask little," Sargos said. He took several deep breaths and found that he could hope to speak instead of gasp. *At least, I will ask little. The gods*

will not help a man who asks more than those who follow him are willing to give. "Little indeed," Sargos repeated. "Only that you follow me in war and peace, save when I ask for war against blood-brothers or peace with blood-enemies. And that you bind yourselves by this oath until I release you or death takes you."

"I swear—" Chief Rostino began, but Sargos stopped him. "Rise, I will have no brave warriors swearing anything to me on their knees. That is more pride than the gods allow."

There was a boisterous round of oath-taking as all the assembled chiefs who had not already done so swore their allegiance to Ranjar Sargos as Warlord.

After all the oaths had been given, Sargos said, "Let us take a visit to the bathhouse, and heat us some beer. Or there is wine should any of you wish it. "

Sargos could not tell what drew more enthusiasm, the gods' judgment, the baths or the prospect of a good drinking party.

VII

Verkan flew his aircar through the Old Town section of Dhergabar, where there were still ground-hugging buildings, a square mile of densely packed ground level residences and commercial facilities. There were even a few buildings which could trace their history back to First Level PP (Pre-Paratime), but most only went back four millennia to after the Religious Wars when most of the city outskirts had been leveled and afterwards had taken its present shape of tall anti-gravity towers and spires. Old Town was where the infirm, those who found it difficult to live in townhouses only reachable by aircar resided; the indigent—even the Bureau of Psych-Hygiene hadn't been able to root out all the bums from First Level society; out of work Proles—which included those studying for their First Level Citizenship; and a small criminal element that not even the most determined Psych-Hygiene treatments and techniques could eradicate, nor the Metropolitan Police sweeps take captive.

Right in the middle of Dhergabar City was the Paratime Commission Building, a two hundred-story edifice, an entire city-block square in size and shielded with a next to impenetrable collapsed-nickel shield. Verkan parked his green aircar on Chief's reserved landing port and took the lift down to the hundred and eightieth floor to the office of the Paratime Commissioner for Security, where he was quickly ushered into Dalgroth Sorn's office.

"Chief Verkan, nice to see you," Dalgroth said, "please, take a seat."

Dalgroth Sorn was a tall, thin man with the air of a scholar, which was belied by both his piercing black eyes and his raspy voice; there were still a few older Paratime Police who could recall, when during his term as an Inspector, that voice could peel paint. Dalgroth was more formal than usual and Verkan wondered if it was because he was aware of the reason for this visit.

Verkan paused long enough to remove his pipe, load the barrel and light it. "This is not easy, Commissioner, but I believe it's of utmost importance—"

"Verkan, you get right to the point. It's one of the things I like about you. But this time, I know what you're here to ask. The answer is yes."

Verkan blew out a lungful of smoke. "Thank you, Commissioner—"

Commissioner Dalgroth held up his hand to stop him again. "I hate to keep interrupting you, Verkan, but I've got some things I need to tell you."

Verkan nodded this time.

"I'm going to keep my job as Commissioner, but not just because you need my help. But, because, there are some serious problems facing First Level society, and I think I can do a better job right here at the Paratime Commission than as head of the First Level Social Stability Project. That was the job I was going to take after I resigned as Commissioner of Paratime Security."

"I am very relieved by your decision. I believe I heard something about this Stability study on the evening news."

"What you heard, Verkan, from some newsie was just window dressing, as our friends on Europo-American call it. The real subject and purpose of this Project is not for public consumption."

Verkan braced himself. "I know I've been spending too much time on Kalvan's Time Line and outtime in general, but—"

"Don't apologize, Vall. I'm one of the few people who completely understand how demanding the Paratime Police Chief's job truly is. I doubt you know this, but once—thirty years before Tortha's reign—I was offered the position of Paratime Chief. Oh, yes. I turned it down flat; I saw what it did to the man they wanted me to replace. Remember, back then I was Chief Inspector. I have seen four Chiefs in my lifetime and Tortha was the only one who resigned without a physical or mental breakdown."

Verkan realized that he had never really known Dalgroth; he'd just been another useful ally who knew how to tell a good tale. Verkan was beginning to realize that even with five times the normal human lifespan, there was still not enough time to do everything that needed to be done—much less what he wanted to do.

"I think your sojourns to Aryan-Transpacific are a great way to get away from the pressures and demands of a job that is simply too much responsibility for one man. Unfortunately, it has come to my attention, and that of several other highly placed persons, including former Chief Tortha, that something is fundamentally wrong with our First Level culture. This is the reason behind the Social Stability Project."

"By fundamentally wrong, just what do you mean?"

"Vall, this time-line stinks! Maybe it's the accumulated sins and bad debt of ten thousand years of living off the labor and sweat of other human beings, but—whatever it is—it's beginning to manifest itself here on Home Time Line."

"I haven't noticed anything. Well, maybe crime is up a little."

"That's just one of the many symptoms. Did you know that First Level population has been dropping for the past four centuries?"

"No. It certainly isn't obvious, Commissioner. There appear to be just as many Citizens as ever."

"True, but only because of the increase in Prole citizenship—even as hard as the tests have become. The Prole problem is another part of this issue."

"I have noticed there is more actual Prole prejudice in Dhergabar than I recall growing up."

"You're right, the prejudice is growing worse. As Scholar Elltar has proposed, the Prole in our society has assumed a place quite similar to that of the Negro in the Europo-American, Hispano-Columbian Subsector, in the political entity still known as the United States, during the period they call the Reconstruction—after the War Between The States."

"The Civil War, I remember that well. I was there during the worst of it and I can see the parallels. The Civil War, in a lesser part, was about freeing the slaves. Separate, but not equal. The threat of slave rebellion."

"Exactly. As you've noticed in your Europo-American Quarantine proposal, this situation has been exacerbated with the passage of time. A number of observers believe there will be large scale race riots on Hispano-Columbian Subsector in the next few years. There are a number of parallels to what's happening here on First Level."

"The Proles aren't slaves or former slaves, but I do see similarities. Do you believe that this is a threat to First Level Security?"

"Not now, but it could be. Are you familiar with a man who calls himself The Leader?"

"No. Should I be?" Verkan re-lit his pipe.

"Not really. However, the man—and we don't know who he is—that calls himself The Leader is becoming more and more influential amongst the youth and the politically disenfranchised Citizens. Those who most feel threatened by the former Prole Citizens and by society as a whole. He's even encouraging his followers to wear a uniform of sorts, blue shirts and pants."

"That sounds similar to the fascist black shirts in Italy, and brown shirts of the old Nazi Party on Europo-American." Verkan shook his head in disgust.

"You're not the only one who has come to that conclusion. There are some frightening parallels."

"Commissioner, as long as I'm Chief, I will not tolerate the harassment and murder of Proles on First Level, such as the Nazis performed against ethnic minorities and religious groups that lived under their rule."

"I don't think it will come to genocide here. It's a completely different situation on First Level," the Commissioner said. "No one here wants to eliminate the Proles, just keep them down and not allow them to become Citizens."

"Well, the whole idea of allowing outtimers to become Citizens is fairly new. Less than a thousand years old."

"Yes," Dalgroth said, "that's when it was first brought to the Executive Council's attention that the population decrease was going to continue, no matter what laws were passed. To counter this, a program was set up to administer citizenship to the best and brightest of the outtimers. It's been one of the last millennium's few successes. But the Proles are not the real problem; the problem is here with the Home Time Line Citizens."

"How bad do you think this problem really is?" Verkan asked.

Dalgroth's brows furrowed heavily. "Bad. Bad enough that I believe it is the biggest problem facing the survival of the Home Time Line."

"More dangerous than the possibility of the Paratime Secret being uncovered?"

"Yes, because it threatens the very core of our society. The fact is, Verkan, our society is crumbling before our eyes. There's enough social and commercial momentum that it might last another millennium—but it is dissolving. That is why, for right now, I decided it is more important for me to stay on as Paratime Commissioner to help stabilize your stewardship as Paratime Police Chief, than it is to delve into First Level social problems. Because, if you fail as Chief, the results will be so catastrophic it will no longer matter what the problem was or is. The Paratime Police are First Level's most stable institution and if the force collapses because it's Chief has been forcibly removed, well—the fact is—this whole time-line will go up like a thermo-nuclear blast!"

For the first time in many years, Verkan Vall was so nonplussed he was actually speechless.

VIII

"Present—aaarrrmmmss!"

Forty bayoneted muskets snapped into position across forty Hostigi breastplates. A hundred sabers leaped to the vertical. Even in the watery spring sunlight, the reflection from all the steel made Kalvan blink.

The herald of Nestros, King of Rathon and self- proclaimed High King of the Trygath, rode forward. His mounted escort rode up on either side, fifty big men on beer-wagon-sized horses. By the customs of the Trygath, heralds went guarded until they were actually in the presence of the men they were sent to parlay with. Also by custom, the horsemen rode with their visors up and their swords held upright by the blades, as proof of peaceful intent.

Kalvan studied the guards as they rode up the slope toward him. They reminded him more than a little of the late—R.I.P.—Harphaxi Royal Lancers, swathed head to toe in armor about as useful as cheesecloth in keeping out a musket bullet or a chunk of case shot.

Except that this was the Trygath, a frontier area where in nine years out of ten the only fireseed available was what neighboring eastern princes were willing to sell illegally, risking both shortages and Styphon's Ban. Against other armored men-at-arms or lightly armored nomads, riding around looking like a blacksmith's version of a lobster made a certain amount of sense.

This had already begun to change, with the emerging trade of Hostigos fireseed for horses, ale, and furs. It was about to change even more, but not quickly or easily. Military technology was generally about as slow to change as priestly ritual. So for now, the Trygathi iron men had a few remaining days in the sun.

The herald signaled; the Rathoni guardsmen reined in, leaving him to mount the slope alone. At a nod from Captain-General Harmakros, Aspasthar rode out, his first sword reversed in his hand and the sun shining on his first suit of armor.

"Who has come to the host of the Great King Kalvan of Hos-Hostigos?"

Aspasthar's voice was high-pitched but steady.

"Baron Thestros of Rathon, herald and envoy of High King Nestros." The herald took another look at the Royal Page. "Does the Great King so lack men, that he has me greeted by a beardless boy?"

"Had he thought you saw wisdom in a beard, my lord, the Great King would have sent you a he-goat!" Aspasthar replied.

In the ensuing silence, Kalvan and Harmakros exchanged eloquent looks. Kalvan's said, If the boy's tongue has run away with him and we have a fight, he is going to get the flat of my saber across his arse.

Harmakros' reply was: Don't worry. The boy knows what he is doing.

The herald was the first to break the silence, with a roar of laughter. Seeing themselves given permission, the Rathoni Royal Guard also broke into laughter. Everyone hooted and guffawed, while Harmakros rode forward to clap his son on the shoulder so hard the boy nearly fell out of his saddle.

At last silence returned, except for the distant rumble of thunder. Baron Thestros wiped his face with a yellow-gloved hand.

"Well-spoken, lad. You do honor to your sire, your King, and your realm. But I think there must be a person of more rank than you in a host as large as this. Might I seek the honor of speech with he who holds the most rank among you? Captain-General Harmakros, I believe."

Harmakros nodded. "At your service. But I am not the highest among those present." He turned in the saddle. "Your Majesty?"

Kalvan urged his horse forward, letting his cloak flow back from his shoulders. The herald did a good imitation of a man whose eyes are about to pop from his head. Then he swung himself swiftly, if not gracefully, from the saddle and went down on one knee.

"Your Majesty! In the name of High King Nestros, greetings!"

"Surely you have more than greetings to bring, Baron Thestros, since you have four thousand cavalry at your summons. Your King has a name for wisdom, and would not send such a host with a message a beardless boy could bring. "

The imitation of eye-popping was even better this time. Kalvan let it go on until he was sure the herald needed reassurance.

"No. I have no demonic arts, only good scouts. They saw your men two days ago and rode swiftly to bring word to me. I came up to the van, so that there might be no misunderstandings about why the men of Hos-Hostigos and its allies have come to the Trygath."

"I believe Your Majesty. But then, pray tell me what *is* the reason for such a host setting foot upon the domain of High King Nestros? He wishes peace with all who wish it with him, but those who wish peace seldom come with twenty thousand armed retainers!"

"Your scouts are not inferior to mine," Kalvan said with a grin. That was a remarkably accurate count of the Hostigi who'd crossed into the Trygath. Another ten to twelve thousand were strung out all the way across Kyblos, ready to either join the main body or cover its withdrawal. Kalvan had hoped for a larger levy from Kyblos, but many of the southern barons had not responded to Prince Kestophes' requests for men and probably wouldn't at anything less than sword point.

"I thank Your Majesty. But—forgive me for being inopportune, but I have only the cause of peace at heart. I ask once more, why are you in my King's realm?"

To call the Trygath King Nestros' realm was more than just an exaggeration, thought Kalvan, since Nestros' sovereignty was only recognized by four of the Trygath's nine legitimate kings and princes. Two of whom, in fact, Ragnar and Thul, were subjects of King Theovacar of Grefftscharr. Diplomacy, however, was the order of the day. "We do not come in search of peace."

Kalvan would have sworn he heard the thud of the baron's jaw hitting the ground. Quickly he added, "We have come to wage war on the nomads, enemies common to all of us."

The herald shook his head. "High King Nestros has taken counsel with his princes and kings, and he has devised ways of meeting the nomad host. It insults him to think that he must wait upon an Eastern realm for the defense of his own."

"I am sure the True Gods fight for your King and his princes and people, likewise. Yet is it not true that the nomad horde counts more fighting men than the Trygath and the Great Kingdom of Hos-Hostigos combined?" Three times, if the estimate of a hundred and fifty thousand on the way northeast was correct.

"It is also true," he added, "that during the last moon riders of the horde reached the Lower Saltless Sea, sowing death with every step their horses took. They did not return, but would it not have been better that they not even start?"

Kalvan wanted to meet the local magnate who'd caught the raiders on their way back from the shores of Lake Erie. King Crython of Ragnar had outthought as well as outfought the nomad raiders. By all reports that kind of ruler would make almost as good an ally as King Nestros. But it was King Nestros who controlled the back entrances to Hos-Hostigos, not King Crython.

"Indeed," the herald said. "No such raids will come again."

"Is this certain? Certainly they will cease after the valiant men-at-arms and footmen of King Nestros have broken the strength of the horde. But Nestros will do this only if he gathers all his strength under his own hand. Then who will be left to defend the lands of those who march against the horde, against raiders and outlaws? Or those nomads who break away from the main body?"

Kalvan had pitched his voice loud enough to be heard by the Royal Guardsmen. All of them would be nobles or sons of nobles; all must share the fear of what would happen to their lands at the hands of nomad out-riders and bandits. None of them dared think of the consequences of a tribal victory over their king.

"Your Majesty, do you swear you can prevent this if King Nestros and you become friends and allies."

"We are not enemies even now, nor shall we be. What you mean is, if we become *allies*. I only say this: if we become allies, there will be thirty thousand Hostigi to strengthen your King's forces."

"And if there is no alliance, there will be thirty thousand fewer?"

"The host of the Great King of Hos-Hostigos will fight the horde wherever we find it. But is it not better that we fight it together? Sticks separated are easily broken. Tied into a bundle, they defy the strength of a giant."

"Your Majesty speaks eloquently. I think, perhaps, it would be wiser if you spoke thus to High King Nestros."

"Nothing would give me more pleasure, if I knew where to find your High King."

"Let Your Majesty ride to Rathon City; I believe he will find no obstacles in his path."

Rathon City was the here-and-now equivalent of Akron, Ohio. About fifty miles away—two days' easy riding.

"The High King will see me in Rathon City before the horde can wreak any more harm upon his vassals. Now, I see that the sky promises rain. Would you and your guard commander care to accept the hospitality of my tent, which I believe is closer than your own?"

The herald and his guard commander exchanged looks, then the herald nodded. "We are honored by Your Majesty's hospitality."

"Call it the first repayment of the hospitality we have received from Nestros' subjects." The herald frowned, and still looked puzzled as he led his guards off behind Aspasthar.

When the Trygathi commanders were safely on their way, Harmakros rode close to Kalvan. "Your Majesty, far be it for me to tell you how to guide the realm—"

"If you ever stop telling me, Harmakros, I'll find another Captain-General. Out with it. I don't want to get caught in the rain if I can help it. A fine spectacle for our allies, me leading a charge with sword in one hand and handkerchief in the other!"

Harmakros quickly ordered the First Royal Horse Guard into a wide circle, then put them in movement toward the tent. Riding practically boot to boot with Kalvan, he grinned.

"Your Majesty is as silver-tongued as any bard, but is this the time to be so truthful about what we want?"

"It is the best time. Any earlier would have given the Union of Styphon's Friends or the League of Dralm time to make noises. Not to mention letting the Zarthani Knights send scouts on to our line of march, and maybe more than scouts. Four thousand Trygathi could give us enough trouble. Think about four thousand Knights."

"I'd rather think about more pleasant things."

"Like that blonde at Mnebros Town?"

Harmakros flushed. "I didn't know Your Majesty noticed."

"Just because *I* slept alone doesn't mean I don't know the officers who didn't." They were silent for a moment, guiding their horses over a rough patch of ground.

"It's Mnebros Town that made me think the time was ripe to tell the truth," Kalvan continued. "Those people were so Dralm-damned *glad* to see us, it was almost pathetic. We could have had anything we asked for, not just wine, women, and banquets. They were *scared* of that horde!"

"What the Styphon!" Harmakros exclaimed. "A horde that size scares *me!* But our lands are farther than they're likely to reach. Around here, nobody knows if they'll have a roof over their heads and all their family alive come winter. Nestros will do his best, but if that isn't good enough..."

"If that isn't good enough, the princes and barons will start looking around for someone whose best might be good enough. Which might not be so good for us."

"Exactly, Harmakros." The gray sky was overhead now, and to the northwest was turning black. The royal pavilion was in sight ahead, and the herald's party was just turning into it.

"The Trygathi nobles here," Kalvan continued, "have always had more independence than the ones in the east, at least since fireseed came along. Things aren't as settled here and a good castle gives you more bargaining power when the only way to take it is by starving it out. Nestros will be down to Prince of Rathon if he lets too many of his nobles' lands be overrun.

"An alliance with us is really a gift from the gods, which Nestros will see unless he is a greater fool than I can believe. An alliance with us would allow him to send home, to defend their homes, all the second-line troops he probably can't feed anyway. We will put our men into line with his, and he'll have twice as big an army as he would otherwise. And a better one to boot! Nestros will keep the loyalty of his barons, defeat the horde and have his title recognized all at once. How could any man—?"

At the word "resist," the skies split apart in a thunderclap that made the horses jump. As the thunder rumbled into silence, the hiss of rain took its place. A few drops spattered across Kalvan's hands, a few more across his face, then the deluge struck.

He reined his horse to a walk and sneezed as drops found their way up his nose. So much for Royal dignity.

IX

Hadron Tharn heard the portal alarm go off and looked over at the privacy screen, seeing the face of his older sister, Dalla. He tapped the release code and the door opened.

"Long time no see, Sis."

Dalla winced. She was still playing mama—a job their birth mother had rejected. They had been close during their youth, until she met the future supercop, Verkan Vall. Actually, he rather admired Verkan's single-mindedness and lack of squeamishness. Verkan's, problem was that he still retained too many of the ideals of the old nobility that he'd been born into. Whereas, he had cast off all those old-fashioned ideas when a visit to Europo-American had introduced him to the works of Friedrich Nietzsche.

"I haven't seen you in a half-year, where have you been?"

None of your business, he wanted to shout, but Big Sis still had her uses. Without her influence, the super Paracop might be taking a closer look at this wanderings and financial dealings. That would not do, at least, now while events were still percolating. "I've been overseeing some my outtime business affairs."

"I understand from cousin Falro that you've been making quite a stir in First Level financial affairs."

Falro was in banking and it was useful to know that he still owed his loyalty to Dalla, who he'd unsuccessfully tried to romance—after her breakup with Verkan. "It keeps me occupied. And, as you know Dalla, the only things our parents left to us were Paratime Exchange Units." That was a sore spot and he knew it, and smacked it whenever Big Sister wanted to play mama. The truth was their mother had left the family for outtime adventure and it had been no great loss to anyone but Dalla. He'd been too young to even remember her. He saw her once or twice every twenty years and oohed and aahed while she treated him like another older sister.

"So what really brings you here, Dalla? I've been a good boy; no more visits to Fourth Level, Europo-America Axis Subsector." He'd been fortunate to make his first visits there, while a student at Dhergabar University, secretly ferreting out future business as an agent with Outtime Foodstuffs before the Big War in Europo-America, when the entire Axis Subsector had been declared off-limits to all First Level commercial and travel bureaus. He still had his contacts, but no one knew of them but Warntha, his personal bodyguard, the only person in the universe he completely trusted.

Dalla blushed fetchingly. She was as beautiful without make-up as most women were with it. She could have been a film star on any Europo-American time-line. If she weren't so useful, he might have been tempted himself. She was so good at protecting him, protecting him from everyone and everything—but himself. It was good to know that she still felt guilty about telling Verkan about his little Axis excursions; fortunately, she hadn't known the half of it.

He decided it was time to punish her some more. "Have you told my esteemed brother-in-law about the Hadron family secret?"

She gasped. "No! No one outside of the family knows about that."

"Supercop hasn't even made a guess. I'm disappointed; maybe he's more smitten with my elder sister then I surmised. Isn't it ironic that your husband's toy policeman—Kalvern, isn't it—drops off rather conveniently on the same time-line created by our esteemed great, great, uncountable great grandfather? Don't they still have some devil god named after the old fossil—rather like the family name? Must be the family curse."

Dalla nodded listlessly.

Hadron laughed. "Good old Arnall. It wasn't enough to violate the Paratime Code, but he had to create his own time-line by scaring away the natives! Now, it's Kalvan—that's the name—who's getting all the attention. The first Paratime time-line observed from the moment of divarication—ha! Maybe it's time we set the record straight. Told them about

how 'ol' Hadron Arnall' arrived on a Europo-America time-line a couple
of thousand years ago and played god to one of the tribes. How he used
to ride around in a big aircar taking the prettiest young girls with him
and how he killed and tortured any of the tribesmen who 'objected.' Of
course, he never brought the girls back—alive. He made such an impression on the primitives that they actually changed their migratory pattern
and created a whole new Subsector—Aryan-Transpacific, if I remember.
They even remember him as some sort of an underworld god. Now, that
story would get good old Kalvan off the home screens, but I doubt it
would enhance the family name."

"Now, that's enough, Tharn. That's not the least bit amusing!"

"I forgot what a prig you turned into when you were around me.
Does supercop get to see this side of you, too?"

"Shut up about him!"

"I see the family temper has bred true."

For the first time since the Big Fight, he saw tears in her eyes. He
wondered what nerve ending he'd struck. Maybe supercop didn't want
to breed—now there was a frightening thought—little Verkans running
around with toy needlers. If Verkan wanted to keep the family unit small,
they were both in agreement; maybe there was common ground between
them.

"Why do you strike out at the only people who love you?"

Oh no, he thought, Big Mama's coming. Time to change the conversation again. "So you still haven't told supercop the family secret. I bet he
already knows."

"What do you mean? That file was purged from the records thousands
of years ago."

"And you believe that! Oh no, I guarantee you that in some secret
data file in the Paratime Police supercomputer there's a flagged file with
our shameful family secret. Probably only accessible by the Chief. Maybe
the reason supercop hasn't brought it up is: he's waiting for you to tell
him. Maybe he does love you, after all!"

"Of course he does. You don't mean that really? There can't be any
such file."

"Oh, yes I do, Big Sis. True, it cost the family a few million units to keep the story away from the newsies, but I didn't think you were gullible enough to think the Parafanatics buried it as well."

There were worry lines creasing Dalla's forehead and he wondered if anyone cared that much about what he thought. Probably not. Big Sis included.

"Enough of your verbal sparring, Tharn. I came here to warn you that the Paratime Police know all about your little spy."

For a second he was worried, but little was not a description that would describe his real agent in any manner. "She of the big mammaries. Yes, I admit she's working for me. One of my subordinate's had a daughter who needed a job; I sponsored her for the Kalvan Study Team. I still have friends at the University, even if they couldn't stop my expulsion. After my Axis studies on their Great Man, I did receive a *lot* of moral support from some of my fellow academics for what the Paracops did to my fledgling academic career."

"You still don't see the danger in what you did?"

"I wasn't telling the natives about the Paratime Secret, if that's what you mean, just soaking up some local flavor and finishing my studies on Great Men in history. A little firsthand research never hurt anyone; not that most of the University professors would agree—it's too much like work. What I want to know is, why do they always proscribe the 'interesting' subsectors and time-lines? And, how, in Zirppa's Foodtube, was I to do original research on Great Men without any subjects! And, trust me Big Sister, the *Führer* is one of the greatest men of any Paratime Level or time-line!"

"There are great men all over Fourth Level; the one you picked may have been a catalyst, but by no other definition could he be called great— especially in regards to height, or any other adjective."

"You're wrong there, Sis, but we could argue over these minor philosophical difference for days. What brought you here this time?"

"I wanted to warn you to be careful. Your tame little spy could get you in serious trouble if she's caught tampering on Kalvan Prime. Verkan and I both like Kalvan and I won't be able to stop him again if he catches you involved in some outtime contamination."

"I'll keep that in mind, Big Sis. Now I know the end line of sisterly devotion. I have no intention of contaminating supercop's toy soldier's field of play. And, as much as I do admire the priestly scoundrels in charge of Styphon's House, I really have no interest in the outcome of their little war. I do like to keep an eye out for any slip in the old family secret. After all, the Zarthani do have written records and who knows what oral history some priestly scribe might have heard around the campfire and saved for posterity."

"You don't think?"

"I really don't, Sis. But anything is possible and it's best to have a 'friend' on hand to help contain the damage, so to speak."

Dalla blanched.

"Sorry to upset your placid existence, but someone has to protect the family name." It was hard to keep from laughing at that lie. His sister was too preoccupied to notice his change of expression; it was amazing how love could screw up your life.

"Oh, at the risk of upsetting you further, I just thought I'd let you know that word of new Kalvan time-lines have reached the University and some of the scholars are quite upset. They propose the novel hypothesis that every time another Kalvan appears on a new time-line: well, the risk of exposing the Paratime Secret grows more real. Some are even asking why Kalvan's not been dispatched for the good of Home Time Line and all that other patriotic self-serving nonsense. Of all people, they're asking why the Paratime Police aren't doing their job. Your husband might want to consider the ramifications."

Dalla's face, if possible, grew even whiter. He enjoyed that even if he didn't give a fig over the Paratime Secret being exposed. *How could some barbarian from Europo-America teach a bunch of savages enough to uncover a technological marvel that had taken three geniuses in three different fields to concoct and had been the life's blood of First Level for ten thousand years?* The probabilities were so low they weren't worth thinking about.

"I'm sorry, Tharn, I don't feel well. I've got to go."

"That's fine, Sis. Be sure and give my best to supercop." For a moment he was bothered by the thought that almost all their meetings ended this way, with Dalla either in tears or feeling sick—sometimes both. Maybe there was something to the family curse. After all, even father had succumbed in his third century and was now a permanent resident of some Psych-Hygiene house of horrors. No, madness was the escape route of lesser men—not an overman such as himself. Not with all that he had left to accomplish.

X

None of the forts and towns Kalvan had encountered in the Trygath had prepared Kalvan for the sight of Rathon City. Unlike the wooden stockades surrounding most Trygathi towns, Rathon City was encircled by immense stone walls—about the size of the Great Wall of China—which dwarfed the out-buildings and storehouses that had sprung up at their base. Not even the great Eastern capitals had such massive stone bulwarks, but then they were not subject to periodic invasions and large-scale migrations.

The Great Gate was large too, wide enough that four of the Zarthani Conestoga-style wagons could pass abreast. Most of the inner city's two- and three-story buildings were of the usual beam and plaster construction. At the center of the city were a score of large public buildings constructed of stone, half of which appeared to have been constructed during the past decade.

Kalvan guesstimated the population at about seventy-five thousand; smaller than a comparable Eastern Kingdom capital, but very impressive for a so-called "barbarian" kingdom. Most of the people he saw in the streets wore homespun trousers and shirts, although there was a goodly number of hunters and trappers in furs and buckskins. The men, with a few exceptions, wore full beards, rather than the trimmed beards and goatees worn in the Eastern Kingdoms.

Kalvan suspected that being in Rathon City was like visiting one of the Eastern capitals three hundred years ago.

At the center of the city was a great plaza, covering about two city blocks. Surrounded by a great garden stood Nestros' palace, a magnificent building that made Kalvan's own "palace" (actually Prince Ptosphes' summer palace) look like a poor relation's summer home. When this Great Murthering War with Styphon's House was over, Kalvan was going to have to build himself a palace more suitable to his rank—maybe something dong the lines of Louis XIV's Palace of Versailles—or he would have problems maintaining the respect of despots like Nestros.

Half a dozen richly dressed ambassadors came to meet the Hostigi party at the garden gates. Kalvan noticed that all of Nestros' retainers had their beards cut and trimmed in the Eastern fashion. To either side of the road leading to Nestros' palace stood the King's Guard, all over six foot, with finely engraved ceremonial halberds and black armor trimmed in gold.

Inside the palace presence chamber, Nestros himself looked every inch the warrior King, from his bright, inquisitive eyes to his big calloused hands. He had the ruddy complexion of an outdoorsman with a face that was dignified if not handsome. He and Kalvan locked eyes and neither turned away until Nestros spoke first:

"Welcome, Great King Kalvan, to our humble abode. Can I offer you some refreshments? Ale or winter wine, perhaps?"

"Winter wine would be nice," Kalvan responded. It took at least two goblets to complete the usual diplomatic niceties. Before starting on his third, Kalvan said, "As I told your herald, we come in peace. I would like to aid you in your war against the nomads."

"If this be true, then fine. Yet, I have to wonder what brings a distant king, like yourself, to our land. Truly, throughout all our history, we have found that the Eastern Kingdoms care little about our wars and struggles. Why should this suddenly change now?"

"There are great changes afoot during these perilous times."

"Change may be new to you in the Eastern Kingdoms, but here it is constant like the seasons."

"Not in all things. Since when have the Zarthani Knights driven nomads into your lands, instead of chasing them back across the Great River?"

Nestros' forehead furrowed as he tried to puzzle out an answer. "Are you trying to say that the Knights are using the nomads as a cat's-paw against Hos-Hostigos?"

Kalvan was impressed with Nestros' instinctive grasp of *Realpolitik*. "Yes, that is exactly what Grand Master Soton hopes to accomplish. And since your lands are in the middle they are going to take the brunt of the bloodletting."

There was a harsh noise as Nestros ground his teeth. "The Grand Master may well think we are but tools to be used, but we have prepared ourselves well for this invasion. I need neither his Knights nor your help to keep my lands."

"How do you plan to keep the nomads away? They are now less than two days' ride from Rathon City itself."

"We are well provisioned here and our great walls will keep out ten times their number. All farms and gardens within a day's march of the city will be burned to the ground. All villagers and peasants will come to the City. There are royal storehouses in every large town in Rathon, Mybranos, Cyros, and Kythax. We shall feed our own while the nomads starve like wolves in the midst of winter famine. When they have grown hungry and weak, my men-at-arms will feed the earth with their blood and till the soil with their bones."

"That may be a good plan for normal times, but not now. You have never fought a horde as large as this one. I doubt there is a town or city in all Rathon, except for this City, which can hold back the nomad flood. But, say that you are right, and the walls of your towns and cities keep the nomads at bay. What then? In their anger they will poison your wells, burn your villages and sow your fields with salt in retribution. What will your people have to return to then? And what will your nobles have to say about a High King who saves lives by hiding behind walls so his subjects can starve once the wolves have fled?"

Nestros' face turned bright red and for a moment Kalvan feared he had gone too far.

"Aargh! As bad as they taste, there is truth in your words. The nomads are as numerous as the great herds of bison on the Sea of Grass whose numbers stretch from horizon to horizon. It is enough to make one believe in the old legends. What help can you offer?"

"My plan is simple. We join both our armies and drive the nomads back south as the Knights have driven them north. Let the nomads find *our* steel even less to their liking than that of the Zarthani Knights."

Nestros' eyes brightened at the idea of a direct attack. "Will we have enough swords even united to drive such a great horde?"

Not if we were facing the Huns or Mongols of Otherwhen, thought Kalvan. But these nomads had fewer horse archers and fought more in the manner of Caesar's Gauls or Hadrian s Britons. *And they lack a great khan like Attila or Genghis Khan.*

"In a way their great number is to our advantage, King Nestros. With so many warriors they are pressed to fight like heavy infantry, yet wear little armor and make massed targets for our muskets and arquebuses. Also, they have many leaders instead of one chief."

Nestros shook his head. "No longer, King Kalvan. We have just learned that the nomads have elected a Warlord, a Sastragathi chief named Ranjar Sargos. He is a former Cyrosi mercenary and knows our way of warfare."

"He may know Trygathi strategy, but I doubt he's ever faced a regiment of musketeers. Also, as a new leader his hold will be uncertain; we must exploit it by moving quickly. How soon can you muster your troops?"

"Most of my army is within a day's ride of Rathon City where there are enough victuals to feed them. However, before we clasp palms on this alliance, I have a request I'd like to make."

Suddenly Kalvan feared for his good sword and his richly-chased breastplate. In another incarnation, Nestros must have been a horsetrader like Duke Skranga. "What can I do for you?"

"I would like to change my title to Great King and claim my lands a Great Kingdom, as you have done in Hos-Hostigos. Will you recognize my claim?"

This looks too easy! There's a catch in here somewhere. If he recognized Nestros as Great King of the Trygath, it might legitimize him in the eyes of his own people, but it wouldn't mean twiddle-dee to the other Five Great Kings—none of whom had yet recognized Kalvan as Great King.

Furthermore, Nestros claimed sovereignty over several princedoms that were within Grefftscharri borders. Kalvan didn't need to start another war in the west with King Theovacar just because he needed to placate Nestros now.

However, if Kalvan worked this right he could bind Nestros to Hos-Hostigos and possibly bring him into the war against Styphon's House.

"King Nestros, I will recognize you as Great King of all those princedoms and kingdoms who agree to be a part of your new Great Kingdom and who are not already under the sovereignty of King Theovacar."

From the furrowed brow on Nestros' face Kalvan knew he had safely navigated one minefield, but if he estimated Nestros correctly this would not be the last, nor the most dangerous.

"I welcome Your Majesty's support of the new Great Kingdom of Hos-Rathon. I only pray you will be equally swift in helping us to modernize our army."

This request was going to be easy to fill since Kalvan still had half the ordnance of Hos-Harphax at his disposal after last year's war—much of it dropped without even being fired. Not that he would ever let Nestros know that.

"Great King Nestros, when our armies have defeated the nomads, I will have two thousand arquebuses and five hundred muskets delivered to Hos-Rathon to finalize the alliance between our two Kingdoms. I will also send five tons of Hostigos fireseed and will train two score of apprentices in its manufacturing and curing at our new University."

This must have struck Nestros as more than satisfactory as he jumped out of his throne to give Kalvan a bear-hug that all but crushed Kalvan's ribcage.

"Truly, Great King Kalvan, you are as generous as you are wise and a master of the art of war. But enough of this, we will have plenty of time to share ale and wine when the nomads have been vanquished. Now we must plan our campaign. I have ten thousand troops billeted in and around Rathon City and two times ten thousand within a two days' ride. And another ten thousand within a five days' ride."

"Excellent," Kalvan replied. "Send riders out to gather all those within a two days' march. Meanwhile, we can gather provisions and prepare our troops for the battle ahead."

King Nestros rubbed his big hands together. "You speak my language, Great King Kalvan. The time has come to teach the nomads that it is safer in Regwarn, the Caverns of the Dead, than it is here in the Trygath!"

XI

Dalla walked into the smoky bar at Constellation House, looking for Tortha Karf's comforting presence. She was still wrung out from her visit with her brother, Tharn. She paused to take out a cigarette and three different men approached her to light it. She smiled graciously and used her own lighter. Verkan would have been proud.

"Over here, Dalla." She heard Tortha's familiar and comforting gravelly voice.

She sat down at the booth and asked the robot bartender for a bourbon and coke. Unlike most First Level citizens, Dalla preferred the unobtrusive mechanical servants to the status enhancing proles that many of her contemporaries preferred. Possibly, it was because her adopted sister, Zinganna, was a former prole, but she liked to think it was that she had more respect for outtime people than to use them as personal servants, no matter what the cachet.

Tortha was wearing breeches and a well-filled civilian tunic; his hair was streaked with gray and thinning in front. He was too practical and too much a stick-in-the-mud to have a hair treatment. He reminded Dalla of a big old cross bear, with a soft heart. She offered him a cigarette and was surprised to note that instead of a lighter he used one of the peculiar Kalvan Time-Line back-acting flint tinderboxes to light it. She wondered if it was significant, deciding he probably missed palling around with Verkan and the other boys.

"Thanks, Tortha, for coming to see me on such short notice. I know you just arrived from Fifth Level, but Verkan's so busy and I really need—"

"It's all right, Dalla. You can stop blathering. I take it you've just come back from another visit with your lovely younger brother."

"How did you know?"

"Hadron Tharn is the only person I know, besides your husband, who can break through your impenetrable good humor. And, since I've stopped my meddling, you and Verkan have been happier than I can ever remember."

"That wasn't all your fault, Tortha. I could have turned down some of those assignments. In those days I was younger and didn't realize how rare it was to meet a man of Verkan's caliber. I do now and I don't ever intend to forget it, or chance losing him again."

"Good. I don't have to tell you that I agree with you wholeheartedly. Now, tell me, what's the problem with Honorable Hadron Tharn?"

"I don't know—he's nastier than ever. I've overlooked his tantrums and mean behavior for years. He was always jealous of Verkan, you know. Before Verkan, he was such a sweet boy."

"Whoa. Now, wait a minute, Dalla. Is this the same Hadron Tharn, I knew? The one who burned your house down? And that was years before you met Vall."

"Yeah, well, maybe I exaggerated a bit. But, his personality took a real nose dive after Verkan came into the picture."

"Dalla, that might be because Verkan was the first man you really fell in love with."

"True," Dalla said, trying not to blush.

"I think Hadron's problems are deeper than mere sibling jealousy. Yes, I know you both were left to fend for yourselves, after your mother went outtime. Your father was always too busy to spend any time at home. He bedeviled the Department as Chief of the Opposition Party. It may sound horrible, but I was neither surprised or disappointed when the Bureau of Psych-Hygiene decided to put him in 'protective' custody."

Dalla felt her eyes begin to well again.

"Sorry, Dalla, damn this tongue of mine. I didn't mean to stick a soft spot."

"It's not father I'm feeling bad about; it's Tharn. Today, I finally saw him for the spoiled, mean, horrible little man that he's become. He's not a boy anymore, flirting with danger and oddball cults. He's a devious and—sadly—unprincipled grown-up, who I really don't know at all. If anything, I think he's—"

"You don't have to say it. I know all about your family."

"I know," Dalla said sadly, "Insanity runs right through it."

"Yes, and no." Tortha replied.

"What do you mean?"

"It always begins in the early thirties after the first longevity treatments. The longevity serum may well be the trigger."

"How do you know?"

Tortha looked very uncomfortable. "After your first companionate marriage with Verkan went sour, I decided to do a deep background check when I learned you two were getting back together. I also learned that the Psych-Hygiene people told this very thing to your brother and he disregarded it. It happened while he was at the University just before he got involved with those awful Axis people and got expelled for going outtime without a proper Paratime Permit. He knew that subsector was proscribed—"

"You don't have to defend yourself to me, Tortha. It was Tharn's decision to spend time with those terrible Nazis. It wasn't your fault he got caught! He still looks up to them, you know; that's one of the reasons I believe he's insane himself. There, I've finally said it—admitted it to myself. He's mad as a loon and it scares me."

"That's not all that scares you, is it?"

"Tortha, you can see right through me! This is a burden I've never told to anyone, not even Vall. Promise you won't ever tell anyone."

"I promise, Dalla, you have my word."

"Good. There's no better bond. I'm worried about my own children becoming like Tharn or my father or his grandfather, well—you get the picture. I love children, but I'm afraid to have any of my own. Look at the horrible choice I have to offer: be sane and die young, or live long and go crazy!"

Tortha shook his head. "That's not what I was expecting. I thought you might be worried about yourself."

"No. The family curse only strikes the males in our family; probably one reason why they marry so badly."

"That I didn't know. You could always adopt or there are ways to guarantee birth sex."

"Sure, and give my daughters the same terrible choice I'm faced with! I won't do it."

"You could adopt, or get a surrogate mother, or clones of you and Verkan. Today on Home Time Line there are lots of choices."

"Yes, I know. But I want children from me—like Rylla and Kalvan are having. Still, the clone idea isn't terrible. It would be nice to have a little Verkan around, one *I* could house train."

Tortha laughed. "Good luck. You can see how successful I was with the original."

Dalla laughed, too, feeling as though a terrible weight had moved from her shoulders. It was almost like having a father, talking with Tortha. "If you've made a study of the Hadron family, I guess you know the family secret too."

Tortha nodded, not saying a word.

"Does Verkan?"

Tortha shrugged. "I've never brought it up. I always believed if anyone should tell it, it would have to be you."

"Thank you, you old bear!"

Tortha actually blushed when she reached over and kissed him on the cheek.

"Should I tell him, Tortha?"

"That's for you to decide. It won't change his feelings for you that I know. Or I'm a complete romantic idiot."

Dalla laughed. "I will, I promise. But not now; poor Verkan, already has more problems than any three people I know; well, except for Kalvan and Rylla—and poor Ptosphes, of course. He still blames himself for the defeat at Tenabra."

"Not his fault; he was up against Styphon's varsity—and he's no Kalvan. But, my advice to you, young lady, is, don't wait too long. Secrets are burdens and no one understands that better than myself."

Rylla nodded. Tortha had spent almost half of his life protecting the Paratime Secret, and many times from the very people he was trying to protect. Now, her man held the same untenable position.

To change the subject, she asked, "What are you doing here so far away from you farm on Fifth Level Litzn-equivalent?"

Tortha shook his big head. "Too much of the same old, same old."

Dalla smiled mischievously, "That's not what I heard from Verkan. He told me about your nieces and their swimming lessons!"

Tortha blushed right down to his hair follicles. "Dralm damn-it! That blabbermouth!"

"Don't blame Verkan, I weaseled it out of him. Why did you really come?"

"Oh, you want the real reason as opposed to the one fit for a broadcast story. The truth is Dalla; I'm bored out of my skull. I'm tired of trapping rabbits and gophers. I'm tired of grapes and silly young girls. I'm tired of myself, I don't wear well; just ask any of my six former wives! I've spent the last two hundred years of my life doing important work and I'm still too young for the scrap heap. Paratime Commissioner—harrumph! It was a rubber stamp job in my day, and even more so with Vall. I came back here to help Verkan, if I can, or just help myself, if I can't."

"I understand. And, really, Tortha, Verkan needs all the help he can get. I've never seen him so 'involved' with an outtimer as he is with Kalvan—not that I blame him, I adore Kalvan and Rylla is already my best friend. Now he's fretting because he's stuck dealing with this Europo-America shutdown project of his! I've been going to all these meetings and I can tell you it's going nowhere. Can you pump him some sunlight on the issue, Chief."

"Ex-Chief—really, Rylla," Tortha said, trying to hide a big grin.

"Sure, but you'll always be Chief to me. Anyway, Europo-America has become the public 'Sector.' It's been that way since Outtime Novelties brought back jazz and flappers. You know how these outtime fads and crazes run; everyone was Indo-Turanian crazy when I was a girl. I still remember practicing yoga, wearing a turban and those tantric exercises, although those still come in handy with Vall."

Tortha turned pink again.

She smacked him on the shoulder, playfully. "You've been with those nieces of yours for too long, Tortha. Anyway, it's gotten worse ever since rock and racket became popular. Remember when every nightclub had to have their own 'Elvis?'"

"What a headache for the Paracops! They were hi-jacking them from every subsector where that crazy noise was still undiscovered. For a while we had to guard that dumb hillbilly truck driver on a thousand time-lines. I'm still surprised we never designated a Presley Subsector!"

"Verkan's really never paid it any attention, because he doesn't hear or see what he doesn't like. I can't get through to my husband, because he's a snob—and I mean that lovingly—he just doesn't realize that everyone on Home Time Line doesn't have his class or taste. Well, it's worse now, since the Beatles. Not the insects, it's another noisy Europo-American singing combo. They're even noisier and louder than Elvis, if that's possible. And then there are the flat screen films and film stars—Marilyn Monroe, Clark Gable, Humphrey Bogart, and now James Dean—and art deco and all sorts of nonsense. Europo-America is—to paraphrase one of their aphorisms—the "cat's pajamas" and if Verkan doesn't quit this silly crusade of his he's going to derail his job and possibly the Paratime Police along with him."

"Wow! Dalla," Tortha replied, "you've just given me a needler shot of reality. Maybe we have the wrong Chief! I'm even worse than Verkan when it comes to these fads. And I never had any children, except you two—by proxy, of course—to teach me any different. I'll try to talk him into stalling this shutdown for a few decades until all this Europo-America sheep-dip becomes old hat. It will; I've seen half a dozen of these crazes just since I've been Chief. Meanwhile, you stay on top of these committees and study groups."

"Good. I need something to keep me occupied while Verkan's glued to his Chief's chair. But what about you? What are you going to do?"

"Dalla, I don't know. Hang around the office, I guess, until Vall throws me out."

"Well, I know two other people who need some help. And you would definitely be an asset to them."

"Really. Who?"

"Rylla and Kalvan."

"I'm an ex-Paratimer. I can't deal in contamination—"

"Oh, stop being so huffy, Tortha. Hear me out. Sometimes you remind me so much of Verkan. The two of you! Anyway, you could give them moral support and be a Dutch uncle. I'm sure Verkan could come up with a suitable disguise. And don't tell me you're not interested—I see that smile."

"Dalla, that might very good idea. I'm curious myself to meet this Kalvan and his lady that I've heard so much about. And, with this Styphon's House Crusade, it sure won't be boring!"

"Tortha, you've just said a mouthful!" They both laughed.

XII

Great King Kalvan dismounted at the top of Gyrax Hill. While his dignity might require meeting King Nestros on horseback, his horse required a rest. The retreat of the Hostigi royal party from the left flank had been more speedy than dignified, over rough, muddy ground. A few of the Royal Horse Guard were still fishing themselves out from under bushes and rounding up their horses.

From the hilltop, Kalvan had his first good view of the battle in more than an hour. The nomad horde was large, maybe seventy-five to a hundred thousand warriors, a flood of men as hard for Ranjar Sargos to direct as for Kalvan to stop. Not much had changed, and that little for the better. The enemy's right and center, under Sargos, still overlapped the allied left. They had even advanced all the way to the redoubt on the banks of the Lydistros, then stopped among the caltrops and pitfalls, under the fire of the four-pounders Kalvan could spare for fixed defenses.

As far as Kalvan was concerned, Sargos could take his men halfway to the border.

On the allied right, masses of horsemen, light infantry (the only kind the horde had), and an occasional chariot surged back and forth. Each chief was giving his own orders to his followers and taking none from anyone else, including Sargos. They were the less dangerous but more numerous part of the enemy army, fifty thousand against Sargos' forty thousand, give or take a few boys.

They faced mostly Nestros' Trygathi, eight or nine thousand heavy horse, with twice that number of supporting infantry, spearmen, gallow-glasses, and missile troops: crossbowmen, archers, and some arquebusiers. They were stiffened by three Ulthori pike regiments, two regiments of Royal Musketeers, a battalion of riflemen, and two four-pounders. Not that the Trygathi needed much stiffening; they were fighting with the knowledge that they had a chance of victory and that meanwhile their homes were safe. The alliance with Hostigos had let Nestros leave a third of his army home to make raiders a poor insurance risk. The twenty-five thousand he had on the field were his best.

"Alkides," Kalvan called downhill. "Is the Flying Battery ready to move?"

"With Galzar's favor, yes," the smoke-blackened artillery general replied. "I wish the guns really did have wings. This cursed mud's going to butcher the horses!"

"Not half as fast as the guns will butcher Sargos' warriors," Kalvan called back. The gun crews cheered their Great King's words. There were only eight guns for the Flying Battery; three were in emplacements and one had been lost in a swamp on the Nyklos Trail. As much as he wished for another battery or two, with maybe some six-or eight- pounders, the Flying Battery was a far cry from the half-a-dozen catapults the enemy was using.

Kalvan walked over to General Alkides and asked quietly, "How is Great Captain Mylissos doing?" Nestros' chief of artillery had started the day a bit peevish over the council of war. It had been agreed that his ancient bombards would remain with the reserves, and not try to advance with the major attacks. Kalvan could even sympathize with him; after all, it was the first time in memory Mylissos actually had enough fireseed to fire his massive hooped-iron pipes more than once or twice without exhausting his magazines.

"A sight happier than he was, now that he's got targets and fireseed to burn on them. I think he shifted a couple of those twenty-pounders without orders, but I'm not complaining. A twenty-pounder loaded with rocks and old nails isn't something I would care to face!"

Kalvan would have said more, mostly to Aspasthar. The boy was fighting his first battle away from his father, riding with Alkides as one of his messengers. But the boy looked as if he would take the encouragement as an insult, and by Dralm, there were Nestros and his guards in their red and white colors coming up the other side of the hill!

By abandoning royal dignity and running back to his horse, Kalvan was mounted by the time Nestros reined in and hailed him.

"Greetings, friend and ally! We are smiting the horde as if the gods themselves fought for us!"

"So we are. Maybe, too hard. Corpses can't fight the Zarthani Knights. Thank somebody for Ranjar Sargos. He made the horde more dangerous, but if we had to take the surrender of every petty chief one at a time we'd be here until winter!"

A Hostigi messenger rode up and saluted both kings. "The lookouts in the Willow Spirit Grove report that Warlord Sargos is advancing on them."

"Tell them to wait as long as they can, and imitate a strong force meanwhile," Nestros said. "Then they can withdraw. Meanwhile, Sargos will be drawn forward. Perhaps we can meet him hand-to-hand!"

Kalvan and Captain-General Harmakros exchanged amused looks. Nestros was no fool; he was learning such Kalvan-style tricks as feints and deceptions almost hourly. He was also an old-style Trygathi warrior, whose highest ambition had to be meeting the opposing leader hand-to-hand and defeating him.

"As the gods will it," Harmakros said. Kalvan decided to let his Captain-General speak, even if protocol said he should be talking king-to-king. Even four-star generals needed something to take their minds off their sons' winning their spurs—or their shrouds.

"The gods willed that Sargos should be a tool," Nestros said cheerfully. "They also willed that Kalvan should come and bring his fireseed and strength to join ours. I think they will give us this one more small favor."

Kalvan doubted the accuracy of Nestros' description of his opponent. The Warlord had pulled his chariots back the moment he realized the ground was too muddy to let them get up speed. He still had his in reserve, while the other chiefs had mostly lost chariots, riders and teams together.

"Let the gods will that all our men hold their fire until they have a clear target, and that be an enemy," Kalvan said. "We have more fireseed than any army ever seen in the Trygath, but not enough to waste!"

"My men are not children," Nestros said with offended dignity.

"Then let the heralds sound for the advance," Kalvan said. Both kings looked at Harmakros; he signaled the trumpeter. The trumpet screeched, triggering the launching of two signal rockets.

When the green rockets rose into the sky over Gyrax Hill, six thousand reserve cavalry would be launched at the heart of Sargos' army.

Sargos flung a light lance high into the willow branches. A scream rewarded him; an enemy lookout toppled from his perch and lay writhing until an archer dispatched him with a knife.

The heavy thud of many horses on the move reached the Warlord over the noise of his warriors clearing the willow grove of enemies. Sargos jerked his horse around and drew his last lance from its leather bucket next to his right stirrup. His tribal guards followed suit, and the whole band streamed at a canter around the left side of the grove.

Ah, would that 1 had men to be my eyes and ears on parts of the field I cannot reach myself! Such is Kalvan's way, or so the prisoners have told us. Yet how could they reach me, in the midst of my foes, to bear their messages? To remain in the rear merely so that 1 may know more—that is a coward's way and no warrior would follow me.

A contrary voice in Sargos' mind muttered: Kalvan leads that way, as often as not, and who says that those who follow him are not warriors? Enough of yours are with the spirits after meeting them!

Clear of the willows, Sargos reined in and stared in disbelief. Down the hill in the enemy's center moved two mighty bands of armored horsemen, like vast steel-scaled serpents. At the head of each band floated

banners, the red and white colors of King Nestros and the red and blue of
King Kalvan.

So Kalvan will take his chance of joining the spirits today? Well and
good. Warlord Ranjar Sargos stood tall in his stirrups. "Meet them at that
hedge. Cydrak and Trancyles, ride like the wind and bring all the warriors
Chiefs Hyphos and Ruflos can spare!"

The two were young men on fresh horses; they vanished in a spray of
clods. Sargos drew his sword and adjusted his throat guard, his one piece
of armor that was metal all through and through instead of metal over
leather.

The sword hummed over his head as he whirled it. The day was too
overcast for sunlight to shine on it, but those close by saw it and heard it
humming. Their shouts told others what was happening, and the war cries
rose until they seemed a solid wall across the front of the advancing foe.

Then Sargos lowered his sword and spurred his horse toward the
hedge.

Only one of the green rockets flew high enough to be seen. That was
enough. The cheers from both armies drowned out the trumpeters and
captains like a hurricane drowning out a mouse's squeak.

Nestros was pointing frantically downhill. "There! Behind that
hedge. Sargos forms his battle line. We must reach it before he brings up
reinforcements."

Nestros couldn't have been in more of a hurry if he'd read Napoleon's
maxim, "Ask me for anything but time." Once again he was doing the tac-
tically sound things, out of a desire to cross swords with an enemy chief.

So be it, Kalvan thought.

No, wait a minute. If Nestros gets too far ahead of you, the Trygathi
will say their Great King was braver than the Great King of Hos-Hostigos.

"Harmakros!" What would have been a shout under other circumstances was about as audible as a whisper.

The Captain-General reined in beside Kalvan. "Yes, Your Majesty?"

"You stay back here with the mobile command post. I have to charge
with Nestros."

"That ass—" began Harmakros, who apparently thought better of using his trooper's vocabulary about an allied King, then mock-saluted. "As Your Majesty wishes."

Kalvan started to count off guards to ride with him, then saw Nestros and his heavies digging in their own spurs. This time Kalvan had to restrain his curses. Instead he signaled his own banner bearer and dug in his spurs.

The banner bearer took the reins in his teeth and drew his sword. Bearing the Great King's banner had been a much safer job than fighting in the front ranks—at least until today!

Sargos jumped his horse over a ditch and turned it, meanwhile drawing his last lance. To retreat was cowardly more often than not, but to stand with the men he had would not even slow the enemy. Like the Great River flooding over its banks, the enemy horse flowed on as if only the gods could stop them.

Archers were running up, but the range was still long. Against armored men they would waste most of their arrows. Against the enemy's horses, perhaps—

"Look, my chief!" Chief Ruflos was pointing. He had just arrived with a hundred and fifty men not six deep breaths ago. "My chief, the kings offer themselves to the gods!"

It was true. The two royal banners were forging steadily toward the head of the enemy horsemen. Under those banners, Sargos could now see tight bands of splendidly-armored men.

"They offer themselves to us!" Sargos snapped. He tried to quiet his own doubts. Have the kings had an omen, that the gods will give victory if they offer themselves as a sacrifice?

"Then let us take what is offered," Chief Ruflos said. He also sounded as if he wished to quiet inward fears.

Sargos patted his horse's neck and looked about him. The warriors he'd summoned were streaming toward him from all sides. Not all would be with him before he had to face the Kings, but the rest would follow to fling themselves upon the foe.

"Hoaa! Tonight we offer two Kings' heads, to the gods of our land and the spirits of our dead!"

The advance of the two Kings was turning into a race. Nestros reached the hedge first. Kalvan swerved without slowing, nearly colliding with his banner bearer. The trooper's sword pricked Kalvan's horse, who protested by nearly bucking his rider into a ditch.

By the time Kalvan had sorted himself out, Nestros was crossing swords with everyone in reach on the far side of the hedge. Nestros had won the race but not by enough to dishonor his ally. In fact, his ally was going to have a busy time in about two minutes, keeping this from being Nestros' first and last battle as Great-King-Elect. On both right and left, warriors were streaming toward the battle of the kings.

"Stands the standard of Great King Kalvan!" the banner bearer shouted. He thrust the butt end of the staff into the muddy ground and drew a pistol. The banner bearer pistoled the first warrior to come within lance-range, but the nomad stayed in the saddle. Kalvan shot him with his last loaded horse pistol, then drew his own sword and cut a second opponent across the face, a third in the arm.

After that Kalvan lost count of his opponents and all track of what he was doing to them. Somewhere in the next five minutes he managed one coherent thought that was not concerned with his own survival.

If I was fighting well-armored opponents, I'd be dead by now.

About five minutes after that, it struck him that armor might not make all that much difference. These nomads were damned hard to kill, like the Moro *juramentados* he had heard an Old Army veteran describe.

Come on, Alkides! Are you the Flying Battery or the Flighty Battery?

A moment later, Alkides' octet of four-pounders signaled their arrival with a blast of case shot that tore into the ranks of friends and foe with awful impartiality. A chunk of lead snapped the banner staff; the banner bearer dove to keep it from hitting the ground and sprawled with his nose digging up the mud. He held the banner clear of the ground, though.

Kalvan leaned down to pick up the banner, then found his horse sagging to one side. As the horse toppled, Kalvan leaped clear, the weight of his armor driving him to his knees. The horse fell on his side, blew blood from his nostrils, and died.

Kalvan waved his sword at the enemy and cursed Alkides' gunners, both emotionally satisfying if not very useful. At least the litter of dead men and horses around him included many more enemies than friends.

Let's hope to Galzar we didn't wing Nestros!

More cavalry were riding up, a second troops of Nestros' Bodyguard. Their captain reined in, shouting a request for orders.

'Look to your King!" Kalvan shouted back. "He's beyond the hedge. If you get no orders from him, advance cautiously five hundred paces."

"As Your Majesty commands, the captain called. "Will you be here?"

"Here or in Hadron's Realm!" was Kalvan's parting shot. The body-guards cheered as their captain maneuvered his horse through the hedge.

Kalvan mentally crossed his fingers, hoping he had not sent away men he would need for his own protection. But no live enemies were within pistol shot that he could see, and Alkides' guns were now firing steadily. That meant Harmakros and the reserves had to be closer than any organized enemies.

He was safe enough, from his enemies. He wished he could say the same about Rylla's tongue.

When my lovely wife hears that I raced a Trygathi king into the enemy lines, the first thing she'll do is laugh herself silly. The second will be to remind me never to complain about her leading from in front again as long as I live!

XIII

Ranjar Sargos awoke with the sense that a blacksmith was driving a chisel into the side of his head. He stifled a groan and tried to reach to cradle the pain.

It was then Sargos discovered his hands were bound.

Outrage gave him a voice he would not have found otherwise. "Is this honor—to treat a warrior like a rebellious slave?"

At least that was what he had intended to say. From the blank looks on the faces around him, he suspected he had croaked like a frog.

A face Sargos remembered thrust itself forward, and the others gave way to either side. It was the last face he had seen before what appeared to be a thunderbolt crashed into the side of his head and flung him from his saddle.

"Ranjar Sargos! Who has bound you?"

"No one, Your Grace," a gray-bearded man said.

"Captain-General Mylissos, he did not bind his own hands!" snarled the man, who must be King Nestros. Nestros drew a fine, if somewhat mud-specked, dagger from his riding boots, knelt, and cut Sargos' bonds with his own hands.

"I trust your honor as I would my own or Great King Kalvan's," Nestros said. "You led your men most valiantly to the end, but the gods' favor was not with you. Yet if you are willing, you may win more in defeat than you could have gained by victory."

It seemed to Sargos that King Nestros was talking in riddles. Beyond him a tall man in fine armor stood, smoking a pipe and nodding slowly.

"Kalvan?" Sargos asked, pointing.

Nestros nodded.

So they have both come to gloat. No, that is not true. Nestros was truly angry with those who dishonored me.

"I have fallen, and doubtless those around me," Sargos said. "That does not mean victory for you or defeat for me."

"Your men from here to the redoubt are trapped against the Lydistros

River," Nestros said. "The rest are fleeing. We are pursuing them, as wolves pursue rabbits. If you will sit down with us and discuss peace, we shall call off our pursuers and spare your trapped men. Otherwise, the Sastragath and the Sea of Grass alike will be lands of widows and orphans."

If he lies, he does so well. If he is telling the truth...but 1 must see for myself.

Sargos tried to rise. He not only failed, but would have fallen if Nestros and Kalvan both had not aided him.

To take healing from one's enemies is a sign of submission. Yet, if submitting will save those who swore to follow me...? Sargos knew from his days as a mercenary and as Warlord of the Great Horde that most casualties came not in battle, but in the headlong flight that followed defeat. Already too many of his people had died between the grindstones of the Black Knights and the two kings.

"Can you summon a healer and a horse? If I see with my own eyes what you have told me, then we shall talk."

The two kings nodded as if their heads were on a single neck.

The next morning Kalvan stepped out of the royal tent and nearly stumbled over Aspasthar. The boy woke up with a squeak of panic.

"Your Majesty!"

"Aspasthar, sleeping on watch is still a serious offense. Even after doing so well in your first battle."

"Your Majesty, I beg forgiveness. But my father came by and said he would watch in my place. He—"

A rumbling snore interrupted the page.

Kalvan looked into the shadows on the other side of the tent door and saw Captain-General Harmakros curled up under a blanket, even more soundly asleep than his son. Making sure that the armed sentries were all in place, Kalvan ducked back into his tent, burrowed into his piled baggage, and came out with a jug of Ermut's Best.

He raised his hand to quiet the panic-stricken boy. "I see your father. All is well."

By the time he came out of the tent, both his unofficial "sentries" were rubbing their eyes and yawning.

Harmakros did a double-take upon seeing his Great King. "Your Majesty, it is not the boy's fault. I relieved him of his duty, then fell asleep myself—"

"Don't berate yourself, Harmakros. There are other sentries, some of whom actually have slept within the past moon quarter. Think no more of it. I feel like celebrating, but I didn't want to drink alone."

"What about our friend and ally, Great King Nestros?" Harmakros asked.

"Please," Kalvan said. "Remember when I said it was all over but the shouting? I didn't know what I was saying. A discreet whisper for both Nestros and Sargos is what you would use for drilling a whole regiment! I'd be as deaf as a gunner if we had any more private sessions. But, Dralm be blessed, that was the last one!"

"Then we have an alliance?"

"Signed, sealed and about to be delivered to Grand Master Soton. Sargos is no fool. The Zarthani Knights are the hereditary enemies of the Sastragathi. He'll fight them rather than anyone else if he has half a chance of victory. We are giving him much more than that."

"And the rest of the nomads?"

"Those sworn to Warlord Ranjar Sargos will follow us. The rest have half a moon to either join us or leave the Great Kingdom of Hos-Rathon. Nestros would like to make it a quarter moon, but he will swallow this."

"I imagine most men would swallow a lot more, to be a Great King."

"Likely enough," Kalvan replied. *Being a Great King must be the dream of everyone who doesn't know what a headache it is!*

Not to mention aches in other places. Kalvan couldn't recall having been out of the saddle for more than twenty minutes at a time from dawn until dusk. He could recall the fields three-deep in dead men and horses, and worse, those who weren't yet dead. He didn't want to recall them, but they had glued themselves to his memory.

Kalvan uncorked the jug and passed it to Harmakros. As the brandy gurgled, Kalvan added, "Even with what we have in hand now, we'll be leading a hundred thousand men south. That should be a real headache for our friend Soton—and no aspirin for it either!"

"Aspirin?"

"An alchemy potion from my homeland. Good for the headaches we'll surely have if we finish this jug."

"I'll gladly take the burden on myself, Your—"

"Hand that jug over, Harmakros, if you don't want to be charged with treason!"

XIV

Hadron Tharn knocked at the door, the peep-hole opened and a gravely voice asked, "The password?"

"Death to all Paratime Police."

The voice answered with a booming laugh. "That's a good one boss. Your 'friend' is already waiting in the privacy booth, like you requested."

Hadron, followed by Warntha Swarn, his personal bodyguard, entered the Blind Pig—one of a chain of speakeasies he owned—patterned on illegal bars on a Europo-American Subsector that had once attempted the 'apparently' noble, but futile, attempt to prohibit the consumption of alcoholic beverages. The effort had barely lasted two decades, glorified a group of sub-moronic gangsters and opened up the Sector to serious penetration by a number of First Level outtime firms.

The loud racket of some new outtime music called rock and roll washed over him. He grimaced, but noted in satisfaction that almost a quarter of the gyrating young people were wearing blue shirts and trousers. He could imagine their surprise if only they knew that the man 'they knew' as The Leader was present! He felt a wave of pleasure, knowing that they were at his beck and call should the need arise—although with Warntha at his back it was most unlikely.

Hadron motioned for Warntha to wait, while he tapped in his private access code on the privacy booth's terminal. The door opened to show a frightened, middle-aged man in a wig and some dark make-up on. A passable, but pathetic disguise.

"Tharn, are you crazy!" the man known as Landon Toldar, Vice President of the Opposition Party, shouted, as soon as the door closed. "If the Metropolitan Police ever found us together—"

"Shut your yap!" Hadron shouted, he liked to use the appropriate slang of whatever milieu he was in. It showed his uncanny ability to adapt to any period or background that he deigned to enter.

Not used to disrespect of any kind, Landon Toldar did just as he was told, Hadron noted to himself. He was not surprised; most First Level citizens were used to giving orders, not taking them and were easily intimidated. Especially those like Landon who were stay-at-homes and had never worked outtime.

In a loud whisper, as though they might be overheard—which was a laugh, Toldar continued. "Tharn, this is dangerous meeting in this part of town in a 'joint' that you own."

Tharn choked back a laugh at Landon's pathetic attempt to fit in. "This is just what the Metros expect from the eccentric Hadron Tharn. You should know, Landon, isn't that why you and the Party used me to head the 'Wizard Traders,' as my brother-in-law so colorfully described *our* Organization? Not to mention any pull that I might have with the Paratime Police is through my sister. Now, there's a laugh!"

Hadron could tell from the sweat beading on Landon's forehead that he had hit a nerve. He wasn't surprised; he'd spent most of his life cultivating his harmless, slightly mad image. If only they knew what really went on behind his masks— Well, someday they would. He had found his true calling almost two decades ago on a major off-shoot of Fourth Level Europo America, the Hitler Belt. There he met, using his disguise as the son of a wealthy South American German expatriate industrialist, Reinhardt Heydrich, one of the major architects behind the Third Reich. Heydrich had recognized a fellow soul mate and introduced him to the real minds behind Adolf Hitler—Goebbels, Himmler, Eichmann and others. That day, despite Landon's misconception, was the birth day of the Organization and his own incarnation as The Leader. He, too, knew his role: to bring order out of chaos and to rid Home Time Line of its own parasitic and outtime vermin—the proles.

Misinterpreting Hadron's silence as intimidation, Landon's voice grew more confident. "We told you to shut down the Organization, after the Paratime Police scoop. We can't afford to have any involvement with them; it would disgrace—if not destroy—the Party."

"Party be damned!" Tharn answered. He enjoyed the shocked expression on Landon's face; it secretly amused him the many ways others saw him. Only a chosen few—like Warntha—recognized and saw the real leader behind the facade.

"I did not create the Organization to fill the Party's coffers, despite you and your friends' misconceptions. Truth be known, ninety percent of the profits went into my own pockets; I've got wealth secreted away beyond your wildest imaginings."

"Why? How!" Landon looked like a man caught in the middle of Post-traumatic Paratemporal Shift Syndrome, as the Bureau of Psych-Hygiene would call it. "That money was for the Party so that we could finally evict Management from power and control the Executive Council and bring truly enlightened government to the First Level."

"Please spare me your Party cant, I've heard enough of it over the past decade! It's time you and your cohorts learned a few hard realities. "First of all, the Wizard Traders are still in business—"

"What! Are you trying to destroy us all? The Paratime Cops are onto the Organization; they've already captured several key figures. Half the Council members who disappeared or discorporated were Opposition Party members. What if they find a way around the narco-hypnotic blocks? Chief Verkan is no fool!"

At the mention of his hated brother-in-law, Tharn felt his blood beginning to boil. He took several deep breaths. *Focus on the moment,* he told himself. "That's not your concern." He neglected to tell Landon that he had come up with a much better method of dealing with Wizard Trader penetration or capture. All Organization members were now given a narco-hypnotic-command that stopped their hearts when facing imminent capture or detainment. Doctor Vermor claimed it paralyzed the Vagus nerve, which controlled the heart, or some such thing. All he knew was the demonstrations worked perfectly; dead men did not talk.

"There will be no leaks from the Organization, I guarantee that."

Landon didn't look convinced.

"However, I'm not so sure I can count on the Opposition Party."

"We know how to keep our mouths shut, even if the Metros should come to suspect us. Men in our position do not get interrogated."

Tharn laughed! "Then you don't know my brother-in-law! In fact, as much as I hate to admit it, Verkan does possess some admirable characteristics, when compared to weaklings such as yourselves."

Once again Landon's jaw had dropped; it was getting to be a habit, Tharn thought. Maybe after all this was over he could find useful employment on some post-apocalypse Second Level world as a flycatcher! "As I was saying, the Wizard Traders are still in business. We still need more units, not only to fund your corrupt friends but to help finance The Leader."

"The Leader—you know how he is? He's doing more to destabilize the youth of our city than Verkan Vall himself, and this King Kalvan the media have chosen to make a hero of!"

Hadron put on his mask, although he felt like screaming: *Who do you think The Leader is, you spineless jellyfish?* Instead, he said, "The Leader is but one more piece of the coalition to unseat Management Party and restore the Home Time Line to proper authority."

The familiar words seemed to calm Landon's fears as the color returned to his face. "Tharn, your rashness endangers all of us. However, the Party could use additional funds in the upcoming Dhergabar municipal elections. And, if as you say, the Organization is still in operation, we could use a 'donation' of half a million units."

It never ceased to amaze him how quickly political types could restore their equilibrium once they were on the familiar grounds of elections and Paratime Exchange Units. "It can be arranged. However, I didn't call you here just to arrange for a campaign donation. It's time to put some political and public pressure on Chief Verkan. Kalvan Prime is splitting into new time-lines. Verkan is endangering the Paratime Secret by protecting his friend King Kalvan—"

"That won't work, Tharn. The public is in love with this Great King Kalvan—he can do no wrong, at least, for now. If his ratings ever slip, then we may have some leverage. Right now every public station is broadcasting the latest Kalvan nonsense."

"Then hit Verkan from another angle. Log how much time he's personally spending on Kalvan Prime and show malfeasance of duty. I don't know; I can't do your job for you. YOU PEOPLE ARE THE OPPOSITION PARTY—" Hadron didn't realize how loud he was screaming until Landon put his hands over his ears.

"Do something, or you'll never see another unit from me—for this election or any other. And don't even think of threatening me, I'll take the whole Party down with me."

Hadron was pleased at how his remarks affected the Party hack; he was cringing with each word, as though he were wielding a nerve whip. He could see that his true self, The Leader, was at last beginning to emerge. The Opposition Party would not take him for granted again.

XV

"How many men does Kalvan now lead?" Grand Master Soton asked. He knew his voice was as high-pitched as the squeak of a new-hatched quail chick. He did not care. The number he thought he heard could not be what Knight Commander Aristocles had actually said.

"More than a hundred thousand men," Aristocles repeated. He sounded like a messenger bringing news so bad that he hardly cared if he was punished for bringing it.

Any gods worthy of their name would know that the news was bad. There was no fault in Aristocles for being unmanned by it. *Forgive me, old friend.*

"A hundred thousand," Soton repeated meditatively. "Is that the grand sum, or only those bound by oath to one of the three supreme leaders?"

"The second, Grand Master. The number of those who will march against us without being oath-bound is not small. It may exceed twenty-five thousand."

"That is very nearly all the rest of the great horde," Soton said. "Also, if the subjects of"—he could not shape his tongue to say Nestros' pre-sumptuous new title —"the Pretender Nestros need not fear the nomads, all their garrisons will march south. Everyone will wish to be in at the death of the Zarthani Knights."

"Then they shall be disappointed, Grand Master. The audience may gather, but the players in the pageant are going to slip out the back door."

"Leaving all their tavern bills unpaid, of course. Are you thinking as I am?"

"What else makes any sense? We face odds of perhaps five to one. Two of those five are civilized soldiers under captains not to be despised, with more guns than have been seen west of the Pyromanes since fireseed was sent by Styphon! Half our strength are light troops or half-trained, or both."

This bald statement of the truth made it neither less nor more endur-able. In the end, that did not matter, if one was the Grand Master and sworn to bear any burden in the name of the Order. Soton mentally ran over his mental army table of organization: fifteen Lances, comprised of nine thousand Order Brethren and two thousand auxiliaries; seven thou-sand levy, mostly Sastragathi mounted archers and lancers; and three to four thousand unreliable nomad light cavalry—who in a pinch might change sides or run off the field.

To stand and fight the great horde would be suicide. Yet it still seemed to Soton that his own death by Kalvan's hand would be easier to face than the orders he knew he would have to give before this campaign was done. Nor could he hope to find peace by seeking that or any other death.

To do that would be to cast the Order into the hands of Archpriest Roxthar, who in the name of Styphon would surely finish the work of destruction Kalvan had begun.

"We must be across the Lydistros within five days. Organize messen-gers and escorts to ride with word to Tarr-Ceros. The bridge of boats is to be ready within three days, or I personally will decorate the battlements of Tarr-Ceros with the heads of those who have delayed it."

"At once, Grand Master," Knight Commander Aristocles said. No one hearing him could have imagined this was one friend carrying out the wishes of another. "Ho, Heron! Summon Knight Commander Cyblon to the Grand Master's tent—at once!"

When he had heard the order repeated by his messenger, Aristocles turned back to Soton, hand on his sword hilt. Soton wondered if the tales of wizardry in Aristocles' sword had any truth to them. Certainly the sword was the better part of two centuries old. By grasping it in times of trouble, Aristocles appeared to soothe himself and sharpen his wits. Also, he had never suffered a sword wound on the battlefield. A half-score of weapons had left scars, but never a sword....

"Grand Master, what about sending some of our boats up the Lydistros to strike at Kalvan's barges?"

"With the river running as it must, after this rain? They would never be able to reach Kalvan's fleet and return in time."

Aristocles wished shameful and wasting diseases upon those who had sent the rains, finishing with some choice comments on the uselessness of Styphon's Archpriests and priests in general.

Soton shook his head. "Guard your tongue, for even I cannot save you from Archpriest Roxthar."

"Roxthar—" Aristocles began, in the same tone he would have used to speak of a pile of dung on his tent floor. Then he took a deep breath. "Roxthar serves Styphon with holy zeal. Doubtless he has done all that mortal men could do even with Styphon's favor. "Yet, I could still wish the rains had not come."

"The gods give with one hand, and take away with the other," Soton replied, glad for the opportunity to change the subject from priestly politics to other less dangerous topics—like war. "The wet ground and flooding will slow pursuit.

"Also, we know the Lydistros River. Kalvan does not. It will take much luck and more boats than he is likely to have just to cross the river. While he is trying to cross, *then* we can attack his fleet."

Conversation died for a while as the messengers rode up to receive their orders. Soton's servants took the opportunity to light the lamps in the tent, sweep the latest coat of dried mud from the floor and ask the Grand Master what he wished for dinner.

"Kalvan's heart," Soton said sharply. "If you cannot produce that, whatever is ready to hand."

The servants departed; Aristocles poured the last wine from a jug into the two least dirty cups in the tent.

"Another message, I think," Soton said after the first swallow. "To the Commander of Tarr-Ceros, to prepare it in all respects for a siege."

"Holding our whole host?"

"Hardly," Soton replied. "We will send to Tarr-Ceros as many as Knight Commander Democles believes he can house and feed for a moon or two. The rest will fall back on Tarr-Lydra and Tarr-Tyros.

"Then we can pray that Kalvan will cross the Lydistros. Once his men have dug themselves into the hills around Tarr-Ceros, they will be like bears tethered in a pit. We will be the dogs, free to move where we will and strike when we think wise. Oh, the bear will take a lot to kill, but we will have him in the end."

It was an improbable vision, unless Kalvan lost his wits, but for a moment it warmed Soton more than the wine. Then he sobered:

"We must keep well ahead of Kalvan. That means lightening ourselves as much as possible. All the artillery, all the spare armor, all the horse bardings—"

"That makes Kalvan a free gift, Soton."

"But a lesser gift than the whole Order! Besides, the gold of Balph can buy blacksmiths to make new armor, saddlers to fit our horses, iron and bronze to recast the cannon. It cannot buy good men. If we save the men, nothing else matters. Nothing!"

Aristocles' eyes over the rim of his wine cup made all the answer Soton needed. He lifted his own cup and drank again.

XVI

Summer heat had come as the united host moved south toward the Lydistros River. The rain had not stopped completely, but it had diminished. So had the depth of the streams and the mud. While saddling up that morning, Kalvan had received a message from General Alkides, who had ridden ahead to the banks of the Lydistros (what Kalvan had once known as the Ohio) to meet the boats coming downriver from Kyblos.

"The high water has left no shallows and few rapids. It has also left less dry ground than one could wish. However, we may thank the gods for this, too. Prisoners say that the Zarthani Knights have withdrawn most of their river galleys and other vessels to Tarr-Ceros."

Thank the gods indeed. Counting bottoms, the Zarthani Knights had the second-largest navy here-and-now. Few of their ships could navigate beyond the mouths of the Great River, but they didn't need to. The rivers of the Sastragath, the Dellos (Tennessee) and Ellystros (Alabama) systems were their domain.

Harmakros was less grateful for what he saw as dubious favors. "His Grand Craftiness Soton may just be planning to lure us across the river. Then he can strike with us bogged down before the great fortress of Tarr-Ceros with the river at our backs."

"We'll play that one by ear when we reach the Lydistros,' Kalvan said. "Meanwhile, I won't have to answer to the Ulthori and Kyblosi for wrecked boats and drowned subjects."

"Your Majesty, with all due respect," Captain-General Harmakros said, "I suggest we decide beforehand. Right now the Sastragathi see us as a gift from the gods. We give them hope of final vengeance on their ancient foes. If we don't cross the Lydistros and besiege Tarr-Ceros, the alliance may wash away down the river with the downed trees and dead pigs."

"We shall see," Kalvan remembered replying. Now he wished he'd delayed his mounting-up to question Harmakros more closely. He should have remembered that Harmakros had commanded Sastragathi irregulars in the original Army of Observation, during the Year of the Wolf. The Captain-General knew more about handling them than his Great King, who was so damned tired he forgot to listen to advice even when he had it ready to hand.

Now sheet lightning played along the darkening sparks of light from the mountain of armor and equipment left by the fleeing Knights. There was enough here to equip an army, and that fact hadn't escaped the nomad warriors. They were swarming over the pile like ants on a heap of sugar.

Shouts of anger joined the shouts of triumph. Kalvan recognized Trygathi accents. He signaled to Colonel Kronos, his aide-de-camp. "Take two troops of the Royal Horse Guard and find out what's happening down there!"

Kronos took sixty men, leaving the rest around Kalvan. The Great King dismounted to spare his horse. If the united host didn't end its campaign with everybody walking and half of them barefoot (half of those who'd had shoes to begin with, that is), it would be Galzar's own miracle.

Harmakros and Aspasthar rode up as the shouts reached a climax, then faded. A messenger breasted the hill, flinging himself out of his saddle as he reached Kalvan.

"Your Majesty, the Sastragathi wish to claim all the Knights' gear, against your orders. They say they're under orders from Warlord Sargos, and you had promised them first choice."

"Dralm-damnit!" Kalvan growled. "First choice" was a fair offer to the unarmored, sometimes unclothed nomads. It wasn't the same as "everything," but try to tell that to a Sastragathi warrior! It was like telling a wolf to take only one bite.

Captain-General Harmakros was carefully avoiding looking at his Great King. Then he turned in the saddle, and Kalvan saw his I-told-you-so expression, quickly replaced by surprise. A moment later Kalvan knew he must be matching expressions with Harmakros.

The Warlord rode at the head of a gaggle of his guards and subchiefs. Maybe they thought they were keeping a precise formation, but Kalvan couldn't tell which was the main body and which were the stragglers—

"Great King Kalvan! Is this the way you keep your promise to the clans? Your men have laid hands on mine, to keep them from their due. A treasure lies down there! Will you have us put it to use, or have a blood-feud with the tribes and clans?"

"I might ask you the same question," Kalvan replied, more patiently than he felt. Not all of the impatience was with Sargos either. "If blood has been shed, it was without my orders or consent. And against my will. Those who shed the blood of tribesmen will be punished (*tough luck, Kronos, but you were sent to find out what the trouble was, not make it worse*) and a blood-price will be paid."

"Will blood money guard the backs of men from the Knights' swords?" someone cried in a high-pitched voice. Kalvan saw that Sargos' teenage son Larkander was riding with his father tonight.

"No," Kalvan answered, raising his voice to keep the argument from turning into a mob scene. There was too much steel and firepower to make this safe; one hothead could blow the alliance sky high.

"No," he repeated, when Kalvan saw the nomads were giving him at least half the attention a Great King deserved. "Yet not all the bare backs are tribesmen. Will not the men of the Trygath fight better against our common foe with armor and weapons from the pile down there?"

"We of the tribes have fought the Black Knights longer," someone said.

"This is well known. Yet if the Zarthani Knights are cast down from their castles and the land cleansed of Styphon's minions, who loses? If they survive to fight us again, who wins? Let us join together and fight as one band."

Kalvan rested his hand on the butt of his pistol. It was a presentation weapon from the Gunsmith's Guild, an unsuccessful effort to prove they could produce elegant weapons quickly. It was a weapon Kalvan carried only when he wasn't riding with the vanguard.

"Let us divide the loot into two piles, one for the clansmen and one for the Trygathi. Then let each chief judge those most in need and give them their pick." This would cost them more than a day's travel time, (he could almost hear Soton's chuckle), but if it would keep his so-called allies from each other's throats, it would be worth the delay.

"I will begin the first pile with this pistol of mine. Whoever carries it, Trygathi or clansmen, he will carry it with my blessing. So speaks—"

"He seeks our Warlord's life!" somebody shouted. Kalvan's hand completed the drawing of the pistol before his ears could signal his mind to stop the motion. Then the sky appeared to fall upon him, a sky consisting of armored bodies.

Two shots crashed overhead, followed by a scream, a babble of curses and war cries, and Harmakros roaring above everything, "Take the bastard alive!"

The weight lifted from Kalvan, enough to let him draw breath for cursing. There was an audible sigh of relief from his Horse Guard. He spat out mud and grass, then rose to his knees. A Sastragathi subchief was on his back, with Aspasthar kneeling on one arm and several hefty Sastragathi warriors holding other portions of the chief's anatomy—none too gently.

"What the Styphon—?"

Warlord Sargos answered. "This fool thought you sought my life. He drew a pistol. Your war leader's son seized his arm so that his shot went wide of you. It struck my son in the arm. Yet with his other hand he joined—Aspasthar—in dragging the fool from his saddle."

"There is more, Father," Larkander said. "Aspasthar shed blood too in the fight, and it mingled with mine."

"You are blood-brothers?" Both fathers seemed to speak at once, then looked at each other. Kalvan swallowed a laugh; he knew just enough about the Sastragathi to know that blood-brotherhood was a deadly serious business among them.

"It is an omen!" cried out one of the chiefs.

"This seems to be so," Larkander said. His voice was no longer high-pitched, but he was holding his arm against his side. His father's face was as white as if he'd seen a premonition of his own death.

Since nobody else seemed to have the wits to do so, it fell on Kalvan to call an Uncle Wolf to tend to the wound. The question of dividing the booty dropped from everyone's mind until both Larkander's arm and the subchief's were tightly bound.

"Question him rigorously," Sargos ordered. "It must be known, whether he was only a witling or a tool of Styphon's House."

Kalvan relaxed. If Sargos was ready to torture one of his own captains to help the alliance, the worst danger of the split was already past. *Note: Have to give Aspasthar something really impressive as a reward—consulting with his father and blood-brother first, of course.*

As the subchief was carried off, Sargos dismounted. He almost stumbled as he touched the ground. Kalvan realized that the Sastragathi Warlord had driven himself to the edge of exhaustion.

"I don't think our dignity will suffer if we sit down and share some wine." Kalvan wanted to wash the grit and grass out from between his teeth. Sargos looked ready to lie down and sleep for a week.

Well, the man is in his forties. He'd probably be just as happy if being Warlord of the Sastragathi was a headquarters job, in a headquarters equipped with cool ale and warm women.

That brought to Kalvan's mind a picture of his own warm woman. He wondered what Rylla was doing. Her last letter had promised to take no drastic action against the Harphaxi unless provoked, but to patrol the borders heavily and keep the Army of Hostigos ready to move swiftly.

Knowing Rylla, Kalvan knew far too well how "border patrols" could be turned into scouts, and they into an invasion. From five hundred miles away, however, he couldn't do much but hope and consider learning how to pray.

XVII

From the grim look on Knight Commander Aristocles' face, Soton knew he was the bearer of more bad news. The Great Master's first thought was that it was too early in the morning to hear any more.

When he had heard Aristocles out, Soton realized there was no time of the day or night fit for the hearing of such a tale. Kalvan was driving his host on as though he truly had demons at his command to put them in fear. The vanguard was already past Xenos Town, two whole days before

Soton had expected them.

"That means they will be up with us in their full strength before we reach Tryphlon."

Aristocles nodded. "Unless they can be delayed."

"By whom?"

The two men looked at each other. The both knew the answer. The rearmost four Lances would have to stand, fight, and most probably die to the last man—like the three Lances at the Battle of Chothros Heights.

"Who is senior Commander among of the rear?"

"Drakmos, of the Sixteenth Lance."

"May Kalvan's own demons flay him alive!"

Aristocles looked startled.

Soton knew that some of the agony he felt must have shown in his voice. "No, it's just that I am growing weary of sending friends to die."

"We could send another—"

"That would take time, which we do not have. His learning the land where he must stand would take more time. Besides, Drakmos would never abandon the Sixteenth." *You are doomed, old friend*, he thought. *All I can do is let you die with honor, as you have lived.*

Soton looked at Aristocles. The hard-bitten Knight Commander was a trusty right arm, a fine captain, and more often than not a wise counselor. Yet he had not been among the company of youths to whose ranks had come one day a peasant boy, small of stature but with an ambition to be a knight burning bright enough for six giants.

Some of the boys had bullied Soton in practice bouts, with wooden weapons or unarmed. Others had held back, out of pity for so small an opponent with such a large and clearly foredoomed ambition. Only Drakmos had done neither, giving Soton his best and taking Soton's best in return. Since Drakmos had been the best fighter among the youths, Soton learned more from the bouts with him than from all the others put together. It would not be too much to say that Soton's own prowess on the battlefield, which had saved his life a dozen times over, was in large measure Drakmos' gift.

And now Soton was repaying the gift of life with one of death. An honorable death, to be sure, but there was something to be said for an honorable life.

"Summon a messenger," Soton growled, to hide his urge to scream curses to Kalvan, the gods, and anyone else who had brought this about. Himself included, since it was his plan that Kalvan had turned so neatly and dropped upon his head! "Drakmos is to attack Kalvan's main body and keep on attacking until he has drawn that main body onto himself. We need not fear barbarians or light-cavalry scouts sent on ahead."

It hardly needed saying that the barbarians and scouts in advance of Kalvan's great host would cut off what little chance of retreat Drakmos and his Lances had. To balance the odds, Soton added, "We will leave a thousand of our Auxiliary light horses and all our Sastragathi irregulars."

The Sastragathi would probably all desert before Kalvan was within a day's ride, but the Auxiliaries would keep Drakmos from being stung to death by the light nomad cavalry. It was the least he could do.

"More orders," Soton snapped. "All the baggage, everything except a man's weapons and what he wears on his back, is to be left for Drakmos."

Aristocles' eyes were eloquent. Soton shrugged. "Drakmos will need what supplies we have left. For the rest of us, it is as true now as when I said it before. Styphon's gold can buy new armor, new tents, new fireseed, before the snow falls. If we lose the many more seasoned Knights, not all the gold of Balph will be able to rebuild the Order before Kalvan has crushed and cast down Styphon's House on Earth. If we do not think to the future, there will be none."

But there will be a large debt to pay, Kalvan Servant of Demons. A very large debt indeed.

XVIII

"Toss oars!"

The cry floated up from the boat on the muddy river to the hill where Kalvan stood gazing at Tarr-Ceros. The great fortress of the Order of the Zarthani Knights marched across nearly a mile of hills on the far side of the river. Some of those hills had clearly been flattened, others carved into the fortress's outworks. Kalvan counted three concentric layers of trenches and wooden palisades, each furnished with artillery positions and covered ways to let ammunition and reinforcements come up.

The stone walls only began beyond the trenches, rising like seats in a theater up the central hill to the massive keep in the middle. Two, maybe three, concentric circles of walls, each with its own moat and array of towers. Armor and guns glinted from the towers and the walls alike.

In the center the keep rose a good hundred feet above the highest tower. And were Kalvan's eyes playing tricks on him, or was the keep faced with something shiny? Marble? There were marble quarries up near the head of the Tennessee River in his own world; why not here? Certainly water transportation for the marble wouldn't have given the Knights any problem, not with their river fleet.

Marble was not the stone Kalvan would have chosen for a fortress. Under artillery fire, it would splinter and the splinters scatter like shell fragments.

But then, Tarr-Ceros had been built when the Zarthani Knights had no enemies who could bring artillery against their citadel. Until recently, neither the tribes nor the Trygathi had much to bring against Tarr-Ceros except numbers, archery, a few arquebuses and the odd wrought-iron four-pounder.

Kalvan signaled to the horse holders, who led Harmakros' mount and those of his aides down to the bank. So far the Tarr-Ceros garrison had paid their visitors less attention than cockroaches. If they changed their mind, some of the guns in the outer fortifications could certainly reach across the river.

Harmakros held his horse to a walk as he led his party up the muddy hillside, then reined in and saluted his Great King. The Captain-General's face was grimmer than ever, and far more than could be blamed on fatigue and the strain of a long campaign.

"Your Majesty, that floating barrier of spiked logs is no tale. There's no way through to the quay until the logs are removed."

"How long would that take?"

"With a few tarred barrels of fireseed and no enemy fire, an hour of any night. But they've got tarpots and what looks like bundles of arrows all laid out in the trenches right behind the quay. They could light up the engineers and pick them off like rats in a kitchen corner. Even if the barrier went, the trenches would be manned and ready for the landing party. "

"So going for the quay would be a waste, even as a feint?"

"The Knights would get a good laugh and we would get a bloody nose,' Harmakros said morosely.

He did not put into words what his tone added: *"And there is no need to send anyone up under the guns of the fortress to learn this. Once Your Majesty decides it has to be done, it becomes my duty. But if I don't have any more such duties for a while, it won't break my heart."*

"Harmakros, for at least the hundredth time—well done. If we find ourselves with a vacant Princedom, would you consider taking it?"

"Once Your Majesty doesn't need my services in the field, I won't say no. But I have a bad feeling that besieging Tar Ceros is going to take a long time. We've driven the badger into his lair."

Kalvan nodded. "The Grand Master spent several of his Lances to delay our progress so that he and most of his Knights could return to this fortress. Do we have any way of getting Soton out and taking his hide home?"

Again, tone spoke volumes, when Harmakros replied:

"Galzar Wolfhead might knock down those walls with his Mace, but nothing we have will even come close. As for a siege, unless you have figured a way to feed any army on air, forget it.

Harmakros was right. Kalvan had known as much the moment he'd laid eyes on Tarr-Ceros. It reminded him of one of the great Crusader castles in the Holy Land—but an aerial photo of a ruin didn't give the full picture. You had to see one of those stone monsters armed and garrisoned and intact, looming over you, ready to defy the worst you could do. And when that worst wasn't enough to do more than give the garrison a few sleepless weeks…what then?

There wasn't a gun in the Hostigi artillery stockpile that could both be moved here and make an impression on the walls. There wasn't enough food to keep a third of the allied host alive long enough to make the Knights tighten their belts. A simple attempt to storm the place would kill half the attackers and demoralize the rest.

Summon Soton to negotiate? That at least would waste only breath, not blood. Grand Master Soton knew the strength of his walls and the men who manned them. Probably less than half his garrison were seasoned fighters, but behind those walls children with croquet mallets could be deadly foes.

"Well, then, we can't do much at their front door," Kalvan said. "Let's wait until the scouts to the east and south return with their reports. If it's good cavalry country, maybe we can do something in his backyard."

That something was likely to be expensive in time, treasure, fireseed, horses and blood—but it had to be discussed. The rest of the allies had very little notion of what a hollow victory they had won. They only knew that they'd seen the Knights in retreat for the better part of a moon. The final battle against the four Lances of the rearguard had given them a taste for Knights' blood—they wanted more.

Kalvan remembered Napoleon's dictum about the advantages of making war against allies. Soton could wield his Knights as a single weapon, like his famous war hammer. Kalvan had to be chairman of a committee as much as a commander-in-chief.

One would think that the last battle would have made even a Sastragathi chief realize that the Knights' blood didn't come cheap. The four Lances and their support troops had numbered perhaps three to four thousand men at the outset; perhaps one hundred and fifty wounded prisoners survived. The allies lost more than eight thousand men, not counting the wounded, and that was with the advantage of artillery.

At least General Alkides had all the horse artillery ready to move. Where cavalry could go, the guns could follow. Something might be made of this—not much, but enough to keep the alliance from falling apart because the Sastragathi barbarians believed Great King of Hos-Hostigos had abandoned his allies!

Something else that might help, even more than artillery, at least right now—

"Harmakros, I forgot. Did we save any of that wine we picked up with the first batch of loot?"

"I had one of the barrels drawn off into flasks and loaded on pack mules under a trusted petty-captain.

"I reckoned we might have a use for it. Another job well done. I think we're going to call a Council of War. Just a small one, so I think one barrel should be enough to keep even Sargos happy." *At least until he finds out that he's still going to have the Knights on his borders, almost as strong as ever and out for vengeance.*

"Then there is *nothing* more we can do against those fatherless Knights?" Sargos glared at the men present in Kalvan's tent as if ready to challenge any king or captain present to personal combat.

Maybe he is. Kalvan began to think that breaking out the best wine hadn't been the best idea. Sargos had grown increasingly belligerent instead of mellow.

"Not *nothing*," Harmakros said, with the air of a man trying for the twentieth time to persuade a stubborn child to go to bed. "But we can't knock down the walls of Tarr-Ceros or besiege it long enough to do any good. What else is there is what we need to ask."

Sargos emptied the last of a jug into his cup and looked into the ruddy depths. He seemed to find wisdom or at least a better-guarded tongue there.

"Nothing that will end the Knights for all time, I suppose. But is there anything else worth doing?"

"Yes," Great King Nestros said. Nestros wore a gold circled crown set with turquoise picked up from the Knights' baggage and hastily set into place by an armorer. "Anything that will keep the Knights quiet for a year or two will be almost as good. United, with no enemies at our backs, we're their match. We know it, they know it and none of us is going to forget it soon. Let us do something to make them remember it as long as possible."

Several faces around the tent wore, "Yes, but what?" expressions. It was time for the god-sent Great King Kalvan to take a hand. The rest had finally wrangled themselves into being ready to listen.

"Now a lot of what we can do depends on how long we can keep the boats and barges in range of Tarr-Ceros—"

"Oh, demons fly away with those boats and barges!" Sargos growled. "If they won't let us destroy the Knights, what good are they?"

"If we have half a moon, we can destroy the Knights' lands," Kalvan answered. "Alkides, do you think we have that much time?"

The grizzled artillery officer sucked on his pipe and released a small cloud of smoke. "Your Majesty, with guns mounted in the right places, I suspect we can keep off anything short of all the galleys at once. That's using mostly the Trygathi bombards, which wouldn't be much good in the field anyway."

Sargos looked ready to curse the boats and barges again, but Kalvan fixed him with a sharp look. "Warlord Sargos, those watercraft are like herds or chosen warriors to the Princes of Kyblos and Ulthor. Would any of your chieftains thank you if you lost all his horses or two score of his best warriors?"

Sargos appeared to ponder the question and came up with an answer that at least kept him quiet. Kalvan signaled to Harmakros, who handed him a map of the area around Tarr-Ceros. It was a rough map, but it was a historical document—the first here-and-now map ever drawn on paper. (There was also a second copy, on the more usual, not to say durable, deerskin.)

"The Knights have left a belt of forest around their fortress, between them and the lands that raise their food and horses. They've always relied on the forest to let their light-armed troops delay an enemy while the heavies moved in.

"Now suppose we throw two forces across the river. One infantry, with light artillery support. They'll hold the forest belt, keeping the Knights *in* instead of enemies *out*. I'll wager half the Treasury of Balph it will take even Soton a while to figure out what to do about that."

"Yes, yes!" Sargos cried. Eagerness crackled in his voice. "Our archers are without peer. Given time to hide themselves, they can hold the forest—"

"Boast about your archers when they've proved themselves!" Nestros snapped. "We of the Trygath are no children with our crossbows, as you yourself—"

"Hold!" Kalvan shouted. "There will be enough Knights to go around, I am sure. To the archer or crossbowman who kills the most, I will personally give ten Hostigos gold crowns and a weapon of his choice. Alkides, can you move your four-pounders in that kind of wooded country?"

"With a little help from Galzar and a lot of help from men who aren't afraid to drag a gun—"

The two allied rulers couldn't promise their help fast enough.

"The second force will be cavalry. It isn't intended to stand and fight. It's going to burn out every farm and village, run off every head of livestock, terrorize every peasant it can reach. If the Knights come out, they will have to fight their way through their own forest belt. If they stay in Tarr-Ceros, they will have to watch their peasants, crops and herds laid waste.

"They can get some supplies from upriver, but not all. It will be a lean winter and a lean couple of years for the Knights. Soton will gladly march the Knights out in their breechcloths with clubs if all else fails, but they won't be nearly so formidable."

The picture made the others in the tent smile. Harmakros produced another jug and began to pass it around. When the jug reached Sargos, he held it high in the air. "To the best ally a man could have in this lifetime—Great King Kalvan!"

XIX

"It's beginning to appear, Vall," Paratime Commissioner Tortha Karf said, "that you're more interested in playing Colonel Verkan of the Hos-Hostigos Mounted Rifles than you are in being Chief of the Paratime Police."

"That's hitting below the belt, Tortha," Verkan said, running his fingers through his blond beard. "I know I haven't been back on Home Time Line for more than a two ten-days, but it's imperative that I establish my cover in Greffa as Verkan the trader. If I don't, one of these days some Grefftscharrer merchant is going to arrive in Hostigos Town and someone's going to ask him about the merchant prince Verkan and he's going to go 'Verkan who?' Then, not only will two years hard work be plunged down the drain, but also the Paratime Secret itself will be endangered, along with Great King Kalvan and his family. You know how those Dhergabar University Professors would like to get their hands on a 'noble savage' like Kalvan and pick him apart in one of their Mentalist labs."

Tortha nodded his head in agreement.

The Paratime Secret was the keystone of First Level civilization. The only inflexible law concerning outtime activities was that the secret of Paratemporal Transposition must be kept inviolate. Home Time Line was the ultimate parasite culture, secretly drawing off the resources and population of tens of thousands of other time-lines. A little here, a little there, but not enough to really hurt anyone. But unfortunately, maybe even tragically, that secret would be discovered on another time-line someday, just as Kalvan had brought an end to Styphon's House fireseed secret and monopoly by re-inventing gunpowder and then telling everyone about it—even his enemies! Which had made him many friends as well as the nemesis of Styphon's House.

When the Paratemporal Transposition secret—a thousand times more complex than the fireseed mystery—was broken; well, it wasn't too much to say that fate and welfare of ten billion Home Time Liners would depend upon the reflexes and ruthlessness of the Paratime Police.

"Verkan, it appears to me you've got a bad case of Outtime Identification Syndrome. As you yourself know, it happens to the best of Paratimers. But don't forget that for twelve millennia First Level civilization has depended on being able to secretly draw upon the resources of millions of alternate time-lines and we can't afford to let any one man—not even the Paratime Chief of Police!—put our way of life in jeopardy. One of these days you're going to have to make a choice between loyalty to a friend and your natural loyalty to the Home Time Line.

"If it ever comes to the point where King Kalvan or his subjects come between you and your job as Paratime Chief of Police, then I'll be the first to recommend the Paratime Commission that you be cashiered from your job." Tortha removed a cigarette from its pack and had to will his fingers to keep them from trembling as he lit up.

"Tortha, you know me better than that. You're the one who talked me into taking over as your replacement! My duty to the force comes first, before everything. Ask Dalla. Yes, I admire Kalvan; he's taken the tiny Princedom of Hostigos and turned it into a first class outfit. Without any real help from me, I might add. And, as much as I admire and like Kalvan, Rylla, Ptosphes, Harmakros, and the rest, I have no desire to go native and throw away three hundred years of longevity just to live a simpler, more honest way of life."

The wistful tone Tortha heard in Vall's voice indicated to him that on some deeper mental level Verkan might be quite willing to do just that, but Tortha couldn't see anything to be gained by picking at that particular scab. He'd just have to keep a closer eye on Verkan, try to help take some of the pressure off and then be ready to jump in whenever it appeared that the Chief's judgment was going awry.

"How is Dalla's work on the Fourth Level Europo-American Study Group going?"

Verkan laughed. "To listen to my wife talk you'd think she'd been shut up in the Innermost Circle at Balph and been forced to listen to one of Archpriest Roxthar's tirades for a year of ten-days! She's not sure what's worse, listening to the representatives from Tharmax Trading and Consolidated Outtime Foodstuffs pleas for open 'trade' lines, or the University cliques talk of the inevitability of outtime social interests conflicting with Home Time Line politics until First Level civilization embraces the benefits of post-industrial socialism, or some such garbage."

"Good, it's going just about as we expected. As long as they keep arguing semantics and ideology they'll never get down to what the Study Group is all about, a full embargo on Fourth Level, Europo-American. That will leave you and the Paratime Commission free to do what has to be done when the time comes. Although, I want to tell you that I hope it never comes. Without a Code Red situation, or all out nuclear slugfest, shutting down Europo-America may not be politically feasible—"

"What you too, Tortha? I get enough of that from Dalla."

"Well, maybe in this case, it might not hurt to listen. We get a lot of everyday products from that Sector, like the cigarettes I'm smoking."

"It would be inconvenient to relocate our sources of supply, but it could be done, Verkan answered. "I can't think of anything critical to First Level life or civilization, though."

"The Europo-America Sector has caught the public's fancy. They're behind the flat screen film craze and are the supplier of that hideous 'rock and roll' music that's been jamming the airwaves."

Verkan's eyebrows shot up. "The first time I heard that jangle of atonal sound waves, I thought I'd tuned into a cat fight."

"Verkan, just listen to yourself! You sound just like me: it must be that crazy horseshoe desk. Or the responsibility of protecting ten billion contrary timeliners who don't always know their own best interests."

Verkan shook his head. "I don't know how you kept going for so long."

"Maybe, just maybe, because I thought I was doing really important work."

"That doesn't sound like you, Tortha. Getting tired of that Fifth Level truck farm in Sicily already?"

"Actually, it's been so dull there this past year I've taken to watching Fifth Level Prole soap-operas."

Verkan shuddered in mock horror. "The only two things worse than prole soap-operas would be either attending an administrator's conference at Dhergabar University, or one of the Kalvan Study Team's argue-fests at the Royal Foundry in Hos-Hostigos."

Tortha laughed. "Actually, I wanted to talk to you about a cover story for a trip to Kalvan Prime."

"That's a wonderful idea. Kalvan and Rylla can use all the help they can get."

"Well, I'm not a military genius, or engineer—"

"I didn't mean that kind of help, Tortha. They need a good shoulder to lean on now, especially since Price Ptosphes took a mortal wound at Tenabra."

"I didn't know he was shot."

"Not that kind of wound—it's worse, he's stopped believing in himself. And that's the most terrible thing that can happen to a man like Ptosphes. There aren't a lot of people in Hostigos Kalvan can really talk with and you might be the best medicine he could get. I know how you've helped me over the years."

"Just my job, Vall." Tortha pulled a pack of Camels out of his pocket and reached for Verkan's tinderbox.

"We both know better. It wouldn't be wise to make you a Grefftscharrer merchant, too. Xiphlon's far enough away that no one in the Northern Kingdoms knows much about it, and it's in a bit of a bind. Another of those Aztec empires—the Zarthani call them the Mexicotal—that crops up on one Fourth Level, Europo-America time-line after another is trying to move their cannibalism racket into the Middle Kingdoms. Somebody's been selling them 'fireseed'—another local term for gunpowder—and last I checked they had some huge slave trains dragging these antiquated hundred and two hundred pound siege guns, old hooped iron bombards, to try and blast through the great walls. The Mexicotal are not familiar enough with gunpowder weapons to know that those stone balls will do about as much damage to the walls of Xiphlon as their ceremonial obsidian blades do on plate armor!

"Xiphlon is one of the most 'civilized' cities in the northern hemisphere. The city reminds me of Byzantium on Europo-America, Alexandria-Roman. Huge outworks and walls as thick as the Great

Wall of China and almost as tall, made of quarry stone that must have been transported by river barges for a hundred years. Very sophisticated inhabitants, they've done it all, seen it all and know it all. The city has been besieged a dozen times; they're got fresh water cisterns and provisions enough for a ten-year siege. Right now Xiphlon's biggest problem is all the trade and portage business they're losing. I wouldn't be surprised that after the Mexicotal have picked up their pieces and gone home, the High King of Xiphlon doesn't try and hire Kalvan to take his army down to their capital and teach those heart-stabbing barbarians a thing or two about gunpowder diplomacy!"

Tortha blew a series of smoke rings. "Sounds like my kind of place. I'll make a covert visit there, first, so I can familiarize myself with the city layout and find a place to set up my cover story."

"Great idea. I'll get Kirv to send in a team to help you. After you leave, they'll stay behind and establish a deep cover. Fortunately, these Middle Kingdom merchants do more traveling than a Paratime Policeman."

Tortha smiled. "This sounds like fun. Do you know how long it's been since I went undercover outtime? No, don't even try to answer."

Verkan laughed for the first time in what felt to be a year.

XX

Grand Master Soton of the Order of Zarthani Knights sat in his private audience chamber at the heart of the great fortress of Tarr-Ceros and stared at the stone walls. Too many good men dead, he thought, and four more banners to hang in the Hall of Heroes. During his term as Grand Master he had now hung a total of seven banners, representing seven decommissioned Lances; more than any Grand Master in the past two hundred years. Those seven Lances also accounted for almost a quarter of the Order's strength.

Am I destroying the Order to salve my own pride?

No, damnit! I am trying to save the Temple, and part of the Temple is the Order of Zarthani Knights —my part. Kalvan means to destroy the Temple and to do this he must destroy me and the Order. Kalvan is the enemy and must be stopped at any cost!

A gentle knocking at the plank door took his mind off Kalvan and these all too familiar thoughts. "Come in."

Knight Commander Aristocles entered the chamber. "Good news, Soton. Kalvan and his allies are leaving—at last!"

"Ahhh. Finally. They must be growing short of rations. Either that, or they have run out of farms and barns to burn."

"True. There will be little produce left to harvest this fall, but we can bring in victuals by boat. The real cost has been time—there we have cost Kalvan dearly. Just as you planned. It is already the middle of summer and by the time Kalvan's tired army marches back to his not-so-grand kingdom, it will be too late in the year to mount a successful attack on Hos-Harphax, or any of our other allies."

Soton paused to strike a flame with his tinderbox and relight his pipe. Suddenly his mood seemed to lift with the fresh smoke rising from his pipe. "Yes, there will be no war this year in Hos-Harphax—our friends there owe us much. I hope they have used this gift of time wisely."

"They have," Aristocles answered. "A messenger from Balph just arrived. Lysandros has used Kalvan's attack on us to persuade the Harphaxi Electors to crown him Great King of Hos-Harphax. Now Captain-General Phidestros will have the full might of a Great Kingdom behind his rebuilding of the Harphaxi Army."

"Good news on an auspicious day. I must go to Balph and take council with the Inner Circle. It is time to make further preparations for the *real* war against the Usurper Kalvan. I will need Styphon's Voice to help to convince Great King Cleitharses to mobilize the Ktemnoi Army for next spring. There are many things to be done and already the summer is half gone. Call my oath-brother, we have a trunk to pack. And a debt to settle with Kalvan—on a bill that is long overdue."

THE ALEXANDER
AFFAIR

JOHN F. CARR

I

1967 A.D.

Davran Thal was sitting at the console in front of the visiscreen as he tallied up the Parian marble statues and red-figure pottery he was about to send back to First Level. He looked up when he heard the whoosh of a door opening into the transposition depot chamber buried deep underneath the factory floor.

Coming out of the portal was his friend and fellow Paratimer, Halthar Varn. "Hello Varn, I expected you back two ten-days ago?"

Halthar shook his head. "I used up some more of my leave time. Bored and tired is what I am. I not only hate this boring time-line, but the people who sent us here!"

They both had five-year outtime contracts with Vendrax Luxury Imports to locate and ship luxury goods from the Fourth Level Alexandrian-Roman, Seleuco-Macedonian Subsector where the civilization was frozen at the pre-industrial stage and the most recent innovation was the horse collar. A stage where it had remained static for the past two thousand years. Progress was as foreign to this subsector as good hygiene. In truth, one became accustomed to the smell of unwashed humanity, but never to the sameness of each day and the dreary stone and mud-block buildings of Alexandria.

In this subsector Alexander the Great had lived long enough to conquer most of the known world. After he died without issue, Seleucia I Nicator became regent of Alexander's empire and eventually consolidated his power by assassination and military domination. Davran doubted old Seleucia Nicator would have found many changes in this time-line, other than its size, were he to be brought back to life. All Davran knew was that there hadn't been anything new or different since he'd arrived some three and a half years ago. Nor would there be when he left in another year and a half—if he could last that long.

"Believe it or not, I've come up with something to break the monotony of this hellhole," Davran declared.

"What?" Halthar asked, frowning. "You're not using Black Henbane again, are you? The last time you used that drug you went into convulsions. Even the priestesses of Apollo have to be careful when using it for their oracles."

Davran dismissed his friend's concerns with a wave of his hand. "I was experimenting with different dosages and additives. I believe I added too much nightshade. But, I don't take Henbane anymore—too dangerous. This is something new."

Halthar gave him the same kind of look his crèche mother used to give him when he returned disheveled and late at night from one of his outings in Old Town Dhergabar.

"No, this is completely different. I've been going to the *taverna*, the Bronze Bulls. I've set up microdots for recording on all the tables so I can overhear conversations."

"Sounds boring to me," Halthar responded.

"Maybe, but not always. But it's not gossip or scandals I'm looking for. I'm picking up background information which I can use later in my new game."

"Game? What are you taking about...? These locals are dangerous. Their man-god emperor has all the powers of a total despot. Insult or inflame the wrong person and the result is death. Remember, they still use scaphism, or the boats."

Davran remembered seeing such an execution: the prisoner was wrapped in rawhide and put between two narrow rowing boats, with holes for his face and limbs. Then he was forced to drink milk and honey until it ran out of his orifices. This attracted swarms of flies and other insects which would feast and lay eggs on the culprit's exposed parts. It often took days for the miscreant to die, all the while suffering horribly.

"No, I'm not stupid. I have no intention of ending up in the lion's pit, or suffering any of the other terrible punishments for capital offenders this dead-end time-line offers. This is just some light-hearted fun, and it's profitable!"

Halthar's ears perked up.

Davran smiled. "They pay up with gold and silver coins to win my favor. I do a little fortune telling, as well. I've been able to get a nice big apartment and buy two more slave girls."

Halthar frowned. "You and your handmaidens.... You know that the Paratime Code forbids slavery. The penalties are severe: you could be stuck on Home Time Line for the rest of your life; that is, if you don't get sent to Bureau of Psychological Rehabilitation for a mind wipe and reconditioning."

Davran laughed. "When was the last time you saw a Paracop at this outpost?"

"Well, never—but there's always a first time."

"That's your problem, Halthar. You never want to take any risks. You live in a tiny sublet that even a prole would disdain. Work with me and I'll see that you profit, too."

That night at the Bronze Bulls tavern, Davran ran his psychic act on a fat merchant and an older woman dressed in colorful silks with gold trim. He told the merchant that his wine caravan headed to Dalmatia would be most profitable, but since the bandit problem was growing he should double the amount of guards. The merchant was thankful and dropped a handful of silver coins before departing. The woman was worried about a faithless lover, and Davran told her that her paramour would never change. It was time for her to cut her younger lover loose. She wasn't as pleased as the merchant and only dropped a few coppers.

"Marks don't always want the truth," Halthar observed.

Davran smiled. "I'm always truthful. Once they realize my prediction was right, they come back for more—and their return visits are far more profitable."

"Yes, but this is a slow way to get rich. What you ought to do is present yourself as a demigod or king, like Alexander."

"That could be dangerous…. But you might be on to something."

II

Davran Thal had to wait three ten-days before he could make an unscheduled trip to Home Time Line to visit a face place for a cosmetic overhaul.

"What if a supervisor makes a surprise inspection?" Halthar had asked.

"When was the last time that happened, two years ago? Don't worry about it; if one does show up, you can tell them I had a medical emergency."

"What kind?"

"Tell him I fell and broke my nose and cheek bones. I needed cosmetic surgery."

Halthar nodded. "I guess that'll do."

After bandaging his face, Davran took the stairs down to the basement, where he used the thumblock to open the collapsed-nickel plated door to the conveyer terminal. Inside, he was met by the two company guards. They ran him through a full-body scanner to make sure he wasn't transporting any of the rare ceramic vases and dishes that were this time-line's only profitable export. After a quick peek, they didn't pay any attention to the box of gold and silver coins he was carrying. Their metal content was worth no more than lead, but they had a special appeal to coin collectors, especially those who specialized in Europo-American sub-sector coins.

He usually earned a few thousand units for those coins he brought back to Dhergabar, since he was careful to choose only select mint specimens.

Davran knew the right places to visit; proof that his childhood visits to Old Dhergabar had not been wasted. Unlike the rest of Dhergabar City, which was comprised of thousand-story towers and spires that reached up to the clouds, Old Town was a place of ground-hugging buildings, all of them millennia old, and the streets that squeezed between them. Many of the buildings housed drug bars, taverns, inns, stim-palaces and under-ground grottos where anything went, limited only by the customers' per-verse imagination and the number of Paratime Exchange units they could raise. Ground cars from every time-line imaginable crowed the streets. Some were sleek as greyhounds, others old wrecks. He recognized a red 1955 Chevrolet Nomad from when he was working on Europo-American.

His first visit was to Rare Outtime Artifacts and Unusual Oddities where the owner purchased most of his mint coins. "Unlike most of these clowns, you know what a mint coin is," Harlon Zald noted. "Unfortunately, for you—and thanks to you—I'm overstocked on Seleuco-Macedonian coins. So don't bring anymore until you get posted to a new subsector. Now, if you could bring me in some of those coffin masks...."

Davran shook his head. "Sorry, Harlon, but they take death far too seriously on that subsector. The penalties for grave robbing are horrific!"

He left the store and looked for The Body Shop. It was no longer in its former emporium, now an empty building housing some empty-eyed stim-glass addicts and a few filthy prole runaways.

His next stop was a nearby bar which featured the latest Fourth Level Europo-American craze, some mop-topped musicians caterwauling away on electric instruments and a drum. He approached the bartender, asking for a highball while palming him a twenty-unit note.

"What happened to The Body Shop?" he asked loudly, trying to overpower the machine-like noises screeching from the bandstand.

"A Metro squad busted them two years ago. You must've been outtime?"

Davran nodded. "Do you know where they've relocated?"

He shrugged. "Haven't heard a word."

As a serious gambler, there were several places he went during his "off-work" visits to Dhergabar. He was well known at the Corkscrew, where he'd dropped a small fortune. If anyone knew where The Body Shop had gone, Jorand Rarth would know. He left the bar and made his way to the Corkscrew.

He was greeted at the front door by a familiar big man with a red scarf, sporting white skulls and crossbones, covering his head.

"I'd like to speak with Jorand Rarth," he said.

The man shook his head. "Jorand is outtime. And we don't know when—or if—he's coming back.

"Maybe, you can help me?" Davran asked.

"Are you in need of a little boost?" the big man asked.

As a good customer, Davran could call on an advance to tide him over. However, the payback rates were astronomical and he'd—so far—avoided that potential tar-pit. He shook his head. "No, Citizen, I'm looking for The Body Shop. It must have relocated and I thought if anyone in Old Town would know where, it would be Jorand."

"It's moved down on Azthal Street, but they don't call it The Body Shop anymore. Ask around back for the Transformer. Tell them Varlan sent you."

He thanked the crime boss, promising to return for some games of chance when his business was finished.

It took some digging but he found the Transformer down a lower level and beneath a bakery. The entrance looked derelict until you passed through the portal. The room was furnished in Second-Level Interworld Modern and probably cost more than he'd earned in the last fifty years. The receptionist was a young hairless woman with fine features; her head was egg-shaped and her eyes big and bright. She was alien-like in appearance.

She looked at him closely, squinting. "Who are you?"

"I'm Davran Thal. Varlan sent me."

"How can I best direct you," she asked.

"I need some cosmetic work done," he replied.

"How extensive?"

He showed her the Tri-D slab of Alexander the Great he'd downloaded from the Dhergabar Outtime Library. "I want to look like this."

"That'll require extensive reconstruction," she said. "It'll be expensive."

He smiled. "I've got means." In preparation he'd just taken out a loan for a new aircar, and had accumulated over fifty thousand units worth of jewelry and coins using his psychic con.

She smiled. "Let me call the Medico and tell him you're here."

III

Davran was under medical care for two ten-days before he was able to return to his time-line on the Seleuco-Macedonian Subsector, Alexander Belt, hitching a ride on a supply conveyer. During his return trip, Davran hypno-meched all the known data on Alexander the Great. When he arrived at the terminal, his friend Halthar didn't recognize him.

"Who are you?" he asked, as Davran exited the conveyer.

"It's me, Davran!" he exclaimed.

"Oh! You did it! I thought your face looked familiar."

"Yeah, it's on every drachma on this time-line."

Halthar looked embarrassed. "I'm sorry I ever came up with this idea. I never thought you'd go through with it."

Davran smiled. "This is my million-unit face. It's going to make both of us rich beyond our wildest dreams."

"If it doesn't get us killed," Halthar muttered.

They left the Vendrax collection depot to go outside to the main street, which was a riot of color and bustling activity: horse and mule-drawn carts, a few camels, as well as men in multi-colored tunics and the occasional barbarian or nomad wearing trousers and shirts. In the distance they could see Alexander's Pillar and the Great Lighthouse.

Suddenly a voice split the air: "By Jupiter and Mars, it's Alexander!"

"Back from the dead!" someone else shouted.

"It's the God Alexander come to help us!"

A tall man grabbed his tunic and tore it. "God, you must help me!" the man demanded.

Davran pushed him aside and tried to turn around.

"It's Alexander!" a dozen voices cried out.

A man with no hair and terrible sores covering his face cried out: "Please help me? I beseech you, Alexander. Remove this terrible curse!"

More people came running. Halthar forced his way forward through the growing crowd, with Davran in his wake.

They reached the factory door and pounded on it. No time to use their keys! Now, more people were shouting and screaming. Hands were grabbing at them. Suddenly, the door jerked open and they slipped inside. They slammed the door closed catching one of the worker's hands, slicing off his fingers.

Outside, people were banging on the door with fists and what sounded like clubs. "We've got to get out of here!" Davran cried.

Halthar said, "I know, but where can we go?"

The workers were beginning to panic.

Davran shook his head. "I don't know.... I didn't expect to be recognized so quickly!"

Suddenly, the banging against the door grew louder.

"They're using battering rams," one of the factory workers cried out.

Guards rushed into the entryway along with some of the local workers. "What's going on?" the chief guard asked.

"Another riot," someone said.

"But why here?" another guard shouted.

The chief guard pointed at Davran. "Who's that?"

"Hey, he looks like the guy on the drachmas."

The chief guard nodded. "Alexander, right?"

Davran nodded.

"What did you think you were doing?"

"I didn't expect all this, Monitor Salar," Davran cried.

IV

"We've got a riot downtown," the Company Supervisor said, as he put down the handset. He pointed to his chief trouble-shooter, Garlen Darl, and said, "Find out why?"

"Where?"

"Near the pottery warehouse."

Garlen Darl went downstairs and took out an antigravity lifter from the shed at the top of the building. The lifter was gold-plated and designed to look similar to the local's chariots in case they were spotted. It wasn't an ideal solution, but better than the alternative of flying over the city in an unidentified vehicle. Both would attract attention, but the golden chariot would fit into local legends about their gods.

It was mid-day and as he glided over the city of Alexandria he was drawing more attention than he'd hoped for. Citizens down below on the streets were motioning upward and shouting things he was unable to hear. He supposed his flight across the city would soon be seen as some sort of omen.

It was against the Paratime Code to use advanced technology devices openly on Fourth Level time-lines, but this was an emergency; he'd worry about the ramifications later. He was sure that losing Paratime lives to a citywide riot outweighed the transgression he was committing. The superstitious locals would view it as some sort of magic chariot, or something along those lines.

Surprisingly, the city was quiet until he approached the quadrant surrounding the warehouse. There the riot was in full swing, the locals were not only attacking the warehouse but the nearby buildings and merchant stalls. A few structures were already on fire and dense black smoke was beginning to rise, like black fingers poking up toward the clouds.

Some of the figures had taken large timbers and used them as battering rams to force open the warehouse door. Now they were smashing the inside walls. *What are they looking for?* He shook his head. *Damn Paratime Police regs*, he cursed. If they'd allowed them to use collapsed nickel on the doors, they would have withstood anything this time-line had to offer, including a brace of elephants.

The front of the warehouse was burning and dark smoke was billowing upward. This was turning into a catastrophe! They had ten company operatives in the building along with over a hundred local artisans. To say nothing of hundreds of valuable pots and statuary. And somehow it was all going to be Vendrax's fault.

Part of the crowd had noted his arrival and were pointing upward, shouting and crying out. He couldn't tell if they were curses or hosannas. He quickly thought of using sleep gas to quiet the crowd, but the sheer number of gathering citizens made that impractical. *I'd have to gas half the city!*

As he neared the warehouse Garlen realized that it was every man for himself. The crowd was tearing the whole place apart, some were making off with pottery and a few were even smashing statues. Others were running from the growing flames. It was a complete cock-up and he had no clue as to why.

Furthermore, since the Paratimers and factory workers were dressed like locals in robes and tunics, he had no way of picking them out of the crowd. The lower he flew the more the crowd roared; now most of them were pointing or shaking fists at his lifter. A few even tossed pots and what looked like spears his way!

Others were crying out: "Another god has arrived on a golden chariot!"

It was time to leave and come back more anonymously.

"What in Great Blaxthakka's Beard is going on?" his Supervisor demanded. "And where are our people?"

Garlen shrugged. "From the air, it looked like half the city was looting our warehouse. I couldn't get low enough to find out why. I'm going to have to go in on foot."

"Put on a better tunic, one with gold-trim, like something the lower-nobility might wear. Use a litter; they're faster," his Supervisor advised. "And take a big purse of drachmas—for bribes, in case you need them. Silver, not gold; you don't want to attract too much attention. Things are bad enough as it is."

"Yes, sir."

"Just how ugly is it?"

Garlen shook his head. "Real bad, boss. It looks like a total loss of inventory! The rioters were taking anything and everything that wasn't nailed or bolted down."

"How about the warehouse?"

"That, too. What wasn't on fire, the crowd was smashing to pieces."

The Supervisor cradled his head. "Oh, no... I wonder what set them off. Damn, I took this post because it supposed to be low-key. We'd better come up with a good answer for why the locals looted our warehouse, or the head office is going to be all over us."

Or the Paratime Police, Garlen surmised, but kept that thought to himself.

"What about our other buildings?" he asked.

"Oh! I hadn't thought of that," Garlen replied. "I'll talk to security and have them evacuated and see what they can do to secure the premises without violating the bloody Code."

"Good thinking. We need to get ahead of this disaster before it takes us all down with it!"

A journey that had taken fifteen minutes by air took over two hours by hand-drawn labor. Plus, Garlen always felt like a fool being carried anywhere in one of these litters. It took one man to clear the way and four bearers to keep the litter balanced and moving at any kind of speed. The local upper classes took them for granted, but he thought they'd do better using their own feet or riding horses if they were in a hurry.

There was still a small crowd hanging around the demolished ware-house, but no one seemed to know what the riot had been about. There was some talk about someone seeing the God Alexander, but he took that for more local hooey. He figured he'd learn more at one of the local taverns. He did know, after a quick tour of the abandoned property, that the warehouse was a total loss.

No one back at headquarters was going to be happy about that.

The nearest tavern was called the Great Heron. Inside the tavern was filled to overflowing, but his litter handler, a big man with rough hands, forced his way inside and cleared a nearby table. Garlen gave him a dirty look and offered to buy drinks for the men he'd just dispossessed. This made him instantly popular and he asked a man in a smoke blackened tunic: "What in Jupiter's name happened out there?"

With a fresh drink in his hand, the man was eager to talk. "Your Lordship, I have a clothes stall down the street from the foreign-owned pottery factory. A few hours after dawn, I heard a loud commotion down the street from my stall. People were shouting 'the God Alexander has come' and praising the gods for his deliverance." He shushed and looked around warily. "Not everyone is happy with the current Seleucus."

Garlen nodded in return. From what he had learned of the current ruler, Seleucus XXI Soter, was an in-bred moron with a taste for rubies and young girls from noble families—and not necessarily in that order. To finance his jewel collection, he periodically raised taxes and generally made the local citizens lives miserable. Having seen the ruler's bow-legged and hirsute sister/wife, he understood why he looked elsewhere for his evening entertainment. However, everyone would have been happier if he'd confined his wandering eye to the merchant or scribe classes, but no, he wanted only the best. Fortunately for the Pharaoh, the locals were frozen in a permanent state of cultural paralysis; otherwise, he would have lost his crown and head years ago.

The shopkeeper continued, "Some voices cried out the name Alexander, as if he had returned to life! Blasphemy! Blasphemy, I say."

Garlen nodded in response. On most time-lines, it was safest to be neutral on religious issues. Other patrons were beginning to listen in. He quickly ordered a round of drinks for the entire tavern, refocusing their attention as well as gaining their favor.

One of the other men at the merchant's small table looked around warily, then added, "But, my friend, you did not see him!"

"That is true," the shopkeeper replied.

Garlen noticed the soot marks on the man's face and hands. He asked, "Did you?"

He nodded up and down, an almost universal human gesture.

"Who did you see?"

Even the shopkeeper was listening intently.

"It was Alexander himself returned to life," the soot-faced man said. Who then paused to spit on his hands, then rub them together. "By Osiris and Isis, I swear this!"

The merchant paled. "Is this true, Amosis?"

He nodded again.

"What exactly did you see?" Garlen asked.

Amosis continued, "I was leaving my shop when I saw the reincarnated Alexander, walking along with one of the foreigners—a Persian I believe—from the pottery factory. I heard several voices call out: "Alexander the God has returned!" Then, I saw the two men turn and run back to the factory, followed by the crowd."

Aha! Galen thought to himself. *The plot thickens.* He wondered what strange plan had been cooked up by indolent fellow Paratimers in amongst the pots and statuary.

"It was as if one of the marble statues of Alexander had come to life!"

Everyone in the tavern was listening to Amosis' story now. They all waited breathlessly for him to continue.

"People in the street stared pushing and shouting so they could see, then rioting broke out."

"He speaks the truth!" someone called out. "I saw the riot with these two eyes."

"Everyone," continued Amosis, ignoring the interruption, "wanted to view the reincarnated Alexander. Me, too. Then he disappeared inside the factory and rumors of his presence spread like a runaway fire causing the multitude to grow, overflowing the street. Before long, the crowd turned violent—too many idlers, vagabonds and master-less men—and began to pound on the doors. I left, in fear of my own stall, when some of the more fervent started lighting fires and using timber rams upon the door.

"The entire block was soon engulfed in flames and I lost everything I own. I curse Alexander and the spell that brought him back to life!"

A patron grabbed Amosis and hit him in the face, screeching, "How dare you speak such blasphemy!"

Another man pulled a knife from his belt and stabbed Amosis in the back. Blood was squirting from the cut and he began to scream. All the patrons were up on their feet, except for a few too deep in their cups to rise. Fists and feet began to fly. The bartender and two bouncers came out from the bar and began to lay into the crowd with lead-weighted saps.

Garlen jumped into the fray, knocking down the knife wielder and two others with First Level hand-to-hand fighting and a quick kick. When the man with the knife started to get up, he kicked him hard in the throat and the man grabbed his neck choking and sputtering.

It took him a minute or two to fight his way out of the tavern, which was now drawing a crowd from the street. From past experience, Garlen knew an inflamed bar fight could quickly turn into a city-wide fracas, especially a city on edge like Alexandria. He pushed past the newcomers and made his way to the street.

His litter handler grabbed him by the shoulder, saying, "Let us leave, Your Lordship, before we get caught up in this madness!"

V

Garlen Darl finished up, "So, boss, it looks like someone from the pottery facility screwed up—big time! All I know for sure is half the city is rioting and the other half is waiting for it to spread. The Pharaoh's ordered his guards to clear the streets, and word is he's called for reinforcements. It'll be a city-wide bloodbath before it's over."

His supervisor groaned. "And you know whose fault it's going to be back at the home office?"

"Sure, who else—you? Not the numbskulls that caused this catastrophe!"

"Exactly. Varthan Nar managed to locate the faux Alexander. He's being held at the Great Amphitheater."

"Is there any way we can extract our man?"

The supervisor shook his head. "He's heavily guarded, I understand. Varthan is in tight with some of the Palace officials."

Garlen nodded. A few bribes to the right people could do wonders for one's status on most Fourth Level time-lines. It always helped an outtime operation to have someone affiliated with the local nabobs. And Varthan Nar was damn good at his job.

"The word around the Palace is that the Pharaoh is worried sick about the sudden appearance of this Alexander," Varthan continued. "He's not sure whether to welcome him or execute him. I believe he's afraid that if Alexander is a god he'll be punished; considering the job the Pharaoh's been doing here—I don't blame him. Even the priests are divided; some believe he's a real deity, others believe Alexander the Great has been reincarnated. A few radical priests are whipping the locals in a frenzy to have him released!"

Garlen shook his head wearily. This just kept getting worse.

"I'm going to have to call in the Paratime Police," his supervisor said angrily."

"You're right, but that's not going to go over well in Dhergabar."

His boss nodded. This fracas would probably cost him his job; Vendrax had no patience with supervisors who called in the Paratime Police to resolve company problems; too many Paratime Police complaints could cost them their outtime license. At best, it could cost them thousands of P. E. units in fines.

"I'll send Varthan to deal with the Paracops, but I don't know what the subsector commander will want to do."

Garlen shrugged. It could be a while before they heard back from the local Paracop inspector, especially at an outpost for a subsector this minor. He'd probably have to send word back to Fifth Level Police Terminal for reinforcements—maybe an Army Strike Team. This could get ugly. Shpeegar help them if they got Paratime Police Chief Verkan Vall involved....

Three hours later Garlen got another call from his boss. He quickly made his way through the boxes and cartons of goods that covered most of bottom floor of the facility. Inside, his supervisor's office, he asked, "Any word from Varthan Thal?"

"No, we heard from one of the factory supervisors. He's on his way in."

A few minutes later, a slightly overweight Paratimer wearing a smoke-blackened tunic came wheezing into the office. He had a black eye and an ugly bruise on his forehead.

"Sorry, boss. I got here as fast as I could," he wheezed.

Garlen identified him as under-supervisor Kaltar Lar.

"What happened?"

"Phew," Kaltar puffed. "I'm still...out of breath." He bent over and put his hands on his knees. When he got back up, he said, "I got knocked out trying to escape from the factory"—puff puff—"It may have saved my life, since I was thrown into an alleyway when it was set on fire. Puff puff—I had a hard time getting here...."

"What do you know about the false Alexander?" the supervisor asked.

Kaltar paused to draw in a deep breath. "I was there when Davran came back inside the factory with his friend, Halthar Varn." Puff puff—He was the spitting image of Alexander the Great! I heard he'd gone back to Home Time Line after a bad fall that injured his face—"

"Probably a ruse to get him to First Level," Garlen interrupted.

Kaltar nodded. "Probably. He and Halthar Varn were most likely in on it together; they're both thick as thieves." He paused to catch his breath. "Halthar's been running some sort of mind-reading scan with the locals—"

"Why wasn't I informed of this?" the supervisor demanded.

Kaltar reddened, then shrugged his shoulders. "It was just a way to make a few units and pass the time. Harmless, we all thought."

"Idiots," the supervisor mumbled under his breath.

Garlen sympathized with the factory workers, although he would have never admitted it out loud. This kind of outtime work—supervising local working class types and artisans in repetitive labor—was deadly boring and didn't pay much, either. It could have been done better by proles, but the Paracops didn't trust the proles and certainly didn't allow them access to the transtemporal conveyers—and for good reason. There'd been more than one prole uprising in First Level history. And no Paratime chief in his right mind wanted to be the man in charge when another revolt broke out.

"Anyway, sir, the two of them must have been up to something. But it didn't get very far...."

"They were playing with incinomite and didn't know it," the supervisor said. "This is why we have Paratime regulations."

Kaltar shrugged again. "Don't look at me like that, it wasn't my idea!"

"We know the locals captured the false Alexander, but what happened to his accomplice?"

Kaltar winced. "I saw Halthar's body inside the factory. It looked like someone had stabbed him repeatedly. Some of these outtimers are pretty fanatical about their religion!"

"And foreigners, like us, are always an easy target," Garlen added.

When Sector Regional Subchief Dalnar Dall arrived, they went over the story one more time. Subchief Dalnar was an older man, probably in his late fourth or early fifth century, who looked as if he'd rather be any place else but in the middle of this cock-up. His face turned into one big frown as he announced: "I have an entire Army Strike Team waiting to pacify the city. Now, where are they holding the guilty party?"

"From what little information we've been able to collect," the supervisor said, "we believe Davran Thal is inside the Amphitheater of Alexander."

"Has anyone tried to negotiate his release?" Dalnar asked.

Varthan Nar spoke up: "Yes, I talked with several palace officials. Unfortunately, the Pharaoh himself is involved. He's convinced himself that Alexander is real and was sent by the gods to replace him as ruler of the Ptolemaic Empire."

Subchief Dalnar shook his head in wonderment. "Why?"

Varthan sighed. "First, the Pharaoh is an overbred idiot. On top of that he's paranoid—probably with good reason. He's just smart enough to know that he's in way over his head as ruler of the Empire. He doesn't trust any of his advisors. Anyone who becomes popular with his subjects, he has executed in a most barbaric and painful manner. As a result, no one wants to make a move without his direct participation or upon his direct order. To add to this quagmire, he takes a long time to make even a minor decision. If this were any other subsector, the Pharaoh's own subjects or outsiders would have had him replaced long ago. However, this particular subsector is in an advanced state of stasis, best characterized as institutional paralysis.

"So, the injection of a new element—in this case the pseudo-Alexander—has everyone involved at the palace in crisis mode. No one is willing to make a move without a direct order from Seleucus the Twenty-first."

Another Paracop came rushing into the room. "Sir, we have a new problem."

Subchief Dalnar sighed. "What now?"

"The locals are attacking the Amphitheater and attempting to free the pseudo-Alexander. What are your orders, sir?"

"Let's take a look."

A technician, wearing a green tunic, sitting at the back of the room flicked on the wallscreen and scanned through several sites until he came upon one which displayed a close-up of the Amphitheater, as viewed from the overhead sky-eye. The large gates had already been knocked awry and the screen showed thousands of ant-sized rioters in and around the large building. Many of the rioters were carrying weapons and torches. Fires were burning out of control at several contiguous sites.

"Where are the guards and soldiers?" the Supervisor asked.

Varthan said, "It looks like they've pulled out. Maybe a palace coup?"

"Look!" someone else cried out. "Isn't that our Alexander?" He pointed to a spot just outside the amphitheater.

Garlen looked closer, as the tech blew up the image. There it was: an image of a tiny man being carried on a silver litter by six or so black litter bearers. He was surrounded by what appeared to be priests.

"Can you magnify that area any better?" asked Subchief Dalnar.

The tech shook his head. "We're at maximum magnification, sir."

They disappeared a few minutes later as the litter went into the palace.

"Where are they going?" the Subchief asked.

VI

Davran Thal rocked back and forth in his litter as his bearers made their way through the endless maze of corridors inside the Seleucus palace. Following behind was the Pontifex Maximus, wearing his ram horns, with a dozen fellow underpriests of Jupiter Ammon. After several days of confinement in the amphitheater, he was unsure if he was being freed or about to be sacrificed by the djedi. No one had told him anything; he might as well have been a statue instead of the living god.

What a stupid idea to come here as Alexander, Davran concluded. *I only wanted to have some fun, not create a revolution!* The entire city of Alexandria was involved now and he hoped that his fellow Paratimers could come up with some sort of rescue—even if it meant an eventual mind-scrub at the hands of BurPsyHygiene. He didn't know why the priests had taken him and what they would do with him; he suspected the worst.

Deep in the palace interior, they came to a halt before stairs leading to a large presence chamber. Inside Davran was allowed to step out of the litter and refresh himself with a flask of wine. The room itself was a large chamber with statues of the gods in the alcoves. Terracotta oil lamps mounted in sconces set in stone walls lit the chamber with shadowy, flickering light. One entire wall was covered by a painting showing the God Alexander attended by Anubis and other Egyptian Gods and, towering above all others, the Greek god Zeus.

Two priests led him up onto a dais where he was seated on a gilded Egyptian throne chair.

The Pontifex Maximus came before him, bowed deeply and intoned: "We apologize, Great Alexander, for the confusion attending your Return. Sadly, it was not prophesized and we Your Servants were not prepared."

He wisely nodded in return, not sure of what his expected response might be.

Four tall Nubian guards, with gold-platted halberds and dressed only in white loin cloths, came forth from outside the chamber. Sandwiched between them was the current Pharaoh, or at least, someone who looked like his statues, since Davran had never been in his presence. There was blood dripping from the ruler's mouth onto his white and gold robes and one eye was blackened.

"Why have you laid hands upon your ruler?" the Pharaoh demanded, his voice high-pitched and slurred.

The high priest took something out of his red robes that looked like a riding crop and struck the Pharaoh in the mouth. "Quiet, fool. You are in the presence of the Reincarnated Alexander!"

The ruler turned his dark eyes upon Davran and they suddenly widened. He started blubbering and sobbing.

"Yes," the Pontifex said. "Now you are the presence of *true* royalty. Many in this great city have prayed to the gods for Alexander's return; it appears their pleas have been answered."

Everyone turned toward Alexander waiting for him to speak. Deepening his voice, Davran spoke up, "For too long I have been aware of how badly my descendants have ruled my city. Yet of the many fools and charlatans ruling in my name, you, Seleucia XXI Nicator, have been the worst. I appealed to Jupiter, God of Gods, and he agreed that it was time for me to return to the land of the living. I am here to render judgement upon you!"

All the priests went to their knees and bowed their heads.

"Have this odious fraud taken before my people and have his head removed from his body," he ordered, not sure if his words would be followed.

A strangled scream came out of the Pharaoh's lips

The Pontifex Maximus rose up and struck him in the mouth again with his crop. "Your order shall be obeyed, Oh Great One, Lord of Lords and King of Kings."

Almost immediately the Pharaoh was dragged from the room, writhing and screeching, with the high priest and his attendants following closely behind. The two priests left behind brought Davran a goblet of wine as well as fresh fruit, dates and honey cakes on plates of gold. *This is more like it*, he decided.

The rioting in the amphitheater had now spread throughout Alexandria. Many of the buildings in the foreign-owned section of town were being looted and then torched. The fires were spreading and the supervisor was getting worried; they could hear the sounds of a growing crowd outside. Wringing his hands, the supervisor turned to Subchief Dalnar Dall. "What can you do to stop this? I, I mean, we can't afford to lose our headquarters."

The Subchief shook his head in disgust. "Civilians," he spat. "Go down below to the conveyer-head depot. You'll be safe there."

The supervisor nodded and made his way to the depot door at a fast trot. Most of his employees followed just as quickly.

Garlen Darl stayed behind with the Inspector and two of his Paratime Police officers.

"Why aren't you running after them?" Subchief Dalnar asked.

"If the rioters break-in, I'll leave. Otherwise, I want to keep an eye on the situation. There should be someone here representing Vendrax's interests."

"Do what you have to, but don't get into my way," Dalnar threatened. "I'm going to use this building as my staging area."

"For what?" Garlen asked.

"For the attack, of course. We're going to have to break into the palace and rescue that fool masquerading as Alexander."

"Why?"

The Subchief looked appalled. "This Davran Thal has violated numerous sections of the Paratime Code. He needs to be removed before he says something that will tip the locals off to the Paratime Secret."

Garlen shook his head. "This isn't Second Level Interworld Empire or Fourth Level Europo-American. Even if the local authorities did torture Davran and he blurted it out, the locals would never put it together. At best, they would believe his words were the babbling of a moron or lunatic. At worst, something to do with their cursed gods. These are superstitious and uneducated natives, not sophisticated city dwellers."

"That's a chance we cannot take," replied the Subchief. He took the hand-phone from his belt and got in touch with the orbiting Strike Team.

"Red Alert. The miscreant, in disguise as Alexander of Macedon, has been taken by the locals into the main palace. Break into the palace, locate the false Alexander and take him into custody."

May the fates save us from well-meaning fools, Garlen thought. This will really stir up a hornet's nest back on Home Time Line.

VII

Paratime Police Chief Verkan Vall was seated at his desk going over the Outtime Duty Rosters on his screen, when Inspector Ranthar Jard entered holding a folder with a red flag sticking out.

"What's up, Jard?" he asked.

"We've got a big dust-up on Alexandria-Roman, boss. It's what they call a snafu on Europo-American."

Verkan leaned back in his seat and took out one of his ivory Zarthani pipes, sculpted into a likeness of Galzar, their war god. He used an out-time Zippo lighter to fire it up. "I'm familiar with the term. Give me a quick summary."

"The problem is on Fourth Level Alexandrian-Roman, Seleuco-Macedonian Subsector."

Verkan nodded. "I'm familiar with it; a dismal and unchanging hellhole, one of the worst postings on Fourth Level. Another plague or rebellion?"

"No, this one's more personal. It appears that one of Vendrax Import employees got a little too ambitions. First, he free-lanced as a prophet, or seer, in a couple of the local bars and taverns. When the scam wasn't profitable enough, he decided to return to First Level and get a face sculpt, as Alexander the Great."

"Ouch!" Verkan replied.

"Yeah, it got ugly in a hurry. The locals saw him as either a deity or the reincarnated Alexander, who had returned to solve all their problems. At first, it was localized in Alexandria, some riots and buildings set on fire. Now word is spreading throughout the Polemic Empire that Alexander the Great has returned and people are inflamed. All of Macedonia is up in arms; they want Alexander returned to his rightful home. Some of the bigger towns are rebelling and the Caucasus' nomads are rising up."

"How did it get out of hand so quickly?"

"You can blame that on Subchief Dalnar Dall."

Verkan cringed. "That old time-waster. I thought he'd retired years ago. Oh yeah, didn't former Chief Tortha exile him to Alexandrian-Roman to keep him from causing any more trouble?"

"Yup," Ranthar replied. "That was like putting out a fire without bothering to smother all the hot spots. The old fool decided the best course was to liberate Alexander from the local priests and return him to Dhergabar for a mind-wipe at BurPsyHygiene. First, he used an Army Strike Team to break into the Pharaoh's palace and liberate him. This set off a firestorm of protests as well as cries of witchcraft and demonic attack. On top of that, this Alexander look-alike was missing!"

"What a mess," Verkan said. "Does anyone know where the imposter is?"

Ranthar shook his head. "The only person onsite who hasn't lost his head is Garlen Darth, a local trouble-shooter for Vendrax. He's been trying to institute a city-wide search but hasn't gotten any cooperation from Dalnar."

"Of course not, it might actually work." Verkan pointed to several piles of papers, video tabs, memory sticks and various report cubes. "I'm still trying to clear my desk of all the stuff that piled up while I was on Aryan-Transpacific. Think you can handle this by yourself, Jard?"

"Sure Chief, but I may have to bust a few heads."

"Do whatever it takes. Just keep it away from the news services."

Ranthar chuckled. "So far that hasn't been a problem. Not too many newsies will voluntarily take an assignment on Alexandrian-Roman!"

The first thing Inspector Ranthar Jard did, after arriving via transtemporal conveyer to Seleuco-Macedonian Subsector depot head and taking over the supervisor's office, was fire Subchief Dalnar Dall. Dalnar protested vehemently until Ranthar showed him the termination notice from Chief Verkan, bearing his official stamp.

"You mean I'm actually fired, Inspector?" he asked, his eyes widening in shock.

It was rare for the Paratime Police Department to fire senior officers, but in view of his Dalmar's mishandling of the Alexander Affair, the Chief had thought it was necessary. The Department couldn't afford anymore screw-ups by this incompetent hack, although Ranthar didn't put it quite so bluntly.

Old Dalmar, his shoulders slumped in defeat, left the Vendrax office without his needler, badge and epaulets.

Next on Ranthar's things-to-do-list was to question Garlen Darth, the Vendrax trouble-shooter. He'd already shooed the Vendrax supervisor out of his office; the man was clearly in over his head. All he wanted was for an end to the Alexander crisis, but had no idea of how to bring it about. Ranthar suspected that this fiasco would follow the supervisor to Home Time Line and cost him his outtime supervisory position—if not his job.

Garlen Darth came into the office, poised and ready for action.

Ranthar approved. "Since you're johnny-on-the-job, what do you suggest we do now?"

Garlen nodded. He didn't seem the least bit intimidated by having this hot potato tossed into his lap. "As I suggested to the last officer, Subchief Dalnar, I'm certain the priesthood is hiding our man somewhere inside the city. We've shut down the harbor and closed off all the roads leading out of town."

"Whose idea was that?" Ranthar asked

"Mine. Once I learned it was one of our employees who was responsible for the rioting, I immediately closed off all the city exits. I wanted to contain the crisis. Unfortunately, word has slipped out of the city and now there are uprisings throughout the Empire."

"As they say at the Academy, the only thing faster than the speed of light is a good rumor. I've sent word to Pol Term Fifth Level for reinforcements. We should have about five hundred operatives arriving dressed as *astynomia*, or local police, and ready to police the city. I want a list from you of all the places we should search first."

"I can do that."

Over the next three days the Paratime Police *astynomia* tore Alexandria apart with no results. None of the locals knew anything other than that the reincarnated Alexander had returned to punish Ptolemy XXI. Ranthar was growing increasingly frustrated when Garlen Darth came into his temporary office with a big smile on his face.

"I've found him, Inspector."

Ranthar rubbed his hands together. "Where?"

"He's hiding in a waterfront warehouse, along with half the high priests in Alexandria."

"How did you pull that off?"

Garlen smirked. "I figured that the best way out of the Alexandria was by boat. So I hit a bunch of the dockside taverns and told the local captains—all who are incensed at being cooped up in the city—that I'd give anyone who brought me information on Alexander's whereabouts his weight in gold staters, if he was captured due to their information."

Ranthar nodded. Gold was one of the first items brought back in large amounts by the earliest Paratime exploiters. As a result, there was so much gold on Home Time Line that it was practically worthless, being used primarily for cheap jewelry and industrial fabrication. Gold was, however, quite useful for both trade and bribery throughout the various Paratime levels.

"The captain gave me the location of where our phony Alexander is hiding," he said, proceeding to give Ranthar all the details on the dockside warehouse. "The priests have been waiting for almost a ten-day for the hunt to die down so they can move Alexander to someplace safe—probably in Greece or Spain."

After checking the data against the detailed city map he pulled up on his visiscreen, Ranthar said, "Good job, Garlen. We'll pick him up tonight at roughly 0300, which should give us the least interference from outsiders. I'll post some men dressed as locals discretely around the warehouse so that Alexander doesn't slip out of our net."

"Inspector, if we want to contain the rumors that will follow

Alexander's capture, I suggest we bring along an actor dressed as Anubis, the God of Death. That way the priests can claim that Alexander escaped from Hades. And that Anubis and his cohorts were sent to Alexandria to bring him back to the underworld."

"An excellent idea! I have just the man for the job." Garlen appeared to be the only competent man Ranthar had run into on this subsector, which gave him a good idea. "Garlen, after this case is wrapped up, would you be interested in joining the Department?"

Garlen stood back for a moment, then smiled. "Aren't I a little old for a Paratime Police recruit?"

Ranthar looked at him closely. "What is your age? I'd say seventy or eighty years old."

"Close, but more like ninety-three."

"Hell, you're still a kid. I'm twice your age. I can fast-track you through the Academy and guarantee you a place on my team."

"In that case, I'm your man."

VIII

Davran Thal was sleeping comfortably on the feather and down mattress provided for his comfort, when he heard the first explosion. He woke up with a start. Before the priests started fawning over him, he would have welcomed the Paratime Police coming to get him. Now, he wasn't so sure.

There was another loud explosion, causing an avalanche of wooden timbers and roofing material to fall, and suddenly everyone was awake. One high priest had been crushed and the rest were squawking like geese. There were some fifty to sixty soldiers inside the warehouse and they were forming up on the floor under harsh orders from their superiors.

Suddenly the interior of the warehouse lit-up as though it were daylight!

It must be the Paracops, he thought. *No one on this time-line has flash grenades.*

Some of the soldiers began to fire their muskets at distant figures which turned out to be a big mistake. The Paratimers shot back with heavy assault weapons and about half of the soldiers were killed or wounded in the initial barrage.

No, this kind of firepower means it's a Strike Team. How many men did they bring?

Davran started looking for a place to hide, but the priests surrounded him with their bodies.

Suddenly one of the priests cried out: "There's Anubis God of Death! We are doomed...."

Another priest screamed as a bullet blew through his torso.

The priests were now crying out and begging for deliverance. Within seconds all the priests were lying face-down on the floor and shouting for the remaining soldiers to do likewise. Figures dressed all in black and wearing beaked masks began stripping all the soldiers of their weapons. Others started tying up the priests. Finally, Anubis himself made an appearance.

"My priests, you have made a terrible blunder," said Anubis in a loud and deep voice that demanded reverence. "This shade escaped from the Underworld and we have come to bring him back."

The Pontius Maximus cried out: "We did not know, Lord. We beg your forgiveness."

"I will consider it. Now, leave us. I will take this shade back to where he belongs."

Trembling, Davran found himself in the grip of two big Paratimers."

"You really screwed up," one said in his ear, as he tied Davran's hands back in flexible restraints.

Ranthar Jard gave Chief Verkan a full account of the raid and subsequent capture of the renegade Paratimer. "The idiot actually thought he was going to get away with impersonating the most famous man on the subsector! What do they teach kids in school these days, anyway?"

Verkan sighed. "Clearly, not enough. You'd think that First Level companies would do their best to weed out the bunglers and criminal types before sending them outtime. It's probably just as well; if they did their job—what would we do?"

Ranthar laughed. "I'm sure we could find something. I did make one valuable find there."

"What was that?"

"I found a new Paratime Police recruit, Garlen Darth. Once he gets though the Academy, I'm going to add him to my special investigator team."

"I'm glad something worthwhile came out of this mess."

"What about our Alexander?" Ranthar asked. "What are we going to do with him?"

Verkan grinned. "He's not our problem anymore. I had him sent directly to BurPsyHygiene; he's their problem, now."

SEA ⊕F GRASS

JOHN F. CARR

I

1967 A.D.

Verkan Vall gazed at the mass of info wafers, message balls and data cubes that covered his desk and sighed. He was cooped up with beeping computers and chirping data writers while outside it was a beautiful spring day. At times like this Verkan wondered why he'd allowed former Paratime Police Chief Tortha Karf to talk him into becoming his successor.

Being the best-trained man for the job did not make him the best man for the job, nor did it make that job any easier—especially when that job was being the final arbiter over a near-infinity of alternate worlds. They all had to be policed. Maybe it was too much job for one man—Tortha Karf had been saying that for years. But committees did not like to make decisions and when they did, too often they were compromises. So, until the Executive Council legalized cloning, it looked as if Verkan was stuck with the job.

Verkan had spent the winter shuttling back and forth between Home Time Line and Greffa, establishing his cover as Trader Verkan. It would not do to have Kalvan bumping into another Grefftscharrer who had never heard of Trader Verkan. The consequence was he had neglected his work here at Paratime Police headquarters and would have to spend the next two or three ten-days catching up. The squawk of his intercom interrupted his thoughts. He touched the com button with his toe and said, "What is it, Orthlan?"

"Inspector Ranthar Jard to see you, Chief. Code Red."

"Send him right in."

Ranthar Jard was a broad shouldered man with a quick step and bright gray eyes; if Dalla was his right hand, Ranthar was his left.

"Hate to bother you, Chief, but this could be important."

Verkan nodded for him to continue.

"We turned up some interesting irregularities on that list of Opposition heavy contributors you had me check out with the Metro Records Division. Our prime suspect is one Jorand Rarth—have you heard of him?"

"No. Who is he?"

"He's an outtime importer with possible connections to the Novilan Syndicate, mostly gambling and prole prostitution."

"Those two Wizard Trader suspects who allegedly committed suicide last year both had connections to the Novilan Syndicate."

Ranthar smiled, showing his well-formed teeth.

"This sounds like the link between the Wizard Traders and the syndicates we've been searching for," Verkan said. The Wizard Traders, who called themselves the Organization, had been a large band of First Level slavers posing as sorcerers. Unauthorized, they had gone outtime, using First Level technology as magic to take advantage of the ignorant and superstitious. The Organization had captured refugees from local wars and other disposable locals on isolated timelines as slaves to be sold for gold and fissionables on other time-lines. The Paratime Police had closed part of the operation down over a decade ago, but were still trying to penetrate the upper layers of the Wizard Trader Organization.

"Where is Jorand now?"

"That's the bad news, Chief. We've had his quarters under close surveillance for the past four hours. Less than fifteen minutes ago, we picked up the landing beam from his aircar. Before we could move in, he fled. We lost his aircar in the city lanes."

"I take it his locator was off?"

"Yes, first thing we checked. Nothing registered for his aircar on the traffic monitors, either."

Verkan sighed. "Where do you think he may have gone, Jard?"

"A syndicate hideout—for now, would be my guess, Chief. Then he'll hop aboard the first illegal outtime conveyer he can find. There's no place on Home Time Line to hide for more than a few days. I'll put out a warning on him to all the registered outtime firms."

Verkan moved his head in agreement. "I want an ID and picture of Jorand Rarth distributed to every Transtemporal terminal on the First Level. I also want his face on every news broadcast in this city by this evening. Arrange a pickup for all known associates. This is one fish I don't want to see slip away."

"Yes, sir."

"Rarth may be the key we've been searching for. So far we've been looking everywhere but in the right places."

"I've got a few suggestions. Take a couple of the Opposition Party big-wigs and put them under narco-hypnosis; we'll get some answers, all right."

"You may be right, but it's prohibited for the Department to question any elected Party official unless he's actually caught red-handed in a violation of the Municipal or Transtemporal Codes. Otherwise our hands are tied."

It was one of the many reasons Verkan preferred to spend his off time on Kalvan's Time Line; there you could cut through regulations with the nearest dirk or sword.

II

Archstratagos Zarphu, who had fought in thirty battles in as many years without giving in to fear, noticed a tremble in his legs as he entered the Lord Tyrant's audience chamber. Dyzar, the Tyrant of Antiphon, was truly one of the greatest rulers in Antiphon's history, but that was not enough to make him a great man in Zarphu's eyes. Neither was the sparse beard that grew upon Dyzar's cheeks.

Dyzar did not view other people as living, feeling beings like himself; instead they were pieces to be moved or removed from life's game board. His outbursts of temper were as notorious as his women's quarters, which were filled with young slave girls and other young ladies 'lost' on the city streets after catching Dyzar's eye.

These days there was more silver than bronze in Zarphu's hair, and despite the recent victory over the Army of Leuctramnos, Dyzar might have finally decided that it was time for a younger man to command the city's army; maybe one more malleable to his will. He was certain he had not done anything recently to make Dyzar doubt his loyalty and good service. Yet, since when had the Lord Tyrant ever needed proof of anything beyond his own whims and suspicions?

The two palace guards, both Eternals, wearing gilded chain mail and sporting red horsehair crests in their helmets, stood as if cast in metal. Zarphu wondered how they endured the constant inactivity; perhaps they were secretly amused by the parade of visitors into—and sometimes—out of Dyzar's chambers.

The door swung open and the Chamberlain bade him enter.

The Lord Tyrant Dyzar wore a rose and black velvet robe and his scruffy beard was intricately braided with gold wire. The Tyrant was reclining on a long red divan trimmed with gold mesh. He indicated that Zarphu was to sit on the other end of the divan.

After kneeling and touching the floor three times with his forehead, Zarphu rose. "Your Magnificence, I am your slave to command—"

"Arch-Strategos, we will dispense with the usual formalities for We

have an urgent matter to discuss with you. Are you familiar with the former refugees from our lands who have settled beyond the Iron Trail?"

"No, Your Magnificence."

"Certainly you have heard the fables from the Time of Troubles about
those who chose to flee to the lands beyond the Sea of Grass?"

"Yes, Your Magnificence. But I did not know there was truth behind
those tales."

The Lord Tyrant nodded his head. "They are mentioned in the Lost
Chronicles of Domitios. These I'm sure you have heard whispered words
about."

Discourse with the Lord Tyrant was like sword fighting against a
skilled blade master; any feigns or missteps could be instantly fatal. "Yes,
Your Magnificence, I have heard about them although I did not believe
they still existed."

The Lord Tyrant grinned. "The Chronicles are part of my secret
library. Of course, any mention of what has passed between us in this
chamber will cost you and your family dearly. Is that understood?"

Zarphu nodded.

"Good. As you know the Time of Troubles began with the Echini War
against the Echanistra Confederation and lasted for almost a thousand
years. Near the end of the war, Echanistra's fleet was nearly destroyed;
so many of the northerners decided to flee their homelands. Invited by
King Chaldorec of Grefftscharr, many of them followed the Iron Trail and
beyond to new lands, where in the winter snow is as common as the sand
on our beaches. There they conquered the Ruthani, as our ancestors did
three thousand years ago, and took the land as their own.

"We know few details about their conquest, but in time five major
kingdoms were established—each dominated by a great city-state, much
like our own rule. For many years they have grown and prospered, all
without tribute or tithes to the lords they fled. Now a new kingdom has
formed and they have asked for our help. Maybe the time has arrived for
us to us to re-establish our dominion over these our strayed children."

There was an intense inner light in the Lord Tyrant's eyes that worried
Zarphu. The Tyrant Laertru, Dyzar's father, had built the greatest army

in the history of Antiphon. His son had used this army to subdue and conquer his neighbors, a feat no one had accomplished since the Time of Troubles. Now the Lord Tyrant's power extended from Amcylyestros in the south to Tyrantor in the north. Apparently, not even the domination of the Great Cities was enough to appease Dyzar's appetite for power. Were the rumors the Lord Tyrant wanted to forge an empire from Great Sea to Great Sea actually true?

"We have been approached by agents of Styphon's House—the Temple of a powerful eastern god—with a request to hire part of our army. The terms are generous and we have accepted their offer. Now that we have wrested peace from Amcylyestros, and have so soundly defeated Leuctramnos that they too seek a settlement—all due to your brilliant generalship—we have an unparalleled opportunity to learn about the eastern lands and their peoples."

"Who is this Styphon, Your Magnificence?"

"Some false god of war they worship." Dyzar continued. "He cannot be a very good god or they would not need our help. According to the Styphon's House emissary, they are embroiled in a war with a demigod named Kalvan and desire our help to defeat him. Demigod indeed! I care not one whit for their petty struggles, but there can be much to gain by going to their aid. We need to know more about these barbarians if we are to exploit their troubles and turn them to our advantage."

"How much of our army do they wish to hire?"

"Four stratgi of horse and fourteen of foot, including two stratgi of plumbati."

"Your Magnificence, that is almost a quarter of our entire army. Can we afford the loss of so many valuable men?"

"Yes. With Leuctramnos suing for peace there is no other city-state left to oppose us but Sybariphon in the north, and they are still at war with Echanistra. We may never have a better opportunity to search out the easterners' weaknesses."

Zarphu felt weak in the knees, as if he had been ordered to run his army into the ocean to fight the waves. What madness was this? He would have to cross the Sea of Grass, fight the warriors of the Iron City and defeat the barbarian kingdoms, who—if stories were to believed—fought with fire and stones, shot by fire sticks farther and faster than the fleetest arrow.

"I need you to lead them, Arch-Stratego. Only you will be trusted with the true secret of our mission."

Yanked out of his reverie by this pronouncement, Zarphu knew chances were small he would ever return and see his beloved city again. Maybe, as his friends had warned, his own success on the battlefield had made him too dangerous to be left alive. Certainly an honorable death on the battlefield, no matter how far from home, was to be preferred to the assassin's dart.

"How long will we remain in the barbarians' employ?" Zarphu asked.

"Until next summer, or whenever this Kalvan—be he man or demi-god—is dead."

Seeing the boy—for boy he still was, to Zarphu, for all his arrogance and lofty ambitions—seated there looking so completely alone, an up-surge of that wretched emotion called loyalty stirred in Zarphu's heart. Without thinking he knelt before his sovereign with the ridiculous gold-threaded scruffy beard, took his hand and placed it atop his head in the older gesture of fealty among the Ros-Zarthani and quietly said, "I will serve Your Magnificence, until I bear Kalvan's skull as a drinking cup or my shield is hung in Hadron's Hall."

"I knew my trust was well founded," Dyzar purred. "I want maps dawn of the entire journey, a list of all cities and fortifications you en-counter, samples of all new armor and weapons, notes on how an army can be supplied on each part of the journey and any documents of mili-tary importance you can obtain. I will send scribes and mapmakers to aid you with these chores. In addition, I will entrust you with a bodyguard drawn from my Eternals; they will guard you with their lives."

The Eternals were the Lord Tyrant's own personal bodyguard, as well as his eyes and ears—and occasionally his assassins. Zarphu was being both honored and kept safe. Why couldn't he shake the feeling that he was caught in an invisible undertow?

"Do not worry about your affairs in the city, Zarphu." Dyzar paused to stroke his beard. "Should you not return to us within five winters, we will gift your heirs our weight in gold."

The Lord Tyrant was notoriously tightfisted; Zarphu couldn't help but wonder why the sudden benevolence. While a few of his friends had whispered their complaints about the Lord Tyrant's growing capriciousness, he had never in any way encouraged this kind of talk. He had also heard from one of his confidants that there were actual factions opposed to the Lord Tyrant's rule, so perhaps Dyzar had some justification for his worries about his own security and the loyalty of his stratgi.

His own loyalty was incorruptible. "I thank you for your generosity, Your Magnificence. I shall return before the passing of five winters so your generosity will not be wasted." Zarphu prostrated himself before the crown again and kissed the Lord Tyrant's feet. He then rose, pausing only as he was about to cross the threshold to ask one last question. "When do we leave?"

"In a moon-quarter, Arch-Stratego. We are having the fleet fitted and provisioned to take you and your command as far as Mythrene. There you will disembark, buy additional provisions and wagons, and take leave for Olythrio. The Styphoni have will have additional guides there to help you with your travels. Now we will give you leave to muster your men and prepare for the coming journey."

III

Jorand Rarth pushed his chair back, to ease his bulging belly, and listened with pleasure to the jingle and clang of the slot machines in the front room of the Corkscrew. The slots were a recent *import* from Fourth Level, Europo-American Sector and they were proving to be—as had so many other Europo-American imports—a great hit. He estimated the average take was up fifteen percent at all three of his Dhergabar clubs since their introduction. He was going to have to *import* more slot machines and send them to his other clubs outside the capital before one of the other Bosses got the same idea.

While the Bureau of Psychological Hygiene saw gambling and play-ing games of chance as evidence of an anti-social character, gambling itself was not strictly illegal. To a society that liked to see itself as free of pre-literate and pseudo-scientific superstition, games of chance were a social embarrassment—a continuing reminder of the irrationality of human nature. As such, Psych-Hygiene agents liked to keep records on those who frequented gambling dens.

In an ongoing attempt to protect customer anonymity, the gambling syndicates carefully guarded the location of their clubs, moved them around at irregular intervals and paid large sums of shush money to cer-tain captains in the Dhergabar Metropolitan Police Department.

Jorand needed to talk to his contacts at Tharmax Trading right away about acquiring more slot machines. It didn't help that they were quasi-illegal on most Europo-American Subsectors, either. If Paratime Police Chief Verkan Vall hadn't been monitoring that Sector so vigilantly, Jorand would have solved his problem very simply. He would have run a big conveyer into one of the Fourth Level Bally slot machine factories, taken all the trained mechanics and setup men, blown a gas main under the old factory and then sent them across time to an uninhabited Fifth Level time-line where he would have set up his own slot machine business.

Making them was clearly not as easy as hijacking them, but then slot machines were not as easy to obtain outtime as Fourth Level jukeboxes or Second Level subliminal hormone exciters. Plus, by using slave labor, the syndicate could save a lot of units as well as create a dependable sup-ply base—one not dependent upon outtime politics and Paratime Police's good will to operate. Wars and revolutions had a nasty way of mucking up supply and delivery, especially when they splashed over whole subsec-tors, containing millions times millions of timelines.

Jorand's door sensor beeped and Metropolitan Police Captain Sirgoth Zyarr entered the room. Jorand quickly rose to his feet. Sirgoth had never physically come into one of his clubs in more twenty years of 'working' together. He wondered if he were about to be raided. Raids were ritual-ized, with both sides warned long in advance so each could play out their part to perfection.

Something big was coming down. "What is it, Cap—"?

"No names."

It suddenly hit him that Sirgoth was not wearing his regulation blues, but a gray street tunic and cape.

"One of my men flagged your name in a data pool we share with the Paratime Police. They've tagged you for pickup. Don't know when or where, but if I were you I wouldn't waste any time finding a hole to crawl into."

"Why the warning?" Everyone knew about the age old antagonism between the Metropolitan Police and the Paratime Police; the Metros— along with almost everyone else—thought the Paracops acted like a second government—with more authority than the Metropolitan Police and the Executive Council combined. Maybe they needed their autonomy to guard the secret of Paratime Transposition, but that didn't mean everyone else had to like it. Or that the Paratime Police had to be so self-righteous in carrying out their job.

"I'll give you one reason. Then I'm getting out of here. As far as you are concerned, you've never heard of me and I've never heard of you. Make any attempt to re-establish contact with me, and I will see that you are terminated."

Jorand gulped.

"Ever since Chief Verkan and his Paratime squads saved our butts on Year-End Day, by helping us put down the riots, we've been given orders to assist them in all on-going investigations and to share our data pool. It's a new game under Chief Raldor and all the old rules are changing. If the Paratime Police get their hands on you, the first thing they'll do is pump narco-hypnotics into your system until you squeal like a frightened little girl. Then you're going to throw up everything you know. My name is going to appear in whatever mess you regurgitate. If I were smart, I would have wired your aircar and cleansed the whole operation in one blast. But there are problems with that approach, as well. So just be thankful that in the past you've always been on time with the slush, and that you haven't splashed any dirt on me."

With that said, Captain Sirgoth spun around and left the small room.

Jorand felt his heart pound like a trip-hammer. *I could have a heart attack right this moment, race to the nearest hospice and wake up with a new heart and a Paratime Policeman at my side.*

He willed his heart to slow down and quickly began to draw up a mental list of what he had to take with him and what he had to destroy.

IV

Jorand Rarth felt weight return as the wheels of the air-car struck the rooftop landing stage of Hadron Tharn's penthouse and shut down the pseudo-grav. His driver opened the rear door and asked, "What should I do with the car, boss?"

Jorand looked around as though expecting a blue Metro or green Paracop police car to materialize on the landing stage. Yesterday afternoon he had been forced to flee his own tower just minutes before a squad of Paratime Police raided the place. Now there was a warrant for his arrest and the cover he had so elaborately devised a century ago was gone.

"The police should be able to ID it before long so drop it off at a public tower and meet me at the Constellation House in two hours. We can steal a new aircar out of the parking lot if we need one."

The driver nodded and took off. Jorand stepped into the lifthead of Hadron Tharn's penthouse; he keyed in his password and pressed his thumb on the thumblock. The lift door rose behind him to cut off the view of Dhergabar City under a winter sky as bright and blue, and as coldly unsympathetic, as Paratime Police Chief Verkan Vall's eyes.

The lift door opened, letting Jorand out into the maroon-carpeted entry hall of Hadron Tharn's private quarters. A robot rolled forward to take Jorand's coat. Behind it rolled another robot, holding a tray with hot spiked simmer-root in a silver cup. Jorand took the cup, triggering the robot's vocal circuits.

"Citizen Hadron Tharn is waiting to see you in the lounge."

Jorand mumbled an automatic thank you in return which told more about his prole origins than he liked known, since Citizens never spoke to robots unless giving them a command. He had spent decades setting up his First Level Citizen identity and had lived it for close to a century. It appeared he'd gotten fat and lazy; he was going to need all his old skills and moxie to survive this fracas.

A century ago he had been the head of an underground gambling syndicate in Novilan City. While all First Level Citizens' children become Citizens, Proles had to qualify by passing an intelligence and general psych test. Proles could be adopted and made Citizens, but even so they must pass the tests. The problem was that few Proles received a First Level education.

Jorand had tried with tutors, but hadn't liked the hard work. Instead he had searched for a decade to find a compulsive gambler within the Bureau of Identification. It hadn't been easy because the Bureau of Psychological Hygiene made periodic sweeps of the Records Division to keep such fraud to a minimum.

When he had his mark hooked and gaffed, he arranged the 'disappearance' of a respectable Citizen and the substitution of Jorand's DNA record for the mark had been affected. No one had been the wiser for ninety-eight years—until yesterday.

Jorand didn't have the time, or the patience, to set up another set of false IDs, so he had no other choice but to go outtime. With his usual contacts under suspicion, he would have to use his influence in the Opposition Party, using the influence he had spent decades building with large donations and conscientious attendance at Hadron's boring political action group meetings.

He had also been a boss in the Organization, a criminal syndicate that had kidnapped outtime peoples and sold them at high profits on other time-lines. Since most of these outtimers had been victims of wars or famines, he had only too happy to arrange their sale to those who could make good use of their labors. After all, they gained their lives while he in exchange made a fair return.

As far as he was concerned, none of those outtimers would have to face anything Jorand hadn't gone through himself during his childhood on Fifth Level Industrial Sector, where his own father had sold him to a slum overlord for drug money. Jorand had been raised by a man who had bought him as a slave, then raised him to second-in-command of a large burglary syndicate.

Now as a member of the Organization's second level, Jorand knew just how 'involved' in the Organization many of the top politicos of the Opposition Party had become. Unfortunately, the Paratime Police had put his branch of the Organization out of business; his boss had been detained and never heard of again. There were rumors that he'd been killed while under Paratime Police interrogation. Recently, Jorand had heard new rumors that the Organization was back in business, but no one had contacted him, or he wouldn't be here trying to cash in on that information—regardless of Citizen Tharn's feelings on the subject.

Fortunately, as a member of Tharn's Opposition Action Team, he hadn't even had to twist Tharn's arm for a private audience. Jorand almost looked forward to the day when the Action Team discovered they had a prole among their membership. Despite all their egalitarian cant, he had heard enough prole jokes to know their true sympathies. It had been his private joke, one that kept him awake through their interminable meetings. Too bad he would not be there when they learned the truth about him.

Jorand gulped the last of his simmer root as he entered the Blue Lounge. He thought of ordering another, then decided to wait since he would need a clear head for today's meeting.

"Welcome, Citizen Jorand," Hadron Tharn said, stepping lightly toward him. "I trust you had a good journey." Unfortunately, the warm greeting didn't extend to Tharn's chilly eyes.

"Except for the stratospheric winds, yes. That's why I'm late."

"It hardly matters. Would you care for another drink?"

Jorand shook his head and sat down in his usual red-leather chair. The only other person in the room was Warntha Swarn, Tharn's bodyguard and who-knew-what-else. Warntha was in his usual stance, hands clasped behind his back and eyes roaming the room, and as usual guarding Hadron Tharn's back.

Citizen Tharn gave one of his famous grins, but the blue eyes were as icy as an arctic gale. "What can I do for you Citizen?"

Jorand didn't bother to return the smile. "I'm in trouble and I need your help."

"I'm sorry to hear that, Citizen, but why me?"

"Call it a return on a three million credit investment. I need to go outtime."

Warntha visibly tensed.

"The only reason I'm not having you thrown out of here," Tharn said, "is that you've been extremely helpful in the past. I don't know what your problem is, but I suggest you go elsewhere for its solution."

"My personal rooms have just been sealed by the Paratime Police and by now I'm sure to be high up on their most-wanted list."

"You have my sympathies, of course." Tharn held both hands out to express his helplessness. "However, my brother-in-law, Verkan Vall and I have an unspoken accord; he doesn't ask me for favors and I don't ask him for any."

"Citizen Tharn, let us get to the heart of the problem. I have been one of the heads of the Organization, or Wizard Traders as the Paracops call it, for about thirty years. Don't look so shocked; I can name a dozen prominent Opposition Party members who are equally involved."

Hadron Tharn nodded, his face expressionless.

"If the Paratime Police pick me up, the lid will be blown off what's left of the Organization and the Opposition Party. Frankly, it is in both our interests to see me disappear from Home Time Line." Jorand saw a stealthy look slip between Warntha and his master and added, "My driver has a message ball he's to take to Verkan Vall if I don't leave this tower according to schedule."

"Where do you get these ideas?"

"Because, like you, I've found that the simplest solution to most problems is often the most elegant—in this case, my disappearance. Therefore, I've taken certain precautions, just as you would have done."

Hadron Tharn leaned back in his chair, his forehead furrowed in what appeared to be concentrated thought. He remained frozen for some time until he sat up abruptly. "I don't have as much access to Paratemporal

Transposition as you seem to think, but we do have one operation where you might fit in."

During the height of the Wizard Traders operation, Jorand would have had his choice of thousands of time-lines to hide on, but now he was forced to take whatever crumb Tharn threw his way. Despite his reluctance to take grudging charity; it was a vast improvement over psycho-rehabilitation, a year of unremitting physical and mental agony, the ignominy of having his private thoughts probed and twisted by psychotherapists and finally the horror of emerging as someone who would not be Jorand Rarth.

"What is it?" he asked.

"You've heard of Kalvan's Time Line?"

"Who hasn't? We've talked it to death at the Action Team meetings. What about it?"

"Kalvan's Time Line has become Chief Verkan Vall's major political vulnerability, one the Opposition Party intends to exploit. One way we can force Verkan's hand is by making life difficult for his outtime friend, Great King Kalvan. If things get sticky enough for Kalvan, Verkan might commit a breach of the Paratime Code—and then we will have him."

Right, thought Jorand, *a scandal big enough to break Management Party's stranglehold on the Executive Council. Sweeping reforms inside the Paratime Police would help many of the commercial houses who felt constrained in their theft of outtime resources.* It was enough to make an honest thief wonder who the real crooks were.

"So where do I fit into all of this?"

Hadron Tharn leaned forward, locking eyes. "Rarth, I could use a trusted agent I can send to Kalvan's Time Line to oversee a very important operation. This last year has been a very good one for King Kalvan. He defeated probably the largest army in his time-line's history. Now he's built up his army to the point where only the most concerted effort will root him out of his so-called Great Kingdom of Hos-Hostigos.

"Fortunately for us, the opposition has some good leaders, Archpriest Roxthar, Prince Lysandros of Hos-Harphax, and Grand Master Soton of the Zarthani Knights. They are planning a major counter-attack but need help. Kalvan has either killed or recruited most of the available mercenaries in the Five Kingdoms and the national armies aren't that strong as of yet on this time-line.

"But the picture isn't all bad. On the west coast there are a number of city-states who have built up formidable armies after a millennium of constant warfare. Now, for the first time in centuries, they have a great leader in one of the city-states, Antiphon. A leader who has become strong enough to conquer most of the others. The problem is that he is unstable and unpredictable, more a Hitler than an Alexander. Like Hitler, this leader—Dyzar—suffered from an untreatable case of syphilis, which has left him with delusions of grandeur, a homicidal temper, and massive mood swings—"

Jorand stifled a grin as he realized that this description might equally cover Hadron Tharn himself, who on occasion had been known to scream and berate his cohorts for hours. "What do you mean, suffered?"

"A month ago my agents used a neuro-prophylactic on Dyzar and were able to stabilize his condition. Due to the primitive conditions, the advanced stage of the disease and the lack of a fully trained medico, they were not able to restore normal mental functions. In the end they were forced to use the rejuvenation treatment to insure he survived the treatment. Dyzar should live a long and painful life."

"You used rejuvenation formula on an outtimer! Next to the Paratime Secret that's the most heavily guarded invention we have. We could all be fried for this—"

Hadron Tharn smiled a most unpleasant smile. "That is why we need an agent of utmost discretion for this job. One who will not be particular about a lengthy and somewhat primitive assignment."

And someone very expendable, thought Jorand to himself. *And unable to return to First Level without Hadron's help.* Unfortunately, for him, there were no other choices. "What is it you want me to do?"

"First, we will put you under narco-hypnosis and give you a pseudo-memory overlay as a merchant from Hos-Zygros; it's as distant as you can go from Balph, Styphon House's administrative center. You will be one of the guides of the expedition, which is under the authority of Highpriest

Prythos. In your guise as a merchant who has traveled the Iron Trail re-
peatedly—under narco-hypnosis you will be implanted with all the neces-
sary details—you will become an essential member of the contact team.
The team, headed by Highpriest Prythos, is currently in the City-Sate of
Mythrene awaiting the arrival of the Ros-Zarthani army. Your job will
be to make sure that the Ros-Zarthani forces arrive intact at the Eastern
Kingdoms where they will be prepared for their role in the war against
King Kalvan."

"Why not," Jorand answered. It wasn't as if he had any place else to
go.

V

The moment Jorand Rarth left, Hadron Tharn turned to Warntha
and asked, "What do you think of that one? Can we trust him?"

"For about two heartbeats after the Paratime Police pick him up. I
tossed a sticky locator on his tunic when he walked by. Do you want me
to follow and dispose of him and his driver? I don't believe his story about
any documents ready to go to the Paratime Police."

Tharn shook his head. "He was flying by the seat of his pants! Still, we
need an expendable agent on Kalvan Prime—Prythos has been useful, but
in his last communiqué he asked for more help. I think he's getting tired
of traveling across the continent by horseback."

They both laughed.

Hadron Tharn continued. "We have to be very careful on Kalvan
Prime; there are more Paracops there than at the Dhergabar Paratime
Terminal. Verkan has been pressuring the Executive Council, to put a
Paracop on every outtime conveyer. Not even Management will go for
it, because there's thousands of firms with outtime licenses and they'd
have to curtail business or increase the Paratime Police Department by
several orders of magnitude! Unfortunately, some of our late friends in the
Organization got sloppy and gave Verkan valuable ammunition. If Verkan
catches an unauthorized conveyer on Kalvan Prime—all bets are off! Still,

it's too good an opportunity to give that sanctimonious bastard a black eye. This Jorand is perfect; no one will miss him and he no longer has any ties to the Organization. When his job is done—"

Warntha smiled. "Do I get to pull his plug?"

"After he's no longer useful, but that won't be for some time. Prythos, though…hmm. The time has come to terminate Highpriest Prythos, but first put him under narco-hypnosis, do a complete memory lift for Jorand—then kill him and dispose of the body. No witnesses, no crime."

"Do you think anyone will notice, boss?"

"Highpriest Prythos has been gone for over a year from Balph and we selected him originally because he was a newcomer from Hos-Zygros that wouldn't be missed. His most memorable feature is his big gut, and Jorand's big belly almost matches his."

They both laughed.

Warntha Swarn placed his palm over the portal plate and the door to the warehouse slid open—poor security. Typical of a University project, he thought scornfully. Inside the room was a large silver-mesh dome about fifty feet in diameter, large enough to hold the two score of scholars and academics moving around the storeroom. Most of them were dressed in homespun wool, leather and buckskin garments appropriate to Kalvan's Time Line.

Warntha wore the full-length, hooded yellow robe of a Styphon's House highpriest. He couldn't help but notice how the academics quickly moved out of his path, as though the trappings of a Styphoni priest had a sinister aura. Upon reflection, the big man decided it wasn't much different than the usual way Citizens usually acted around him—just more pronounced.

As a counter-military specialist, Warntha had spent over a century on the Industrial Sector, Fifth Level worlds, where he had infiltrated and helped to neutralize Prole resistance groups. Warntha had liked this work and had been very good at it. Unfortunately, he had single-handedly killed the top two leaders of a Prole Independence Movement cell unaware that there had been another active agent in the cell. Command had judged him as 'over-zealous' and given him the choice of Psycho-Rehab or retirement at half-pay. He had taken the latter. If Hadron Tharn had not seen some value in his services, he would be living on Home Time Line at about the same economic level of the Proles he had once overseen.

In the farthest corner of the warehouse, all by himself, Warntha spotted Jorand Rarth, wearing a battered back-and-breast—that hid most of his potbelly—a large floppy black hat and leather trousers with a buckskin fringe. He approached Jorand from his blind side to gain the maximum advantage of surprise. Warntha hoped this fool proved as useful as Hadron Tharn anticipated. If not, Jorand's life would come to an abrupt and permanent end.

"By Dralm's white beard!" Jorand cried upon seeing Warntha in his Styphoni robes. He quickly reverted to First Level language when he recognized Warntha as Hadron Tharn's bodyguard. "What are you doing here?"

"Councilor Tharn decided I should accompany you on this mission as a highpriest of Styphon's House. We will be accompanying the Hos-Harphax Study Team, which will be dropped off at the new Harphax conveyer-head in Harphax City. We have a small aircar secreted inside one of the conveyers. From there, we'll take the aircar across the continent to the City-State of Mythrene, the seaport where we're meeting Arch-Stratego Zarphu and his army. I will be accompanying the expedition across the Sea of Grass."

"Won't the locals see our aircar as some king of omen or premonition?"

Warntha laughed. "They won't see us without night goggles! We're traveling after dark; once we cross the Mother River it won't matter who sees us. They're all outies!"

"What'll we do with the aircar after we arrive?" Jorand asked.

"One of our agents has purchased a small warehouse where it will be stored in case we need to bug out in a hurry. It's getting more and more difficult to make unscheduled drops on Kalvan's Time Line. The Paratime Police are paying more attention to the University's use of Transtemporal conveyers. The University doesn't like it, and neither do we. But, it's the way things are now."

Jorand nodded wryly, as though he understood, but didn't like it much, either. Warntha suspected Jorand enjoyed his company about as much as he enjoyed spending time with the former Dhergabar crime boss.

"I've got some additional instructions for you as well. Instead of guiding the Arch-Stratego to the Hyklos River to where it meets the Great River, we're going to lead the Ros-Zarthani over the Old Iron Trail into Grefftscharr."

"But why?" Jorand asked. "It'll not only add at least a full moon to the trip, but it might draw us into a fight with the Grefftscharri. They're not going to look kindly at what they could easily perceive as a nomad invasion."

Maybe Jorand isn't a complete fool, after all, Warntha decided. "That's what the Councilor wants. The Ros-Zarthani haven't fought against gunpowder weapons before. It's important they have the opportunity to test their mettle before fighting Kalvan. If they break, then we abort the mission—"

The fat man turned pale. "Yeah, but where does that leave me? In Greffa as a prisoner of war or a galley slave on the Great Seas?"

"Then I guess it's important to see they don't break, Jorand—since it is only our necks at stake." Warntha wasn't the least bit worried, if things went wrong; either he'd get killed—in which case all his problems were over, or he'd find a 'job'—probably as a bodyguard, since they were always in fashion—in Greffa. "If the Ros-Zarthani show real mettle, maybe King Kalvan will have a big surprise next year."

"I guess it wouldn't help Chief Verkan's position in Greffa either," Jorand said, "if his patron, King Theovacar, loses a major battle to a bunch of barbarian spearchuckers. Nor would he be in a position, the following year, to help Kalvan with men and supplies."

"Very good. You're beginning to pick up the lay of the land. Just look at these kings as syndicate bosses and you'll get along just fine."

"When can I come home?" Jorand asked.

"After we get the army safely back across the Sea of Grass, or when it has ceased being an effective fighting force, our job is over. If they survive the fight with the Middle Kingdom forces, we'll lead the Ros-Zarthani to

Dorg where they will be Styphon's House's problem. Then we will make our way to Balph where you will assume Highpriest Prythos' identity—"

"How are you going to do that?" he asked.

Warntha quickly made a slicing motion across his throat with his index finger. Then continued:

"That should give our friends on First Level time to create a new cover and identity for you. Once the Ros-Zarthani are on the way back home you'll be able to return back to leading a civilized life on First Level."

Jorand appeared so pleased by this news that Warntha had to choke back a laugh. If the fat fool really believed that anyone on Home Time Line would go to that much expense and trouble for a drone like himself, then he deserved his fate. Jorand was nothing more than an over-weight, smarmy ex-Prole. Warntha stroked the hilt of the dirk hidden in his gold and leather girdle and repeated to himself, *Your time will come, my fat little friend. Yes, it will come—I promise you that.*

VI

Arch-Stratego Zarphu made room on the cluttered table for a freshly scraped deerskin parchment. He dipped his quill into the inkpot, making a notation that two hundred barrels of salt fish would be arriving from Hellos within the moon half. Zarphu knew that most soldiers considered provisioning and buying victuals scribes' work, but he knew that an army marched on its belly as well as on its feet, and woe to any Stratego who forgot that fact.

The sea journey from Antiphon to Mythrene had taken over a moon quarter, as the ships had been forced to go against the current and prevailing winds. Even with rowers it was a long, arduous trip and, praise to the weather god, they had only lost one ship to foul winds and none to pirates. Best of all, his stomach was once again his own and not leaping at every lurch of the ship.

Their greeting from the Lord Tyrant of Mythrene had been gracious, befitting an ally who came at the head of an army. The Lord Tyrant had offered him rooms at the palace, but Zarphu had refused. As long as he was in Mythrene, the local Tyrant's spies would be weighing their every move. Still there was no gain in making their job an easy one. Instead Zarphu had hired out the Black Thorn Tavern as his headquarters.

The army was garrisoned outside the city walls, although keeping them outside the city was a major headache. It would not be wise to have some of them mugged by cutpurses and the rest given the pox by local whores before they left the coast. In truth, Zarphu could hardly wait until they were on their way. He was going to have to wait for another moon— at the earliest—before his quartermasters could collect enough foodstuffs for the initial leg of their journey. He would have to place his faith in the stories the merchants told about great herds of bison and cattle moving across the Sea of Grass like schools of tuna and albacore. In case it was the stuff of legend, he intended to send several large pack trains out ahead of the army to set up depots, since there was no conceivable way they could take enough victuals along with them to cover the entire passage.

A hearty knock at the plank door told him his Eastern visitors had arrived. "Enter."

A big priest, with a shaved head and hard eyes, wearing a yellow robe—raiment of the god the barbarians called Styphon—was the first to enter. After him came several lesser priests in black robes. Next came the merchants, led by a portly man with a solid-metal breastplate chased with silver and gold that Zarphu would have traded his favorite horse for. The portly man had a wine merchant's smile pasted on his face. Zarphu wondered which, if any, of these foreigners he could trust.

The big highpriest, who he had met before and called himself Highpriest Prythos, was the first to speak. "My fellow priests, except for two, will return on your galleys to Antiphon as agreed by your Lord Tyrant. I will accompany your army to the Five Kingdoms as advisor and priest to those who need me."

Prythos spoke to him as if he were a lesser form of animal; the high-priest reminded him of Dyzar's Immortal Bodyguards. Zarphu didn't trust him the width of a lady's dagger. He would like to know more about this 'fireseed' that the priest had shown him the day before. Still, the priest had already crossed the Sea of Grass and, along with the portly merchant, had survived the journey, so he might prove helpful in their passage.

"Who will we be fighting when we reach the Five Kingdoms?" Zarphu asked.

"A usurper and blasphemer who goes by the name of Kalvan. I have been sent to aid you in bringing your army to join the Holy Host. You will have your part in what will be a great victory."

Zarphu could tell by his tone that the highpriest didn't think much of that part or his mission. Good, the priests of Styphon's House underestimated him. That would make his job easier. He was sure that once they arrived in the Five Kingdoms an opportunity would arise where he return this oafs' disdain. The Zarthani, as they now called themselves, might have better weapons, but he was certain they didn't have any better soldiers than his own—even this so-called Usurper Kalvan. If they did they wouldn't be riding the width of the continent for mercenaries.

One thing that he was certain of, not much good would come of an alliance with these priests of the false god Styphon. What he really wanted to know was why the other priests were returning to Antiphon. Just what kind of deal had the Styphon worshippers struck with Lord Tyrant Dyzar?

After he'd dismissed the foreigners, he had one of the merchants brought in. Garnoth was rapidly approaching old age, most of his teeth were gone and his hair and beard were braided with silver. But he dressed like a nobleman and the rings on his fingers were worth a small fortune; it was obvious that financial necessity was not his primary reason for joining the expedition. It was also known that he'd traveled the Iron Trail more times than any man alive.

"Trader Garnoth, I'm curious as to why you want to join our expedition." He rested his eyes on the trader's jewel encrusted fingers. "It's not as if you need the fee."

"This is true, Stratego," he answered, his words mushy because of missing teeth. "I lack little either in comfort or wealth, after fifty years of traveling the Iron Trail." He held up his right hand which only had two fingers and a thumb. "I lost those when a barbarian's spear clipped my hand; I was twenty-six winters old then. But we beat the Ruthani back, killing thirty of their bravest warriors. There was a challenge like that for every journey, although I never lost any more body parts."

He paused to make a wheezing sound that Zarphu took for laughter.

"It's a good thing, because we lost a lot of good men over the decades. My father was killed by a tomahawk blow to the head; my uncle was shot in the neck with an arrow. Fortunately, few of the Ruthani on the Sea of Grass have iron weapons; although more do now than when I was a youngster. The new breed of traders will make exchanges with anyone, if they can meet their price. We had ethics—" He paused to cough, an awful hacking sound that made Zarphu wonder if he'd even finish the journey.

"How do you think the barbarians will react to a force this large?" He was worried that the savages might believe they were an invasion force or guards for a rich caravan, since they were bringing three thousand wagons of victuals, supplies and weapons with them.

Garnoth repeated the wheezing sound that passed for laughter. When he ran out of air, he sputtered: "They'll run like the wind, Stratego. The tribes and clans rarely join forces, and even then only rarely to attack trade caravans. It takes them too long to band together, they have to have pow-wows and tribal get-togethers, before they can pick a war leader. They'll still be jawing about your Army three winters after you've departed. If they do attack, use your superior training and organization to grind them into the ground. Fear is the only thing barbarians respect!"

"You still haven't answered my question: Why do you want to join the expedition?"

The old trader grinned. "I'm dying of boredom, pleasant and enjoyable boredom, but dying just the same. I need to get away, to see and"—he paused to sniff the air—"smell the Sea of Grass one more time. And this appears to be the expedition of all expeditions!"

"You do understand, I do not know when, or even if, any or all of us, will return."

"Yes, Strategos, know. I also know that you are traveling to the lands beyond the Sea of Grass, places I've never seen. I would never forgive myself, if I missed such a grand opportunity."

He nodded, the old man made as much sense as anything else on this gods-forsaken expedition. He was fortunate to have the old trader; the younger merchants had refused the moment they learned that their destination was not Grefftscharr, but Hos-Ktemnos. Several traders had agreed to accompany the party as far as Greffa, where they planned to take their own wagon trains of goods. He was agreeable, since he might find their goods useful. Whether the merchants were allowed to depart would depend on the circumstances of their journey. Garnoth was the only one traveling to the lands of the Zarthani.

"There will certainly be new and strange sights, and as much adventure as any man can stand," he said.

Garnoth started wheezing again, while pounding his knees with joy. "The stories I'll be able to tell."

He didn't want to say it out loud, but Zarphu doubted the old man would survive the war against Kalvan the Usurper. Still, there were worse ways to die. He questioned the trader about his previous travels along the Iron Trail and made notes of the important things. Later he would have one of his scribes gather the old man and the other merchants to go over the old maps he'd brought from Antiphon. Together they should be able to provide a more accurate map than the one he already had. This Kalvan was said to positively dote on maps; it was a feature they both shared. After this expedition, he would have maps that would be the signposts for future armies.

VII

When he'd exhausted the trader's storehouse of information, Arch-Stratego Zarphu decided it was time to get to the meat of the matter. "What do you know of these priests of *Styphon*? They seem to be an untrustworthy lot in my estimation."

Garnoth the Trader nodded. "A nasty clutch of thieves masquerading as priests, Arch-Strategos. The Grefftscharrers don't trust them, and neither do I. There's not many of their heathen temples in Greffa, only one or two small ones. They do have several large banking houses. The

Styphoni priests over-charge for their fireseed, then sell the dregs to the Grefftscharrers. And only small amounts at that; they absolutely refuse— to sell their precious fireseed or their firetubes—to us! As if we were bar- barians, ourselves, instead of the oldest civilization in the world. It's an abomination, Strategos!"

"I agree, but we were forced into an alliance with them by our Lord Tyrant."

The old trader made a sly grin. "By the *madman*. I've heard tales—are they true?"

They're worse than your feeble mind can conjure, old man, but he kept his thoughts to himself. "We have enough to worry about on this journey without fishing for more, trader."

"Aye, Your Excellency. However, beware of any deals you make with the House of Styphon. Their highpriests are not to be trusted."

VIII

After leaving Mythrene, the army made very good progress through the foothills, Zarphu considered, having covered almost a hundred marches in three days mostly in pouring rain. They made camp around a former stone way station for the Iron Trail; the old way stations were po- sitioned a day's travel apart for a heavy loaded caravan. This station only had all four walls and none of the roof timbers had caved in, although the slate roof was long gone—probably scavenged by the locals. It showed signs of recent occupancy, but the scouts found no one in the vicinity except an abandoned lumber camp about twenty marches away; the land was heavily forested, mostly second-growth trees.

He made the way station the officer's bivouac. They erected a tem- porary roof and, after three days of riding in the rain, he welcomed the respite from the constant drizzle. The previous way stations had been re- claimed right down to their foundations. If their guide hadn't pointed the previous one out, he would have thought it was just another ruin. This station was far enough away from Mythrene to make hauling the stone too costly. Several centuries ago, it had been the Tyrant of Mythrene's responsibility to keep the stations manned and maintained; now, they were just a memory of the olden days.

From what his agents-inquisitory had been able to determine, less than four or five expeditions left Mythrene for the Iron Trail annually. Two-thirds returned each year, and those that did turned a good profit. Trade was mostly for copper, brass, glassware, furs, jewels and buffalo hides. Occasionally, one or another party would return with a firestick, usually rusted and useless, and less frequently some of the fireseed powder. He had promised the Lord Tyrant that he wouldn't return until he had both firestick makers and the secret of fireseed manufacture—even if he had to kidnap a highpriest of Styphon's House.

If he didn't return without them, it would cost his family their lives. Of course, he had to cross the Sea of Grass first and help the false priests win their war against the man they called a demon in human form.

He heard the noise of leather chafing metal and the sounds of boots on stone, indicating that the Zarthani merchant had been brought to the guard station.

"Strategos, sir."

"Yes, Baltrath."

"The Trader Jorand has arrived, sir."

"Good. Bring him in."

The portly merchant followed Sergeant Baltrath into his chamber, their footsteps echoing within the stone walls.

"Your Excellency, Captain-General Zarphu, I am delighted to meet you at last."

He doubted the veracity of those words; the merchant was sweating profusely and even his thick robe was stained around the armpits. The rain had ended half a candle ago and it was a cool evening.

"What can you tell me about the House of Styphon?"

"I try to avoid them whenever possible, Your Excellency," he said, with a sickly smile.

His tongue was heavily accented, but the words were similar to Ros-Zarthani. There was a falseness to the man that made Zarphu distrust him even though he was obviously doing his best to please him. However, in the merchant's favor, there was none of the false priests' arrogance or disdain in his manner.

"What about this fireseed? Where does it come from?"

"The priests make it from a formula given to them by their god, Styphon. The war between them and King Kalvan came about because he also knows the Fireseed Mystery."

"Does he...?"

"Yes, and Styphon's House says he has released it to the world; this has gained him the undying hatred of the Temple. They will do anything to bring Kalvan and his House down."

Maybe we hired out to the wrong party, he thought. Still, it appeared that half his worries were solved even before they crossed the Shield of God mountains. "Can you teach me how to make it?"

"No, I do not know the formula. There are princedoms in Hos-Hostigos and Hos-Harphax, where it is known. But not in Hos-Ktemnos, where even talking about it is worth your life."

That was unfortunate. He wasn't sure he believed the trader; on the other hand, he had no reason to lie. Maybe he was afraid of the priests.

"What about the firesticks?"

Jorand shook his head. "I'm not an artificer. I know you use an iron tube for the barrel and wood for a stock, but I wouldn't know how to make one of those tubes or flintlock gadgets."

"We have working models. Maybe if you had some encouragement...."

The merchant paled. "I'd have to do a lot of tinkering to get it right. Who knows how long it might take?"

Trader Jorand appeared to be all thumbs. It didn't appear that Zarphu was going to get out of this expedition that easily. *Too bad*, he thought, although, he might have had a tough time explaining to the Tyrant why he reneged on his contract, just to save the lives of a few soldiers. It wouldn't take long for their master artificers to produce the *calivers* and *arquebuses* in large quantities; the only thing holding them back had been the lack of fireseed. Once they got the formula from the Hostigi, then they would be able to make their own firetubes, too.

IX

Jorand looked down at the passes and mountains below and felt his breath grow short; the view was as magnificent as it had been the first time he'd come up the mountains, back when he was a forty-niner and working undercover. "The Rocky Mountains," that's what they were named on Europo-American, he recalled. The wilderness was as unspoiled as it had been over a hundred years ago, when he was passing himself off as a gold miner. At the time, he'd needed a quick source of money to pay off the last of his debts; purchasing illegal longevity treatments had cost a bundle.

True, gold was almost worthless on Home Time Line. There was enough cached in vaults and on the moon from uncountable expeditions to make it as common as iron. However, outtime it was still a very valuable commodity. With the gold he'd got from his mines, he'd built up quite a fortune in only a few years. It really helped when you knew where the good ore and rich veins of gold were before you left Home Time Line; all the unclassified data collected outtime was available to any Paratimer in the Master Resource Data Bank. Metals were useful, but of no great value.

The really valuable outtime resources were original artworks, jewelry, ancient artifacts, furs, incunabula, recordings of rare or new music, unknown fossils, secret knowledge and rites, new inventions, master paintings and, maybe the most valuable of all—beautiful women.

Jorand had specialized in providing gorgeous young girls, sold as mistresses or slaves or wives; he was indifferent to their fates. They were as lovely and as insubstantial—with their short lifetimes—as butterflies. In San Francisco during the Gold Rush, there had been plenty of gorgeous girls and women, many of them prostitutes or gold-diggers, most of them untraceable. He had secretly traded them on Home Time Line for Paratime Exchange Units and for influence. Those were the good old days....

Now, he was stuck in an even more primitive milieu on Aryan-Transpacific, dependent on a crazy man for a way home. He shook his head. He would have to make the best of it, but it wasn't easy. Everywhere he went, he felt Warntha's eyes on him. His impersonation of a Styphon's House highpriest was frightfully good. Even the real priests were afraid of him. Oddly, Warntha got along very well with the Ros-Zarthani soldiers; at least, the rank and file. He wondered what the Warntha's real mission was....

The trail leading down through the mountains was about the width of one of the primitive horse-drawn wagons, or as wide as the tracks on those railroads he'd rode when he crossed the great divide on his way from San Francisco to New York. He wondered what he'd do once the journey was finished. No one had told him anything; Tharn had told him to follow Warntha's lead, but he didn't trust the former mercenary. He suspected his life would end when the journey finished. He needed to prepare for that eventuality, which meant he needed currency, or what passed for it here on Kalvan's Time Line. And he needed a place to go....

X

Verkan was beginning to feel—and not for the first time—that his time on Kalvan's Time Line was more and more turning into a job rather than a hobby. The problems there followed him to Home Time Line, just like problems here followed him to Kalvan's Time Line. The mess on Alexandrian-Roman, Seleuco-Macedonian Subsector had been easy to clean up in comparison. One of the employees of Vendrax Luxury Imports had freelanced in local dives as a mind reader, using a miniature radio and a local confederate. The problems started when his confidence game began to bore him and he decided to return to First Level for help with his new con, becoming the God Alexander.

The would-be mind reader saw this as the opportunity of a lifetime, hypno-meched all the available data on Alexander the Great, had a cheap face sculpt. Unfortunately, he was recognized by the locals as Alexander as soon as he exited the Vendrax pottery factory. The locals went gaga and started a city-wide riot.

They overthrew their local tyrant and were threatening to restore the false-Alexander to Imperial greatness when the Paratime Police were notified of the problem by a supervisor at Vendrax who didn't buy his corpse switch.

Unfortunately, the local Paratime Police Inspector in charge of operations on that subsector was a drone waiting for his retirement and had botched a rescue job, killing several hundred locals and using enough technology for cries of witchcraft to be uttered in the streets. Verkan had been called in because the Inspector refused to leave and he had to personally fire him and those subordinates stupid enough to go along with his plan instead of notifying Paratime HQ.

By the time Verkan arrived, it was obvious the Paratimer was terrified at the havoc he'd caused and really only wanted to get out of town. However, he had his own bodyguard and several advisors who saw him as their ride to the top; they weren't going to allow anything to get in the way, including the false Alexander's desire to do a quick skip. Meanwhile, a major war was brewing and very little trade was happening at Vendrax Luxuries.

It had taken Verkan and his investigators three days to find out where they were keeping the false Alexander, on the top of a four-story warehouse in Alexandria. They came in at midnight on an airbus, dusted the place with sleep gas, landed on the roof, broke in and 'liberated' Alexander, who was now in the hands of the Bureau of Psych-Hygiene for a memory wipe and psycho-social adjustment.

Verkan had returned to his office to find Kostran absent-mindedly twirling his pipe, sitting across from Verkan's horseshoe desk. "You're supposed to be in Greffa representing the House of Verkan—what are you doing here?" Verkan asked, as he sat down.

"Chief, we've run across a real anomaly. Zinganna and I agreed that you needed to be brought up to speed on what's been happening in Greffa the last couple of days."

I haven't been gone that long, Verkan thought to himself. "What happened? A palace coup?"

"Nothing that bad. We've just verified local reports that a large army from the West Coast of the Northern Minor Land Mass is traveling north across the old Iron Trail. It will be arriving on Grefftscharrer territory in two or three days."

"What? Isn't that the home of the Ros-Zarthani—the supposedly decadent ancestors of the Zarthani populations on the East Coast? What are they doing on the old Iron Trail?"

Kostran shrugged. "Their army is too small to be an invasion force, but it's too big for anything but trouble—at least, that's how the Grefftscharrers see it. We believe they're from the city-state of Antiphon, but have been unable to verify this since we don't have any agents there. The Ros-Zarthani army has all of Greffa in an uproar."

"I don't doubt it. The Grefftscharrers usually expect their enemies to attack from the east or south, not from the west. What are they going to do about it?"

Kostran stopped twirling his pipe, loaded the barrel and lit up. "The Council of Merchants wanted King Theovacar to raise an army and send them packing. The Assembly of Lords was in agreement."

"That's a first. I can't remember the last time those two bodies agreed on the color of the sky! I take it that Theovacar wasn't too anxious to take on this invading army?"

"You're right, Chief. There's no gain for him no matter what he does. If Theovacar raises an army and defeats the barbarians, so what—they're just a bunch of hicks with spears. On the other hand, if he loses— Theovacar is in a mess of trouble and could lose his throne. Not that either the Council or Assembly of Lords would shed any tears. Neither body is happy about the way King Theovacar has been centralizing his authority in Grefftscharr."

"That's a given. So what did he do?"

"Theovacar told them that as long as the barbarian army did not commit an act of war he was not able to justify attacking them. However, if one of his barons or princes felt threatened, they were free to raise their own army. The Prince of Thagnor, who's been trying to slip out of Theovacar's leash for years, decided to raise an army of his own. Prince Varrack did a pretty good job; about six thousand levy, three thousand mercenary horse and the Army of Thagnor—another four thousand men."

Verkan nodded. "Good move, you've got to hand it to King Theovacar. Even if the Prince wins, he'll lose a lot of troops; if he doesn't win, he might not only lose face but his life as well. How did Varrack get his troops into Greffa without starting a civil war?"

"He's having them ferried over now. They'll be arriving in a few days. One might almost think Varrack had something to do with this invasion, if we didn't know better."

Verkan nodded. "You're right. I bet Theovacar isn't sleeping well these days. After all, it's Theovacar's job, not his nobles' place, to defend his kingdom from invasion, whether they can be classed as 'hicks with spears' or not."

"I think Theovacar's afraid that if he moves the Royal Army away from Greffa City, his enemies will attempt a coup—or start a civil war, while he's out of town. It's the same problem Great King Lysandros faces if he heads up the Harphaxi Royal Army and chases after Kalvan in Hos-Hostigos next spring. If Theovacar stays in Greffa while his troops march off, he's even more of a coup target."

Living in Greffa hadn't slowed Kostran's mental muscles; if anything it had quickened them. "So what's Theovacar's answer?"

"So far, he's not talking. There's lots of grumbling in the streets about Kings who don't honor their oaths and obligations—mostly from his petty barons, at this point. The commoners don't care since they feel safe behind the city walls. The merchants are too busy rubbing their hands together over all the profits they're making selling fireseed, food stocks and weapons to Varrack and his crowd. Meanwhile, Theovacar's most vocal opponents are playing soldier with Prince Varrack. Maybe he's hoping they'll get their heads handed to them on a platter!"

Verkan laughed. "I wouldn't put it past him. I'd like to see him work the Executive Council."

Kostran joined in the laughter.

After he'd stopped laughing, Verkan asked, "Kostran, what are Prince Varrack's chances?"

"It's hard to tell. We know very little about the West Coast city-states.

I've already picked two agents to infiltrate Mythrene City. They'll find out what's going on since that city is the drop-off point for Ros-Zarthani expeditions along the old Iron Trail.

"We have done some nighttime aerial surveillance and it appears that this Ros-Zarthani army is a first class operation by the way it's run, but they've never encountered firearms before—that's a big liability. On the other hand, the Greffans are over-confident and Prince Varrack's never been in a battle this size. I'd call it a tossup."

Verkan shook his head. "I hate to take sides, but I hope Varrack beats the iron pants off the Ros-Zarthani and sends them back to Antiphon where they belong. Kalvan's got enough problems without another army to worry about."

XI

Captain-General Phidestros watched as the two Knights, in blackened armor and white capes with Styphon's black sun-wheel emblazoned on the back, brought Grand Master Soton's chair in and then waited at attention while the Grand Master strutted in and took his seat. Phidestros was surprised to note how much Soton had aged; there were sharp lines around his eyes and mouth, and his beard had turned mostly gray. He wondered what had caused him the most pain, losing thousands of his beloved Knights on Phyrax Field or having to explain to the Inner Circle of Styphon's House his 'retreat' from Kalvan's army? Neither could have been easy, but knowing Soton as he did, he suspected the former.

"Grand Master Soton, can I offer you some winter wine?"

Soton excused one of his Knights, but the Sergeant stayed. "Yes, I could use a drink. I have spent far too many hours talking to nobles with more iron between their ears than in their spines." He sounded weary and a little hoarse.

"We could always meet tomorrow, Grand Master."

"No, I can only stay for a moon-quarter more, and then I have to return to Balph. We have a lot to discuss if the invasion of Hos-Hostigos is to be successful."

"Agreed. Mynoss, serve us some wine." After his servant had brought them all, including Sergeant Sarmoth, goblets of red winter wine, Phidestros made a toast. "To Styphon and the fall of the false Kingdom of Hos-Hostigos."

After a long swallow, Soton offered up another toast. "And to Great King Lysandros!"

"To Great King Lysandros."

"Unfortunately, that is about the only good news to come from the Sastragathi debacle."

"That is hardly true, Grand Master. You drove the barbarians into the Trygath, threatening western Hostigos, which prevented Kalvan from invading Hos-Harphax, something he could have done with ease this spring. Instead he spent the campaign season chasing you."

"I am glad to see *you* believe our sacrifice was not in vain."

"I don't just believe it, I know it, Grand Master. If you had not divert-ed Kalvan's attention to the west, Hos-Harphax would be no more—and Harphax a princedom of Hos-Hostigos! If you still believe, as you did last year, that Hos-Harphax is the anchor of the Five Kingdoms, then your sacrifice was well-made."

"I hope you are right," Soton said. "The entire campaign was a night-mare I'd just as soon forget...."

"We have made great progress here."

"Tell me about it."

"By Styphon's Grace and much of his gold, I have completely rebuilt the Army of Hos-Harphax; it now musters over eighteen thousand men: two thousand Royal Pistoleers, eight hundred of the King's Royal Lancers, four thousand Royal Foot Guard and four thousand Mobile Dragoons—mounted infantry much like Kalvan's Mobile Force, made up of the best of the City Militia—and a dozen mercenary regiments. I've recently hired another six thousand mercenaries, four thousand foot and two thousand horse; all have agreed to join the Royal Army—for a price. I've formed two mobile batteries of four six-pounders and six four-pounders each and one Royal Rifle Company with seventy-six riflemen.

"Excellent!—Captain-General. You have been busy. But how well trained are these troops?"

"Every third man in each company is a veteran, and we've been drill-ing them six days a moon-quarter since spring. They're not seasoned yet, but they are in good spirits. I'm paying them twice the usual salary and year round—"

"So that was how you convinced the mercenaries to join the Royal Army." Soton nodded thoughtfully. "Year round! I can hear Archpriest Drayton, the Temple's Treasurer, screaming all the way from Balph."

"No you won't. I'm not paying them all in gold. Half their salary is paid in iron coin, redeemable in gold *only* when Kalvan's army has been defeated."

"Brilliant." Soton shook his head as he took out a burl pipe with silver inlay. "By what spell do you convince soldiers to accept iron in place of gold?"

"All soldiers are gamblers and see nothing ahead but the piles of gold they will win when the Army of Hostigos has been vanquished. It has also given them a great incentive to work on their drills. Besides, many of the local merchants, ladies of the evening and gamblers accept the iron coins at a discount."

"If that is true, truly you have brought about Styphon's Own Miracle! Styphon be praised! If the local slatterns and sharpers are willing to take these iron rakmars in trade, then even the scum must believe that we will prevail. I wish the Archpriests of the Inner Circle shared their faith."

"They will, Grand Master. They will. The City Militia is now more than ten thousand strong, and are better armed and better drilled than in living memory. Every moon I have a thousand of them brought to Tarr-Anibra where they are drilled from first light to dark. They do much better away from Tarr-Harphax and the City walls. They will not run as they did at Chothros Heights."

"You have made great progress in the past year—even more than I ex-pected. Yet, this shortage of mercenaries may yet prove our undoing. I had hoped you would have twelve to fifteen thousand Free Companions by this time, but far too many have died in this Ormaz-spawned war against the Usurper—or worse, have taken his colors. Archpriest Anaxthenes put before me an idea that may help solve our problem. Let me present it to you."

Soton explained how Styphon's House had merchants and agents-inquisitory who traveled as distant as the far off West Coat settlements of the Ros-Zarthani. One of these agents had been authorized by the Inner Circle to hire an entire army of Ros-Zarthani. Word had recently arrived in Balph that they were almost across the Sea of Grass.

"This is interesting news," Phidestros said, his face trying to hide his disappointment. He needed these western barbarians like he needed another regiment of royal lancers. "How do we know they will not break the first time Kalvan's guns fire?"

Soton shrugged. "They may be sounder troops than you suspect. The agent-inquisitory has informed Archpriest Anaxthenes that the Ros-Zarthani know neither kingdoms nor princedoms as we do. Each city acts as its own kingdom—yes, a chaotic system of rule that leads to much fighting. A highpriest was sent by Archpriest Roxthar to 'hire' an army from one of the larger cities to aid in our war against the Usurper Kalvan. The army will march from their home, across the Sea of Grass and through Grefftscharr."

"You mean some highpriest, who doesn't know a rake from a ramrod, has hired an unknown army and believes it will pass unmolested through the Sea of Grass? The Grefftscharri will pulverize it as grindstone mills wheat. Why not skirt Greffa all together, by taking the—"

"Fighting the Greffa Army is be their test, as I understand it. These troops have never faced fireseed, and it is well that they do so before they meet the Royal Army of Hos-Hostigos in the field. It will take Styphon's Own Miracle for them to arrive as an intact unit. Yet, this Highpriest Prythos believes that these Ros-Zarthani can more than hold their own against the nomads and Grefftscharrers. At least he has convinced Archpriest Anaxthenes and Roxthar that this is so."

"Anaxthenes may know all there is to be known about running temple services and pulling Supreme Priest Sesklos' strings, but he knows nothing of war."

"Don't underestimate Archpriest Anaxthenes. Any Archpriest who has survived for twenty winters in the Inner Circle has more understanding of command than you might think. There is even talk that he will become the next Voice of Styphon."

Suddenly all is clear, Phidestros thought. Lysandros might believe the gathering host was his army, but Styphon's House had a different opinion. "Since the Temple pays, we cannot lose. What weapons do they use?"

"They still fight in full armor and on destriers, much as our ancestors did and your Royal Lancers do now."

"Oh no, more iron hats! Kalvan's artillery will harvest them before they have time to set their lances."

"Not all of them. Many use bows or carry heavy throwing darts."

Phidestros shook his head. "Darts and bows! They will probably run when the first shot is fired."

"If half of what this Highpriest Prythos claims is true, they may surprise both you, me and—most importantly, Kalvan. At worst, they will serve as a screen for our own troops."

"For how long has Styphon's House purchased these *soldiers*?"

"Styphon's House has paid their city well; they are under contract to fight for two years, or until the Usurper Kalvan is dead, whichever happens first. Scoff if you must, but answer me this: where else do you intend to find more mercenaries to fight under our banners?"

Phidestros shook his head. "There are no more mercenaries to be bought in the Five Kingdoms, not for gold or glory. No, bring these iron hats, and we will find some use for them—if they ever arrive! If nothing else, they will give Kalvan's guns targets while my men do more serious work."

XII

A cloud of dust on the far horizon usually meant a herd of buffalo or cattle were moving across the Sea of Grass. Today Arch-Stratego Zarphu knew it was neither; it was the advancing Grefftscharrer Army. His scouts had already told him the disposition of the enemy army: six thousand infantry, mostly carrying long spears and firesticks, four thousand heavy cavalry and two thousand light auxiliaries, mostly Ruthani cavalry recruited from the grasslands. He told one of his orderlies to fetch the Highpriest.

Highpriest Warntha rode quickly to his side in a very soldierly and un-priestly manner that of which heartily approved. "I see the enemy is closing."

Zarphu ignored the snorts of disapproval from his senior officers; he knew the difference between priests and soldiers even if his officers didn't. "This is not an ideal place for a battle." He paused to indicate the flat lands on all sides. "Nor is it a good place for an ambush."

The Highpriest, who no longer wore his yellow robes, nodded. "If we can defeat the Grefftscharrer Army here, we can perform both a service to Styphon and a disservice to the Usurper Kalvan. The Kings of Grefftscharr only rule as long as they show enough strength to cow both their under-lords and the powerful merchants of Greffa. It has been rumored that arms have been shipped from Greffa to the false kingdom of Hostigos. A win here will be the first victory of next year's campaign!"

Zarphu was impressed with the priest's knowledge of things other than arcane rites and offerings of his trade and wondered if he had served in a military order before putting on his robes. He'd learned from the fat merchant that Styphon's House had two military arms of its own. Zarphu had tried to question Highpriest Warntha about his past but might have had better success with a stone, could any be found on this endless grassland.

Zarphu was not as convinced as the priest that his army—though greater in size—would be able to seize the battlefield. His knowledge of the enemy was negligible and his own army had no experience fighting against the firesticks. The Highpriest had demonstrated the noisy and smelly "muskets" and they had proved to be capricious. The fireseed had to be dry or they would not fire. However, the muskets were deadly when fired—if they hit their target. Unlike his archers, who could hit the eye socket of an approaching enemy from a hundred paces.

His soldiers were all experienced troops—fourteen maniples of a thousand men each, eight of horse and six of foot soldiers. Plus, two maniples of the Lord Tyrant's own Immortals—heavy armored cavalry who fought with spear and broadsword.

Zarphu turned to Stratego Lyphar and ordered, "The enemy is two marches away. When they are one march, have the foot archers and skirmishers run ahead and engage the enemy. They are not to hold, but fall back and draw the enemy in."

He turned to another general and ordered him to support Lyphar's foot with his light cavalry, mostly horse-archers and javelin throwers. Then he addressed Highpriest Warntha. "I would have taken the river route that my scouts recommended, but I also thought it might be best to test the mettle of the Eastern ironmen."

Warntha looked over in surprise, and even had the grace to blush. It was the first time Zarphu had read any emotion on the priest's face. If these priestly troops of Styphon's were not soldiers at arms, they were soldiers of the heart.

"You must remember, Highpriest, our records go back almost two thousand winters. We have traversed these lands and trails more times than there are nomads upon the Sea of Grass. While it is true that trade between us and the Middle Kingdoms has dwindled to a trickle, there are still among us those who trade along the old routes. Several of these are among our scouts. I am as anxious as you are to see how well my men hold up against the firesticks. However, I suspect you will be the more surprised."

It was also true that Zarphu sounded more confident about his troops than he felt. His people had heard stories about these fire weapons for centuries, and had obtained more than a few over the years of trading.

However, as long as the fireseed was scarce, they were more curiosities than real weapons. One of the traders had told him that the fireseed mystery was no longer a secret. If this were true, he would take back more than gold from these distant lands. With the firesticks, the Lord Tyrant would be able to complete his conquest of the city-states and expand his reach into the Sea of Grass and maybe even farther.

The light foot soldiers began to run forward and the heavy infantry, with full body shields and long spears, went into a double time. The massed heavy cavalry followed to exploit any breaks in the enemy lines. If all went well, the archers and javelin throwers would sting the enemy army, bringing forth the more impetuous cavalry and foot. Then the skirmishers would retreat behind the shield wall and the slaughter would commence; at least, that was how it was done in the homelands. Nothing was certain against an unknown enemy—except uncertainty.

XIII

Prince Varrack, purple plumes jutting out from the back of his burgonet, pointed to the growing mass of men, the sun sparkling off their armor, in the distance. "There are the Ros-Zarthani barbarians. We shall ride over them as the buffalo trample the Ruthani tent cities!"

"Your Lordship, I suggest we move to the rear just in case a stray spear comes our way," one of the Barons suggested. "Let the professional soldiers do their work."

"There will be few casualties today, my friend." Prince Varrack said, slapping the Baron on the back with his gauntleted hand. The nobleman, who wore no more armor than a silvered breastplate over his red and black velvet doublet, staggered forward, almost falling off his mount. When he had regained his poise, he gave Varrack a pained expression. "My back hurts!"

Varrack had to choke back a laugh. Such weakness was all too typical of Greffa's decadent nobility. Many of them wore more perfume than his courtesans. *This will all change after the vile dog Theovacar is put in his place. I will return the Middle Kingdoms to their past glory, with Thagnor the king of cities, and it all begins today with my crushing defeat of these barbarians.*

Another noble, this one with a cultivated lisp, announced, "Please, let us stay at the front, Varrack, so we can watch these creatures die up-close!"

A young Count, with a wispy blond beard, cried, "This is so much better than one of Theovacar's Spectacles. One grows tired of pantomime sea battles and bear fights."

Captain-General Errock said with gritted teeth, "Your Lordship, my men need to prepare for battle. We will be hampered if we have to spend our time protecting your guests." The way he stepped on the last word left no doubt about his own feelings concerning the martial ability of Grefftscharrer nobles in general.

"We shall retire, Captain-General. It is your job to win this battle." Under his breath, Prince Varrack added, "And win me the glory I need to challenge Theovacar in his own city."

XIV

The battle opened almost like a scroll-written exercise out of Arch-Stratego Zarphu's library. It appeared the Grefftscharrer soldiers held his army in contempt, allowing their own front ranks to break as they attempted to chase down the annoying skirmishers. The archers and spearmen quickly pulled back behind the now stationary shield wall and—once the enemy was within bow range—began to fire at will. Several hundred disorganized enemy light cavalry ran into the shield wall; many of them were impaled on spears or shot out of their saddles by arrows. When an enemy fell, a skirmisher would rush from behind the shields and dispatch him with a quick sword thrust.

When enemy cavalry advanced to the shield wall, the surviving skirmishers and light cavalry moved to the wings. Meanwhile the enemy foot soldiers marched forward, setting their long spears and firesticks. The archers continued their steady stream of arrows, with gratifying results as the enemy was forced to close ranks and cease forward movement. Now the Grefftscharrer cavalry was forced to stand and take fire until their own infantry arrived. Meanwhile the archers and spearmen killed hundreds of Grefftscharrers, since only the front ranks of the Grefftscharrer cavalry wore full armor.

The enemy horse parted and a large body of firestick men and others carrying short bows with stocks moved forward. Suddenly, the firesticks crackled and sputtered, and a cloud of smoke with the stink of brimstone filled the air.

A noise like thunder hammered Zarphu's ears! For a moment he thought his horse would buck him off its back. Several of his officers were thrown, but most quickly remounted. For a few moments there were holes in the shield wall, and the entire line buckled, until the rear ranks moved up. Only a few men broke ranks and they were cut down by the swords of their comrades. It appeared to Zarphu that most of the firesticks' force was spent on the shields. The flight of arrows fired in answer inflicted many more casualties among the unprotected Grefftscharrer infantry, especially the firestick men who were not wearing steel chest plates.

The firestick men fired several times, but the shield wall held. The enemy's own lines took many more casualties from bow fire and javelins.

Out of the cloud of smoke a large body of enemy horse, mostly armored, rushed forward striking the shield wall. Again the wall held, while the spear points spitted horses that screamed and bucked off their riders. Skirmishers rushed forward with long knives to slash the throats of the fallen horsemen and their mounts. The stalled enemy cavalry milled in front of the shield wall, futilely hacking at it with their swords or firing short firesticks, until their commanders ordered a retreat. When their surviving cavalry were back behind their own lines, the firestick men fired off their firesticks in unison.

One of his chief officers dropped off his saddle, sprouting a red hole just above his left eye. Zarphu cursed and wondered how many more irreplaceable troops he would lose in this battle.

The infantry battle continued, with the bowmen's arrows inflicting three times as many casualties as the firesticks. The enemy infantry began to bunch-up even tighter and the slaughter mounted. The Grefftscharrer foot became bunched together so closely that the enemy cavalry were forced to fight along the wings, where they were sternly rebuffed by the Immortals. Zarphu decided it was time to order forth his own heavy horse.

The horns sounded, and the infantry pulled back into lines. The iron-scaled cavalry moved forward through the infantry, while the shield wall reformed behind them.

The three maniples of plumbati pushed forward until they were within range of the enemy, then took out their heavy darts, casting them into the massed infantry. The enemy infantry were momentarily paralyzed, then forced together so closely only a few of the firestick men could shoot their weapons. The archers ran forward again, supported by horse-archers and began firing point blank into the massed Grefftscharrer foot. The slaughter was horrific, causing many of the enemy's long spearmen casting their weapons aside and trying to break rank—only to find there was nowhere to go. The ground ran with streams of the enemy's blood.

The plumbati pulled out their swords and cut their way through the ranks. Suddenly the entire body of enemy foot broke ranks, trampling those who stood in their way. The heavy spearmen now moved forward, cutting and slicing those left behind by the forward movement of the heavy cavalry. The enemy cavalry, spurred by the sight of their own re-treating foot, rode over and through their own ranks to reach the plumbati—and died by the score.

Zarphu nodded and another horn sounded. Both left and right wings of heavy cavalry moved out in a flanking pincers movement to surround the enemy army. He was sorely disappointed when the enemy horns sud-denly rang out, and the Grefftscharrer horse turned and retreated, leaving behind several thousand foot soldiers. The enemy horse reformed ranks before the wings could close, but the plumbati struck them hard from the rear.

The Grefftscharrer infantry were completely surrounded and disor-dered; the battlefield was littered with their brightly colored corpses. The cavalry reformed to chase the enemy horse, which fled so hurriedly they left behind their wounded.

Seeing their own cavalry flee, the Grefftscharrer foot surrendered, putting their helmets upon their swords. The survivors numbered less than half of those who had joined the battle. Zarphu rubbed his hands— a nice ransom.

Highpriest Prythos, too, had a big smile. He nodded, saying, "I am impressed, Arch-Stratego." They both watched as the enemy horse, under withering fire, left in a massed but orderly retreat. "Are you going to ride them down?"

"We could grind them into the dust, but they are not cowards. We would take unnecessary losses. Also, another army lies in wait some forty marches away. There is no profit in goading them to attack. Better to let them hide behind their walls and lick their wounds, Highpriest. They will not forget us soon. We have other more important battles to win. And there will be no reinforcements."

"Wisely put," the Highpriest said. "I think many will be surprised by the Iron Men from across the Sea of Grass. None more so than the Usurper Kalvan!"

XV

"What happened to my army?" Prince Varrack cried when Captain-General Errock pulled up alongside, his horse breathing and snorting like a bellows.

The Captain-General's face was white and there was blood splattered across his breastplate. "A lot of good men died because we underestimated the enemy. It's the Trickster's own luck that the Ros-Zarthani didn't decide to chase us to the City walls."

"This is good fortune?" Varrack screamed, looking around at the rag-tag collection of horsemen that surrounded him, their finery soiled and their plumed helmets discarded. "We have lost a great battle, and you talk of luck!"

"We will be laughed out of the City," one of the Barons shouted.

Varrack punched the Baron in the face with his gauntlet, knocking him off his horse and onto the ground, where he was stretched out frozen as if he'd been poleaxed.

"You've killed him, Varrack!" the young Count cried. "This day has been a disaster for all of us."

Except Theovacar, thought Varrack, *who right this moment is laughing himself off his throne!* He ground his teeth until they squealed. *If we'd had King Theovacar's support, this defeat would never have happened. He withheld his soldiers to play us as fools! This disaster is his fault. Theovacar is in the pay of the Usurper Kalvan, as the priests of Styphon's House claim, otherwise he would have helped us take the field. Yes, this disaster is the result of Theovacar's treason! Wait until the City learns of it.*

XVI

Warntha Saln was sitting by the campfire drinking the piss-water the Ros-Zarthani called beer and discussing close-order tactics with an under officer of the Fourth Maniple when he felt the vibration from his locater alert. He quickly excused himself from the conversation, using the time-tested excuse of going to the latrine. Instead of heading straight to the trenches, Warntha swung around to the northwest where his locater indicated, through increasing vibrations, the homing signal was originating.

Warntha spotted the silver mesh of the twenty-foot Transtemporal conveyer in a small glade. He had been wondering when Hadron Tharn was going to send someone to pick him up. After their defeat of the Grefftscharrer army, the Ros-Zarthani army had followed the trail to Dorg where water transport was being arranged to ferry the army down river south of Wulfula to Tarr-Ceros, where they would winter. The Dorgi had refused transit rights to ship Zarphu and his men down the river until the defeat of the Grefftscharrer army. Now they couldn't get the Ros-Zarthani across the Great River fast enough.

Warntha wouldn't have minded staying with the Ros-Zarthani; the company was good—mostly fellow soldiers who had accepted him as one of their own despite his disguise as one of Styphon's highpriests. The possibilities for future fighting seemed endless, so he was content. He was especially looking forward to fighting against Kalvan and his Army of Hos-Hostigos.

On the other hand, things were never dull when Hadron Tharn was around. Warntha was surprised to find he actually missed his crazy boss.

The conveyer door opened to show Tharn with a welcoming smile, flanked by two guards in the black uniforms. "How was your exercise?"

Warntha took a seat inside the conveyer across from his boss and said, "It was a nice vacation. The Ros-Zarthani soldiers are good troops, even without gunpowder weapons. They'll give Kalvan fits, but not enough to be decisive."

Tharn's face blanked. "None of my plans are working. I'm hemmed in on every side by morons and incompetents! The Opposition Party has refused my latest donation! They claim that Chief Verkan's new policy of phased harvesting of the Europo-American Sector is workable and acceptable by all parties. So Verkan wins once again!"

Warntha was used to his bosses' sudden mood shifts, but this one took him by surprise. He wasn't exactly sure why his boss hated Paratime Chief Verkan Vall, but he suspected it had something to do with his sister Dalla. Or maybe the fact that he was the more powerful of the two. "What about Jorand? I didn't have time to make the memory transfer."

"Leave him here to rot. He can't do us any harm at this point; besides, living here is punishment enough."

Warntha nodded. "So what's the next move, boss?"

"We're on our way to Fifth Level Base One."

Warntha, as an ex-military specialist, had been originally recruited by Tharn's Organization to help train troops, mostly proles being trained for military action, at Base One and Two, on the Fifth Level, Industrial Service Sector. This had been going on for almost twenty years and Tharn had created quite the private little army. The proles he was using as shock troops believed that Hadron was a supporter of the Prole Liberation Movement. Warntha, knowing Tharn's prejudices regarding proles, seriously doubted that. He still didn't know Tharn's plans, but he knew that Tharn had no good purpose in mind for any of the proles, whom he regarded as little less than beasts of burden.

Warntha had just finished cleaning his kit when the overhead flickering ceased and the silver mesh began to solidify, signaling that they had arrived at Fifth Level, Base One. The conveyer came to rest in a small room. The two guards remained behind.

From there the two of them entered a gravlift and went to the surface where they boarded a rocket and traveled to a large island. This island was at the base of the largest southern continental mass, one that usually served the Home Time Line people as a recreation spot, meaning there was very little possibility of a Paratime Police conveyer dropping in unexpectedly.

Warntha, who was dressed for higher latitudes, felt himself began to sweat as they arrived at a large military compound. There were hundreds of bat-wing fighter craft in the base airport. It took a great portion of Tharn's assets to keep this place running, but he had six air-strike teams and fifteen divisions of infantry for his own personal army. To the best of Warntha's knowledge, it was a bigger force than First Level's own military which existed primarily to put down prole insurrections and revolts.

He followed Tharn into a large conference room with a large visiscreen dominating one wall. A dozen proles in military uniforms decorated with gold braid sat around a long trestle table.

They all rose to their feet as Tharn approached.

"Citizen Tharn, when can we mount our attack?"

"General, the time has not yet arrived. More work needs to be done on Home Time Line. I advise patience.

Warntha choked back a laugh. Having Tharn advise patience was like having someone advise a friend to take a vacation on Second Level Arzl Dykx, a subsector where the survivors of an ancient nuclear holocaust still killed each other for table scraps.

One of the generals, an older man with a gray beard, said, "Citizen, with your long life, you can afford to wait. I was a young man when I joined the PML—look at me now!"

The other proles nodded in agreement.

"If all goes as I have planned, you will all receive longevity treatments. You and your children will live a long life, indeed."

Tharn's promise appeared to settle them down and the generals went back to the business of plotting the overthrow of Fifth Level Home Force Headquarters.

As a veteran of the Home Force, Warntha knew the headquarters would have to be taken by surprise for this band of half-trained and inexperienced resistance fighters to overthrow their base. *What kind of surprise attack does Thran have planned? By definition, as a Hadron Tharn plan, it would be irregular, dangerous and with total disregard to casualties—one either side.* He almost felt sorry for the proles, to say nothing of Home Time Line....

<h2 style="text-align:center">XVII</h2>

Jorand carefully approached the big-eared soldier who'd been identified as one of the last to see Warntha. "Do you know where the big priest went?"

The soldier, who was still drunk, said, "Naw, last I saw, he was off to the privy pit." He pointed to a nearby copse of trees.

"When was that?"

"Last night. Ahhh, curse and blast it! My bleedin' head hurts." He reached down and rested his hand on his sword pommel. "Enough with the questions!"

Jorand turned away and went back to the camp. *It looks like I got left behind,* he decided. If he was going to be stuck here on Kalvan's Time Line, a backward place at best, he needed a better cover than that of trader. He went back to the wagon he shared with Warntha and quickly searched it. Most of Warntha's possessions, and there weren't many, were still there; however, the money chest had been pried open and all the gold and silver removed.

"How could I be so stupid!" he asked the universe, as he quickly pawed through the remaining possessions and blankets looking for the lost coins. Only a few coppers turned up. *Now I'm broke and stranded!*

Jorand needed a new cover ID and quickly, being a broke merchant, with no friends and contacts, was not going to get him anything but a very nasty and short future. He thought rapidly and decided that he needed to learn more about Styphon's House, which seemed to be the biggest and most successful racket on Aryan-Transpacific.

He went over the Highpriest Prythos' wagon, which was bigger and better outfitted than the one he and Warntha had shared. He knocked on the side and Prythos' head emerged from the canvas slit. "What do you want?" the priest demanded.

Jorand drew out his tobacco pouch. "I thought we'd share a smoke."

The priest nodded. "Come on in."

The inside was lit by a flickering oil lamp; there were two benches, covered in thick bearskin, to sit on. He filled his pipe and then passed his pouch to the highpriest. Not being much of a smoker, he had a lot of his original supply left. The way the priest grabbed his tobacco pouch made it clear that the heavy-set man had either run out of tobacco or was down to his last few flakes.

"I can't wait till we get back to civilization so I can get some quality leaf." The Highpriest paused to shake his head, as he filled his pipe. "This journey will be my last, by Styphon's Brass Balls! Too much heat, too much dust and too many barbarians. Plus, no respect from Zarphu and his commanders, either."

"This was an important trip, wasn't it?" Jorand asked.

Highpriest Prythos nodded, and visibly swelled. "I was given this assignment by Holy Investigator Roxthar himself. The Archpriest promised that if I made a good deal with the barbarians and brought back the soldiers he wanted, I would be well rewarded."

Jorand eyes widened and he nodded, as if highly impressed. He also noticed that Prythos, with his bald head and shaved faced, looked pretty much like any other bald and shaven heavy man with a pot belly—rather like himself, less hair. The yellow robe would hide any physical differences. A plan began to blossom.

Prythos continued, "He even suggested that I might be elevated to archpriest! With no payment, either. What about that?"

"Very impressive," Jorand said, stroking his goatee. He used his First Level memory to pick up on the highpriest's voice and syntax so that he could impersonate him later on. "I suppose, as a highpriest you have your own manor in Balph?"

The priest practically preened. "Yes, it's in the northern quadrant, outside the city gates. A very nice twenty-room mansion, but nothing compared to what I'll have once I'm elevated to the Inner Circle." He went on in great detail to talk about all the slaves and servants he would purchase and what he would do to several of his enemies once he was an archpriest.

"An Archpriest! I'm fortunate to have known you." Jorand continued to fawn over the highpriest and ask him detailed questions about the Styphon's House racket and his own background. It turned out Prythos was new to Balph and didn't have a lot of friends there.

Prythos pulled out a goatskin bag of wine. "How would you like some of this? It was a present from one of the barbarians. He gave me six of them; this is the last bag."

"Sure," Jorand replied. He spent the next two candles plying the high-priest with more wine, while drinking sparingly himself. When Prythos left to visit the latrine, he used that opportunity to drug the wine. After the priest passed out, he used his knife to slit his throat, then waited until dark to dispose of the body.

Jorand dragged the body to his own wagon and put the priest inside. Then he went back to get the oil lamp. He spread the remaining oil inside his wagon and lit it on fire before returning to the highpriest's vehicle. The wagon was completely engulfed in flames before anyone in the camp noticed and no one made an attempt to try and save the merchant sup-posedly inside.

The next morning, using his knife, he cut off his hair and beard, then shaved any remaining hair with the priest's straight razor. Since the old robe had been fouled when Prythos' died, Jorand put on the dead man's cleanest yellow robe. Then he went outside to view his former wagon.

No one questioned him and took it for granted that he was Highpriest Prythos.

"What do we do with the merchant's remains, Your Worship?" one of the unkempt muleskinners asked. He looked as though he wanted to poke through the wagon's blackened shell to see if there were any coins or other treasures the fire hadn't consumed. No one appeared the least bit concerned about the dead man inside.

"You have my permission. The merchant was an unbeliever and does not merit our rituals."

"Praise Styphon!" the greedy muleskinner proclaimed.

Nor did it hurt that the dead highpriest hadn't been close to anyone in the party. The common soldiers and wagoners were intimidated by his rank and association with Styphon's House, while their commanders regarded him as a necessary pest. Jorand imitated the priest's bluff and hearty manner with the guards, telling them that it was time they made their way to Dorg. If he was going to be stuck in this wasteland, he might as well be at the top of the heap.

SIEGE AT TARR-HOSTIGOS

JOHN F. CARR & ROLAND GREEN

I

1967 A.D.

PARATIME POLICE CHIEF VERKAN VALL TRIED TO SORT HIS atypically jumbled thoughts as the transtemporal conveyer carried him toward Fourth Level Aryan-Transpacific, Kalvan Subsector. The civilized Second and Third Levels were behind him now. Once in a while he caught flickering glimpses of Fourth Level—buildings, airports, occasionally a raging battle.

Fourth Level was the highest probability of all of the inhabited Paratime Levels. There the human First Colony had come to complete disaster, in the past fifty thousand years losing all knowledge of its origins.

It was the most barbaric level, as well as the biggest. Its cultures ranged from

344

idol worshippers to the technological sophistication and social backwardness of the Europo-American, Hispano- Columbian Subsector.

It was from one of these Europo-American lines that Corporal Calvin Morrison of the Pennsylvania State Police had accidentally traveled in a conveyor to Aryan-Transpacific, Styphon's House Subsector. Thrust into a ruder and deadlier culture, Calvin (or Kalvan, as the inhabitants of that time-line called him) not only survived, he prospered—until just a few days ago. In less than four years he'd married a princess, founded an empire, broken Styphon's House's monopoly of gunpowder, and more than held his own against the worst that band of priestly tyrants could do.

No more. Styphon's House had gone on the offensive and assembled their Styphon's Grand Host; at the Battle of Andros Field the Host—after numerous ten-days of fighting—broke and defeated the outnumbered army of Hos-Hostigos. Verkan had been there on an anonymous Beshtan ridgetop, fighting with his Hostigi Mounted Rifles until wave after wave of battle-crazed Harphaxi cavalry and infantry had broken their line. In the final push, he had taken a frightful chest wound, when an infantryman had fired a big-bore musket at close range. Unfortunately, the rest of the Army of Hos-Hostigos had fared almost as badly as his command; last he'd heard was that Kalvan and what remained of his Army were retreating to Hostigos Town and its nearby castle.

He was still officially recovering, although the Opposition Party members were still calling for his resignation in the Executive Council for abuse of power and violating the Paratime Code. Until the waters settled, Verkan had been tied to his desk on First Level by piles of routine business and some non-routine schemes by his political enemies. To put it mildly, his conscience was nagging him because he couldn't be there when his friend needed him most. He refused to think about what the Bureau of Psychological Hygiene would say, if they discovered that the top Paracop was suffering from Outtime Identification Syndrome. He'd already had enough headaches for one day.

The biggest of those headaches was the fate of the Dhergabar University Study Team which had been caught up in the Hostigi rout. Like all outtime researchers, they worked under Paratime Police protection.

That might not be enough, on the kind of Fourth Level time-line where civilians were likely to end as part of the body count when a victorious army swept through hostile territory. Too many members of the University Team were still unaccounted for; every casualty among them would be a gift to the Opposition Party.

Kalvan would have to fight his own battles for a while, against even longer odds than before. He'd need skill as well as luck to save his own life and Queen Rylla's, never mind refounding his empire.

Already the Grand Host's cavalry scouts had raided almost to the outskirts of Hostigos Town. Its main body could hardly be more than a day behind. Kalvan's father-in-law, Prince Ptosphes, might be able to hold Tarr-Hostigos for a few days. If the Grand Host had to stop and lay siege to the castle, Kalvan still might never rule a kingdom again. He and Rylla might at least escape westward, to sell the services of their army somewhere in the Middle Kingdoms, menaced by barbarians and now by the Mexicotal.

The conveyer dome shimmered into material existence. They had reached Kalvan's Subsector. Verkan checked his personal equipment and headed for the hatch. Somehow four Paracops reached it before him, all with drawn Fourth Level pistols and palmed First Level sigma-ray needlers.

"Sorry, Chief," one of them said. He didn't sound sorry. Verkan looked behind and sighed. The other eight men of his personal guard had closed tightly around him from the rear. Swaddled in bodyguards like a baby in cloth, Verkan stepped out into a large storeroom. The rest of the conveyer-load of Paracops followed, lugging equipment or pushing lifter pallets.

From the outside, the conveyer-head was disguised as one of four large storehouses attached to the Royal Foundry of Hos-Hostigos. The room before them held a desk, some First Level monitoring equipment, racks of muskets, two field-gun carriages, and hundreds of sacks of oats and corn.

No good to anybody except maybe the Grand Host was Verkan's thought as he strode across the room. Like the other Paracops, he held a flintlock pistol nearly two feet long, loaded and cocked. On his head he wore a high-combed morion helmet; his clothes were a sleeveless buff jack, dark blue breeches, a bright red sash, and thigh-high boots. Nobody from Kalvan's Subsector would have thought him anything but a Hostigi light cavalry officer.

As he'd expected, the storehouse was empty of anything except mice and rats. He opened the keyed magnetic lock, stepped back, let the four point men go first, then followed at their hand signals of "All clear."

The door was intact, as he had expected. Under local oak planking, it had a collapsed-nickel core. Nothing local could even dent that, not even a two-hundred-pound stone ball from a siege bombard.

Nothing else in sight had been as lucky. The main Foundry buildings had all burned; some had collapsed. Most of the outer buildings also showed battle scars, and bodies lay everywhere.

Smoke still rose from most of the buildings. That confirmed Verkan's guess that the attack had come only hours before. The half-dozen survivors of the University Team who'd reached First Level's Kalvan Subsector Depot had been incoherent with fright, except for Baltov Eldra, who was unconscious from a head wound.

"Too many tourists," a Paracop said.

Verkan nodded. The University had insisted on doing their own investigation of Kalvan's Time Line. Short of imposing quarantine, there'd been no way to stop them. For a moment Verkan wished himself back as Special Chief's Assistant, where he could do the sensible thing without having a dozen political potentates baying at his door.

The Paracops spread out, leapfrogging from building to building, covering one another until they'd reached the edge of the Foundry on all sides. Then they posted sentries, sent a miniature spyeye to hover a thousand feet up, and began the grisly task of recovering the bodies.

Verkan turned over the nearest civilian casualty with his sword. It was the Team's expert on pre-industrial sociology, Professor Lathor Karv. He had a gaping hole in his forehead and several stab wounds in his torso, but no signs of torture.

First good news all day.

No signs of torture meant that none of Archpriest Roxthar's "Holy" Investigators had ridden with the cavalry. Hypno-mech conditioning or not, it was asking a lot of anyone to resist the kind of torture the Investigators handed out. Not that they were as efficient as the Second Level priests of Shpeegar or some Europo-American secret police agencies, but they would improve with time and practice. The Grand Host's victory had bought them the time, and Roxthar's fanatical determination to find and extirpate heresy everywhere would guarantee the practice.

Of the fifty-odd bodies in the open, some were here-and-now Foundry workers, the proverbial innocent bystanders. About twenty were mercenaries of various persuasions or undercover Paracops, and the rest members of the University Team.

"Fiasco" is a mild term for this, was Verkan's first thought. Nobody is going to be happy about it.

"Chief!" the head guard called. He ran up and lowered his voice. "We've found Agent Skordran Kirv."

Nobody, starting with me.

Skordran Kirv's dead mouth was twisted into the parody of a smile, but it looked as if he'd fought as well as he'd lived. Five troopers in yellow Harphaxi sashes lay dead and bloody around him.

Verkan cursed out loud. There went an old friend and one of the few Paracops he could still trust absolutely.

The lifter teams started loading bodies for shipment back to First Level, while the rest began the house-to-house (or ruin-to-ruin) search. In spite of the danger from smoldering embers and falling beams, they turned up twelve more Paratimer bodies, three of them Paracops. Seven skeletons too badly burned for field identification made the last load before the conveyor headed back to First Level. Paratime Police Headquarters had a full medtech team on standby, for DNA identification.

Verkan spent most of the time before the conveyer's return wandering aimlessly among the ruins. Every Paracop on this team knew when to steer clear of the Chief; Verkan knew he was being guarded but so tactfully he couldn't complain.

One thought dominated Verkan's mind. He'd thought he had a crisis, with an alliance of Opposition Party chiefs and outtime traders after his scalp over closing Fourth Level Europo-American. He had a case—too many nuclear and chemical weapons in the hands of national governments. However, he and Dalla would live through it even if he couldn't persuade anyone else.

Kalvan and Rylla were running for their lives, which might not be very long if Ptosphes's garrison of the lame and the halt couldn't hold Tarr-Hostigos for at least a few days.

As the day wore on, Verkan began to hope that the Grand Host's scouts would reappear. It was out of the question to seek the main body and tear it apart with First Level weapons. A few hundred dead cavalry troopers, however, could be labeled "noncontaminating self-defense" in an Incident Report. Their demise would make the Grand Host only a little less strong but a lot more cautious.

Or it might make people genuinely believe that demons fought for Kalvan, and create enthusiastic support for Roxthar's fifty-times-cursed Investigation! That was the problem with contamination—you couldn't control how people would interpret your intervention. Good Paracops always remembered that.

Verkan Vall gritted his teeth and decided to be a good Paracop again. He hoped his present set of teeth would survive the experience—

"Vall?"

He started to glare at the interruption, then recognized Kostran Garth, his wife Dalla's brother-in-law, and another of that handful of good friends and reliable Paracops. The conveyor must have returned with the lab test results—although from the look on Kostran's face, he was not the bearer of good news.

"I'm sorry, if that helps any," Kostran said.

"Some. Better security would have helped more. Dralm-dammit, we could have had it!"

"By Xipph's mandibles, Chief, you did all you could!" He added several more curses from a particularly vile Second Level time-line where spiders and beetles were sacred fetishes. "They sabotaged everything you and Kirv tried to do."

"They paid for it, too. But keeping that from happening was ultimately the Chiefs responsibility. *My* responsibility." Verkan managed a wry grin. "Wasn't it Kalvan's own—'Great King Truman'—who said, 'The buck stops here'?"

The grin faded, but Verkan managed not to sigh. "All right. Who did we find?"

"Five locals, Gorath Tran, and Sankar Trav, the Team medic."

"That leaves Danar Sirna and Aranth Sain unaccounted for." The two Paracops' eyes met. If the two missing people were prisoners, they were probably on their way into the hands of the Investigation. Then they'd soon wish they had burned to death instead.

"Danar Sirna. Doctoral candidate in history?"

Kostran nodded. "Right. Tall woman, auburn hair. Great figure too."

"Let's wish her better luck in her next incarnation. The soldiers here-and-now have rough-and-ready notions about dealing with enemy civilian women. What about Aranth Sain?"

"He's ex-Strike Force, one of the few Team people with survival skills. He was their expert on pre-industrial military science." Kostran hesitated. "I wonder if he was forced to try putting some of his theories into practice?"

"You mean, take an unscheduled field sabbatical?"

"Exactly. His cover is an artillery officer from Hos-Agrys and you can bet he won't break it by accident. If he catches Phidestros' eye, he may even be safe from the Investigation!"

It rubbed Verkan the wrong way, to possibly owe anything to the man principally responsible for Kalvan's defeat. Still, if under the circumstances Aranth had succumbed to the temptation that most outtime workers felt every so often—Verkan could only wish him luck.

Now, to interrogate the surviving Team members thoroughly.

Verkan wasn't looking forward to the job, but maybe it would turn up some clues. He decided to start with Baltov Eldra, if she was ready; she had the reputation of both a cool head and a keen talent for observation.

II

The climb to the gun platform on top of the north tower of Tarr-Hostigos left Prince Ptosphes unpleasantly short of breath. Old age had been pursuing him for a long time. Now it had finally caught him. Under other circumstances he would have been angry at the prospect of not seeing his grandchildren grow up, but that matter had been taken care of four days ago at Ardros Field.

"Should we summon Uncle Wolf for you, my Prince?" the gun captain asked.

Ptosphes shook his head. "No. Just let me sit down and catch my wind."

He lowered himself on to an upended powder barrel and was about to light his pipe when he remembered what he was sitting on. The gunners and sentries, he noticed, had returned to their work as soon as they knew he needed no help.

Good men, and more than ever a pity that they had to stand here and face certain death even if most of them were like him, a bit long in the tooth. At least they were the last good men he'd be leading to their doom. No more battles like Tenabra, to haunt him during the long winter nights. Kalvan and Rylla wouldn't be so lucky, and Kalvan at least liked such work even less than Ptosphes. Kalvan would just have to endure Rylla's tongue on the subject, as Ptosphes had endured Demia's.

Ptosphes chuckled, as he thought of Rylla's mother for the first time in nearly a moon. Rylla had much of her mother in her, both the strengths and the tongue and temper. Ptosphes remembered Demia asking (at the top of her lungs) whether he hated war too much to hold even the little Princedom of Hostigos.

Well, she'd been right in a way. He would have lost even that to Gormoth of Nestor, for not wanting to fight the battles of Styphon's House, if the gods hadn't sent Kalvan. Why, then, had those same gods turned their faces away when he needed their help most? What had he or Kalvan done to earn their wrath?

Great Dralm, I ask nothing for myself. Let your wrath fall on me, and spare Kalvan, Rylla, and my granddaughter Demia.

Ptosphes's breath came more easily now, and he badly wanted that pipe. He rose and was turning toward the stairs when he saw a horseman riding uphill toward the castle. He wore armor but no helmet, and a sash with Prince Phrames' colors. Probably one of Phrames' loyal Beshtans.

"Ahoooo! Prince Ptosphes! Prince Phrames has sent me back to warn you. The Styphoni are on the march once more. Their scouts are barely a candle from Hostigos Town!"

"Thank you, and carry my thanks to Prince Phrames." *So the siege begins even sooner than we expected.*

The trooper made no move to turn his mount. Ptosphes glared down at him. "No, you can't come into the castle. Your Prince and your Great King need you more than I do."

"Prince—"

"Now, Dralm-damn you, turn that horse around and get it moving! If you're not gone before I count to ten you'll be the first casualty of the siege of Tarr-Hostigos."

Ptosphes drew his pistol but his roar had already startled the horse into movement. It wheeled, nearly losing its footing on the steep slope, then broke into a canter. By the time Ptosphes had counted to five, it was out of pistol range. The Beshtan was still looking back at the castle. Ptosphes hoped he would turn around and look where he was going before he rode into a ditch.

Once his pipe was drawing well, Ptosphes walked around the walls to where he had a good view to the southeast. That was the likely direction for the Grand Host, or at least where he hoped most to see them. Anyplace else would mean they had a too-godless- good chance of cutting off at least Kalvan's rearguard.

The southeast was empty of smoke clouds, and so were all the other directions. Were the Styphoni advancing along roads where there was nothing left that even a fanatical believer would consider worth burning? Or was the vanguard mercenaries, who would be thinking of having roofs over their heads and food in their bellies during the siege?

Tarr-Hostigos should have a bit of time before its walls *had* to be manned and kept manned until the Styphoni stormed them. Plenty of time, for what Ptosphes intended.

He pointed the stem of his pipe at the nearest sentry. "Take a message to Captain-General Harmakros. Summon everyone in the castle except the sentries to the outer courtyard."

"Every—?" the man began, then broke off at Ptosphes' look. "Everyone. Captain-General Harmakros. Yes, my Prince."

The soldier hurried off, as if he wanted to open the distance between himself and his Prince before Ptosphes showed any more signs of madness.

Ptosphes followed at a more leisurely pace.

III

By the time the garrison was gathered in the outer courtyard, the sun was high overhead. Even the twenty-foot walls cast short shadows. Ptosphes sweated in his armor, wishing the laggards would hurry and resting his hand on the hilt of his sword.

It was a newly forged Kalvan-style rapier, balanced for fighting on foot but quite long enough for his purposes now. The Great Sword of Hostigos, which he'd belted on the day he was proclaimed Prince, was on its way westward with Kalvan and Rylla. His grandson would need that Sword some day, when he ruled a realm so huge that Old Hostigos would barely rank as a respectable Princedom.

If the gods are merciful.

Ptosphes saw no more men joining the crowd. He drew the sword and raised it overhead in both hands. Sunlight blazed from the steel.

"Men of Hostigos. You all know why you are here. You all were told, when you offered to hold Tarr-Hostigos until our Great King and his family might reach safety. Every one of you has already earned honor in the eyes of Dralm Allfather, Galzar Wolfhead, and the other true gods, the gratitude of your Prince and Great King, and the goodwill of your comrades.

"Styphon's Grand Host is approaching faster than we thought. Within a candle, two at most, this castle will be surrounded by the mightiest army in the history of the Great Kingdoms. For every one of us, there will be a hundred of the enemy. When they camp, a mouse won't be getting out of this castle.

"Any man who wants to leave can still do so. I'll say nothing against him nor let anyone else say a word. He'll have to hurry, to catch up with our rearguard before nightfall, but there's an open road for any who want to take it. " He pointed toward the castle gate with his sword.

"For those who stay—you all know what kind of quarter Styphon's dogs gave us at Ardros. The lucky ones will have a quick death. The rest will have an appointment with Roxthar's Unholy Investigation."

A few hollow laughs sounded from the ranks; most faces were set and pale. All knew what had happened to the Hostigi prisoners after Ardros Field; few had not lost kin or friends in that butchery. Most of the prisoners not slaughtered outright were in the hands of the Investigation, doubtless envying their dead comrades.

Ptosphes lowered his sword and strode to the door of the woodshed on one side of the courtyard. Then he drew a line with the sword's point, through the dirt and straw covering the flagstones of the courtyard, from the woodshed to the blacksmith's forge on the other side. He then took a deep breath, sheathed his sword, and turned to face his men.

"All who want to stay—cross over this line and join me. Those who want to die somewhere else—stay where you are!"

Silence. Ptosphes could hear the stamping of horses from the stables on the far side of the courtyard. An unnaturally complete silence to be hanging over five hundred men. No one coughed, no one shuffled his feet. Ptosphes could have sworn some had ceased to breathe.

A thickset man in battered armor pushed his way from the rear into the open. Ptosphes tried not to stare too hard. It was Vurth.

Vurth, the peasant who'd been Kalvan's first host in this land, who owed his life and his family's to Kalvan's fighting skill. Who'd sent word of the Nostori raiders to Tarr-Hostigos, so that Rylla could lead out the cavalry who had cut off the raiders and found Kalvan.

Vurth, a peasant who might really be called Dralm's first chosen tool for bringing about everything which had happened since that spring night almost four years ago. Ptosphes wondered briefly what Patriarch Xentos would have to say about the theological propriety of that notion—if presiding over the squabbles of the League of Dralm in far-off Agrys City left him any time for such matters.

Much good may that do Xentos in the eyes of the gods, when the League sends only words of condolence instead of soldiers and muskets to those who fight its battles against Styphon.

Ptosphes examined the gray-haired peasant. His clothes and face were caked with mud and powder smoke, one shoulder was bandaged, and he limped. He wore the breastplate of some Harphaxi nobleman, once etched and gilded, now hacked and tarnished, over his homespun smock. On his head was a battered morion helmet, on his feet cavalry boots from two different corpses. He still carried the cavalryman's musketoon he'd acquired the night of Kalvan's coming, and both it and the powder flask at his belt were clean.

"First Prince, Captain-General Harmakros, people," Vurth began. "This isn't really a Council, so maybe I don't have the right to start off, as if I was Speaker for the Peasants like Phosg, Dralm keep him. I think I've a right to be heard, though."

Ptosphes would have cut down anyone who disagreed. The men saw this, and Vurth went on.

"Prince, most of us here either can't run, don't want to run, or don't have anywhere to run to. My farm has burned, my wife is dead and one son too. The other son's off with King Kalvan, in the Royal Dragoons, and my son-in-law Xykos is Captain of Queen Rylla's Lifeguards. Dralm keep all the daughters who ran off with mercenaries.

"Styphon's taken or chased off everything I had except my life. All I want to do with what's left of it is kill Styphon's dogs until they kill me. I'm too old to go climbing trees or hide in caves like a thief, even for that. I'd rather sit here and kill the bastards in comfort!"

Vurth shouldered his musketoon and stepped forward across the line before anyone could cheer.

Ptosphes felt his eyes burn and quickly blinked back the threatening tears. He stepped up beside Vurth and put his arm around the peasant's shoulders. Any land that bore men like this would be barren ground indeed for Styphon's House. Such men could be killed; they could not be frightened.

Harmakros' voice cut through the new silence.

"Lift that litter, you fools! You don't have to stay yourselves!"

The bearers' reply was nearly inaudible and totally disrespectful. They had the Captain-General across the line before Ptosphes stopped grinning.

Another man stepped out, then two more, then five, then a band of ten, then a band too numerous to count, and after that it was a steady stream. Ptosphes saw one gray-haired man telling a club footed boy no more than ten to stand where he was, then step out. The boy looked sullenly after his grandfather until he was sure the man couldn't see him, then slipped across the line.

Ptosphes turned his back on the men. He didn't want them to see his face until he could command it as a captain and a Prince ought to.

By the time he turned around, the space on the other side of the line was empty.

Ptosphes ran his eyes over the garrison, with the care of a man trained at the quick counting of large masses of men. There'd been just over five hundred before. No doubt a few had slipped off, perhaps as many as a man could count on his fingers and toes. Call it four hundred and eighty left behind, quite enough to do all the work Styphon's Grand Host would allow.

Ptosphes was fumbling for words of thanks when a sentry on the keep shouted. "Prince Ptosphes! Enemy scouts in Hostigos Town! On the east side, cavalry with two guns."

Guns up with the scouts meant they had orders to fight instead of hit and run. Who would have such orders? Perhaps the Zarthani Knights.

Ptosphes swallowed; the lump in his throat twitched but remained where it was. "What colors?" he managed to shout.

"King Demistophon's and a mercenary company's. Looks like a rearing white horse on a blue field."

The lump shrank. Mercenaries wouldn't burn a town they expected to provide them with dry beds and hot food, unless they had other orders. Such orders might not be obeyed, either, unless the man who gave them was watching.

With Grandbutcher Soton not up yet and Phidestros himself a mercenary, there might be no such man here. If Soton arrived after the Grand Host's advance guard had settled in—well, making mercenaries in another king's pay burn their own shelter and food was a task Ptosphes wouldn't wish even on Soton.

IV

Grand Captain-General Phidestros of Hos-Harphax felt his guts twist as the vanguard of his Iron Band rode by a burning farmhouse. A child lay on the steps, skull split.

In the farmyard itself, three of Roxthar's Holy Investigators were "questioning" a Hostigi woman, no doubt the child's mother. The Investigators wore hooded white robes with a red sun-wheel over the breast. The robes were well stained with mud and blood—some of the blood long dry.

"They can fight women and children well enough!" growled Grand Captain Kyblannos, commander of the Iron Band. "Where were Styphon's swine when we charged Kalvan's artillery at Ardros Field!"

Phidestros leaned out of his saddle to grip his friend's hand before he could draw a pistol and do something foolish. Not that half the Iron Band and Phidestros himself didn't feel the same.

Phidestros shut his ears against the woman's screams. Why in the name of every god couldn't the Styphoni at least find more private places to torture and maim? It was Roxthar, of course—Roxthar, with the fanatic's blindness to the opinions of others and total sense of his own rightness. He'd still better learn discretion, before half the Royal Army of Harphax and more than half the mercenaries started hunting Investigators instead of Hostigi.

Phidestros led veterans, men accustomed to danger, wounds, and death, for themselves and for others. He didn't lead butchers who reveled in killing like weasels set loose among turkey chicks!

Curse and blast the Holy Investigation and all its works! They were dragging honorable soldiers down into the same kind of sty they enjoyed, without doing Styphon's House on Earth all that much good. These priests seemed to forget too easily what soldiers learned young if they wished to grow old: men made desperate by fear will fight to the last.

Phidestros twisted his head and flexed his shoulders as much as his armor would allow, to ease the tautness. He should be the happiest man in the Great Kingdoms, yet he felt more fear of the future than he had ever felt of Kalvan.

Kalvan was not invincible. Ardros Field proved that. The greatest victory since Erasthames the Great defeated the Ruthani Confederation at Sestra more than four centuries ago, and won by a man who three years ago was lucky to count two hundred soldiers following his banner! A victory so great that the Grand Host had already released some of its mercenaries and set others to garrisoning captured castles. Five thousand of the best were hard on the heels of the fleeing Royal Army of Hos-Hostigos.

Phidestros knew he should be riding with those men, instead of playing steward to Archpriest Roxthar and his Investigators. Let Grand Master Soton invest Tarr-Hostigos while Phidestros pressed the pursuit until Kalvan was no more! As long as Kalvan was alive, he might rise again. A man who could conjure a Great Kingdom out of not much more than the gods' own air was no ordinary foe.

But try telling that to anyone else, including Grand Master Soton, who ought to know better! Phidestros could not understand why Soton deferred so much to Roxthar. The Grand Master was not only the highest-ranking soldier of Styphon's House, he was an Archpriest in his own right, the Investigator's equal in priestly rank.

A mystery, and one that demanded an answer soon. Otherwise they'd never run that wily fox Kalvan to earth before he found another burrow.

It would not be an answer easily come by, either. Undue curiosity about the affairs of the Investigation was a short road to a charge of "heresy."

The Iron Band started down the last slope into Hostigos Town, laid out on its alternating hills and dales. In the distance, Phidestros saw the

Kettlepot Mountains and Hostigos Gap, with Tarr-Hostigos perched atop two formidable mountains to the right of the Gap.

The first mountain held the main castle with its great keep surrounded by walls and gun towers. The second and higher peak held a tower with its own walls.

Removing Tarr-Hostigos from the path of the Grand Host was not going to be as simple as taking a splinter from a child's foot, regardless of what Roxthar thought. If Phidestros had his choice, he would leave a detachment to blockade the castle and let starvation do the rest.

But he was merely a Grand Captain-General, in a war run by priests. Also a Captain-General who answered to a Great King who'd mortgaged everything but his concubines' shifts (if they had any) to Styphon's House!

It was time to send the priests back to their temples and the counselors back to their castles so the soldiers could go on with finishing off Kalvan.

As they rode down toward Hostigos Town, Phidestros was pleased to see only two columns of smoke rising from it. There'd be dry beds at least for the next quarter-moon.

A rider galloped up, shouting for Phidestros. From his silvered armor and black-caparisoned horse with a silver sun-wheel on each quarter, he was a Knight of the Holy Lance.

"Hail, Grand Captain-General Phidestros! I am Commander Rythar of the Holy Lance, with a message from Grand Master Soton."

"Greetings, Commander Rythar. What is your master's pleasure?"

"The Grand Master requests your presence upon yonder hill."

The Commander raised his visor and pointed to a nearby hill. A Blade of sixty Knights stood in attendance on the diminutive figure of the Grand Master, whose blackened armor made a stark contrast to their polished finery.

Phidestros nodded to Kyblannos. The Grand Captain told off sixty of the Iron Band and placed them around his Captain-General until Phidestros felt like a babe in its nurse's arms. He held his peace; Kyblannos would be like a she-wolf with one cub toward his old captain until the day he died.

It took a few moments for the horses of Phidestros' party to get used to rough ground again, after several candles on the smooth paving of Kalvan's Great King's Highway. *Kalvan is a hard man not to respect, even in defeat,* was Phidestros' thought. *Many saw the wisdom of such roads. None were built, until Kalvan came.*

A quarter-candle took Phidestros up the hill to Soton's outpost. Phidestros dismounted and advanced to greet Soton, as Banner- Captain Geblon arrayed the Iron Band facing the Knights.

The two commanders clasped hands. Soton pointed to Tarr-Hostigos.

"A hard nut to crack, aye, Captain-General?"

"One to give any squirrel a bit of work. It's big enough to hold two thousand men and supplies for a year, if they don't mind horseflesh. We may see snow before we see a breach in those walls!"

"Rest easy, Captain-General. We've interrogated some prisoners—*not* as the Investigation does it, by the way. Kalvan's left only a skeleton garrison, five hundred men and some of those wrinkled like crab apples. We should have the castle invested in a few days. Then we can see about tracking Kalvan all the way to the Great Mountains if we must!"

Phidestros wanted to sing, dance, and embrace Soton, but dignity and caution shaped his tongue to a question. "Will His Bloodiness let us show such wisdom?"

"Guard your tongue, Phidestros. You are not so high that you cannot be made to lie down on the rack!" Soton's look would have stopped a charging bull.

This time frustration and disgust kept Phidestros altogether silent. Just how far into Roxthar's pocket *was* Soton? Before this year he would not have believed a man lived who could bind Soton to his will. Surely the mystery of Soton and Roxthar demanded a solution, before it threatened the victory so dearly bought with the blood of men Phidestros had led to battle!

When Phidestros found his tongue again, his voice was cold. "Yes, Grand Master. I have seen the fate of women and children who defy the Holy Investigator."

Soton's face paled and he looked away. "It is our duty to obey the

Temple's will," he muttered. "This war against women and babes is not my choice, either, Phidestros. But when the Hostigi heresy is scourged from the land, the Investigation will be ended."

If you believe that, Phidestros thought, you aren't half the man I'd thought you are.

"The commanders are to be billeted at Ptosphes's new palace in Hostigos Town," Soton continued. "I'll be going there myself, as soon as we finish this drawing of Tarr-Hostigos."

He pointed at a Knight sitting on a stump with a slate and charcoal in hand. Phidestros peered over the man's shoulder, to see a fine rendering of the castle, with every tower and gate clearly shown.

Best round up Kalvan's mapmakers as soon as we're settled in, he decided. *Some may have fled, and doubtless Soton will want his share. But this, please Galzar, is something soldiers can settle between them without listening to priests' babbling!*

V

A hundred petty matters kept Phidestros and his Iron Band out of Hostigos Town for much of the morning. By the time they'd covered the last furlongs of Old Tigo Road, the few fires were out. The streets were deserted, except for soldiers and chain gangs of prisoners, led by Roxthar's Investigators and Styphon's Own Guard, resplendent in their silvered armor and red capes.

Phidestros was hardly surprised to see the Guard acting as the Investigators' allies. The Temple Bands had a reputation as stout fighters, who neither asked nor gave quarter. That last habit had given them the nickname of "Styphon's Red Hand."

The chain gangs all seemed bound for Hostigos Square, which Phidestros found already half-filled with slave pens of Hostigi prisoners. The palace itself was garrisoned by Guardsmen standing practically shoulder-to-shoulder, and Investigators darted in and out like rats from a half-eaten corpse. Phidestros led the Iron Band toward the palace, ignoring the curses and threats of Styphoni brusquely pushed aside.

The Iron Band replied only with silence, and occasionally with a hand rested lightly on a pistol butt. Before it reached the palace, the Styphoni were giving way without protest.

As Phidestros dismounted, he knew one thing. He'd be cursed if he billeted any of his men in this nest of temple-rats! He'd say that the siege demanded all his attention and find quarters elsewhere! Otherwise the Iron Band would start the war against the Investigators here and now, and he'd be lucky to end up back commanding a company of every other captain's leavings!

VI

Danar Sirna's first thought on waking up was to wish that she hadn't. Being dead or at least asleep seemed the best solution to quite a number of her problems, starting with her crashing headache. The last thing she remembered was trying to escape from the Royal Foundry.... The screams and cries of her dying colleagues still ran through her head.

The first thing Sirna saw clearly was a dead man. Beyond him lay two more dead men, one with half of his face blown away. Was she in what passed for field hospitals here-and-now?

She was lying on a straw pallet, with a wood-beamed roof over her, whitewashed plaster walls around her, and a window in one of those walls. The warped wooden shutter was ajar; through the gap she could see what looked like a cobblestone street in Hostigos Town.

She must have been picked up and brought in by one side or another, and put in here because she looked dead or dying. The whole left side of her head not only throbbed horribly but felt caked and stiff with dried blood. A scalp wound like that could make you look dead to people in a hurry.

Sirna had just decided that sitting up was a bad idea when a board creaked behind her. She decided to face her visitor sitting.

She struggled up, groaned, and turned to see a woman well past middle age, made up in a fashion that would have announced her profession on many other time-lines besides this one.

"So you're alive," the painted lady said. "They call me Menandra. What's your name, sweetheart?" The voice was gruff and coarsened by alcohol, but not unfriendly.

Better say something. Sirna didn't dare nod, but her mouth was so dry that only a croak came out.

Menandra bawled something in a voice that would have rallied a cavalry regiment. Sirna winced. One of the house women appeared with a jug and a cup.

"Drink this."

Sirna rinsed her mouth out, then swallowed. It went down, heavily watered wine with some herbs in it. When she thought it was going to stay down, she asked, "What's been happening since—Ardros Field?" She realized she didn't know how long she'd been unconscious.

Menandra looked at the ceiling as she spoke. "Well, King Kalvan is on his way west with what's left of the—his men. Prince Ptosphes is holding the castle, to let him get away. We're playing host to Captain-General Phidestros' Iron Band. Does that answer you, girl?"

"What's Phidestros doing here?" Sirna asked.

Menandra's reply was a hoarse whisper. "I hear that the Captain-General's not too pleased with how Roxthar's Investigators are tearing up this town. He's supposed to be staying over there at the big headquarters, in what used to be Ptosphes' palace. But he spends most of his nights here or over by the siege works." She grinned. "Once he sets eyes on you, he won't be staying anywhere else."

Sirna strangled another groan. Menandra shrugged. "War's like that. Now, the next question is, what do we do with you now? Some peasants picked you up, thought you fit for ransoming. They had you in a cart when the Iron Band passed by. They ran you on into town in the cart, facedown on top of a load of squash with your skirt up to your arse."

"With my skirt—?"

The picture made Sirna giggle, then laugh. Once she started laughing she couldn't stop, although it made her head hurt worse. It also shook her stomach, which finally rebelled.

When Sirna stopped retching, Menandra was still standing over her, trying to look stem but not entirely succeeding. "As I said, what about you, girl? You're a long way from home and your friends at the Foundry are either dead or run off, the true gods alone know where."

"Run off?"

Menandra couldn't give many details, but what she said told Sirna very clearly that the survivors of the University Study Team had left her for dead. It took all her self-control not to cry. She not only felt sick, she was frightened.

"Not good for you, the more so since the Styphoni will be looking for people from the Foundry. Outlanders especially. I can probably protect you here at the Gull's Nest, if you're willing to work."

This was more than Sirna could digest in one gulp. Clearly Menandra was the owner and madam of the Gull's Nest (and why that name, this far from the sea?) and was quite willing to let her earn her keep, sick or not.

"No!"

"It's how I started out in Agrys City, girl. More years ago than either of us wants to think about. There's worse things than making a living on your back. Gives you a new view of the world, you might say."

There probably were worse things here-and-now than making a living as one of Menandra's whores. Right now Sirna couldn't think of them. She shook her head slowly.

"Well, you're handsome enough for it, and to spare."

Sirna shook her head again.

"I'll leave it be, then. Just remember, though—anything you make in the house, half goes to me. Or you go to the soldiers!"

Sirna closed her eyes and wished it all away. The smoke-blackened timbers were still there when she opened her eyes. She really was in a situation where she could be turned over to a band of mercenaries and passed from man to man until she died or they got tired of her. It was a long way from reading or even writing about "the inferior position of women" to experiencing it.

Deliberately, she closed and locked a door in her mind, on First Level and all the pleasures and privileges she had there, even on her chances of ever seeing it again. (Which were slim enough at best, with Kalvan defeated and her left for dead.) She would look forward, look this Styphon-cursed time-line squarely in the eye, and dare it to do its worst.

Not that it hasn't already given me its best shot—

She came back from this mental exercise to see Menandra looking positively concerned. "That crack on the head didn't addle your wits, did it?"

"I—don't think so. I must have slept off the worst of it. I was just thinking—what I'm going to do to those fatherless sons of the gods who ran off and left me."

That was no lie, either. She now understood emotionally as well as intellectually the concept of the blood feud. If she ever caught Outtime Studies Director Talgan Dreth alone in a dark place—

"By Yirtta's dugs, girl, I can't give charity! Phidestros' men may pay me if Styphon's House ever pays them. Then again they may not. If they don't want to and I ask, they may burn the place down!"

And pass the women around among themselves, Sirna added mentally. Somehow the idea was no longer so paralyzingly frightful, now that she'd closed that door to First Level.

"If you know anything about healing, even the smallest bit, you might make yourself useful. Phidestros is going to be sending his sick and hurt here. The Iron Band's Uncle Wolf was killed in the battle, and there aren't so many priests of Galzar that even a Captain-General can conjure them up. You help patch and purge Phidestros' men, and there won't be any trouble keeping you."

"Help those damned filthy Styphon's sons of—?" Sirna began.

Gently but emphatically, Menandra slapped her. At least it was probably intended as a gentle slap. Sirna had to shake her head a couple of times, to make sure her neck wasn't broken. Through the ringing in her ears, she heard Menandra warning her against saying anything less than complimentary about Styphon.

"Archpriest Roxthar's here with his Investigators. Anyone who blasphemes Styphon within a day's ride of him will wish she *had* been turned over to the soldiers. Yes, and the stallions and the draft oxen too!"

From what she'd heard of Roxthar, Sirna saw no reason to argue the point. "I'm sorry, Menandra. I'm still a little confused."

"Well, unconfuse yourself, girl. You might start with that head wound. Clean it up, and I'll think you're good enough to turn loose on Phidestros' men."

Menandra bawled for scissors, a mirror, hot water, and bandages, while Sirna took off her mud and blood-smeared clothes and examined her body for other injuries. A prize collection of black-and-blue marks was all she turned up. Her anger toward the people who'd abandoned her grew. If they hadn't been too panic-stricken to spend ten seconds examining her, they'd have learned she was alive and fit to be moved.

The head wound was a long shallow gash, probably a sword cut. She must have picked up the concussion when she fell. No signs of infection, but she made a thorough job of cleaning the wound, starting with cutting off the hair all around it. It was bleeding again by the time she was finished, and so was her lower lip where she'd bitten it. She finished by trimming her hair all around.

"You're cutting off one of your best parts, you know that, girl?" Menandra said.

Persistent, aren't you? "I'll be hard to recognize with my hair short. Maybe they'll even think I'm too ugly to bother."

"With a figure like yours? You've got a lot to learn about men, girl. Somebody's going to want what you've got if you shaved yourself bald! Best arrange to give it to a man big enough to fight off the rest. Or else you'll wish you'd taken my first offer."

What am I, a mare to go with the strongest and fiercest stallion in the herd?

Exactly.

Sirna sighed and stood up, swaying slightly but not really wanting to lie down again. That was one good sign. Another was that she was hungry.

"Is there anything to eat around here?"

Menandra chuckled. "You'll do, girl. Come on down to the kitchen and I'll see if the bread and tea are ready."

VII

Tiny clouds of white smoke rose three times from the Styphoni siege battery. Ptosphes started counting. At "five" the three shots crashed into Tarr-Hostigos. One struck the face of the outer wall, the others hit the left side of the breach. Rock dust as white as the powder smoke whirled up, carried down toward Ptosphes on the morning breeze. He tasted the grit on his tongue and teeth. It was a familiar taste by now, with the siege into its tenth day.

The men working on the barricade rising inside the breach barely looked up from their work. The barricade was made of heavy timbers from the buildings of the outer courtyard, flagstones from the courtyard itself, and stones from the breach itself. The men at work were lacing the timbers together with ropes and strips of leather, while others stood by, ready to haul a cannon on to the top of the barricade.

"Pretty old-fashioned way they have of doing things," said Master Gunner Thalmoth, who was standing beside Ptosphes. "Without those captured guns and the slaves to haul 'em up, they'd be sitting down on the level making faces at us."

Thalmoth was old enough to remember standing in the crowd with his father to see the newborn Ptosphes presented to the people of Hostigos as their future Prince. Too old to take the field, he'd taught at the University as well as lending a lifetime of artillery experience to testing the new Hostigi guns.

Ptosphes wondered if Thalmoth had volunteered to remain behind entirely because of his age. He'd been seen to lift powder barrels and wield handspikes on balky guns. Or did he perhaps hold himself responsible for the proof-testing explosion that killed four men and took off Captain-General Harmakros' leg on the eve of the campaign that led to Ardros Field?

Thalmoth owed an answer to that question only to Dralm or Galzar, not to an overcurious Prince.

"It's the Host's first big siege," Ptosphes said tolerantly. "No doubt they'll do better next time."

This morning he felt almost benign even toward the besieging Styphoni. It was a beautiful day, and not too hot. He'd eaten a good breakfast. The garrison's wounded were doing as well as could be expected. Best of all, the men of Tarr-Hostigos now knew they'd won the victory they *had* to win.

Last night a party of picked men had slipped into the besiegers' forward positions. Their score was twenty-eight taken prisoner, more than fifty killed, a magazine blown up, and three bombards spiked, all for the price of one man dead and four wounded.

All the prisoners claimed that Kalvan hadn't been overtaken. Some added that the men chasing him had been ordered back to join the siege. One said he'd heard a whole band was wiped out in an ambush by Kalvan's rearguard. Ptosphes suspected that the last man was trying to please his captors, who had nothing to lose by shooting him from a cannon.

The last stand at Tarr-Hostigos was *not* going to be a waste of lives. If that wasn't worth celebrating, then nothing was.

Of course, the odds against the besieger would rise still higher now that the Grand Host was bringing back their vanguard. Since those odds were already close to a hundred to one, who cared? Ptosphes rather liked Harmakros' way of putting it:

"Aren't we lucky? We'll *never* run out of targets now!"

That might have been Harmakros' fever speaking. In spite of his stump having been cleaned to drive out the fester-demons, Harmakros had been working far too hard for a man so badly hurt. However, most of the rest of the garrison seemed to feel the same way.

Prince Ptosphes continued his walk around the castle walls, Thalmoth following ten paces behind. The riflemen in the towers encouraged enemy musketeers to stay beyond accurate range, and the besiegers didn't waste cannon shot on single men. Ptosphes suspected that they were short of fireseed and saving what they had for the storming. No trouble of that kind for his people, even without the reserve of twelve tons of Styphon's Best in the cellar of the keep.

He inspected the gunners at the main gate and the siege battery at the bottom of the draw leading up to the gate. The battery had been laid out by someone who knew his business, which was also why it had no guns in it as yet. They would be needed for the storming, to keep the Hostigi on the gates from having target practice on the men coming up the draw. Until then, they would simply be on the wrong end of plunging fire from the gate towers.

Another hundred paces along the walls, and some of Ptosphes' good mood evaporated. On this side Archpriest Roxthar had his prison—really more of a stock pen—for the people he was Investigating. Like most of the besiegers' works, it was walled in timber and stone carted by slave gangs from Hostigos Town, but lacked their roof of old tents. At the rate the besiegers' works were swallowing the town, it soon wouldn't matter if they burned it or not.

A long line of gallows rose by the gate of the prison pen, most of them dangling bodies, and continued on down the road halfway to Hostigos Town. Ptosphes could smell the bodies that had been dangling more than a couple of days, even over the stable-and- powder-smoke reek of the siege.

The gallows seemed to be more burdened now than even a few days ago. No doubt the Styphoni had finished with their Hostigi slaves after they'd sweated and bled to haul the captured sixteen-pounders up the slope to the siege battery.

That whole affair had been as bloody in itself as some of the battles of the days before Kalvan. The Styphoni had killed a fair number of their own men, mining the places where Ptosphes' grandfather had carved the slopes into vertical faces. The Hostigi had also had to kill some of their own folk, weeping and cursing as they flailed at the gun teams with case shot and rifles.

The end of it was what had to be, when one side could spend men like water. The guns were in place and hammering at the walls of Tarr-Hostigos in a way even those ancient stones could not endure forever. Hostigi guns, Alkides' prize sixteen-pounders. No surprise that, considering that all of them except "Galzar's Teeth" had been lost at Ardros Field.

No surprise, and therefore something Ptosphes *should* have been able to do more about. He'd forgotten Kalvan's advice, given late one night when they'd all been emptying a jug of Ermut's brandy.

"Always plan against the worst thing your enemy can do. That way you'll be safe, no matter what he does. If he doesn't do his worst you'll win more easily."

Wise words. Clearly the army of Great King Truman had taught its captains well.

Ptosphes shook his head and lit his pipe. There was no call to feel sorry for himself. He had done too much of that. Besides, while he might not be fit for service in the hosts of Great King Truman, he was no bad captain for Tarr-Hostigos when every day it held was another victory over the Styphoni.

VIII

The man on what had been Menandra's best table writhed and twisted, and almost but not quite screamed. The four mercenaries holding him strained to keep him still.

"Lie quiet," Sirna muttered. "You lie quiet, or I'll have to use a sandbag on you. I don't want to do that. You may have already hurt your head, when the tunnel fell on you."

The soldier on the table sank his teeth into his lower lip. Blood came, but he lay still as Sirna cut open the flesh of his cheek over the finger-length splinter there and drew out the bloody wood. More blood flowed freely. Sirna let it flow while she picked out the last bits of wood, then bound up the wound in a dressing of boiled rags. By the time she'd finished the bandaging, the soldier had fainted, but he came awake as his comrades lifted him off the table.

"Sorry to be so much trouble, girl," the soldier said between clenched teeth. "But I wanted to look at something pretty."

Sirna grinned. "With the gods' favor and no fester-demons, you'll have two eyes to look at pretty girls. And a fine scar to attract the ones you want."

The scar would be a lifelong disfigurement—no reconstructive surgery here-and-now. Still, if the soldier was able to contemplate life with it....

She'd thought she'd been used to what people on Fourth Level could face, after almost three years with the University Team. Still it made a big difference, to live alone among such people, with the nearest person who would have ever heard of First Level at least a hundred miles away—farther if they'd kept on running. Not to mention the possibility of spending the rest of her life here-and-now.

On top of everything else, Styphon's soldiers! It wasn't easy to accept that men who fought for something as silly, irrational, even barbaric, as Styphon's House could be like other men. But they fought just as bravely, cried out just as loudly for their mothers when they hurt, and made just as many bawdy jokes that could still turn her face brighter than her cropped hair.

Or rather, it hadn't been easy to accept this, ten days ago. Now it sometimes seemed that she'd never believed anything else.

No more sick or wounded seemed to be coming, so Sirna sent one of the women with the knife and the salvaged bandages off to the kitchen to boil them clean. She also made at least her twentieth mental memo: *Borrow some better instruments from a priest of Galzar, or have the Iron Band's armorers make them.*

Another woman, face streaked with makeup, wiped down the table with a bucket of boiling water. Menandra herself brought Sirna a cup of hot turkey broth.

"You'd better eat something solid, you know," the madam said. "Even if it's only an omelet. Won't do, having you faint on top of men too hurt to enjoy it!"

"Oh, I'll eat something tonight." At the moment, the mere thought of solid food made her gag.

"Tonight—" Menandra began, then lowered her voice to a whisper so that none of the wounded on pallets along the other side of the room could hear.

"The talk in town is that it's tomorrow they go for the castle. So you'd *better* eat and sleep tonight, or by Yirtta I'll turn you over my knee and spank you!" She ran her fingers through Sirna's hair with one large greasy hand.

Sirna gulped her broth with both hands clasped tightly around the cup so Menandra wouldn't see that they were shaking. Seventeen wounded men in one day was bad enough. If they stormed the castle, it could be more like seventy—or seven hundred! Although she might have more help from the priests of Galzar if the promised reinforcements came up. Had they? She was trying to think of a tactful way to ask when the door to the street opened and a suit of armor wearing dusty leather breeches and boots strode in.

The suit of armor also had a brown beard and wide gray eyes, but it wasn't until the high-crested helmet came off that Sirna realized there was a man inside. When she saw that the man had a high forehead and a long scar across his right cheek, she knew who'd come to visit his wounded.

Grand Captain-General Phidestros waved the men trying to rise back on to their pallets with his free hand, set his helmet on the table, and took off his mud-caked gloves. Then he grinned at Sirna.

"You randy bastards! You've been keeping secret the best thing this wreck of a town has to offer. Where's your loyalty to your commander, you—?" The term would have been insulting as well as obscene in any other tone. The men replied in kind, except for Banner-Captain Geblon, on light duty today because of an attack of dysentery.

"She is Menandra's healer, Captain-General," Geblon said, trying to both look and sound innocent. "She has been marvelously chaste."

"I'm sure she has," Phidestros replied. "But has she been caught? If she hasn't, you aren't the men I thought you were!"

Sirna stopped blushing and started giggling. Phidestros bent down and gripped her by one arm, pulling her to her feet as easily as if she'd been a child. Seen close up, his long face showed deep lines, apparently gouged with a blunt chisel, then filled with dust.

By the time he'd led her into the hall where no one could see her, she was trying to stop giggling. Somehow she wanted to impress him favorably, and not only because he had the power of life and death over her.

"To speak plainly—what is your name, by the way?"

"Sirna."

"Speaking plainly, Sirna, I owe you for a good thirty of my men helped and at least two saved outright. Where did you learn to treat burns like Aygoll's?"

"My father had some skill in healing, and was always quick to learn anything someone else would teach. One year we lived not far from a smithy. They knew how to heal burns from molten metal."

"Curious. What you did for Aygoll is very much like what Kalvan is said to have taught, about driving out the fester-demons."

"Is it not possible that the gods can send wisdom to both good and evil men, and leave it to them how it shall be used?" She looked up to meet his eyes as she spoke, and she thought she kept her voice steady.

"It's not only possible, it happens all the time," Phidestros said. "Only don't try arguing the point with Holy Investigator Roxthar. He's threatening to purge the hosts of Styphon once he's finished with Hostigos."

"Aren't you speaking a little freely, if he's running—if he's that suspicious?"

Like most of the surviving population of Hostigos Town, Sirna had stayed indoors. Those whom urgent business or the search for food drove outside too often found themselves confronted by white-robed Investigators or squads of Styphon's Red Hand. Few of those returned. Now only rats and fools strayed outside: rumor had it that the Investigators were turning to house-to-house searches in East Hostigos Town.

"Afraid you won't be paid, Sirna?"

"That's not it at all! I just—I'm not like Menandra, you know. I'd feel sorry for a thrice-convicted rapist facing the Investigation."

"So would I, believe me." He grinned, displaying a mouthful of almost intact white teeth, which meant not only good health but good luck in battle.

"Menandra is no worse than the gods made her, but they were drunk that day and perhaps a little careless. No, Sirna. I'm in no danger. Not unless the Archpriests decide they don't need good soldiers anymore. That won't be until Kalvan's dead, and somehow 1 think that man is going to take a lot of killing."

Sirna would have kissed Phidestros if she hadn't known he would misinterpret the gesture. "I wouldn't be at all surprised if it did," she said.

"Which means that Roxthar is going to be dealing lightly with soldiers for a while. Healers who may be tainted with heresy aren't quite as indispensable. Remember that, and you may live to be paid for your work with the Iron Band.

"Oh, and by the way; I'll pay it right into your hands. If Menandra asks for a single brass piece, tell me. We'll roast our victory ox over her furniture."

The way Phidestros' voice and face changed in those last words made Sirna want to flinch away from his touch. She forced herself to stand still as he put a hand behind her back and urged her back toward the main room.

"Let's join the men, before they gamble away all their money wagering which one of us was on top!"

IX

Phidestros woke up the instant a hand pressed over his lips. Instinctively his right hand snaked underneath the bedroll his head rested on, to grip the poniard there.

Now another hand gripped his right wrist. Phidestros used his left hand to reach for the single-shot widow-maker he kept in a pouch next to his heart.

"For Galzar's sake, sir! It's me, Kyblannos!"

Phidestros stopped struggling when he recognized the voice, but didn't let go of the still-undrawn widow-maker.

"What in Regwarm's Hidey-hole is up now?"

"A parlay, sir. Some of the mercenary captains would like a private word with you, out of Archtorturer Roxthar's hearing."

"By the Wargod's Mace, couldn't they pick a more civilized hour?" Phidestros groaned.

At least the captains had picked the right place. The tent Phidestros used when he spent the night at the siege lines was a thousand paces from the nearest other tent. Men like Kyblannos guarded it, men who had been with Phidestros in the early days of the Iron Company, men who had no fear of priests or torturers. Men who had guarded him with their lives and would go on doing so.

Phidestros cursed again and sat up.

"Who wants to talk with me?"

"Grand Captains Brakkos, Demmos, and Thymestros, Captain Phidammes, Uncle Wolf Eurocles, and three other captains I could not recognize."

That was five of the best freelances in the Grand Host, leading about a sixth of its strength. Now that he was awake enough to think clearly, Phidestros found himself not altogether surprised.

The first attempt to storm Tarr-Hostigos had been a disaster. The attack up the mountainside at the breach and up the draw toward the gate had been bloodily repulsed. The Hostigi had thrown everything from barrels of fireseed to ordinary rocks at the storming parties, reducing them to bloody rags fifty paces from the walls.

In the northern work, a handful of Hostigi had slaughtered twenty besiegers for every man they lost before the scaling ladders finally reached the walls. They might have held as firmly as they had in the main castle, if it hadn't been for the newly arrived siege rifles.

Converted from the heavy boat swivels used by the Zarthani Knights against the Ruthani of the southern swamps, they could go anywhere three men could climb. Once in action, they outranged even a Hostigi rifleman perched on a tower. Ten of them had given the Grand Host the northern work of Tarr-Hostigos. Fifty might have given them the main castle.

At least they now had a place where heavy guns might play against the keep, once they were hauled up there. Given time, those guns would finish the work with no need for another attack.

Time, though, is just exactly what I won't have, he thought. *If the freelance captains don't take it away, Roxthar will. He knows only one way of solving this problem, and that's the bloodiest. Does he plan to bleed the Grand Host to a shell, so it cannot turn against him after Kalvan is overthrown?*

Phidestros began pulling on his clothes. "By the way, Kyblannos.

What do they want? More gold?"

"I don't know, sir. Truly."

"Help me get my breastplate on, then let them in."

The captains slunk into the tent like foxes into a turkey yard. Uncle Wolf Eurocles was in the lead, chief among the Host's Uncle Wolfs and formerly a freelance Captain-General of some note in his own right. His hair was almost white and his beard iron gray, but his face was still ruddy and his back straight as a musket barrel.

When everyone was inside, Phidestros rose. "I won't apologize for poor hospitality. It's too late for that. What can I do for you gentlemen?"

Eurocles spoke first. "In the name of Galzar, can you bring this mad siege to an end?"

"Not without putting my jewels between the blades of Roxthar's clipping shears."

Nervous laughter skittered around the tent.

Grand Captain Brakkos spoke up next. "I thought you led this army, *Grand* Captain-General, not Roxthar's regiment of bedgowns."

"I command, but only so long as I do nothing to offend Archpriest Roxthar or Great King Lysandros. Where do you think I would have been if we had lost at Ardros Field? Even now, I have Grand Master Soton, Roxthar, and would-be successors all tugging at my swordarm.

"The real commander of this Host is the one who fills your pay chests with gold—and you all know it."

"Then not even you can stop this senseless assault on Tarr-Hostigos?" Eurocles asked.

"No, Uncle Wolf. Were it up to me I'd leave a blockading force with a few heavy guns, to starve the Hostigi out of their fortress or knock it down on their thick heads. I would take the rest of the Host after Kalvan until I caught him, then pickle his head as a gift for Lysandros.

"But our Holy Investigator decrees otherwise. As I would like to survive this siege, I am not going to disobey."

"May Galzar strike that blasphemer of Galzar dead!" Brakkos shouted.

"Hush, man! Even the walls have ears," a captain urged.

"Curse and blast Styphon and all his Archpriests!" Brakkos raved on.

"This isn't the only gap in the mountains, for Galzar's sake! None of the others are half so stoutly defended. Let us push through one of them and fight Kalvan's fugitives, not sit here like owls in a thunderstorm!"

"Silence, Brakkos," Eurocles replied. "Your flapping tongue is a danger to us all." His steely gaze finally reduced Brakkos to stuttering.

"Captain-General Phidestros, *you* are the leader of this Host, and that is a sacred trust given by Galzar. You must stop this madness."

"If I had Galzar's hand to guide mine, I would. I do not. Only Styphon's branding iron and the headsman's ax rule here. I say again, and I hope for the last time—if I order the Host to do anything whatsoever that displeases Roxthar, my life will be forfeit and leave the Host under the command of Soton."

"Then stay and be Roxthar's slave if you will," Grand Captain Demnos snapped. "We shall do otherwise."

"Do anything else and your life won't be worth a bent pfennig," Phidestros replied. "Roxthar has a memory like Galzar's Muster Book."

"Styphon's tentacles do not cover the earth," Brakkos replied. "King Theovacar is always ready to hire freelances, and I've heard there's a revolt in Wulfula and a king taking oaths. Too, there are no Investigators in Hos-Zygros or Hos-Agrys."

"Not yet, my friends," Phidestros said, wearier than even the hour and a moon of work could explain. "Leave at your own risk. The day is Styphon's and his sun burns hot and reaches everywhere.

"If you must leave, do so at night, without a word to anyone. If Roxthar hears of your plans, the Red Hand will drown you in your own blood.

"Let it also be said that this is oathbreaking and I speak against it. Uncle Wolf, what say you?"

Eurocles shook his head. "The Captain-General speaks the truth. Any of you who desert this siege without his permission will be under Galzar's ban. I have no choice."

Brakkos spat on to the ground. "Priest, you are as weak-spined as our *Grand* Captain-General! Don't you see, when Roxthar and his butchers are through with Kalvan they will next turn on Dralm, then Lytris, then

Yirtta Allmother, finally on Galzar himself! Fight before it is too late! We betray Phidestros, but we do not betray our god!"

In a thunderous silence, Brakkos left the tent.

It was Eurocles who broke the silence. "He and his men will be gone before dawn," the priest said in a hushed voice. "By Galzar's Mace, they are doomed. Yet I fear he may well be right."

X

Prince Ptosphes looked around him at the battle-strained faces on the keep's roof. At dawn they would face the twenty-first day of the siege; almost certainly they would face the second storming attempt.

The first one ten days ago had cost the garrison a hundred men, the Styphoni three thousand. It had gained the enemy the north tower, but shellfire from the keep had kept them from mounting guns there.

The second storming would be more dangerous. The enemy would certainly have some tactics devised to meet their shells. Those heavy rifles would come into play against the Hostigi marksmen who had butchered the mercenary captains.

Worst of all, this time Styphon's Red Hand would be clutching at Tarr-Hostigos. Their massed columns had been gathering in Hostigos Town all day. Would they lead the assault, or bring up the rear to remind the vanguard that there was something more to be feared than Hostigi shells?

Two men carrying Captain-General Harmakros' chair set it down with a thump. The two men carrying Harmakros himself gently lowered him into the chair, arranged the cushions behind him, and stepped back.

Even in the twilight, Ptosphes could see that Harmakros' cheeks were too flushed for a man who was supposed to be healing well.

"Did you have wine at dinner?"

"Why not, Prince? It will take more wine than we have in Tarr-Hostigos to kill me before Styphon's House does."

Ptosphes sighed. With variations, he'd heard this at least twenty times today, since it had become obvious that the Styphoni were gathering again. No one expected to see tomorrow's sunset. Nobody seemed to care, either, so long as they could take a proper escort with them. To be sure of doing that, everybody had worked all day as if demons would pounce on them the moment they dropped their tools or even stopped to take a deep breath.

Ptosphes looked the length of what was, for another night at least, *his* castle. The work done to protect the mortars showed most clearly. The four small ones now had stones banked around them, so that the shells bursting outside wouldn't do so much damage. The three larger mortars were back on their field carriages. They could move to prepared positions all over the courtyard as fast as the men on the ropes could pull them, then be firing again almost as soon as they stopped.

The four biggest "mortars" were still in the pit in the outer courtyard. They were really just an old twelve-pounder and three eight-pounders, with their breeches sunk into the earth and their muzzles raised. They were too heavy to move or mount anywhere else, and in any case they could reach everywhere around Tarr-Hostigos from the courtyard. Their crews were finishing a magazine of timbers covered with stones, to protect their shells and fireseed.

"Prince Ptosphes!" One of the riflemen on sentry duty was pointing toward the siege lines on the west side of the castle. "They're starting to move around before the light goes. Think they'll come tonight?" He sounded almost eager.

Ptosphes stared into the dusk, wishing for the hundredth time in the last four years that he had one of the far-seeing glasses of Great King Truman's army. But they were like Kalvan's old pistol—the Great King couldn't even teach his friends how to make the tools to make the tools to make the glasses!

Yet those skills *would* be learned. What the gods had taught once, they could teach again—and more easily, because they would be teaching men who were trying to learn and knew what power the new knowledge might give them.

If Kalvan's luck continued to hold, his children might live to look at a battlefield through far-seers, or even ride into battle aboard one of those armored wagons that moved without horses and carried guns that fired many times while a man was drawing a deep breath.

Ptosphes put aside thoughts of the future he wouldn't see and looked to where the rifleman was pointing. The man was right. Guns—heavy ones from the number of horses drawing them— were rolling slowly along behind the lines. It was too dark to make out more, but Ptosphes suspected that the missing Hostigi sixteen-pounders had just been found.

"Should we try a few shots, just to remind them that we're awake?" Harmakros asked.

"Not with the mortars. We want to save their shells. That little rifled bronze three-pounder on the inner gate, though—it might have the range."

"Kalvan said we shouldn't use case shot with rifled guns," Ptosphes said. "It damages the rifling. With solid shot, that three-pounder will do more good up here."

Harmakros' face asked what he was too tactful to put into words: how likely is it that any gun in Tarr-Hostigos will last long enough to damage itself, once the Grand Host advances? Perhaps he was also chafing at waiting like a bear tethered in a pit, for the dogs to come down within reach.

The hoisting tackle on the keep easily hauled the three-pounder up on to the roof, but not before darkness fell. Half a dozen shots produced a satisfactory outburst of shouts and curses from the Styphoni, but otherwise they seemed to have fallen off the edge of the world. After the half dozen failed to start a fire, Ptosphes ordered the gun to cease fire.

He made a final inspection, counting with special care the torches and tarpots laid ready, in case the Styphoni came at night. It wasn't likely; the chance of hitting friends in a night attack would not please the mercenary captains. It wasn't impossible, either, and Ptosphes was determined to follow Kalvan's teachings to the end (not far away now): prepare for *everything* that isn't impossible.

At last Ptosphes returned to the Great Hall, to find Harmakros asleep in the chair of state and snoring like volley fire from a company of musketeers. Ptosphes rolled himself in his cloak without taking off his armor, on a pallet as far from Harmakros as he could find.

He'd thought he might be too tired or uneasy to sleep, but instead he was drifting off into oblivion almost as soon as he'd stretched out his legs and lowered his head on to the dirt-stiffened cloth.

XI

Phidestros brushed the sleep out of his eyes and stared through the valley's early-morning shadows at the Grand Host's encampment. A splendid sight with its thousands of campfires—until one remembered that all these tens of thousands of men were chained to this desolate valley by a castle held by some five hundred old men and walking wounded. Meanwhile, the Usurper fled into the wilderness.

Phidestros realized now that it was in some measure his own fault that he was not free to ride on Kalvan's trail. He had not questioned Lysandros' orders that he should not go against the will of Grand Master Soton. Apart from the folly of divided command, he respected the man too much.

He had not realized how completely Soton would be in Roxthar's pocket. Nor had he considered the possibility with as much attention as he would have given to the effect of rain on the roads he needed to bring up fireseed! Had he done so, a few discreet questions at least might have already been asked, and the mystery closer to solution. Certainly he would have been able to do more than he had, against the Grand Master's seeming need for Roxthar's permission to break wind!

As it was, he was chief over the Grand Host only in name. In truth, he was first among equals—all of them hamstrung by Roxthar. The Investigator was utterly convinced that the root of Kalvan's heresy was to be found in Hostigos and equally determined to extirpate it if he had to Investigate every person in the Princedom! He would not allow any stone to be left unturned, including Tarr-Hostigos. Against that particular stone the Grand Host had bruised its foot for the best part of a moon, but with Galzar's favor that was about to end!

Phidestros also asked for Galzar's favor, to keep Investigators out of his promised lands of Beshta and Sashta. A small forest of poles already held the bodies of more than a quarter of Hostigos Town's people, those who had failed the Investigation. Add to that those who had fled with Kalvan, and by spring there would hardly be enough Hostigi left to bury their dead!

If the Investigation came to his lands, Phidestros resolved it would not be *his* subjects who decorated gallows. He somehow doubted that Investigators with iron pincers would do as well against soldiers as they did against women and children. It might cost his own head to take Roxthar's, but he would have the pleasure of harvesting the Investigator's first!

The shadows began to fade. From his high vantage point, Phidestros saw the camps coming to life, like kicked anthills. He'd wanted to lead the Iron Band in the first assault himself, but Soton insisted on his staying safely in the rear. Captain-Generals, Soton stated emphatically, were *not* meant to be fired off like barrels of fireseed!

Soton was right, of course. Had Phidestros been in the vanguard during the first storming attempt, he might be dead along with so many others from Ptosphes's exploding cannonballs.

He might also have kept more influence over the mercenary captains. It would have been worth risking Soton's wrath to forestall the hornet's nest Brakkos' departure had unleashed. Or would unleash, as soon as the Red Hand could be spared from the siege to go and hunt the captain down. Roxthar had somehow realized that sending away his picked troops at this moment would end the siege and might end his own existence.

It still rankled, to be leading from behind. One more thing he would have to get used to, he supposed, along with asking who had married whom *before* he swore unquestioning obedience....

Phidestros cupped his hands around his pipe bowl and used the tinderbox to get a spark. When the pipe was drawing, he blew out a long plume of smoke, watching the rising morning breeze chase it away.

"Please, Captain-General," Banner-Captain Geblon said. "Would you get down? Otherwise the Hostigi will aim at your smoke."

Phidestros doubted that in this breeze even a Hostigi rifleman could hit a man at this distance, but obeyed. He could see as well, and make

Geblon happy to boot.

The guns newly emplaced in the battery at the foot of the draw thumped. Their shots tore masonry from a gate tower. Another salvo followed, and white smoke rose in place of the morning mist.

Phidestros puffed on his pipe and prayed to all the true gods that today's butcher's bill would be a light one.

XII

Ptosphes was leading a cavalry charge at the climax of a great battle. The guns thundered and something else was growling like a whole forest full of hungry bears.

He looked down. He wasn't riding a horse, but standing on top of one of Great King Truman's iron wagons with its strange gun. Except that the wagon wasn't quite as Kalvan had described it—it had the head and tail of a horse, the mane flying into his face. As they rode downhill toward the lines of an enemy in the colors of Styphon's Red Hand, the wagon-horse turned its head to look at Ptosphes. Its eyes glowed a sinister green, and he knew that he was riding a creature possessed by demons.

He clawed for reins he couldn't find, trying to turn the creature so he wouldn't have to look into those eyes. No matter how desperately he groped, he couldn't find the reins. At last his fingers closed on something that felt like woolen cloth, which was a strange thing to make reins out of—

"Prince Ptosphes! Prince Ptosphes! Wake up!"

Nobody should be telling him to wake up in a dream and this was still a dream. He could still hear the thunder of guns, even if he couldn't hear the bearlike growling of the iron wagon.

"Prince Ptosphes! The Grand Host is coming!"

"Hu-rmipppp!" Ptosphes lurched into a sitting position before he realized that he was awake and clutching his blanket.

He also heard guns thundering and someone shouting in his ear that the Styphoni were attacking. The window showed gray instead of black. Two men ran toward it, carrying a heavy rifled musket and nearly tripping over Ptosphes as they came.

Ptosphes threw off the blanket and stood. The air of the keep already held a sodden heat. He felt obscurely resentful that so many men should have to fight their last battle on a miserably hot day.

Someone was pushing a cup of tea into his hands. He emptied it in three gulps and held it out again for more. The second cupful was half Ermut's brandy. He set the cup down on the nearest chest, retrieved his sword, and buckled it on.

Harmakros was sitting in the chair of state, wide awake and barking orders. His stump was propped up on a pillow-padded stool and two pistols hung from the arm of the chair.

"Good luck, Prince."

"The same to you, old friend."

That was all the speech Ptosphes allowed himself, even if it was probably the last time he would see Harmakros. If the riflemen were taking position before the arrow slits, there was hardly time to talk.

Chroniclers a hundred years from now will probably make up fine farewell speeches for both of us. Tutors will torment children by forcing them to learn those speeches.

As Ptosphes passed through the keep door on to the outer stairs, the gun-roar doubled, then doubled again. The mortars had opened fire. Whatever was coming at Tarr-Hostigos was now within their range.

Ptosphes hurried down the stairs as fast as he could without appearing uneasy. At the bottom he saw that the guards who saluted him were also busily piling tar-soaked brushwood under the timbers of the stairs. One torch and the easy way into the keep would go up in flames, making another line of defense for the last of the garrison.

From the tower over the gate between the courtyards, Ptosphes could see everywhere except directly behind the keep. Three large storming parties were advancing, one toward the breach made by the siege guns, one by the main gate, and one holding well back on the northeastern side. At a single glance, Ptosphes knew that nearly half the Grand Host must be hurling itself at the castle.

Heavy guns were now firing from the battery at the foot of the draw, over the heads of the column climbing. Big guns, too, even if maybe not the Hostigi sixteen-pounders. Ptosphes saw half the main gate flung backward off its hinges into the portcullis, which bent ominously.

A less well-aimed shot ploughed through the infantry of the storming column. They halted, giving the guns and musketeers on the gate towers an even better target. Their firing sounded like a single volley, and they fired three more times before the column moved again. It moved more slowly now, leaving behind it a trail of writhing, bloody bodies, like a dying bear dragging its guts behind as it sought to close with the hunter.

The column coming at the breach was taking most of its punishment from the mortars, whose crews were firing too fast to be much concerned with safety. Ptosphes saw one man knocked down and crushed as a mortar shifted on its base, and a shell with a fuse cut too short blew up just above the walls. A dozen defenders went down. The ones who rose again shook their fists at the mortar crews.

Now the guns beside Ptosphes were shooting. Another regiment was coming into sight behind the first one—armored men, marching under a black banner with a silver sun-wheel. Soton's Knights were fighting on foot today.

The Zarthani Knights lumbered through the gaps in the first line to take the lead. Ptosphes shouted, "Change to case shot!" It wasn't going to make any difference to the fate of Tarr-Hostigos now, but the more dead Knights, the better for Kalvan.

The guns aimed at the main gate were firing higher now, trying to silence the guns in the gate tower. One of them was disabled, but the other was still hurling case shot straight into the column, inflicting hideous losses. Guns from the other towers were now hammering at the column as well, scything down entire companies like farmers scything wheat.

Smoke gushed up from the enemy battery, more than one could expect from the discharge of even the largest gun. Ptosphes saw men flying into the air and others running with their clothing on fire. He heard the double-thump of an explosion—someone careless with fireseed—as the rate of fire increased.

More Hostigi case shot tore the main column—then suddenly it was breaking up and the men were running back down the draw in a futile effort to escape, some of their officers beating at them with halberds and swords, others joining the rout. From the walls of Tarr-Hostigos, cheers joined the gunfire.

Ptosphes had a moment of thinking that perhaps their doom wasn't so certain after all. One column broken, and its men looking as if they would be hard to rally for another attack. Do the same with the other two columns, and at least the mercenary captains might have the same second thoughts they'd had during the first storming attempt. If they had second thoughts and let Styphon's House know them, the False God himself couldn't keep the Archpriests from having to listen. And if the Archpriests chose to turn the Red Hand loose on the mercenaries, the Grand Host's war against Hostigos would become a civil war within its own ranks—

Ptosphes's moment of hope ended as he saw the column approaching the breach suddenly sprout scaling ladders. They were going to get in or at least close; the heavy mortars had fired off all their shells and round shot wouldn't do so well even against packed men—

The twelve-pounder on top of the barricade let fly with a triple charge of musket balls. Like a volley from a massed regiment it smashed into the column. Already ragged from climbing the slope, the column now barely deserved the name.

Hard on their heels came point-blank musketry that melted away more of the column. Every musketeer within range had six or seven loaded weapons ready to hand for just this moment. For a brief space, they could fire as fast as the rifles of Great King Truman's host, with their "magazines" of eight rounds.

These foes had their blood up, though, or maybe better captains. Then Ptosphes saw the blue and orange colors and recognized the Sacred Squares of Hos-Ktemnos, the best infantry in the Seven Kingdoms. They rose across the rubble before the breach like a blue wave, with clumps of musketeers on the flanks firing over the heads of the storming parties to keep down Hostigi fire. The crews of the useless heavy mortars drew swords and pistols and joined the mass of men struggling in the breach. Ptosphes drew his own sword, ready to join them if they showed signs of flagging.

One of the overheated four-pounders beside Ptosphes recoiled so violently that it snapped its breechings and knocked down Thalmoth. He lay with his thigh a mass of blood, white bone shining through the torn flesh, cursing the gun crew for not remembering what he'd taught them and asking for a pistol. Ptosphes gave him one of his own, as scaling ladders suddenly sprouted to either side of the breach.

The first ladder rose, then flew to pieces as a shot from nowhere split it from top to bottom. At least it came from what seemed like nowhere to Ptosphes, although he knew that what he could see and hear must be rapidly shrinking. This storming of Tarr-Hostigos was already making every other battle he'd seen sound like a mother's lullaby.

The rifled boat swivels were coming into action now. Dead men around them showed that the Hostigi riflemen weren't out of the fight yet. New gunners moved up to replace the dead, though, obviously eager to claim their share of glory. Ptosphes wondered what share of glory they would have if they hit more of their own men than the enemy's. Share of broken bones and heads, more likely.

More ladders rising now. The men on them must be some of the southern swampmen Soton had brought north—no armor, no clothing except leather leggings, and no weapons but hand axes and long wicked knives.

The mortar emplacement spewed flame, smoke, slabs of stone, and flying timbers. An enemy shot or a stray spark had touched off the remaining fireseed in the magazine. Most of the men in or around the pit went down where they stood.

Flying debris scythed into the rear of the Hostigi infantry holding the barricade at the breach. Their line wavered. Some charged forward, grappling with Styphoni and rolling down the rubble to die in the moat with them. Others gave way, and a volley of musketry cleared a path through the ones who stood. Across the dying and the dead of both sides, the Sacred Squares poured over the barricade and down into the outer courtyard.

It seemed to Ptosphes that the Styphoni reached the gatehouse where he stood in the time between one breath and the next. Bullets whistled around him; the men atop the keep were now firing on the inner wall without caring much who was there. His reluctance to turn his back on the enemy gave way to an indignant refusal to be shot in the back by his own men. He ran to the edge of the gun platform, sheathed his sword, dangled from the battlements with both hands until he was sure his arms would pull out of their sockets, then dropped to the inner courtyard.

It was a long drop for an armored man no longer young. Ptosphes went to his knees and was quite sure all his bones were jarred loose from one another. Thankfully, all of them seemed intact when he stood. Smoke was rising from the base of the stairs to the keep. He sprinted for them without stopping to take a breath.

Bullets tore through his jack and glanced off his breastplate, clipped his beard, and seared one hand. At first they came from both sides, then he heard a shout from above, "That's Prince Ptosphes, you wolf's bastard!" and the bullets from the keep stopped. A moment later a crash like the end of the world sounded from behind, followed by screams and curses that penetrated even the ringing in Ptosphes's ears and a choking wave of fireseed smoke. Some Styphoni with more zeal than sense must have used a petard on the inner gate, no doubt blowing it open but also demolishing a good many comrades as well!

Two of the swamp warriors reached the foot of the stairs before Ptosphes. He cut one down with his sword, knocked the ax out of the other's hand, leaped on to the stairs, and dashed up them with flames rising behind him almost as fast as he climbed. By the time he reached the top, the blood pounding in Ptosphes's ears drowned out every other sound. He leaned against the wall beyond the doorway, feeling the cool stone against his forehead and not hearing the outer door being shut and bolted behind him.

By the time he'd been led to a chair and had a cup of wine thrust into his hands, Ptosphes had enough of his wits back to think about what to do next. This was no normal siege, where the garrison of the keep was always given one last chance to surrender. This one would end with the Styphoni trying to bury the Hostigi under a pile of their own dead flesh if they couldn't finish the battle any other way.

If Phidestros and Soton and their captains had the wits the gods gave to fleas, they would launch the last attack as soon as they could, before their men had time to lose their battle-rage. Otherwise those men might start thinking of the kind of fight waiting for them behind the walls of the keep.

When Ptosphes had drunk the wine and could stand, he walked over to Harmakros in the chair of state. He had to walk carefully, to avoid stepping on exhausted men catching their breaths, cleaning their weapons, or just lying staring at the ceiling. The lightly wounded were taking care of each other; the badly wounded hadn't reached the keep.

"I lost sight of the column on the ridge. What of them?" he asked.

"They started to close when the column at the main gate ran," Harmakros replied. "Then the breach fell, and the ridgerunners drew back. Not without leaving a good many men behind, to be sure."

"What do we have left?"

Harmakros shrugged. "A hundred, maybe a few more."

"They'll come soon, wherever they do it." Ptosphes leaned against a stone archway and propped himself up with his sword. By the Twelve True Gods, he was getting old!

"I have men watching on the roof, and more men on the stairs relaying messages, my Prince. They won't catch us napping."

"Unless they kill the men on the roof."

"Not without shells, and maybe not even with them. Anyway, I'll wager a cask of Ermut's best brandy that they don't have any shells."

"Done," Ptosphes said. "But just in case they do...?"

"I've had the men on the roof build themselves a shelter with chests and rolled-up tapestries."

Some of those tapestries, Ptosphes realized, were probably part of his wife's dowry. Not that anybody except Rylla would be left to care before long, of course, and this was a better end for the tapestries than being looted or burned, eaten by vermin, or left to rot in the crumbling shell of the keep....

Ptosphes forced his mind away from such thoughts and climbed the stairs to the roof of the keep.

XIII

Seeing the Styphoni swarming over the shambles that had been his seat and home didn't improve Ptosphes's mood. It helped to see the men on the rifled three-pounder actually smiling as they carved notches in the smoke-stained oak of the gun carriage.

"The big one's for smashing the wheel of one siege gun. Didn't hit any of our people, either," the gunner added. "The four little ones are banners we knocked down. The circle is one of the swivels. We'd have got ourselves a second, but the Styphoni were too cowardly to man it again."

Never mind that the gunners probably hadn't done half the damage they thought they had. If they spent the last candle of their lives grinning and the last moments killing more Styphoni, what did anything else matter to them now?

Ptosphes had just descended to the Great Hall when a messenger followed him down the stairs. "They're moving a heavy field gun into the inner courtyard. One of theirs, though, from the number of men they've put to hauling it."

"Everyone to your places, men," Ptosphes said. He hesitated, then added, "It's been an honor to be your Prince and captain."

A ragged cheer rose, then outside the musketry began again, heavy, rapid fire. The expected message came down from the roof—bullets were mostly coming up, to keep the gun there out of action. Even a three-pound ball could wreck a gun carriage.

"Wait until they attack," Ptosphes ordered. "Then they'll have to cease fire or have spent bullets falling back on their friends." He doubted that the mercenaries or even the Knights would care to risk much of that. It had been a bad day for self-inflicted casualties on both sides; for the Styphoni it was about to get worse.

Galzar's muster-clerks are going to be working long hours today, Ptosphes thought both irreverently and irrelevantly.

Chrunngggg!

Something struck the outside of the wall—a solid shot, the report of its firing lost in the roar of musketry. "Not bad," Ptosphes said. "Sounds as if they hit just to the left of the door."

It took three more shots before the smashing of wood and the ringing of iron signaled a direct hit on the outer door. Two more shots completed the work. A rifleman crept into the doorway and peered over the wreckage.

"They're reloading, but they've lined up a storming party too. They can't be going to fire right over—here it comes— ayyyyhhhh!"

The pieces of the door flew into the Great Hall. So did the pieces of the rifleman. A cannonball rolled in after them, making the Hostigi do spritely dances to avoid it.

Harmakros unhooked his pistols from the arm of the chair of state, cocked them, and laid them in his lap, then raised an empty wine cup in salute to Ptosphes. "I'll claim that brandy, Prince. If they had shells, they'd have used one then."

"So it would seem."

Then from all the firing slits the sentries shouted that the storming party was on the way. The gun on the roof let fly, although no one bothered to tell Ptosphes if it hit anything. It fired a second time, a third.

As the fourth shot went off, the Styphoni burst into the Great Hall.

A ragged volley of pistols and muskets half-deafened Ptosphes. He saw the leading rank of the enemy stagger and go down, but realized that the men behind them now had shields of once-living flesh. He drew his own pistol and fired it over the heads of the six men who'd appointed themselves his last bodyguard. Then the Styphoni were everywhere.

Ptosphes decided that if demons ever really came into the world, they might look like Styphon's soldiers. The attackers wore every sort of armor and clothing except for those who wore little of either. They were black-faced, red-eyed, stinking, shrieking cries in no language intended for human ears, and waving strange weapons in more arms than the gods gave men.

The massed Styphoni gave Vurth a fine target for his musketoon. He shot one man, smashed in a second's face, then got a third in a wrestler's headlock and broke his neck before someone else ran him through. Vurth's diversion let Ptosphes break away from his bodyguards toward the fireplace and the concealed ladder leading down to the cellar. He had to be down there to do his last duty as Prince of Hostigos—not last Prince, the gods grant it!—and knew he might have already waited too long.

Four of the bodyguards stayed alive to reload their weapons and see that their Prince no longer needed them. They fired into the Styphoni, then closed with steel.

The first man to make a way past them, Harmakros shot in the head. The second man ran Harmakros through the stomach; the Duke returned the compliment with his second pistol. A third man wanted to either help his comrades or see if Harmakros was dead. Harmakros snatched the pistol from the man's belt, rammed the muzzle up under its owner's jaw, and pulled the trigger. The chair of state fell over, spilling out Harmakros' body as Ptosphes swung himself into the chimney.

He forced himself to go down the iron rungs of the ladder one at a time. It would help nobody except Styphon's House if he failed in his last duty by falling down the chimney and dashing out what the siege had left of his brains.

By the time he reached the bottom, he knew that if he had to climb back up again his heart would burst before he finished the climb. He'd been right; he would not have lived to see his grandchildren grow up even without this Dralm-damned war! However, this way he was at least spared years of listening to old Tharses and Rylla fussing at him, making him eat and sleep and rest as they thought proper, and generally trying to turn him into a corpse while he was still alive.

The blessed coolness of the cellar revived him a little. He found that he'd brought, his pipe, tobacco, and tinderbox with him, started to light up, stopped as he remembered the ironclad rules about smoking near fireseed, then laughed. It made precious little difference *what* anybody did down here now.

Ptosphes found the fireseed intact, all twelve tons of it minus a barrel or few. He also found the last of the magazine-keepers sitting at the foot of the stairs, along with his clubfooted grandson. The keeper was an old soldier past campaigning, with the grandson to support and no other kin. Ptosphes had given him the magazine by way of a pension.

"What can we do for you, my Prince?"

"If you have pistols—?"

The keeper showed an old cavalryman's matchlock. The boy produced a heavy-barreled boar-hunter's pistol.

"Good. Keep watch on the stairs."

With his pipe in his mouth, Ptosphes walked over to a row of small barrels, chose one, cracked it open, then laid a trail of fireseed a thumb wide and a finger deep to the main pile of larger barrels. Just to be safe, he borrowed one of the keeper's handspikes and knocked in the head of one of the larger barrels. Fireseed poured out, until a helmetful lay waiting at the end of the train, with the twelve tons waiting beyond.

By the time Ptosphes was finished, fists were hammering on the outside of the cellar door. Then he heard the more solid sounds of a chest or bench being swung against it. Wood cracked and metal pulling out of stone screeched, as a hinge gave way. The door half-swung, half-fell inward.

All three Hostigi fired together at the first silhouettes to appear. The answering volley sent bullets spanging around the cellar. One hit the boy in the thigh. The Styphoni drew back, except for the one who fell forward and rolled down the stairs to land at Ptosphes's feet.

He was as filthy as all the others and no more than eighteen. He was crying for his mother as he clasped his hands over a belly wound that under other circumstances would have killed him slowly over the next few days. Well, he'd be spared that, and he'd already lived longer than the keeper's grandson would, or Harmakros' son if the Grand Host overtook Kalvan.

Except that they wouldn't. Ptosphes knew this, although he couldn't have explained how he knew it. He was sure it was true knowledge, not a dead man's dreaming to make his death easier.

Since he was dead, why wait any longer, in case one of those Styphoni cursing so loudly at the top of the stairs wanted to come down and argue the point?

Ptosphes finished tamping the ball and wadding of his new load, checked the pan, then rested the pistol on one knee as he knocked the live coal from his pipe into the train of fireseed.

XIV

"Damn you, Sirna! What are you using in the wound? Galzar's Mace?"

Sirna ignored Phidestros' blustering. She knew she must be causing him agony, probing his wounded thigh with her limited skills and instruments improvised by the Iron Band's armorers from Menandra's kitchen utensils. He'd refused a sandbag, though, and she had to go on and extract that last piece she felt in the wound. Otherwise he would certainly lose his leg and probably his life. Then what would happen to her? Sirna told herself that her concern was thoroughly practical and continued digging.

Finally the probe clicked on the fragment again, this time loosening it until she could grip it between two blood-slimed fingers. It was a piece of stoneware, sharp-edged but solid. It wouldn't leave any more fragments in the wound (or so she told herself, because she knew that her hands would start shaking uncontrollably if she had to burrow back into that mangled flesh).

She held up the stoneware. Phidestros managed a grin. "So that's why they didn't run out of bullets. They saved up their last moon's trash and shot it at us!" Phidestros made a face and groaned. "That's not all the trash I'm going to get shot at me when Soton learns I got this kiss from Galzar rallying his swivel gunners not a hundred paces from the breach! My ears will hurt worse than this leg!"

Petty-Captain Phyllos lifted Phidestros' leg so that Sirna could bind it in the boiled remains of a shift. Phyllos' wrenched knee made him slow, but as long as he could stand he felt that he had to be on duty. Certainly he'd had more experience dealing with battle wounds than any of Menandra's girls, didn't mind taking orders from a woman who knew her business, and whipped into line any soldier who did.

At last Phidestros was bandaged. Sirna came as close as she could to offering a prayer for his recovery. She could no longer tell herself that her wish was entirely practical, either. Phidestros was too good a man to die, even if he was serving a particularly murderous brand of superstition

"Sorry to give you such a bad time," she said as four of the hastily recruited orderlies lifted Phidestros off the table. Half the Captain-General's bodyguard had escorted him to the Gull's Nest after he fell. She'd drafted most of them into helping with the wounded who'd been streaming in since dawn. And this was only one of the besiegers' hospitals! Galzar's Great Hall was going to be crammed to the rafters tonight.

"Menandra runs a fine whorehouse, but it's not much of a hospital," Sirna went on. "If I had some proper tools, or the help of a priest of Galzar—"

Phidestros sighed. "My lovely Sirna, if I knew where to find an Uncle Wolf who didn't already need two heads and six hands, I'd have him dragged to you. You're going to be all we have for today. When they carted me off I heard we already had two thousand men down."

"Two thousand!" Sirna shuddered at the implications. Phidestros had been hit early enough to reach the Gull's Nest before the storming of the keep. Two thousand men down in the time it took the Styphoni to close the walls. How many more in the fighting since—?

Thunder battered at her ears and the floor quivered. The door and all the window shutters banged wildly and dust rose until the room looked as if someone had fired a small cannon. Sirna looked frantically out the window, saw nothing but people gaping idiotically, knew she must be doing the same, and dashed out the door.

A vast cloud of gray smoke towered over Tarr-Hostigos, blotting out the whole castle and slowly swallowing the hillside below it. The top of the cloud was already several thousand feet high, spreading into something dreadfully like a fission bomb's mushroom. Sirna lived a moment with the nightmare that Kalvan had done the impossible, taking his time-line from a poor grade of gunpowder to fission bombs in four years.

The mushroom shape started to blur, and Sirna breathed more easily. The top of the cloud was simply spreading in a breeze not felt here in the lee of the hills. She watched the cloud start to trail off toward the southeast, bits and pieces of smoking debris dropping from it as it went.

Prince Ptosphes had given himself and the last of his men over to a quick death, destroying Tarr-Hostigos and more of his enemies than anyone would ever know.

Sirna wanted to weep, scream, pound her fists against something. For a moment she even wanted to die herself. There had to be something wrong with her, if she was still alive with so much death around her. The battle, the flight, her surgery at Menandra's, Roxthar's Investigation, and now the storming of Tarr-Hostigos—dead men and women, and children were everywhere.

Sirna didn't die. She didn't even have hysterics. Instead she gripped the porch railing until she knew she could stand without help. Around her Hostigos Town awoke from a stunned silence into a hideous din of bawled orders, howling dogs, shrieking women and children, horses neighing or galloping wildly about in panic, and an occasional pistol shot.

Menandra was standing in the doorway when Sirna turned. "Better come in quick, girl," she said. "The soldiers who lost comrades up there—they'll be wanting someone's blood for it. Can't keep it from being yours if you stand out there."

Sirna followed the older woman inside. She wasn't afraid of death itself. After today she never would be again. Ptosphes had shown her that death could sometimes be your best friend.

He'd also shown her that there were good and bad ways to die. No, not good and bad. That implied a simple moral distinction. If there was anything simple about death, Sirna hadn't seen it.

Wise and foolish ways? Better, but still an oversimplification.

Useful and useless? Yes. That wasn't a universally sound way of distinguishing kinds of death, but there probably wasn't any such thing. It certainly made sense here.

Staying outside to be shot or raped by soldiers mad with rage or wine would be a *useless* death. She wouldn't risk it. What she would do another time, she would decide when that time came.

A phrase from one of Scholar Danthor Dras' seminar lectures came back to her: "*The only universal rule of outtime work is that there are no universal rules.*"

XV

Soton cursed the Hostigi and their stubbornness that was costing the Grand Host so many lives. Half the storming party was inside Tarr-Hostigos, swarming over it like bees. Both courtyards were littered with bodies, most of them Styphoni. Clouds of smoke wreathed the keep, but before they rose Soton had seen even from his distant post the savage struggle to enter it.

Why in the name of all the gods hadn't Phidestros kept back, instead of closing the breach? Then there would have been someone to go down and put matters in order.

Instead Phidestros was wounded—badly, the tales ran. Small loss, with the last defenders of Hostigos dying even now and Kalvan fleeing toward the Trygath. If Phidestros was going to make a habit of such follies, perhaps it would be best if he stormed Hadron's Caverns the next time. If he didn't, Soton would make him wish he had!

The smoke around the keep eddied. Soton turned, to summon a messenger.

He never completed the turn. Instead something as invisible as the air but as hard as stone flung him to his knees. Thunder swelled until it seemed that someone was beating on his helmet with his own warhammer. Three Knights flew off the ledge, along with a shower of rocks. Soton knew he cried out at that sight, but couldn't hear his own voice.

He lay, gripping the ground as closely as he ever gripped a woman, until it stopped shaking. Then he rose to his knees, and when they did not betray him, to his feet.

The air was filled with acrid smoke and fine ash. Looking toward Tarr-Hostigos, he saw only a vast swirling cloud of smoke. Somewhere in that smoke was the entire storming party—one man in three of the Grand Host's strength.

One of the Knights was shrieking. "It's the Demon Kalvan! He's come to save his people! Great Styphon, save us!"

Soton smashed his gauntleted fist into the Knight's face. The man fell as if poleaxed. Soton didn't know what he was really smiting, the Knight or his own fear.

Slowly the air around what had been Tarr-Hostigos cleared. The slopes around it were alive with men, thousands of them all streaming away from the castle. Soton let out a deep breath he hadn't even known he was holding.

Another quarter-candle showed him what was left of Tarr-Hostigos. The keep was only a pile of smoking rubble, the towers had mostly lost their tops, and the walls looked to have been chewed by monsters. How many of the Grand Host lay there under the fallen stone or in fragments strewn across the hillside? The Grand Host would be far less grand by the time they were all counted, Soton was sure.

Yet—this should not have been a surprise. Desperate men will take desperate measures. Who had more experience fighting the desperate than Soton, Grand Master of the Zarthani Knights?

Soton smashed his fist against his armored thigh, insensible to the pain.

"Kalvan!" he shrieked. "Kalvan, you will pay for this! By Styphon's Wheel, I swear it!"

XVI

Verkan Vall finished lighting his pipe with an Aryan-Transpacific silver and ivory inlaid tinderbox, then turned back to the data screen and its display of information on one Khalid ib'n Hussein. The second cousin of a minor Palestinian prince assassinated five years earlier—on his sub-sector branch—Khalid was putting together a Mideastem superstate that included just about every Moslem nation except Turkey and Libya.

As this new Islamic Caliphate emerged, on most of its time-lines its pro-Western leanings seemed to be toppling the balance between Communism, that strange atheistic religion, and the so-called Free World. Another case of the inherent instability of the entire Europo-American, Hispano-Columbian Subsector!

Verkan made a note to send out some investigator to see if the Mideast had acquired some transtemporal hitchhiker like his friend Kalvan. One of the problems with transtemporal history was that it was always easier to spot the important historical turning points after the damage was done! There was that Paracop chief two thousand years ago, who hadn't paid any attention to an anonymous carpenter's son until the religion his death launched was already shaking whole subsectors to the foundations—

The red light on Verkan's desk lit up, announcing an important visitor. Verkan looked up to see Kostran Garth enter. The man's face was red from exertion, his breath came short as if he'd been running, and he was holding out a data-storage wafer in one hand.

"What is it?"

"This just arrived from the surveillance satellite on Kalvan's Time Line. I scanned it briefly—Dalla had it red-flagged—and I knew you'd want to see it right away."

From the look on Kostran's face, Verkan knew the wafer wasn't good news; only bad news ever traveled that fast. Verkan slipped the wafer into his viewer and watched the screen light up.

The views began with a satellite's-eye scan of Hostigos and the surrounding Princedoms, from an altitude that made them all look deceptively peaceful. The next shots were close-ups of Tarr-Hostigos. Verkan sighed with relief; at least he wasn't going to see Kalvan and his remaining soldiers caught like fish in a net.

The camera panned in closer, suggesting manned control of the cameras (remember to commend Dalla for that precaution). A human wave was approaching the beleaguered castle; almost the whole Styphoni host seemed to be on the move. Closer still, and Verkan saw whole units going down under Hostigi shells and musketry.

Verkan sped up the fast-forward. Whatever was coming, he wanted to get it over with.

The attackers poured into the castle like ants over leftover dog food. Muzzle flashes showed that the keep still had some live defenders. Were Ptosphes and Harmakros among them—Ptosphes, who'd refused to leave his home, and Captain-General Harmakros, still worth any three men with two legs?

Suddenly everything vanished in a cloud of smoke. Verkan held his breath until the smoke began to clear. Slowly Tarr-Hostigos reappeared— or what had been Tarr-Hostigos.

Half the walls still stood, battered and leaning. Otherwise Ptosphes's seat was a pile of smoking rubble. Verkan saw where one aircar-sized chunk of stone had crushed an entire company of Styphoni. The slopes around the castle were covered with more Styphoni—lying still, crawling, stumbling, a few lucky enough to be able to run.

Verkan's fist slammed down on his desk. "By Dralm, Ptosphes did it!"

"What?"

"He did what even Kalvan couldn't do. He stopped the Grand Host in its tracks! Look at that mess! The bastards must have taken five, ten thousand casualties. That, my friend, is no longer a Grand Host. It's hardly even an army! By the time Soton and Phidestros sort things out, Kalvan will be safe in Grefftscharr."

Verkan rummaged a flask of Ermut's Best and two cups out of a drawer. "A toast, Kostran. A toast to the memory of a valiant Prince and his last and greatest victory!"

Kostran gagged at the taste of the brandy, but he was smiling as he said, "To Prince Ptosphes!"

XVII

Considering the Hostigi resistance, the four to five thousand casualties taken in entering Tarr-Hostigos surprised no one. From the stories brought in during the day with the wounded, Sirna concluded that another eight thousand at least must have been casualties of the great explosion. Including the earlier sortie that made roughly fifteen thousand casualties. Over half were dead, and half the wounded wouldn't fight again this year if at all. Sirna would have liked more accurate figures, but she was relieved to know that she could go on doing a University outtime observer's work even in the middle of a battle.

It would be embarrassing if she ever returned home and had to confess that she hadn't taken advantage of her "unique" opportunity to observe historically significant Fourth Level events. It would probably cost her that doctorate!

Sirna told herself this over and over again, to keep some grip on her sanity, as the wounded poured into the Gull's Nest. It was the first time she'd allowed herself to think of First Level since the day she woke up in Menandra's back bedroom. Somewhat to her surprise it helped.

Having some extra hands helped even more. More of the lightly wounded men turned to changing bandages or helping comrades to the privies. Menandra rolled up her sleeves and went to work setting bones, a skill she'd acquired in her younger days from cleaning up after tavern brawls in Agrys City. She also turned out all of her girls who could be trusted to know a clean bandage from a dirty one, which was more than Sirna had expected.

Another of Scholar Dras' bits of wisdom kept running through Sirna's mind: "The danger of paratemporal contamination doesn't come from the stupidity of lower-level people. It comes from the fact that they're inherently just about as smart as we are. Once they've been shown that something is possible, you would be surprised how fast they can pick it up and even start filling in gaps on their own."

Sirna knew that would never surprise her again.

By the time the western sky turned an appropriately bloody color, the flow of fresh wounded had stopped. Sirna trudged through the house on feet that felt shod in lead boots, checking splints and dressings she hadn't put on herself.

In the twilight outside she heard shouts and screams. Men, drunk or avenging dead comrades or simply celebrating being alive when they'd expected to be dead, were sacking Hostigos Town. The hard-eyed mercenary guards from the Iron Band kept the noise and the noisemakers safely outside.

At least she didn't hear the sinister crackling of flames, as she had during Rylla's campaign in Phaxos. The Styphoni weren't going to burn the town as long as they needed its roofs over their heads.

Sirna felt like a deer who'd somehow managed to be adopted by a pack of wolves. The Captain-General's men would protect her against all the other packs as long as she did what they expected. But that didn't make her a wolf. Somehow it was no longer hard to take for granted a situation she would have found unbelievably degrading two years ago. Not hard at all, when she listened to the screams outside.

She was changing the bandages on the stump of a man's arm when someone banged on the door to the street, loud enough to be heard over the din outside and the cries of the wounded inside. One of the house women looked through the peephole. Then she unbarred the door and jumped aside, with a look on her face that brought every fit man in the room to his feet.

Two of Styphon's Guardsmen strode in, their red cloaks flapping dramatically. Two more followed their white-robed charge inside, then stood flanking the door. Sirna saw hostile glances flicking over the Red Hands' clean clothing and silvered armor.

At least Holy Investigator Roxthar looked as if he'd worked today, and worked hard. His long hollow-cheeked face was coated with dust and soot and his robes were bloodstained and frayed. He reminded Sirna of a Fourth Level Judeo-Christian representation of the Devil.

For a moment she wondered if Kalvan was the only cross-time hitchhiker around. Then she remembered the file on the control time-line equivalents to the major Archpriests. On one other time-line Roxthar was purging Styphon's House almost as spectacularly as he was here. On several others he'd died mysteriously, doubtless courtesy of one of Archpriest Anaxthenes' handy little vials.

Phidestros smuggled to a sitting position and raised a hand in greeting. "Welcome, Your Sanctity. Today Hadron's Hall is filled to the bursting, but the first and vilest of the demons' nests has at last been burned out."

Roxthar nodded, as though acknowledging a remark about the weather, then looked around the room. His nostrils flared.

"So this den of flesh-selling has served as the Captain-General's nest. I wondered why we had so often lacked your esteemed company at the Palace."

From the Captain-General's face, Sirna knew his patience was strained nearly to the breaking point.

"I must admit, Your Sanctity, that I much prefer the cries of honest passion in this house to the constant uproar at the Palace. No offense meant, of course. Let Styphon's Will Be Done!"

Roxthar's face paled. "Do not presume, Captain-General, or you may yet find yourself enjoying the hospitality of my Investigators."

"They might find a soldier too much work, after so many women and children."

Roxthar's gray eyes turned into steel ball bearings. "Enough of this babble. We have the God of Gods to serve today. The Daemon Kalvan has fled, with the remnants of his host. The land he left behind is tainted with the evil he wrought, and the servants of his demons lurk everywhere. Let the Investigation of Styphon finish its work, *then* we can attend to lesser duties."

It was just as well Roxthar didn't smile. If he had, Sirna knew she would have laughed out loud, hoping to wake up on the other side of the abyss between her and the sane reality of Home Time Line, where people didn't blow up castles in wars over non-existent gods. Instead she bit her lip and unwound the last strip of bandage, then stood up to take the sterilized fresh dressing from the soldier holding the basin.

The movement drew Roxthar's eyes. Sirna felt their hard, unclean gaze on her all the time she was binding on the dressing, emptying the water into the slop bucket, and putting the old bandages into the empty basin to be returned to the cauldrons boiling in the kitchen. She was proud that her hands didn't tremble once.

At last there was nothing more to do except stand up and face the Investigator. He was now smiling, an expression to which his gaunt features hardly lent themselves. Sirna decided that she much preferred him expressionless.

"Those bandages have been boiled to drive out the fester-demons, have they not?"

"That is so, Your Sanctity." Sirna was relieved that she'd kept all traces of a tremor out of her voice.

"That is knowledge given by the servant of demons, Kalvan, you know."

You're not afraid of death anymore, Sirna reminded herself. *Besides, Roxthar won't spare a heretic even if she goes down on the floor and kisses his feet. Do as you please and at least you can hope to go out with dignity, like Ptosphes.*

"That is so, Your Sanctity. Yet the new compounding of fireseed was also brought by Kalvan. With the blessing of Styphon's holy priests, the new fireseed has been used in the guns of Styphon's Grand Host, to smite Styphon's enemies. Is it not possible that the knowledge of smiting the fester-demons may also be used to aid Styphon's cause?"

Roxthar's vices did not include being at a loss for words. "This may be so. Yet I see no priests of Styphon's House here, to bless your work so that it may drive out demons instead of letting them in. Also, it is too soon to tell what may come of this day's work. Not all demons leap forth at the wave of their servants' hands. Some bide their time."

If it weren't that her life was at stake, Sirna would have believed this conversation about demons and their servants totally absurd. "In your own words, Your Sanctity—that may be so. Yet I have been healing the men of the Iron Band since the siege began. In all of them, the wounds are cleaner than they would have been without my work. Ask the Captain-General or the men themselves!

"As for there being no priests here—today there were many wounded and few hands to heal them. Should I have let men who shed their blood for Styphon die, their wounds stinking and festering, because there is no priest to bless work that I *know* is wholesome and good? If I did that, then you *would* have good cause to bring me before the Investigation. I think what I have done is good service to the God of Gods, and I will pray for his blessing, and also for his mercy on you if you falsely accuse me."

She knew that the last sentences must have been audible on the streets outside, from the way the door guards were looking behind them. Roxthar's smile froze, then he shrugged.

"As Styphon wills it. I only know what I must do in his service, and also pray for his mercy if I misjudge what that is. You must come with us before the Investigation, and hope that witnesses may be found in your behalf."

Sirna knew that her last moment was close at hand, and also that she was going to spend it as a woman of this time-line rather than as a scholar of First Level. Her right hand was at waist level, closing around the hilt of a non-existent dagger, and she'd shifted her footing to open the distance between her and Roxthar. One of the Red Hands stepped forward—

—and stopped a yard from Sirna, as a dozen mercenaries drew entirely real swords and daggers. Two more armed with half-pikes appeared on the stairway and a third in the door to the hall, with a pistol.

"Archpriest Roxthar," Phidestros said, in a tone that reminded Sirna of a baron she'd once heard sentencing a poacher. "There is nothing but the truth in what this woman says. This I swear, by Styphon God of Gods and Galzar Wolfhead, by Yirtta Allmother and by Tranth who blesses the hands of the craftsman. My men will swear the same."

"How many of them?"

"As many as needed to make it unlawful for this woman to go before the Investigation, and ten more besides. The Iron Band knows good healing when it sees it."

One of the Red Hands started to draw his pistol at Phidestros' tone. An imperative and slightly frantic gesture from Roxthar stopped him. The Archpriest's good sense clearly extended to recognizing when he saw it a situation where one false move would leave him and his guards dead on the floor and the Investigation of Styphon's enemies in chaos.

"We value your judgment and honor you for your good work in the Holy Investigation," Phidestros went on, as big a lie as Sirna had ever heard anyone deliver with a straight face. "Therefore we will also swear to watch this woman day and night, and bring word to the Investigation of any evil effects from her healing."

Phidestros paused, then fired his final shot. "And is not one of Styphon's own signs of his presence among us his gift of healing?"

Roxthar's head jerked, but to Sirna's relief he stopped short of smiling. "As you wish, Captain-General. Clearly Styphon's favor is with you today, but this may not always be so. I shall return tomorrow, to see those wounded who have been healed in days past and to take the oaths you have promised."

The Investigator whirled and strode out so fast that his Guardsmen had to scurry to catch up with him. A chorus of harsh laughter and obscene remarks about why the Guardsmen had unbattered armor after a battle like this hurried their departure. Sirna also heard a few bawdy remarks, about who would have the job of watching her by night.

Sirna was told afterward that she didn't faint. She certainly remembered nothing until she found herself in a chair, her head pushed down between her knees and Menandra and Banner-Captain Geblon chafing her wrists so vigorously that they felt ready to catch fire. She kept her head down and let the chafing go on until the giddiness and the urge to vomit on an empty stomach passed.

"Sirna—"

"Get back down on that pallet, Captain-General!"

"I need to talk—"

"When you're down on the pallet. Not a word until then!" she demanded. Sitting cross-legged by Phidestros' pallet, Sirna could hear him without anyone else being able to eavesdrop. Geblon made sure of that, with help from Menandra.

"I'm sorry if I put you in danger," she began. "But I couldn't—"

"And you didn't, and there's no need to apologize," Phidestros interrupted, with a grin. "We are the Iron Band, and we can do nicely without temple-rats chittering in our ears in our own quarters. You, on the other hand—"

Phidestros reached over and put a hand on her knee. "You've got a petty-captain's share of pay for this past campaign coming, and more if Styphon's House pays any of the victory gift they've promised. That's enough to be a good dowry for you, or buy you a horse and cart with traveling rations and servants to take you home—if you have any home left."

"Or you could stay here and buy into a partnership with me," Menandra put in. "I'm not as young as I once was. Somebody I could leave the place to would be a comfort to me now."

Phidestros gave Sirna a smile that showed what he thought of the Gull's Nest's prospects after the Grand Host departed.

"A partnership—" Sirna began, then pressed her palms into her eyes until the pain and the swimming red fire killed the desire to laugh. She owed Menandra too much to ridicule the idea of staying in Hostigos Town and becoming assistant madam of a bordello!

"I don't advise any of those," Phidestros went on. "Roxthar can't try anything with us—or at least anything the rest of the Inner Circle or Grand Master Soton won't stop, as long as I'm Captain-General of the Grand Host of Styphon. Soton and Anaxthenes know good mercenaries are valuable, as long as Kalvan's still on the loose.

"You, on the other hand, he'll snap up like a weasel grabbing a new-hatched chick the moment you're out of our protection. You've humiliated him before men he distrusts. He'll forgive that the day Queen Rylla begs on her knees for a pardon from Styphon's House."

Phidestros was making sense—too much sense—but not telling her what to do. Or perhaps he assumed she already knew, and was waiting for her to offer it freely.

"I...1 suppose I could ride with the Iron Band, that is, if you've a place for a healer. I'd like to train some of your men to help me, if that could be arranged, because I really can't do it all myself—"

Phidestros was kissing her eyelids and cheeks as well as her lips. Sirna wasn't quite ready to kiss him back, but she didn't stop him, either. She managed to be deaf to the new chorus of cheers and bawdy remarks around her.

"Some of my girls may want to come with you," Menandra added. "Hostigos Town may not be the most comfortable place for a while. I've three or four who've earned out their time and may want to travel on. If you could train them too—"

It's insane! Here she was, planning to live as the healer to a band of Fourth Level mercenaries and madam to their field brothel. Not to mention, probably, mistress to their Captain-General—an idea that now left her feeling curious rather than degraded. *Although please, let the contraceptive implants not run out before I find a way home!*

It was insane—and it would keep her alive. If Roxthar's Investigators had to fight the Iron Band to reach her, they probably would give her up as not worth the trouble. If she had to sleep with Phidestros to keep his favor, she would at least be sleeping with an interesting man—and not interesting in a purely academic sense, either....

She would go with Phidestros and his men. She would do what they wanted her to do, and they would keep her alive until Great King Kalvan returned and took vengeance for this day and all the other crimes of Styphon's House.

Sirna was sure that day would come. It would be worth enduring much to be there to see it, and maybe, Dralm willing, help bring it about.

XVIII

Tortha Karf, former Paratime Police Chief and now a Paratime Commissioner, ploughed his way through the guards and secretaries into Chief Verkan's office. He found his successor sitting behind his horseshoe desk, face buried in his hands. Verkan's face reminded Tortha of his field-hands' wives back on his Fifth Level Sicily retreat. When he'd announced that he was forsaking his retirement, the women acted as if half the tribe's men had just died in battle!

"What's the matter, Vall? Has Dalla decided on another divorce?"

Verkan looked up, startled as if he hadn't known he had a visitor. "Oh, Tortha. It's just wool-gathering. My friend Kalvan's lost damned near everything. I just finished reviewing the tape on the fall of Tarr-Hostigos.

"Instead of leaving anything for the Styphoni, Ptosphes blew up the castle, the whole Styphoni storming party, and himself. Roxthar has turned his Investigators loose, and they're busy murdering, torturing, or harassing any Hostigi who didn't flee with Kalvan."

"Sounds as if Ptosphes made the best of a bad job. Nothing sad about taking that big an escort with you. As for the other Hostigi—they're just getting now what they've already had on all the other Styphon's House time-lines where they didn't have a Lord Kalvan to save them."

The Commissioner leaned over the desk and quietly continued. "Vall, you're a realist and a historian as well as a Paracop. You know all this. What's really bothering you?"

Verkan winced as if he'd been slapped, then laughed. "You really know how to go to the heart of things. Maybe I will too, if I sit at this desk another century or so."

Not much chance of that if he keeps taking every friend's bad luck so personally, thought Tortha. A shame, really, because apart from his Kalvan problem Verkan showed every sign of being an above-average Chief for the Paracops.

"Now, once again. What's eating you this way?"

"I let a good friend down, a friend who was counting on me. Here I've got all this power and I can't do a Dralm-damned thing to help without upsetting some bureaucrat or breaking some Paratime regulation."

"You're not making sense. You're falling into outtime guilt and loyalty patterns. If you weren't Chief I'd suggest you make a short visit to our Bureau of Psych Hygiene clinic."

"I'd rather be in the hands of Roxthar's Investigation!"

"That's where you might be right now, if you'd been captured at Ardros Field. There, or just one more corpse in a mass grave. You came close enough with that sucking chest wound you took. What good would either have done Kalvan? He's alive and so are you, and I think you can do him a lot more good that way. Where is he now, by the way?"

"The Hostigi survivors are gathering in Ulthor Town."

"Why haven't they crossed into the Trygath or Hos-Rathon, as it's called now?" Tortha asked.

"Because the traitor Nestros has been suborned by the Styphoni. If Kalvan leads his people into the Hos-Rathon, they'll have to face another army. One without tens of thousands of refugees tagging along."

"That doesn't sound too good," Tortha observed. "So, where will Kalvan go from there?"

Verkan shook his head. "He'll either gather all his forces and fight Nestros, or hire enough boats to take him across the Aesklos Sea."

"What will King Theovacar have to say about that?"

"He's not going to be happy, but he's in no position to stop Kalvan. He doesn't have a fleet near enough to make a difference, even if he knew what was going on. Remember, communications on Kalvan's Time Line are at best slow."

"What about the Grand Host? Archpriest Roxthar's not going to give up just because Kalvan's evaded his host. He'll be marching west as soon as the dust settles."

"He probably will be, but it's going to be a while." Verkan seemed more at ease now; his analysis of the situation began to flow with his usual fluency. "Ptosphes inflicted heavy casualties on the Grand Host and gave their morale a nasty jar. They're probably not fit for a long pursuit into hostile country now.

"Besides, the victors will be dividing the spoils. Probably falling out over them, sooner or later. This much land hasn't changed hands since the Zarthani Knights broke the Great River Confederation. Then there was only one real claimant, too. Now there are about six arguing over the pie."

"Then Kalvan should have a while to figure out what to do next," Tortha added. "In his place, I'd build a power base so that I could be a valuable ally to anyone who felt he didn't get his share of the pie."

"He could do that, selling his services in the Middle Kingdoms as a mercenary leader. Everybody's going to need soldiers, until the barbarians are beaten back. The only thing holding the Middle Kingdoms to Styphon's House was the fireseed secret, and that's blown away. King Theovacar might even find Kalvan useful against his own barons, if there aren't enough barbarians to fight."

"Vall, I think you've just described your own next opportunity," Tortha said. "King Theovacar knows Verkan the Trader. He also knows that you're a Baron of Hos-Hostigos. Who knows, you might lead him to make you one of his negotiators with his new royal guest, King Kalvan."

"Of course! It's going to take some planning and all the supplies I can beg, borrow, or steal on a few next-door time-lines, but—" Verkan frowned, then laughed out loud, a sound that made Tortha Karf want to do the same.

Tortha held his tongue, as Verkan tried to glare at him, then laughed again.

"You sly old dog! You planned this all along. Well, the penalty is going to be taking me and Dalla out to dinner at the Constellation House.

We can finish roughing out the plans there."

Verkan started to swivel his chair, then stopped. "Just as a suggestion, why don't we sit on the fact that I've recovered. The rumors that I'm sitting staring at the wall and still recovering from my wounds have already brought out into the open a few mice who think the cat's out to lunch. If we keep the rumors going a few more days, we may find a few more mice."

"You're not thinking of hiding it from Dalla, I hope?"

"If I did that, I *would* belong in the clinic!" Verkan said with a laugh. He swiveled his chair, and the rest of the world might have vanished in mist as Verkan started punching requests for data into his computer keyboard. Tortha Karf found a comfortable chair and leaned back with a contented sigh. The Verkan Vall he'd known for fifty years was back—and on the hunt again.

THE WIZARD TRADER WAR

JOHN F. CARR

I

1971 A.D.

Ex-Paratime Police Chief Tortha Karf entered the Chief's office and looked around in surprise. Hadron Dalla, the new Paratime Police Chief, had redecorated Verkan Vall's former office to the point where he hardly recognized the place. Gone was the chief's horseshoe desk—a signature piece of furniture that had survived the reign of four chiefs—along with Verkan's curio cabinets and all his assorted weaponry and framed paintings. Dalla had replaced the old desk with some modern monstrosity that was all glass and mirrors. The walls were covered with living pictures, wall screens and shimmering metallic hangings from Second Level Interplanetary while the old couch had been replaced with a divan from Imperial Macedonia, fit for an Empress.

The biggest surprise, however, was Dalla herself; she looked harried and her usual impeccable coif was in disarray, strands of hair shooting out of her upswept hairdo. Her Paratime Police greens looked as if she'd slept in them. She was crouched around her reading-screen as if it was a precious tablet someone was about to hijack.

"Chief Hadron, I got your message ball. What's going on?"

Dalla shook her head as if waking from a deep sleep. "Sorry, Tortha. I've been swamped for last five ten-days. You just can't believe…well, I guess, maybe you can."

Tortha laughed. "I've been through my share of crises."

"I'm sure you have," she said with a tone of reproach. "But not like this! We've got riots going on in Old Town Dhergabar and two tower bombings in the last ten-day. The Dhergabar Metropolitan Police Chief wants to borrow ten thousand of our field agents to help patrol the City and find the miscreants. The Prole Liberation Movement is demanding representation on the Executive Council, or else—"

"Back when I was Chief, we used to get the same kind of ultimatums from the Prole Protection League. The PPL was making those kind of demands even before ex-Chief Tharg was on the job. Nothing new there."

"You're wrong, Tortha. Things have changed. The Prole Liberation Movement is the militant arm of the Prole Protection League. They weren't kidnapping citizens and bombing towers when you were in office."

Tortha shook his head, sputtering like a big walrus surfacing for air. "I apologize. Things do sound as if they've gone to Nifflheim in a hand basket! What's Metro doing about it?"

"Metropolitan Police Chief Vothan Raldor believes that someone the proles call The Leader is behind all this."

"Are you telling me this is a religious issue?" Tortha asked. "Because if it is, we're all in trouble." The worst wars in Home Time Line history had occurred during the Mystic Rebellions.

"No, The Leader's just the 'man' who's supposed to lead the proles into citizenship and give them all longevity treatments. I haven't heard of any religious rites connected to his demands. No one knows who he is or what he represents. He's got the proles all lathered up and rioting in Old Town."

It would be hard to riot elsewhere, thought Tortha, *since the rest of Dhergabar consisted of anti-gravity spires and towers stretching toward the sky. Still, the proles far outnumbered citizens, many of whom were working or vacationing outtime. If they continued to attack the towers things could get messy in a hurry.*

"Have you thought of calling in the Army Strike Teams?"

"That's why I asked for your advice, Commissioner. Things are in a real precarious place in the Executive Council ever since Vall resigned and left office. The last Crisis of Confidence vote almost brought down Management. It wouldn't take much for the Opposition Party to wrest control of the Council."

Then calling in the army, Tortha decided, *would be a complete disaster. The Opposition Party would use it to show that Management has lost control over the capital. I know they're somehow behind this fracas, but proving it is almost impossible. The Opposition Party included almost as many scoundrels and scalawags as that Styphon's House racket on Aryan-Transpacific. He couldn't remember the last time things on Home Time Line had been so out of whack. What's going on in Dhergabar, other than politics as usual?*

It hadn't been that long since he'd retired, only a decade or so, and things had been going fine when he'd resigned. Verkan hadn't caused this mess, he hadn't been Chief long enough. Although, spending most of his time on Kalvan's Time Line hadn't helped the situation. He'd spent enough time there that he'd resigned his office—before he'd been forced to—and left it in Dalla's capable hands. No, this was a large scale operation put together behind the scenes over decades. Someone had to be behind it, but who? Dralm-damned if he could come up with anyone or a group that powerful and sinister. Opposition Party contained too many hacks and has-beens; they certainly weren't pulling the strings...dancing to them maybe, but not yanking them.

"Chief Vothan's a good man. Give the Metro Police whatever manpower he asks for and put some of our top Investigators to work and find out who or what's behind all this PLF nonsense. This mess stinks all the way up to Mars."

"I'll do that," Dalla replied. "Any other ideas?"

Tortha took a long drag on his pipe, drawing the smoke deep into his lungs. Fortunately, lung cancer and emphysema had been conquered eons ago by First Level medicine, so smoking was a harmless pastime. And one he could enjoy without any unproductive emotional and physical consequences.

"I think it's time to call an emergency meeting of the Paratime Commission. I'll give Dalgroth Sorn a call and have him set it up. It's time we did something about this prole problem for once and for all."

"Thanks, Tortha. I really miss Vall; he'd know what to do."

Tortha shrugged. "Maybe." He was still disappointed in Verkan Vall, even though he was the one who pushed him into becoming Paratime Police Chief. *Admit it, old man, he fought you all the way. It's time you shouldered some of the blame.* The boy had talent and good instincts, but he wasn't willing to wear the harness. Too bad. It looked like Home Time Line needed all the help it could get.

"How's Vall doing?" she asked.

Tortha took out his pipe and began to recharge it. "Well enough," he said, nodding. "He's busy now that Kalvan's crowned him King of Greffa. Verkan was forced into the position by Kalvan, almost the same way I got him to take my chair. Regardless of whose fault it is, once word hits First Level, the newsies will say he's gone native."

"I don't care about any of that. Is Vall in any danger from King Theovacar? I know Theovacar won't rest until he's back in Greffa and on the Iron Throne."

Tortha shrugged. "Kalvan left Verkan a couple thousand Hostigi regulars and he's been busy building his own little army. He's smart enough not to commit any obvious Paratime Contamination, but he's forgotten more military strategy and tactics than all of Theovacar's commanders combined. Plus, he's got Kalvan to back him up. If anyone's way in over his head, it's King Theovacar. He just doesn't know it yet."

II

Tortha and Vothan Raldor, Dhergabar Metropolitan Police Chief, took an air-taxi to Dalgroth Sorn's private residence in Dhergabar City to avoid any premature public notice of the special session of the Paratime Commission. They flew to the Trapezoid Tower and exited the taxi on the launch pad on the eightieth floor. They were met at the door by one of Dalgroth's household robots who took their coats and led them to the Commissioner for Security's study. Inside the other eight members of the Paratime Commission were seated at a U-shaped table.

Dalgroth, who had the face of an elderly lion with a toothache, offered drinks and *hors d' oeuvres*. Vothan ordered a Manhattan, while Tortha settled for a Scotch and water from the auto-bar. The other eight Paratime Commissioners already had their cigarettes lit and drinks in their hands.

"I'll assume this is important, or we all wouldn't have been called here to meet in private," Dalgroth stated. "What's on your mind, Tortha?"

Tortha stood up and said, "I'm going to let Police Chief Vothan Raldor get you up to speed before I make my recommendations."

He sat down and Vothan rose to his feet. The Metro Police Chief quickly sketched out the problems he was facing from the prole riots and the difficulties he was running into from influential Home Time Liners trying to protect their prole charges. "It's gotten so bad that we've got over two thousand men on permanent guard duty protecting the shops and townhouses in Old Town. It doesn't seem to matter to the proles; there's another riot almost every night. I'm at my wits end. I've had to stop dealing with non-violent crimes just to keep enough active men on riot duty. I need help and I need it now."

Vothan Raldor sat down.

Commissioner Armtar Rana, the only woman Commissioner, asked, "What do you expect us to do? Maybe it's time to call in the Army Strike Force to restore peace. This sounds like something you need to bring up before the Executive Council, not the Paratime Commission."

Tortha rose. "Good point, Commissioner Armtar. However, there's a good reason we're not bringing this before the Executive Council; it's too explosive. Plus, we need to act quickly and decisively without endless debate and backbiting. The Paratime Commission has the power to act on this issue. Quote: 'whenever Outtime conditions threaten the stability or safety of Home Time Line, the Paratime Commission has the authority to declare Martial Law.'"

"That maybe so, Commissioner Tortha," Commissioner Dalgroth noted. "But how do these riots, surely a matter of internal security, have anything to do with Outtime events or actions?"

Tortha took his pipe out of his mouth, pointing the stem at Dalgroth. "Because, this problem is caused by outtimers. These rioters are proles, not Citizens, workers and drones from Fifth Level Servsec and Industrial Sector."

Commissioner Lagrath Sart interjected, "Some of these so-called proles have been living on Home Time Line for four and five generations. You can't call these people outtimers, not in the usual sense. Many of them are Citizens in all but name."

Tortha took his time responding. Commissioner Lagrath Sart, a tall man with a short well-trimmed beard, was one of the few political appointees on the Paratime Commissioner and the only one who hadn't served with the Paratime Police. His loyalty, as far as Tortha was concerned, was suspect. Another reason he hadn't informed the Commission beforehand about why he had called the meeting. He'd have to convince the Commissioner for Security to isolate Lagrath after the meeting until the proposed actions were completed; otherwise all of Dhergabar would know about their deliberations by the following day.

"I don't care if these proles have families going back fifty generations, by law they're still outtimers. As I've said in the past, we've allowed far too many proles to immigrate to Home Time Line. They now outnumber Citizens four to one. When you consider that at any one time more than eighty percent of all Citizens are outtime, this means that the proles could easily take the upper hand on Home Time Line by sheer numbers alone."

"I've been having nightmares about that since the Prole Insurrection some two hundred years ago," interjected the Paratime Commissioner for Security. "That one made the Industrial Sector Rebellion look like a backyard picnic. Back then the Home Time Line didn't have a quarter of the proles we have today and there were over a million casualties. Some two hundred million proles were evacuated to Fifth Level during that fracas."

"Things are different now. People are attached to their servants," Commissioner Lagrath Sart rebutted. "The Citizens won't put up with the Paratime Police taking away their friends, lovers and servants."

"I believe they'd prefer it to having their throats slit in the middle of the night," offered Commissioner Valtan Ryk.

Lagrath shook his head in dismay, as though dealing with a person of limited intelligence. "Removing the proles won't wash no matter how you do it. The Proletariat Protective League will never allow it."

"Since when does the PPL dictate Home Time Line policy?" Tortha asked, his voice reverberating loudly through the room.

"Since they threw their units and support behind Opposition Party," Lagrath continued. "The people of First Level, Citizens and proles alike, have grown tired of Management arrogance and complacency. Management's run Home Time Line, and by extension Paratime, for several thousand years. And they've done it badly! The Party's out of touch with both the people and with the times."

"Are you running for office now, Commissioner Lagrath?" Dalgroth Sorn asked.

"No," he answered, no longer bothering to keep the snugness out of his tone. "I've been promised your office when Opposition Party takes control of the Executive Council. Once they hear of this cockamamie plan, that won't be long!"

Tortha looked around at the other seven Commissioners, as if to say "I told you so." He nodded to the Commissioner of Security. Dalgroth keyed in a code on his wrist com. Moments later three field agents of the Paratime Police entered the room, needlers drawn.

The Security Commissioner pointed out Lagrath Sart. "Take him to Fifth Level Police Terminal for questioning. I'll forward further instructions later."

They nodded and moved forward. Lagrath rose up spitting, "Don't you dare lay a finger upon my person!"

Tortha shook his head. *These youngsters sure have a lot to learn.*

Meanwhile, one of the Paratime Policemen jerked the Commissioner up out of his seat and took hold of his thumbs, pulled them behind Lagrath's back, forcing him to frog march his way out of the room.

"Do you think there's anything to his threats?" asked the woman Commissioner.

Tortha shrugged his shoulders. "We've put off this day of reckoning for far too long. It's possible we may no longer have the political muscle to do what we have to do. But that shouldn't stop us from trying."

Dalgroth Sorn nodded. "Tortha's right. We've sat on the prole problem, let the PPL organize and infiltrate Left Moderate and Opposition Parties. We only have ourselves to blame. When Verkan suggested dealing with the prole problem two years ago, we almost had the Chief investigated at that traitor Lagrath's instigation. He's been our leak all along. I should have had him hypno-meched years ago...."

"Why didn't you?" Tortha asked.

"You know why, Karf. He's my son-in-law. As it is, my daughter will read me out of the family, and my wife will go right along with her."

"Then you no longer have anything to lose, Sorn. It's time to bring in the strike teams and start a mass evacuation. I'll talk with Dalla about setting-up an evacuation conveyer-head to Fifth Level. We don't want them on Pol Term. Or even more than a few a few hundred thousand on any one time-line. Commissioner Galvath I want you to oversee a study on the best distribution sites. Commissioner Sorn and I will discuss the best way to present our conclusions to Management. The rest of you leave and work out some plans for the evacuation. And, remember, don't say a word about this meeting to anyone, not even your families—especially your wives!"

Dalgroth Sorn shook his head wearily. "Let's just hope this doesn't start the rebellion we're trying to fight. If word of this gets out, we're all finished!"

Tortha could only nod in agreement.

III

"How dare you go over my head like that!" Dalla demanded. "You old fools, you'll pull Management Party right down with you if you try to enforce any such draconian decree. What the Paratime Commission is committing is political suicide! I don't think any of you appreciate just how much the average Citizen values his proles, whether they be servants or friends—or in some cases, lovers."

Tortha recoiled. "It's the only reasonable and efficient way to deal with the prole problem, Chief—"

"Not on my watch!" Dalla interjected. "You think we've got riots now, wait until the Citizens learn that the Paratime Police are about to eject all their proles from Home Time Line. That's if the proles roll-over and accept being deported by the tens of millions. And where are we going to get the staff to herd them all, to say nothing of all the additional transtemporal conveyers we'll be needing for an operation this size? Even if everything went smoothly, which it won't, it could take years, and that's only if we stopped using most of our conveyers for Outtime work!"

"We thought we'd start with the most rebellious proles first—"

"Oh, like the Prole Liberation Movement members. And what do you think they're going to do while you attempt to arrest them? They'll either go into hiding or break into open rebellion. Now, wouldn't that make a pretty picture for the newsies!"

"No, of course not, Chief Hadron," said Paratime Security Commissioner Dalgroth Sorn. "We were just trying to come up with a permanent solution to a problem that's only going to get worse over time."

"Well, your solution is too late and too drastic," Dalla replied. Management will never go along with it, nor will the Paratime Police as long as I'm in charge. If the Paratime Commission tries to enforce such a decree, it will be the beginning of the end of First Level civilization as we know it."

In the cold light of day and faced with such determined opposition from someone he had counted on as an ally, Tortha could only agree. "You're right, Dalla, we really didn't think this through."

Dalgroth Sorn looked at him as if the whole thing were his fault.

"Maybe we have become a bunch of 'old fools,' like you say," Tortha added. "But that doesn't solve the prole problem, either."

"I don't know if it can be solved at this late date," Dalla said, shaking her head. My adopted sister Zinganna's a former prole; or maybe you forgot?"

Tortha shrugged. Yes, he had forgotten.

"What we need to worry about first," she said, "is how many people outside of the Paratime Commission know about this cockamamie idea of yours. Any answers, Commissioners?"

The Paratime Commissioner of security answered. "Only the members of the Paratime Commission were informed. Tortha and I were to inform you of our decision. We thought you'd help us work out the details before we announced the decree."

"First thing you do, is forget there ever was such a decree. Destroy all recordings and records of your proceedings."

They both nodded.

Tortha winced, "We do have another little problem."

"By the Fangs of Fasif, what now?"

"I had to use my authority to arrest Commissioner Lagrath Sart, who appears to be a spy for Opposition Party, and had him sent to Fifth Level Pol-Term."

"You did what?"

"He threatened to expose our Decree."

"So you arrested him. Did you think of contacting me before you sent him to Police Terminal?"

"We didn't have time. Temporary arrest and deportation are within the sphere of the Paratime Commission's authority," Tortha said

"Lucky for us," Dalla replied sarcastically. "Now, how are you going to explain his disappearance? He's very popular, being the youngest Paratime Commissioner, and has a number of important friends, including a lot of newsies. Now, Opposition's going to know something is up."

"But as long as they can't prove anything—"

"There'll be a big investigation over his disappearance, you have my personal guarantee! We need a cover story, Tortha. And it better be a good one."

"I have an idea," Tortha said. "Since Lagrath's been a critic of the Force, we can say he requested a trip to Police Terminal to see in person if there were any abuses going on. While there he had a fatal accident."

"Oh, great. This is your 'idea.' That must have taken all of ten seconds of thought."

"Cut the sarcasm," Tortha bellowed. He wasn't used to being talked to as if he were an idiot! Vall might have to put up with Dalla's sharp tongue, but he didn't have to. "We only did this at your instigation. You're the one who asked me for help!"

"I asked for help, not another disaster," she bounced back.

"That's enough out of both of you," the Commissioner of Paratime Security snapped. "We need to do something about Commissioner Lagrath. He's a loose cannon and there's no telling how much damage he could do to all of us if he ever got interviewed by the media."

"He has to disappear for a while," Dalla said. "Otherwise, we'll lose control of everything. It'll be the end for Management, the Paratime Police Department, all of us."

Tortha nodded. That was the first comment she'd made that he could agree with. "What if we say that Lagrath, as part of a Commission Inquest into the treatment of proles by the Paratime Police, was sent to Fifth Level Police Terminal? While he was interviewing one of the proles, he was snatched by the PLM."

The Commissioner of Security said, "I like it. It not only takes care of a big problem and potential leak, but it casts the proles in a dangerous light."

"I don't like it, but it does the job," Dalla said. "I'll have Gathon Dard, one of my special detectives, handle the operation. I'll get him on it right away. You two need to lay a paper trail and cue the other Commissioners onto what's going on. I'd suggest a hypno-mech block for the other Commissioners after you fill them in. This story is too hot for anything else!"

IV

Two ten-days later, Karoth Barg barged into Chief Dalla Hadron's office without a by-your-leave. "Chief, here's an update on the Shimmer Spire disaster."

Dalla winced. The Shimmer Spire, one of the largest apartment towers in Dhergabar and home to half a million citizens, had been A-bombed earlier that morning. There was a recorded message on Tri-V from the PLF, Prole Liberation Front, claiming responsibility. Half of Dhergabar City had to be evacuated due to high radiation and the other half was on standby. Paratime Police HQ had been so bombarded with calls and messages that she'd ordered the entire system shut down except for Code Red transmissions.

"What's the latest, Karoth?"

"Twenty-five thousand casualties and less than a dozen survivors. Those being residents leaving via one of the landing ports or the main landing stage. Everyone else is presumed dead, including over a hundred thousand Proles. They don't even care about their own kind, the bastards. The good news is that two-thirds of the citizens living there were outtime when the blast occurred."

The small atomic bomb had gone off in the early morning hours. It had been detonated on the bottom floor of the Shimmer Spire; the spire's collapsed-nickel exterior walls had acted like a chimney, sending the sun-hot blast of plasma upward through three thousand floors vaporizing everything and everyone in its path until it blew through the ventilation shafts at the top. No living being inside that inferno could have survived.

The explosion had reverberated throughout Dhergabar, as residents fled the City to escape the fallout and the possibility that other buildings had been sabotaged. Shelters across Home Time Line were filled to the bursting with evacuees from the capital city. Hospitals were overflowing from those with radiation sickness, heart-attacks and other aliments related to the bombing. While there had been previous terror attacks by the PRL, this was the first nuclear one.

There were political reverberations as well; many of the cities and towns refused to accept any Proles from Dhergabar and there was a growing call to ship all prole dissidents to Fifth Level Industrial or Service Sector. The Executive Council was in an Emergency Session attempting to come up with a solution to the growing prole unrest. Dalla was scheduled to give a report in less than an hour to the Executive Council, which meant she had lots to prepare.

"Plus, the PLF has released their demand," Karoth said, pausing dramatically.

"What is it?" Karoth was a hold-over from Verkan's administration and, if she ever got any time, Dalla planned to have him replaced with someone less in love with their own voice.

"The PLF demands Citizenship and longevity treatments for all proles on Home Time Line and provisional Citizenship for all those on Fifth Level."

"Ludicrous and unacceptable!" Dalla blurted.

Dalla was considered a liberal on the Prole Question, since she'd gone so far as to adopt one, Zinganna, as a sister. However, even she realized that was no way that Home Time Line could make all the Proles citizens, especially since proles outnumbered First Level Citizens several times over on Home Time Line alone. The result would be political chaos as the former servants paid back real and imagined slights and feuds; to say nothing of the actual costs of giving billions of new citizens the dole, housing, medical and longevity treatments. It would bankrupt the entire system, and that was just for starters....

Only an Opposition Party member would welcome such chaos. Not for the first time, Dalla wondered if they were actively behind the PFL.

Maybe next time it'll be the Paratime Building. "Karoth, I want radiation detectors as well as metal detectors placed on all entrances and landing ports of the Paratime Building. No one is to be admitted to the Building who isn't in the Department or with the Dhergabar Metropolitan Police."

"Yes, Chief."

"I'm expecting Metropolitan Police Chief Vothan Raldor; let me know when he arrives."

Secretary Karoth nodded, then handed her an info wafer and quickly exited her office. Dalla put the wafer into the slot and watched the explosion on her viewscreen. The five mile-high tower on the screen rocked from the force of the atomic fire inside, even as most of the force and radiation was contained by the building's collapsed-nickel walls until it reached the air vents on top. From a distance, it looked like a fireworks display as the vents at top of the Shimmer Spire blew off and a huge flare lanced into the sky. The flame was so bright that it briefly turned the screen completely white despite all the camera's special filters.

As visibility returned it was possible to see the other nearby towers and spires rocking back and forth as if caught in the throes of a major earthquake. *This is where most of the injuries occurred outside the stricken spire,* she thought. *People, furniture, robots and appliances were tossed around like toys as the great towers rocked back and forth.* The physical injuries were in the millions, filling every hospital and medical facility on Home Time Line to the bursting.

The political repercussions would be just as bad. Dalla wondered how deeply this attack would unsettle First Level firmament. She suspected the repercussions would shake the foundations of Home Time Line for the next thousand years.

She herself had been awakened as her apartment, in the Silver Spire, thrown off her bed at 0244 in the morning. Her first thought had been earthquake, even though they were rare in this section of the Major Landmass, or what was called Europe on Fourth Level Europo-American. She had, however, experienced quakes while outtime.

Karoth came bursting into her office again.

"What is it now?" she asked, biting her tongue.

"It's Yadd's *The Day in Dhergabar* show; you need to watch this!"

She hit the button that turned on the wallscreen at the front of her office. Yandar Yadd's supercilious face filled the screen. "What we should be asking ourselves is: How were the PLF able to smuggle an atomic weapon onto First Level? As we all know, it's the Paratime Police who are responsible for protecting us from smuggling and outtime contraband, especially weapons. Obviously, the Paracops haven't been doing their job.

"This has been true for a number of years, ever since Verkan Vall took over from former Chief Tortha Karf. Things have gotten even worse under Verkan's wife and replacement, Chief Tharn. I think it's time the citizens of Dhergabar demanded some answers." He paused to point his finger straight into Dalla's face. "Chief Tharn, you owe the people the truth about what's really going on."

Then he turned back to his audience. "Send those messages and electronic letters to the Executive Council and maybe we will get some answers!"

V

Hadron Tharn watched with great pleasure as the first airborne transports arrived from the Fifth Level Industrial Serv Sec world he'd named Revenge. Finally, he was getting his just desserts. The Wizard Traders would shortly be in charge of Home Time Line. It was in his power to make life on First Level a living nightmare for all of his enemies and detractors. He was going to enjoy every bit of their suffering. *The fools never realized my greatness! They will learn, and soon.*

He watched with glee from his penthouse high atop the Vothran Spire as the fighters began to drop their bombs on the Dhergabar Spaceport.

The first tower bombing had gone off this morning without a hitch. The sky was filled with fleeing aircars that buzzed across the city like mosquitos run amuck! They would all soon learn there was no refuge, no place on Home Time Line he could not reach out and destroy.

He heard a buzz from his personal communicator. Only one person alive had that number, Warntha Sarn, his Number One.

"Yes," he said into his lapel mic. "What is it?"

"Leader, the proles are exceeding their warrant. They're butchering every Citizen they come across."

"All of them?"

"No, some fools are actually trying to protect their masters. But many of the proles, especially those from the Serv-Sec Level, are running amuck killing any and all Citizens. They're using the weapons we provided to break into the towers and butcher the inhabitants, even the tame proles. I thought you'd want to know since it wasn't part of the *plan*."

"See if you can bring them to heel, Warnatha. There's no sense in all of this if all of Home Time Line is brought down!"

"I'll do what I can, but our own force is hugely outnumbered. We gravely underestimated the hatred they have for us!"

Having used that hatred and resentment to further his ambition to rule the world, Tharn understood that he may have unleashed a whirlwind. One not even The Leader could harness. For the first time in ages, he began to feel a sense of dread that he could not shake off....

VI

Karoth Barg brought in a platter full of coffee cups for the members of the Paratime Commission who were crowded into Dalla's office, then closed the door.

"As you all heard in my initial briefing, the proles are making an all-out assault on Home Time Line," Dalla announced. "They're attacking their owners in their own homes, in many cases murdering whole families! Others are ransacking entire buildings, going from apartment to apartment, looting them and murdering any Citizens they come across."

"This is unfathomable!" the Commissioner of Security yelled. "We must bring this to an end, even if it means the extermination of every prole on First Level!"

"I don't think we need to go that far, Commissioner," Dalla replied. "I've already sent orders to Pol Term for five Army Strike Teams to arrive in Dhergabar. They'll be arriving within thirty minutes. That should take care of this revolt—if that's what this whole thing is all about."

Commissioner Tortha Karf nodded. "They should have matters in hand in a few hours. Where are they arriving?"

"The big transposition depot outside Dhergabar city."

Tortha said, "Good. That's near enough the rocket field that they can go wherever they're needed."

Karoth Barg barged into the room. "Chief, the prole attacks are spreading. There are now reports of major prole uprisings in the following cities: Ravartol, Jarnabar, Sohram, Tergostar, Bongaran, Thalna-Jaarvizar, Synalyan and Vathardt. With lesser action in another thirty to forty locales."

Chief Dalla ordered, "Inspector Karoth, assemble as much information as you can on the worst of these hot spots. Have them ready before the strike teams arrive. I will pass the information on to Commander Verdar Zoln. I'll let him sort out what needs to be done."

Dalgroth Sorn, the Paratime Commissioner of Security, nodded his approval.

"What'll we do until then?" one of the Commissioners asked.

"I've already issued a red alert for all Paratime Police officers on Home Time Line ordering them to come to the Paratime Building immediately and sent a red warning boomerang ball to all those who are outtime. We'll assemble our forces here and give whatever help Commander Verdar determines he needs."

All the commissioners nodded. Dalla was glad to see they were accepting her leadership, since she hadn't been Chief long enough to give them much confidence in her ability to run the Department. Nor had her reputation before taking over as chief had much to recommend itself. She needed their full support if they were to survive this rebellion.

Suddenly Dalla's viewscreen turned red with black shooting arrows. An alarm filled the room with shrill screeching.

Everyone turned to stare. "What is it, now?" Tortha Karf asked.

Bad news, very bad news, she thought, but kept her thoughts to herself. "Let me find out, Commissioner."

First she turned off the klaxon and cleared her screen. Suddenly it was filled with a shot from the spaceport. A harried-looking traffic control officer with his blue cap pushed halfway off his head, cried: "Chief, some fifty to sixty unknown warships showed up on the field without authorization. Nor or they responding to my requests for information!"

"Give me a screen shot," she ordered. "Maybe an Army Strike Team arrived early?!"

A score of bat-winged fighters suddenly filled the screen. They lacked their normal insignia and were painted a matt black.

The commissioners crowded around.

Dalgroth Sorn cried. "What are they doing here?"

"What do you mean?" Dalla asked.

"Those ships are part of the mothballed fleet stationed on Fifth Level Industrial Level. Why are they here? Did you call them up by mistake?"

"How could I!" Dalla shouted. "I didn't even know they existed."

"By all the gods!" one of the commissioners cried out. "They're attacking all the ships at the spaceport. They're not supposed to be doing that!"

The screen was filled with the resulting carnage. Passenger ships and space yachts were disappearing in balls of red fire and back smoke. Tiny panic-stricken figures were running helter-skelter across the landing field. Suddenly the screen went black as the transmitter or station itself was destroyed.

The room was filled with questions and exclamations.

"Shut up!" Dalla shouted. "I need to think." If they no longer controlled the spaceport itself that meant the attached transposition terminal was broached. The strike team ships would be vaporized the minute they appeared at the depot!

Then some outside force took over her viewscreen and it went blank for about ten seconds, then a familiar figure dressed all in black, adorned with the usual military accoutrements typically worn by Fourth Level dictators or overlords, began to talk. "Fellow Home Timeliners this is The Leader speaking. The Prole Liberation Front, acting under my orders, has taken control of Dhergabar."

She knew that voice: it was her crazy little brother's! Was Tharn completely out of his mind? Of course he was! And it was partially her fault, too. As his surrogate mother, once her parents had abandoned them, she had covered-up for Tharn, even going so far as to use Verkan's influence with the Paracops to keep him out of the hands of the Bureau of Psychological Hygiene numerous times. What a terrible mistake!

"I want everyone to lay down their weapons and stop all resistance. And that includes the Paratime Police."

"What is this madman doing?" Dalgroth Sorn shouted. The rest of the commissioners broke out in a babble of questions, orders and exclamations.

"Shut up!" ordered Tortha Karf. "Let's find out what he wants."

"I want to tell the Paratime Police specifically to lay down their arms and cease all resistance."

"He's completely insane!" someone shouted.

Tortha Karf slapped a huge hand across the speaker's mouth. "Quiet!"

"Isn't that your brother, Chief? Can't you stop him?"

Dalla shook her head. No one controlled Tharn, not even he was in control of his unpredictable whims and rages.

"I want you to know that my followers are—at this moment—destroying every transposition conveyer depot in Dhergabar and every other city and rallying place on the planet."

Dalla's hand flew over her mouth. This was bad, really bad—actually terrible. By destroying all the First Level depots, Tharn was stranding every poor bastard from Home Time Line who was working or visiting outtime—billions of innocent people! Well, maybe innocent was the wrong word....

Tharn made a nasty smile, like an evil little boy who'd just torn the wings off a fly. "And as far as you parapolice creeps are concerned, if there's any more resistance I'll blow the entire Paratime Building sky-high. There's a thermo-nuclear device in your basement with a dead-man's switch so don't even think of trying to find it. You've got fifteen minutes to evacuate! After that, it's all GONE!"

The screen sent completely blank.

"My wife! My family!" someone shouted. "Let me out of here!"

Everyone was speaking at once.

Dalla made a loud piercing whistle. "Quiet down and listen! We don't have much time. It's obvious this operation is not only well planned, but completely out of our control. We must get everyone in this building down to the Main Depot Terminal and its affiliates, then get everyone transposed out of this building before it blows!"

"But where?" Dalgroth Sorn shouted.

"Who cares?" Tortha shouted. "To your outtime villas or whatever.

That's where I'm headed. Maybe later we can figure something out. But as far as I can determine, we've lost the battle, if not the war for First Level."

"Right," seconded Dalla. She fiddled with the screen until it went back on. "All Paratime officers evacuate the building immediately! There's a bomb set to go off in fourteen minutes. Evacuate to a safe place outtime. We will attempt to contact you later." She knew that was probably a lie, but it would help the exodus. Maybe Verkan would have a solution—if only she could get to Kalvan's Time Line in time.

Commissioner Dalgroth was already out the door on his way to the descent shaft. The others commissioners were milling around like lost sheep.

"Move!" she shouted as she headed for the door. She followed Tortha, grabbing his arm as he quickly exited the office.

"Where are you headed?" she asked.

"To my retreat on Sicily. This time I may be retired for good. What about you, Dalla? Are you going to Kalvan's Time Line to get Verkan?"

She shook her head. "It might attract my brother's attention, which is the last thing we need. In an emergency, we agreed to meet at our hideaway on Nerros. After that, I don't know. Now, let's get a move on!"

VII

Verkan felt the vibration of his kit-phone disguised as an idol of Wotan. Talking to one's personal idol was considered normal behavior in the Middle Kingdoms, as long as one wasn't too loud or obnoxious about it.

He quickly excused himself from the King's Presence Room and went to his private chamber. There were a number of advantages to being king, one of them being able to clear your schedule on a moment's notice.

"Verkan, here," he said, pressing the transmit button.

"Chief, it's Kostran. We've got problems."

"What?" he asked.

"You know the conveyer problem we've been having?"

"Of course, we haven't seen one in almost two ten-days."

"Well, one just materialized."

"Good!" he exclaimed. "It's about time."

There was a pause before Kostran continued. "It was a Paratime Police conveyer and it was badly damaged."

Verkan didn't like the sound of that. *By Blaxthakka's Beard, what's going on?* "Any survivors?"

"Yes, just one," Kostran said. "He's coming around now. You'd better get down here and interrogate him yourself."

"I will as soon as I can get Maldar and Kiro Soran to join me."

He sent out a red field alert and within a few minutes Maldar Dard and Kiro Soran showed up.

"What's going on, boss?" Maldar asked.

"Trouble with the conveyers."

Maldar nodded. "I was wondering if there was something going on. Traffic's been nonexistent the last week or so."

Shortly after taking over as king of Greffa, Verkan had done some remodeling on Theovacar's former summer palace. One major improvement was a conveyer-head built into a large section of what had been the original dungeon. He'd also had a lift put in from his private audience chamber to the collapsed-nickel lined conveyer-head station.

Verkan pressed the idol's ear and twisted, and a door slid open. They all entered and Verkan hit the keypad combination to the conveyer-head and the lift began its descent to the former dungeon. After landing and opening the door, he stepped out into a room large enough to hold a hundred-and-fifty foot conveyer with plenty of room for supplies and holding parties. There were about fifty cases of flintlock smoothbores resting against one wall and another couple of boxes containing high-density armor for his operatives to wear during hostilities.

He saw the ripped and scorched silver mesh dome of a fifty-foot conveyer sitting at the staging ground. Smoke was still coming off the mesh and he could smell the astringent odors of burnt permaplastic and metal. Someone had used a cutting tool to remove a large section of the dome and inside were five figures, in Paratime Police issue greens, lying on the floor. One Medico was bent over one of the figures, while the other two were examining the other bodies.

Chancellor Kostran Galth, still in his robes of office, was running towards him. "Chief, we've got four dead and one badly-wounded officer."

"Are they from here?" Verkan asked. There hadn't been any recent arrivals, nor any that were scheduled, either.

Kostran, his face pale, shook his head. "No one I know." His wife, Zinganna, had left over three ten-days ago to visit Dalla on Home Time Line.

Verkan ordered, "Everyone step back except the Medico."

After about a brief wait, that would have been interminable except for Verkan's First Level mental control, the Greffan team Medico got up and called Verkan to his side. The wounded officer had a gash in his forehead that had bled out into a large pool, but his worst injuries were from a series of bullet wounds to his torso that opened him up from his belly button to his breast bone. The Medico had stabilized the bleeding and had hooked him up a blood pump. It would keep him alive until they got to a robo-doc; although he needed a major trauma center rather than a field robo-doc.

The cloying smell of death filled the conveyor. The Medico looked at Verkan, saying, "I gave him something to ease the pain, but he won't remain conscious long. He can talk a little so you'd better make it quick."

Verkan got down on his knees, leaning over. "Officer, can I have your name and rank?"

"Sardrath Darn, Field Agent Second Class, sir," he mumbled.

"What happened, Darn?"

"We were returning to Home Time Line from Fourth Level, Viking-Vinland Subsector. When we arrived at the subterminal head at Synalyan, we were fired upon by troops dressed in bluish-gray uniforms." He paused, while a series of coughs wracked his body. "I was hit bad…."

"Fired upon at Home Time Line?" Verkan asked. "What's going on?"

"I don't know, sir. We bugged out as soon as we could set the controls, but some soldiers in blue uniforms started shooting…then something hit our conveyer."

He started coughing again. Verkan wasn't sure he'd survive this bout.

"Where are we, sir?"

"Fourth Level, Aryan-Transpacific, Styphon's House Subsector, Kalvan's Time Line."

"Oh…we were trying to make our way to Pol Term."

Police Terminal, Verkan thought. *The Synalyan Equivalent? That was Greffa here-and-now, but on Fourth Level Europo-American it would be Chicago. They were fortunate that the conveyer hadn't ended up there. All hell would have broken loose…if it hasn't already!*

VIII

"Where are you going, Chief?" the Commissioner in charge of Security asked, as Dalla made her way to the antigrav shaft with Tortha Karf.

She thought for a moment. "I'm going to meet up with Vall. We need him to take over. This is way too much for me to handle!"

"But…but you can't—" he blustered.

"You need to get moving yourself, Commissioner Dalgroth. Don't you have a wife and family?"

"Yes, but I'll need an aircar to get to our apartment. It's not safe to fly anymore!"

The Commissioner's eyes were bugged out and darting around as if he were looking for a bolthole for himself. She knew that it was already too late for anyone in Dhergabar outside of the Paratime Building—and they only had minutes.

There was the sound of another blast, strong enough to rock the Paratime Building as if it were made of straw. "There's no time. Either leave now and look for them, or join me at the antigrav shaft."

She left with Tortha before he could make up his mind and ran to the shaft, where they quickly made their way—although the descent seemed to take forever—down to the Paratime Building Main Depot Terminal. The place was crowded with Paratime Police officers, some in their official greens, others in outtime costumes. Cops were moving around as if in Brownian Motion, as though most of them had no idea of what to do.

Tortha bussed her on the cheek and said, "Give my best to Vall, will you?"

"Good luck," she said, as the ex-chief tore off on his way to his personal conveyer.

One of the Paracops ran up: "Chief, thank the heavens you're here! What are we supposed to do now?"

It was Dalzar Holk, her old bodyguard on Kalvan's Time Line and one of Verkan's key men.

"This building's set to go in minutes. We need to leave now—there's my personal conveyer." One of the privileges of being chief was she had her own conveyer parked in an easily assessable parking spot.

"Come with me! Before this place is blown sky high!"

She spotted a group of her personal bodyguards. She whistled loudly and they came running, ignoring the chaos all around them.

"We've been waiting for you," Dalon Sath, her head bodyguard said.

Dalla felt a wave of gratitude, but shook it off; she didn't have time to make nice. "Good." She pointed to Sath and the man next to him. "You two come with me and Dalzar. There's no room for any more. The rest of you find a conveyer and get the hell out of Dodge!"

These were veterans familiar with Europo-American slang and aphorisms. They took off at full speed to the nearest unoccupied conveyer.

IX

Hadron Tharn sat in his underground bunker and imagined the chaos happening all around him. He would have preferred to watch it in person, but even he was not immune to radiation exposure, explosions—or even a stray bullet. All local and satellite transmission lines were down so there were no longer any newscasts to watch. Every once in a while the ground would rumble or shake, indicating that chaos and destruction were nearby.

"Tharn," his private com announced. "Warntha, here."

"What's going on?" Tharn asked.

"The prole bastards have shafted us!"

"What do you mean?" Tharn barked.

"General Rammos is no longer working for us. He and the other pro-les are liberating Home Time Line for themselves."

Tharn ground his teeth together so hard he saw stars.

"What should I do, boss?" Warntha asked.

"Nothing! What about our team—can they do anything to stop them?"

"No. The proles hit us hard when we least expected it—most of the team has been discorporated. Me and a few others were busy setting the bombs at the University, so they missed us."

"Blaztha be damned! What do they think they're going to do, take over and run things? Not likely." Being the Leader in charge of First Level had long been his dream—no ungrateful band of ragamuffin proles were going to usurp his vision. Not if he had anything to say about it.

"Is there any chance we can still execute our plan?"

"No. Not with all our loyal commanders and most of our troops dead. The treacherous swine—"

"Enough! Then let's go to our scorched earth plan."

"Really?"

"Yes. You have more than enough bombs."

"I do."

"I want you to destroy Valdar Engineering and Manufacturing's plant." That was the facility that made all the Transtemporal conveyers. They'd already taken out the Central Administration Tower which had housed the Executive Council as well as the main library. "Next you need to destroy the Rhogom Institute and the Hydrax Scientific Center. Let the damn proles see if they could reinvent Transtemporal transportation all by themselves."

Warntha laughed. "Good luck with that!"

"I know."

"Were do we go, boss?"

"Not to any of the Fifth Level bases. When you're done, join me at my villa on Roman-Imperial." It was one of his secret hideaways that no one but Warntha knew about. Besides, if he had to live outtime, he might as well do it in style and in a place where he could indulge all his appetites without censure.

X

"What do we do now, Verkan?" Kostran Galth asked.

Verkan paused to light a cigarette. "That's a very good question. I can't stay here while Dalla might be stranded on First Level, or who knows where. It doesn't sound as if it's safe to transpose to Home Time Line, but that's where I'm needed. I wonder if this disaster could have been prevented if I stayed on First Level and done my job?"

Kostran shook his head. "Dalla is a damn good Chief, boss. You wouldn't have let her take the job, if you hadn't thought she could do it. If she and Commissioner Tortha didn't pick up on anything unusual, what makes you think you might have?"

Verkan let out a string of curses, then finished with, "You're probably right. Home Time Line has been riding on its merits for a long time; too busy robbing other time-lines to take care of itself. No innovations, no new scientific research, no new art, we've gotten fat and lazy—and maybe stupid as well. Look as this Wizard Trader mess. We've been picking at it for almost fifteen years and we're no closer to getting to the bottom of the Organization than we were when we started."

"But what about the people stranded on Home Time Line," Kostran said, as he ran his fingers through his hair.

Verkan suddenly realized that Kostran was very likely worried about his wife, Zinganna. She'd left some time ago to visit Dalla and was staying at their apartment in the Space Spire. Kostran was more worried about her than he was about his own wife. However, Dalla was very resourceful and if anyone could come out of this mess alive, it would be her.

The big problem they faced was while Paratime Police conveyers, which could theoretically travel to every and any time-line—or at least those that had been surveyed and entered into the time-line data base—could only travel spatially to wherever they were physically located. That was to Synalyan City on Home Time Line, which was a major terminal hub. Since they'd wanted to keep their presence out of the public eye, the Greffan base in the summer palace was located more than a mile outside the city of Synalyan itself, which like most First Level cities was comprised of tall anti-gravity towers and spires.

It might be possible for them to pull off a small reconnaissance mission. In fact, it was damn well necessary, if he was ever going to get to the bottom of what was going on.

"All right, here's what we're going to do," Verkan said. "It's too dangerous, since we don't have a clue as to what we are facing, to travel during day. So, instead we'll visit Synalyan in the middle of the night."

"What if the area's monitored?" Maldar Dard asked.

"The Greffan/Synalyan conveyer-head is underground. I had it put in and camouflaged the area around it so no one could stumble upon it. Otherwise, I was worried that some of the First Level newsies might find out about it and put it under surveillance in order to keep an eye on my comings and goings."

"It's a good thing you did, boss," Maldar said.

"If we detect any surveillance at all, we'll bug out immediately."

Kostran nodded in agreement. "Should I come along?"

Verkan shook his head. "I'll take the Medico, Zalthar Valn, as well as Soran and Maldar with me and leave you the rest of the Greffan team. You need to stay here in Greffa and run things as Chancellor while I'm gone."

"What'll I tell Kalvan when he asks where you are?" he asked.

"Tell him, Dalla's in trouble. He already knows she left Greffa to visit relatives in Xiphlon. Tell him she got kidnapped on her way there and that I've gone to rescue her."

"Do you think he'll buy that?" Kostran asked.

"Sure. It's exactly just what Kalvan would do if someone waylaid Rylla."

XI

Dalla sent her personal conveyer to a Fourth Level, Europo-American time-line where she and Verkan owned a villa outside the city in the Dhergabar Equivalent—Nice, France. The half-hour journey seemed to take forever as they passed a near infinity of time-lines on the way to their destination. For some reason, brief scenes of battle and violence seemed to predominate; she wasn't sure if it was the outside itself or the turmoil inside that was causing her to see so much violence all around her. Everyone else in the conveyer was strangely quiet, as if there was little left to say. She wondered how many of them had abandoned family and friends to join her in her feeble crusade to save some part of Home Time Line.

They reached the villa and left the conveyer at the hidden basement. Dalla checked the motion sensors, hidden camera footage and the other detectors to make sure that no one had been there since their last visit some three years before. Everything was clean and the small group made their way upstairs into the house itself.

They all took seats in the dining room while one of the men heated some of the hidden rations and prepared a meal for the team. Everything tasted like ashes in Dalla's mouth, but she knew it wasn't the reconstituted food, but her own emotions that were tainting everything. Her home, her family and friends—everything on Home Time Line was gone!

Dalzar finally broke the silence. "Chief, where do we go from here?"

"Nerros."

"What's that?"

"It's Verkan's and my hideaway. It's located on a small group of islands called the Bahamas on Fourth Level Europo-American, Hispania Subsector. It's a primitive subsector where the Office of the Holy Inquisition is still in operation in both the Old World and New World and the mechanical arts have not evolved much above the windmill and horse-drawn transportation, which is why we're not traveling there directly."

Dalzar grimaced. He knew all about the Inquisition, having been stranded on one of those time-lines a decade or so ago.

"Not only would we have to have the right papers and documents to travel to the New World, as they still call it, but we'd be subject to the Inquisition if somebody didn't like our looks or thought we spoke funny. Plus, it would take weeks, if not months, to travel from this equivalent to the Bahamas."

Dalla went on to fill them in on the particulars: There had been little development on most of the Caribbean Islands on that subsector. Verkan had possession of the island called Cayman Brac on most Hispano-Columbian subsectors and used it as their vacation home. He had named it Nerros after his hereditary home on Venus.

"But why live on a dangerous time-line in the Hispania Subsector? Why not have an outtime villa on one of the uninhabited Fifth Level time-lines?"

"Yes, that's the popular remedy. But you know Verkan; he follows his own path. He doesn't want to be surrounded by robo-servers or Fourth Level outtimers dragged away from their homes to be his servants, even if it might save their lives."

"So how did Verkan find this place?" one of them asked.

"Early in his career in the Department," Dalla answered, "Verkan rescued a party of Paratime tourists on the Hispano Subsector, who had run afoul of the local Inquisition. While he was there, he made the acquaintance of a Grandee, Luis Fernández, who was in charge of the expedition. In thanks for saving his clients and himself from the *Tribunal del Santo Oficio de la Inquisición*, Duke Ferandez granted Verkan Vall the small island almost forty years ago. Under Verkan's stewardship, Nerros has done well; at least, compared to the neighboring islands. The local villagers consider Verkan their patron and they grow tobacco and sugar cane. That's where we go when we want privacy and to spend time together."

Dalzar smiled. "I've had some of Verkan's hand-rolled cigarettes before. They're an excellent smoking experience."

"How long since you've been there?" Dalon inquired.

She sighed. "It's been almost five years since our last visit. We picked this time-line as our link to Nerros, because we could travel incognito—which we couldn't do on First Level—and because it is possible to travel from France to New York in six or seven days."

"Why don't we use an aircar?" Dalon asked. "That way we could get there by tomorrow morning."

Dalzar smiled. "You haven't spent much time on Europo-America, have you?"

He shook his head.

"Our aircars look a little too much like the 'flying saucers' the locals are always seeing in the skies. We don't use them on this sector anymore because they bring too much attention. The locals are dotty about aliens and unidentified objects. Plus, they have pretty advanced radar and other visual sensors on the sector. So it's safer to use the local transportation methods whenever possible."

"How long will it take us to get this show on the road?" Dalon asked.

"Not long," Dalla answered. "Let me plug in what the locals call a 'telephone' and I'll contact our usual travel agent. I expect we can find comfortable ocean transportation within a few days."

XII

Verkan's conveyer reached the Synalyan conveyer-head just after midnight. The small bunker was equipped with the usual surveillance devices so that Verkan could exit and enter without attracting attention.

The first thing he noticed was that the airwaves were dead, both local and transcontinental. *What in Great Blaxthakka's Beard is going on?*

He quickly used the big nightscope to check out Synalyan proper. The city was pretty much blacked out. Usually, the air space over the city would be surrounded by thousands of aircar running lights, darting and hovering around the city like fireflies. Some of the towers were at weird angles and none of the usual warning lights showed. He noted a few stuttering ground fires and wondered just what had happened to the city?

Maldar cried, "By all the gods, the rad meter is picking up all kinds of radiation! What just went down?"

"Let's see if we can find somebody and find out. "Maldar, what's the meter reading just outside the bunker?"

"A much lower radiation count locally. Nothing we can't tolerate for a short time. But it's hot as hell closer to those towers."

"How long can we stay here before our conveyer is detected?"

"That's a good question, Kiro. From the looks of things upstairs, I don't think there's anyone capable of doing a proper search. However, it's best to assume the worst. So we don't want to stay here much longer than an hour."

"Okay," Kiro replied.

"Take out your needlers and let's see what we can find upstairs," Verkan ordered

It was only a short way to the top of the bunker; no need for any lifts. Instead they walked up a short stairway leading to the bunker outer exit. The permasteel portal was bolted and only responded to Verkan's code which he keyed in.

The portal pressed upward through the camouflage and they walked into the still night air. Occasionally, the air was rent by a distant scream or the sounds of gunfire. Verkan felt as if he were walking in a graveyard.

Their personal nightscopes gave them almost perfect vision despite the dark of night.

"I see something, or someone!" Kiro Soran announced. He pointed to the left where there was a huddled form hidden in the bushes. They would have never seen it without the scopes.

"Are they alive?" Maldar asked.

"Let's find out," Verkan replied.

They approached and found a man who was shaking with fear as he heard their approach.

"We mean you no harm," Verkan said.

"Who are you?"

"Paratime Police."

"Pa...Police. I thought you were all dead or gone. That's what the newsies claimed after the Paratime Building went up."

"What happened to the Paratime Building?"

"It was hit with an atomic bomb The Leader had placed in the basement. They say it went off like a hundred-megaton firecracker—a total loss!"

Verkan shuddered. He hoped Dalla made it out in time but, regardless, thousands of his coworkers and friends must have died in that blast.

"Who is this 'Leader'?" he asked.

"I don't know. No one does. He claimed responsibility to the attack. Maybe he's a prole; there are enough of them running around. They're blood crazed—killed almost all the Citizens in my spire. The Serv Sec Proles are the worst!"

Verkan turned to the others. "This is what we've been warning the Executive Council about for years. Let's get back down to the bunker."

"What about him?" Maldar asked, pointing at the shivering man.

"Take him with us. I've got more questions to ask."

Back in the bunker, the Medico left to check out their captive while Verkan and the others discussed what to do.

"There's no use hanging around here," Maldar said.

"Right," Verkan answered. "First Level's done. Let's head back to Greffa. I want to brief Kostran on what we've learned."

"He deserves that, at least," Kiro said.

Verkan nodded, wondering what to tell someone when everything and everybody they had known outside the Department were gone. And that even the force was done. What any of them would do?

They waited for the Medico.

When he returned it was with a sour look on his face, shaking his head, he reported, "The poor bastard, he's done for. I don't know how many rads he took in, but he won't last until daybreak."

"Can I talk to him?" Verkan asked.

The Medico shrugged. "It won't hurt. He's in and out of consciousness, so make it quick."

Verkan returned a few minutes later. "He doesn't know any more than what he already told us. I fed him a few lies about getting better so he'd die in peace."

"It's time we leave and go back to Greffa City."

"Right, we might have searchers coming soon," Maldar said.

They all went back into the conveyer and Verkan keyed in their destination.

"Where do we go from here?" Kiro asked, as the near-infinity of time-line flashed by.

"Yeah, can't we fight back?" Maldar added.

Verkan sighed. "With what and whom? From what our wounded friend from Police Terminal told us, things aren't any better back on the Fourth Level than they are here on First Level. It's not like we have any special meeting places for outtime police to gather. We're on our own and I don't believe there's much we can do here. Does anyone disagree?"

They all nodded in agreement.

"Here's what I suggest. I'm going to find a way to get to Nerros, my hideaway on Fourth Level. It's a nice little island in the Bahamas with friendly islanders. Anyone who wants, can come with me. Or I'll help them get to wherever they want to go."

"That sounds more than fair," the Medico said. "I don't have a personal retreat; I was always too busy to set one up. So, if you don't mind, I'll go with you."

"That's fine," Verkan replied. "You can help take care of our island friends."

Maldar was the next to speak. "I'm like Valn; I don't have a place to go to, either. I'll go wherever you want, boss."

"Good."

"What about you, Kiro?"

"Sad to say it, but I've been married to my job for so long I don't have a personal life. I'm good to go."

Verkan smiled. "Maybe once we get to Nerros you'll have time to make one. It's not exactly a hot spot! Although, once in a while, we may have to fend off some of the local cannibals—"

"You're kidding, boss. Right?"

"No. Some of the local Caribs have been known to partake in the unspeakable. I've got a deal with the local Viceroy of Cuba so they don't bother us much. Although, every once in a while a few go off reservation."

"Sounds like fun," Maldar joked.

"So how are we going to get there?" Kiro asked.

"Well, for starters, we're on the right landmass. We'll take the conveyer to a spot on Fourth Level, Europo-American I've setup. From there, we'll take a plane ride to Miami. It won't be hard to get a boat to take us to Nerros."

"When are we leaving?" Maldar asked.

"Not for a ten-day or two. Remember, I'm king here and I've got a lot of responsibilities. I owe it to Kalvan to get the army ready just in case King Theovacar wants to take his former home back. Plus, I've got a lot to talk over with Kostran."

"Will he stay or go with us, boss?" Maldar asked.

"I really don't know. I'd prefer that he stay since I don't have any other replacement and I'd hate to leave Kalvan in the lurch."

Maldar winced. "Yeah, with his wife stranded or....dead on First Level, the poor bastard has got nowhere else to go. The rest of us are married to the job and don't have any close family to worry about."

Verkan nodded. "Normally that wouldn't be something to be happy about, but in this case it is. I just hope that Dalla made it out of the Paratime Building safely. I'm not going to get any sleep until I find out."

"You think she'll be at Nerros?" Maldar asked.

"I hope so. I've told her more than once it's our bolthole; the one place no one—other than Tortha—knows about. A place where we can be safe. I just hope she can get there."

XIII

Dalla sat inside the solar at their Nerros villa smoking and drinking a cocktail. She had actually enjoyed the trip over on the *Queen Mary 2*. It had been a welcome relief; for days she hadn't had to worry over what she needed to do—or could or couldn't do. Then a quick trip to the Nerros Equivalent on Fourth Level, from where they had transposed to Verkan's hideaway.

The natives had welcomed her and her guests with great glee. She got the idea that they were bored when nobody was around. Here on the island they lived a carefree life of fishing and hunting. Verkan, early on, had made a deal with the Viceroy of Cuba and he had ordered a series of punitive raids on the nearby Carib and Arawak Indians, letting them know that Nerros was off-limits for their raiding parties.

Since the villa's conveyer-head was in a sealed-off basement, she wondered what the natives thought when visitors magically appeared at the villa. From the special way she was treated, she suspected the tribespeople thought she and Verkan were minor deities who could appear and reappear at will, like some sort of island guardians. Their cohorts, like Dalzar and Salon Dath, were probably viewed as their agents.

She heard the door open as Dalzar and the others entered the solar, taking seats around the big table. They had brought their own drinks, and several of them were smoking pipes. Something most of them had taken up after spending time on Aryan-Transpacific.

Dalzar was the first to speak. "Any ideas on what to do, Chief?"

"I've been giving our situation a great deal of thought. With the Paratime Building destroyed and Pol Term on Fifth Level a wasteland, we don't have many options. Most of the Paracops who've survived the initial attack are stranded outtime—somewhere. Unfortunately, there was a major leak in the Department, so we can safely assume that all our usual hideouts and gathering places are either destroyed or are being watched. Since the Department conveyers are the only ones without governors tying them to the usual commercial and passenger routes, we can pretty much land on Home Time Line wherever we wish.

"Although, I can almost guarantee that wherever we land we'll find a reception party since our tracking devices will give our location away."

"Can't we disengage them somehow?" Salon asked.

Dalzar shook his head. "No. They are integral to the Transtemporal guidance devices. They were designed that way to guard the Paratime Secret and keep us from going wherever we wanted. That way the Survey Bureau knows just where we are and if we need help, they know where to send it."

"Or if someone wants to set up their own racket, they can find him."

Dalla nodded. "It was part of the original pact the Department made with the Executive Council. The Council wanted some tethers on the Department since we have the only conveyers that can go to any level or sector in Paratime."

"Can't Hadron and his minions use them to track us here?" Salon wanted to know.

Dalla made hand washing motions. "Not now. Since the Paratime Building was destroyed, all the tracking device registers and information on outtime conveyers is gone. Of course, we can't track them, either."

"So what are we doing here, other than surviving?" Dalzar asked.

"We're waiting for Vall. We have a pact: if there was ever a major emergency where we were cut off from First Level, we would meet here and figure out what to do. Or…?"

"Any idea when Verkan will arrive?" Salon wanted to know.

Dalla shrugged. "They don't get a lot of conveyers coming and going from Kalvan's Time Line. We'll just have to wait and see. I expect that there'll be some indication within the next ten-day. Until then, boys, try and relax."

She knew after what she'd witnessed on Home Time Line that was an impossible request. She was still in mourning for all the lives lost, friends gone forever—either discorporated or lost in Paratime. She hadn't even had time to warn her adopted sister Zinna. However, as a former prole, Zinna might have escaped the pogrom that would take the lives of most the remaining Citizens on First Level. Life as she knew it, as all the

Paratimers knew it, was over. Ten thousand years of civilization—gone!

And, most likely, never to return.

All due to the efforts of one man, a madman—her brother! She wanted to scream at the top of her lungs, but didn't want to upset the others. *How could he?! And how much of this is my fault?*

XIV

Several ten-days later, Dalla and her friends were sitting at the dining room table discussing what to do when a "ping" sounded.

"Someone's just arrived," she said, leading the way to the basement conveyer-head. They made their way cautiously down the stairs, needlers drawn.

Below they saw a thirty-foot conveyer with Verkan Vall standing beside it. "Darling," he cried, opening his arms.

Dalla rushed downstairs losing herself in Verkan's arms. "You made it!"

Verkan, still dressed in his Aryan-Transpacific royal robes, said, "Yes, just barely."

"They haven't attacked Kalvan's Time Line?"

He shook his head. "It was still clear when I left Greffa City. We made a quick stop at First Level. It's mostly inhabitable. What happened?"

Dalla shook her head and shouted: "It's all due to my sick little brother, blast and curse him! I always knew he was disturbed, but this!!! Tharn's behind some kind of prole-takeover of Home Time Line. If he was here, I'd wring his bloody neck!"

"Is he completely insane?" Verkan cried out.

"I fear so. He calls himself The Leader and he brought prole strike teams from Fifth Level to make attacks on Home Time Line. They went so far as to use atomic and nuclear weapons on Dhergabar, as well as the Paratime Building."

Verkan turned white and looked sick. "Is there anything we can do?"

"No, I don't think so. He launched an attack on Fifth Level Police Terminal, too! Now, with the Survey Division gone there's no way to track the Department conveyers and coordinate with the surviving police. He's also fixed it so none of the First Level people outtime can get back home since his agents have destroyed all the conveyer depots and rotundas on Home Time Line."

"This is an unmitigated disaster! But it doesn't look like there's a damn thing we can do...." Verkan trailed off. "From what we saw, First Level is in as bad a shape as some of the Second Level time-lines we used to quarantine."

"I don't believe there's anything we can do, either, Vall. And, I've had a lot more time to think about it. Now, it's time for us to figure out what *we're* going to do."

"We could leave for Aryan-Transpacific and join up with Kalvan and Rylla. What do you think of that idea?"

Dalla shook her head sadly. "It wouldn't work for long, dear. Kalvan's already in his forties.... And we're supposed to be his age. How long before we have to start dying our hair, use makeup and create phony wrinkles? Besides, do we really want to stay in Hostigos and watch all our friends grow old and discorporate, while we remain young?"

"No, you're right. I don't want to see Kalvan and Rylla in their dot-age...with us unable to do anything to help. I see you brought some friends with you. We'll just have to stay here for now and make the best of a bad situation."

"What about Home Time Line?"

Verkan shook his head. "As a society, we bought and paid for this. It's a wonder it all lasted ten thousand years...."

Dalla nodded. "In a way, we're the fortunate ones. Just think about all those poor Paratimers who are permanently stuck outtime and don't know how or why."

Verkan summed it up. "They'll have to come to terms with it and make adjustments. It could be a lot worse."

"Yes, they could be dead. But what about the Paratime Secret?"

Verkan shrugged. "At this point, who cares? Let somebody else worry about it. Now, what's for dinner?"

The End